PRAISE FOR *ALIAS EMMA*

"One of those wonderful thrillers you read in a day and know you'll remember for years . . . Emma Makepeace is a worthy heir to the James Bond mantle." —James Patterson

"A thrilling read, with brilliantly likeable protagonists, nonstop heart-pumping action, and multiple twists and turns. I could not have loved it more." —Lisa Jewell

"Totally addictive . . . *Alias Emma* is that perfect combination of exciting new character, explosive action scenes, and a thrilling cat-and-mouse chase through the streets of London. Once you start reading, you won't stop." —Lisa Gardner

"Excellent escapism." —Ruth Ware

"Turbocharged pacing, vivid sense of place, and unforgettable characters add up to Thriller with a capital T." —Jonathan Kellerman

"There are fast reads, and then there are reads that throw you right out of your chair. *Alias Emma* is in the latter category." —Linwood Barclay

"Nonstop adventure with all the action taking place within a twenty-four-hour period. Tremendous fun." —Anthony Horowitz, *New York Times* bestselling author of *The Magpie Murders*

"Cinematic and complex . . . a fun thrill ride and an incisive look into one woman's motivations for pursuing a dangerous career."

—*Shelf Awareness* (starred review)

"A breathless race across London. The pace never lets up before a heart-stopping conclusion."

—Robert Gold,
author of *Twelve Secrets*

"An enthralling, unputdownable read, with a breakneck pace and a premise that sometimes felt all too plausible."

—Elizabeth Kay,
author of *Seven Lies*

"*Alias Emma* is one thrill of a ride! Action-packed and fast-paced . . . I was riding shotgun alongside Emma and lapped up every spectacular twist and turn. A not-to-be-missed thriller!"

—Kathryn Croft,
author of *The Mother's Secret*

"I raced through this taut, nail-biting, twisty spy thriller. *Alias Emma* is a wild ride through the streets of London that moves so quickly it'll leave you breathless."

—Robin Morgan-Bentley,
author of *The Guest House*

ALIAS
EMMA

ALIAS EMMA

A NOVEL

AVA GLASS

B

BANTAM BOOKS

NEW YORK

To PM.
My first real spy.

ALIAS
EMMA

1

THE SUN WAS setting over one of the most expensive streets in the world when the assassins arrived.

The CCTV camera on the central London corner recorded long blades of golden light stretched out across limestone walls as two men walked down the exclusive avenue. As if invisible, they passed unnoticed by a nanny pushing a buggy, and a trio of well-exercised women, thin as wraiths, chattering as they ambled to the gym.

It was a bright autumn day, but the men kept their heads tilted down so no camera recorded their features as they slipped out of the shadows and approached a six-story building where the last apartment sold went for £14 million. The camera above the door captured one of them standing guard, his face turned away, while the other bent over the handle. After a few seconds, the door opened.

In another city there might have been a doorman, or a security guard, but residents in this neighborhood never liked to be observed going about their business. The most prized buildings had long been the kind where you can walk from the front door to your flat without seeing a soul. This was one of those. Bypassing the art deco cage elevator, with its modern security camera, the men climbed the red-carpeted stairs without being challenged.

All the way to the top floor.

Outside, Knightsbridge went about its elegant business. A scarlet Lamborghini rumbled by with a panther's purr, pausing at a red light. A delivery truck idled behind it, the driver leaning his elbow against the open window, ogling the car's voluptuous lines. The three women reached the corner and waited for the signal to cross. The noise of the traffic passing on the cross street must have hidden the sounds of struggle from the building behind them because no one looked up as a body plummeted from the window of the top-floor apartment. It fell from the sky with strange grace, a white dressing gown fluttering in the air like wings, before it slammed into the top of the idling van, striking it with such force the vehicle rocked on its wheels. The air was split by an agonized screech of bending metal and crushed bone.

Later, none of the women could remember how they reacted, but footage from a CCTV camera showed them crying out, reaching instinctively for each other's hands as they scrambled away from the carnage.

In the ensuing chaos—cars stopping, the truck driver and the Lamborghini owner emerging bewildered from their vehicles, talking and gesticulating, the women sobbing and pointing, the nanny pausing to look back—no one noticed two men step out of the pale-stone building and close the door behind them before walking swiftly in the opposite direction, heads tilted slightly down.

The job was done.

2

THE T-SHIRT SHOP smelled overpoweringly of patchouli oil. Perched on a stool near the cash register, Emma wondered if she'd ever get the musky, sweet scent of it out of her clothes.

"Put these in that corner." Raven held out an armful of hand-made signs and tilted his head toward the back of the shop, beyond the stacks of T-shirts with peaceful slogans, beaded necklaces, and carved wooden symbols.

"Sure thing." Emma jumped to her feet and bounded over. There were about fifteen signs, the paint barely dry. They swung as she walked to the back of the small shop, sending random words flashing in vivid red, green, and blue: EMERGENCY, DANGER, STRIKE.

It was after closing time but Raven had asked her to stay late and help him get ready for the protest march planned for the weekend. A shaggy-haired political zealot, Raven managed this north London shop and spent the rest of his time organizing a left-wing protest group. He was thirty-three years old but looked younger because of the hair and the tattoos. His birth name was David Lees but he'd changed it legally eight years ago to the more memorable "Raven Hawkhurst." In action on the streets he was the protest equivalent of a lightweight boxer, small and relentless, jabbing black-and-red anarchy flags at riot police, his thin face disguised behind a checkered scarf. In person, he was resentful and paranoid—convinced the government was after him.

Which, to be fair, they were.

It had taken weeks working undercover for Emma to make her way into his inner circle, and even longer to get close enough to earn his trust. Almost as soon as she'd done it, though, she'd decided he wasn't ever going to pose any real danger. He wasn't smart enough or organized enough to bring about the revolution of his dreams. He liked the drama and distraction of a punch-up with the cops, but he was no terrorist.

She'd told her bosses as much more than once but they'd overruled her, insisting she stay and dig deeper. The group's online fundraising received a surprising amount of money funneled through a number of sources, but originating in Russia. And so here she was, stacking protest signs in a fug of patchouli.

Setting the signs down, she turned back. "It sounds like the march'll be massive on Saturday." In character, she gave her voice a flat-edged northern accent. Raven believed she was an activist from Manchester.

He barked a bitter laugh. "You know how many people live in this city?" He didn't wait for her to answer. "Fourteen million. You get ten thousand at a protest? That's not success. That's abject failure." Grabbing the remaining signs, he lugged them to the back without waiting for her to help. "People want to drive their SUVs to their kids' private schools and think they'll save the environment by not using plastic straws."

He was always morose the day before a march. Emma left him to rant and headed back to finish her work with the cans of paint as he warmed to his topic. He'd got as far as "They'll care when we take their mansions away" when her phone vibrated.

She pulled it from her pocket and glanced at the screen. It held only one word: "Home."

"Raven," she said, raising her voice to break through his familiar liturgy. "I've got to take this call. Be right back."

There was an indignant pause, and then she heard him mutter, "Oh, typical."

She hurried out onto the pavement, hitting answer as soon as the door closed. "This is Makepeace 1075."

An unfamiliar female voice said, "Hello, Emma. I've got a message from home. Are you safe to take it now?"

Emma looked up and down the quiet street—there was no one nearby. "Now is fine."

"The message follows: 'Your mother is ill. She needs you urgently.' Do you need me to repeat?"

Emma's heart began to race, but she kept her voice cool. "Got it. Thanks."

When she ran back into the shop, Raven was at the front, gathering the last of the paint.

"I'm really sorry, I have to go home. There's an emergency." Emma raced behind the cash register to grab her bag.

Exuding silent condemnation, he fixed her with a beady look.

"That was my mum," she explained, giving her voice a worried tone. "She's ill, and there's nobody else to look after her. I've got to go."

"Oh, fine." He gestured at the shop with an arm that had the words "NO JUSTICE" tattooed from wrist to elbow. "And I'll just do all this myself, I guess?"

Deliberately misunderstanding him, she cast him a grateful smile. "That'd be fab. You're a star. See you later."

She hurried through the door, his words floating after her: "It was *sarcasm.*"

By then, though, she was already running toward Camden High Street, her biker boots clunking hard on the pavement.

She couldn't care less about Raven right now. She was being called in.

It took her just over thirty minutes to get to Westminster at full steam. There was no time to change out of her Climate Panic T-shirt, or to remove the torn jeans or blue hair extensions. Her appearance raised a few eyebrows on tweedy Rochester Row as she raced from the tube station, crossing against the traffic lights, but she was in too much of a hurry to care.

On a quiet street built along a scimitar curve, she stopped in front of a narrow brick building. Nothing about it stood out. It looked exactly like the other neat four-story offices. Above the nondescript entrance, a plain blue-and-white sign read THE VERNON INSTITUTE.

Emma let herself in and hurried across the empty Georgian front hall to where a set of opaque black glass doors blocked access to the rest of the building. Unlike the front entrance, these doors were modern and bulletproof. A gleaming device was mounted on the wall to one side. Leaning forward, she stared at her own iris reflected in dark glass, as three lights blinked. The first was red, the second amber, the third green. When the third light appeared, the lock released with an audible click. She pushed the door open. On the other side was a busy office building.

A woman at the front desk glanced up from her work and said, "He's upstairs."

When Emma reached the first floor, she found Ripley on the landing, hands in the pockets of his suit trousers, his long, complicated face impassive.

"Got here as fast as I could," Emma told him breathlessly. "What's wrong?"

The message she'd received was an emergency code Ripley had established when she first went undercover. In the two years she'd been working for the Agency, she'd only been sent it once before. That time, Ripley had told her right away it was a test. This time, she knew before her handler spoke that it wasn't.

He indicated the door behind him, gravely. "We need to talk."

Charles Ripley was somewhere between fifty and sixty years old, just over six feet tall and thin, with a strong jaw and short hair gone gray at the temples. His suit of a good navy wool was neither expensive nor cheap. Hundreds of thousands of suits just like it were worn in London every day. His shoes were decent leather but not highly polished. His watch wasn't designer. His white shirt was neat but not overly crisp. In fact, he was so unmemorable in appearance that if he crossed the street in front of you, you'd be hard-pressed to describe him five minutes later. As he'd told her when they first started working together, "Invisibility is a spy's greatest asset."

He'd had thirty-five years in government service to learn how to hide his thoughts, but she sensed trouble as she followed him into his office.

The room Ripley led her into was spacious with dusty, oak-paneled walls and a tall, arched window. Aside from a desk, two worn leather chairs, and a coffee table, it was completely empty. No pictures on the wall. Nothing to indicate who worked here, or that anyone worked here at all.

Motioning for her to sit, he walked to his desk.

"There's been another murder. In Knightsbridge, this time." He pulled a black cigarette case from the breast pocket of his jacket. Late-afternoon light slanted through the blast-proof glass, making it hard for her to make out his expression as he picked up a much-used silver lighter. "Professional job, precisely like the others. Two-hander." He paused to light a cigarette, the last words coming out in a stream of smoke. "Thrown from a window. No DNA evidence. No face capture on CCTV."

Everyone in the Secret Service knew about the killings. The murders were brazen—most taking place in the middle of the day with people all around, but the methods were clean and effective. Each killing was an unmistakable message to the British government from the Russian military spy agency, the GRU: "We do what we want. You can't stop us."

Emma did a quick calculation. "That's four, isn't it?"

Ripley pulled an ashtray closer with a sweep of his fingertip. "Yes, this makes four. All Russian scientists. All under the protection of Her Majesty's Government. All dead in the last two weeks. Killed in ways that could plausibly look like suicide. It's causing a shitstorm in Whitehall, and I believe there's more to come." He fixed her with a steady look. "I'm pulling you off the Camden group as of now. You're working on this."

"Thank God for that." Emma dropped back in her chair, not bothering to hide her relief. No more protest signs. No more patchouli oil.

The faint hint of a smile flashed across his stern features and evaporated just as quickly. "Perhaps you should wait to celebrate until after you've read the brief. This one won't be easy."

Reaching down, he pulled a photo from the black briefcase at his feet and slid it across the desk. Emma looked down at a picture of a heavy-set man with thinning salt-and-pepper hair. His pale blue eyes squinted at the camera through folds of flesh.

"Yesterday's victim." Ripley tapped it with a long index finger. "Uri Semenov. Russian nuclear specialist. Emigrated fifteen years ago. Has provided invaluable information to us about the Russian weapons-manufacturing program."

"Was he still working with us when they killed him?" Emma asked.

A slight headshake. "We got everything out of him that we needed years ago. Just like the rest."

She looked up. "I don't get it. Why are they doing this?"

"Well. That is the question." Ripley took the picture back, pulling out another. "Two things connect the four victims. All of them worked for us, and all of them were close associates of this couple." He slid another image across to her.

Emma looked down at the image of a tall, dark-haired woman with fiercely intelligent eyes. Next to her stood an even taller man, so lanky he verged on cadaverous. Between them stood a boy of about seven who bore both of their features in some way. His mother's eyes. His father's sharp jaw. Each adult had a hand on his shoulder and she could sense the connection between them—they were as close as a tied knot.

"Who are they?" she asked.

"Dimitri and Elena Primalov. They were both highly placed nuclear physicists in the Russian weapons program. Both were assets for

MI6 until someone betrayed them. They fled to the UK twenty years ago. Since then, Elena in particular has been incredibly helpful in our work." He leaned back in his chair, his cigarette smoldering in one hand. The light from the arched window highlighted his features, and Emma noticed for the first time how tired he looked—the creases on his face were carved deeper than usual. "We think she's the one the Russians really want."

Emma looked again at the photo, as if she might find clues in the woman's angular face. There was a kind of beauty to her intense features, she thought. A fire simmering behind those dark, enigmatic eyes.

"What makes you think she's the main focus?"

Ripley slid another paper over to her. This one was stamped TOP SECRET in bold, black letters. In terse, emotionless language it explained that Elena Primalov had invented parts of the centrifuge the Russians used to speed the development of weapons-grade plutonium. And much more. She'd become the face of the Russian nuclear program—frequently appearing on television.

Emma blew out a long breath. Ripley hadn't been exaggerating—she'd been close enough to the Russian leadership to be invited to the president's home for parties. Her betrayal must have burned.

There was no question Elena Primalov had to rank among MI6's biggest prizes. In return for the information she'd provided, her family had been granted full British citizenship and protection. They'd lived in anonymity in rural Hampshire for nearly two decades.

"I can see why the Russians might be a bit cross about losing her," Emma said with dry understatement. "But how can you be certain she's the main target of these murders?"

The sun suffused the room in a warm apricot glow that seemed out of place in this coldly realistic environment. Emma could hear the traffic in the distance as rush hour geared up to grind the city to a halt.

"We've been talking to our allies on this one. It appears a GRU assassination team has been tracking down and killing former Russian scientists around the world for more than a year," explained Ripley. "Everyone they've killed has had some connection with Elena Primalov. Uri Semenov used to share an office with her." He paused. "His murder is the one I can't understand. He saw his Secret Service handler the day before. We knew the danger was high, so he'd been relocated. He'd moved into that apartment one week ago. We put him there to keep him *safe*." He stamped the cigarette out with savage impatience. "I'm putting everyone I can on this. We have to put a stop to it."

It wasn't like him to get angry about a case. Emma let a moment pass before saying, "It's odd. These are all old cases. The Russians are taking huge risks to kill these people, and for what? Revenge?"

"I'm not sure," he said. "The whole operation makes no sense to me. It's too bold. Too extreme. I'm concerned that . . ."

Someone tapped on the door. Ripley stopped mid-sentence.

"Enter."

The door opened and a tall man with neatly combed fair hair stepped in. "Rip, I just . . ." Spotting Emma, he drew back. "Sorry, old chap. Thought you were alone. Hello, Emma."

"Hi, Ed," Emma said.

Ed Masterson was Ripley's second-in-command. His job was mostly communicating with the government officials who paid the bills. The Agency's work straddled a lot of governmental lines between MI5, MI6, and the Foreign Office. It was easy to tread all over someone else's operation if you weren't very careful. Masterson made sure that didn't happen.

Ripley tilted his head at her. "I was just briefing Emma on the Semenov case."

Masterson winced. "Bloody nightmare." Glancing at her, he said, "Good luck with it." He held a folder in one hand, which he lifted for Ripley to see. "The usual complainers at HQ have a couple of questions about this. Let me know when you're through."

"Fine, fine," Ripley said with a hint of impatience.

When the other man had gone, Emma gave her boss an inquiring look.

"The killings have Cabinet Office worked up. They want it stopped and so do I. That's where you come in." Ripley's eyes met hers. "We have reason to believe our Russian friends are planning to move on Elena Primalov and her family very soon. We're bringing the family inside. All of them. And this time there will be no mistakes."

A quick job, then, Emma thought, a little disappointed. Pick them up and lock the doors. Still, it was high-profile, and it got her out of Raven's T-shirt shop.

"What do you need me to do?" she asked.

"This is your target." Ripley slid another photo across the desk. This one showed a strong-jawed man with thick brown hair. There was something familiar about his thoughtful dark eyes, but it took a moment for her to work it out.

"Is this the kid? The Primalovs' boy?" she asked.

Ripley nodded. "That's Mikhail Primalov. Or Michael, as he's now known. His parents were taken into protective custody this morning. They're already in a safe house outside London. We attempted to bring in Michael as well, but he declined our offer of protection. His parents, as you might understand, are frantic. Elena . . ." He paused. "She says she won't stay under our protection unless Michael comes, too. And we have *got* to protect her."

There was an odd note underlying his voice when he said the woman's name—a kind of possessiveness. Emma wondered if he and Elena might not be strangers.

She examined the picture again. "Why did he refuse protection? Is he crazy? The GRU must be dying to hurl him out a window."

"His explanation is that his job as a doctor is too important to him. He refuses to leave his patients. He's worse than a lunatic. He's a martyr."

"And you want me to convince him he needs our help."

"If Michael Primalov doesn't let us help him, we believe he'll be dead within twenty-four hours," he told her bluntly. "As soon as the Russians figure out his parents are under our protection, they are going to go looking for him. Michael's parents adore him—he's their only son. If the Russians get their hands on him, Elena will do whatever Moscow wants her to do. Nobody will have to push her out a window. She'll jump."

His voice was steady and cool, but there was steel in his gaze when he looked at her.

"Elena is one of our top assets, and that makes Michael critical to us. We need to get him to safety as quickly as possible. Do whatever you must to convince him to let us protect him. Be his friend. Earn his trust. Whatever it takes. Just bring him to safety before they kill him."

3

THE NEXT MORNING at seven o'clock, Emma stood at the edge of Clissold Park in north London trying to keep warm. The blue hair extensions were gone, along with the T-shirt and biker boots, replaced by black exercise leggings and a snug, long-sleeved navy fleece, zipped up against the early-autumn chill. Her shoulder-length brunette hair was pulled back in a neat ponytail. To a casual observer she would look like a young professional heading out for a run before work.

As she waited, she stretched out her stiff muscles. She'd been up late reading Michael Primalov's file. If the Russians were as eager to grab him as Ripley believed, this operation needed to be clean and quick.

Rescuing someone who doesn't want to be saved isn't easy. Somehow, she had to make him believe that he wanted to come with her. Once she had him on the hook, the plan was simple: the Agency would send a unit to spirit him away to a heavily guarded safe house far from London. From there, the family would go into hiding. And everyone would live happily ever after.

First, though, she had to bring him in.

All night long excitement and nervousness had dueled for dominance. This was the biggest assignment Ripley had ever trusted her with, and she still didn't know why he'd chosen her. Emma had only been with the Agency two years. The long stint with Raven's group had been her biggest undercover job until now.

In their meeting the day before, Ripley had said, "We tried sending more experienced agents to talk to him. He threw them out. You're almost exactly his age. Maybe he'll listen to you."

When she'd pressed for more details he'd ended the conversation, handing her a stack of papers. "Memorize it," he'd ordered. "Primalov isn't someone you can order around or threaten into making the decision you want. He's smart and he's stubborn. You're going to have to convince him to trust you. And everyone else who's tried so far has failed."

All night she'd immersed herself in Michael's life. She knew all about his schooling, his sky-high scores at university, his rapid progression through medical training. She knew that he'd specialized in pediatrics, that he'd moved to a new hospital a year ago because of its work with young patients. She knew it all, down to his hatred of eggplants and his allergy to codeine. She just hoped it would be enough.

Emma glanced at her watch, hopped up and down a couple of times to get the blood moving, and then joined the flow of runners and cyclists moving through the wrought-iron gate and onto a smooth, flat footpath. Even at this hour, the park was busy. She kept her pace slow, observing the faces around her. There was a woman with a baby that wouldn't rest, tiredly pushing it in a dark blue carriage as it wailed a weary objection. A tall brunette running steadily, her eyes straight ahead.

Mostly, though, there were commuters, jackets buttoned up, cutting across the park, cardboard cups of coffee clutched in their hands.

There was no sign of Michael.

After ten minutes, Emma stepped off the path, pretending to stretch as she surveyed the fast-moving crowd. He had to be here. The man described in that file was a creature of habit. He not only ran at the same time every day, he also ran the same route. Seven days a week. Fifty-two weeks of the year.

She was just beginning to run again when a man hurtled by, headed in the opposite direction. His dark hair was unruly and tangled, his face damp with perspiration, but she'd stared at his picture enough yesterday to recognize him instantly.

Thank you for being predictable, she thought, and turned to follow him.

But it wasn't easy. Michael Primalov moved fast. She had to push herself to stay close to him, and in minutes she was panting.

He did this run every day, while she'd been sitting in a shop in Camden for three months, pretending to be vegan.

Somehow, she needed to slow him down.

In the distance, she could see a point where several paths crossed. If she timed it right, she could use that.

Putting her head down, she ran past him. When she reached the intersection of paths, she veered right onto the side path and immediately crumpled to one knee, grabbing her ankle.

"Shit," she swore. "Ow."

Michael dashed by her, his head turning only briefly to glance at her. Then he slowed, looking back over his shoulder. When he saw her hunched over holding her leg, he stopped, pulling out his earbuds.

As she'd always known he would, he jogged back to her.

"Hey." He crouched a few feet away, shoving his tousled hair off his forehead. "Are you hurt?"

His accent was pure north London. Not a hint of Russian to it.

Feigning embarrassment, Emma gestured at her leg. "It's my ankle. I'm sure it's nothing. I probably just sprained it. I'll be fine." She tried to get up and then dropped back down again, breath hissing between her teeth. "It just bloody hurts."

He grew more serious. "I better have a look at that." He made a self-deprecating gesture. "I'm a doctor, by the way. Believe it or not."

"Are you really?" She gave him an amazed look. "Oh my gosh, this is so embarrassing."

A slight smile quirked the corners of his mouth. "Don't be embarrassed. It happens."

There were no pictures of him smiling in his folder. It changed his face completely, giving him a boyish, approachable look.

"It's all my fault. I took that turn too fast." Hesitantly, Emma stretched her leg out.

"It's easily done. There's loose gravel at that junction. It can be treacherous. I run here every day so I know to avoid it." His hands were gentle as he rolled her sock back to see her ankle. He pressed his fingers against a spot above her ankle bone. "Does it hurt when I do this?"

She shook her head.

He pressed lightly against several other points around the ankle. "There's no swelling." He raised his face and she looked straight into the large dark brown eyes she knew from his file. He hadn't shaved yet, and there was a shadow of stubble on his cheeks. "Can you stand?"

"I think so."

He straightened and bent over to help her up. He steadied her with one hand and she hobbled cautiously as if testing the injured leg, taking the opportunity to look around. Other than a cyclist disappearing in the distance, the two of them were completely alone.

"Try putting weight on it," Michael suggested, still looking down at her ankle.

Emma set the foot down firmly on the ground and abandoned the pretense. "I'm not actually injured," she said quickly. "I need to talk to you."

He opened his mouth and then shut it again, a doubtful crease forming above his eyes.

"My name is Emma Makepeace. I work for a government agency that has been assigned to protect you. There is a credible threat against your family. I want to help keep you safe, if you'll let me."

His face hardened and he dropped his hand from her arm as if it had scalded him. "What is wrong with you? Why would you pretend to be hurt?"

"Because I knew you'd stop to help, and I needed to talk to you without being seen," she said honestly. "I'm not sure you understand the danger you're in. They are looking for you right now. And if I can find you, they can find you."

"They?" He made a dismissive sound. "Who are *they*?"

"The Russian Secret Service. They are coming for you. We believe they intend to use you to get to your parents."

"Oh, come on . . ." he began, but she didn't let him finish.

"Listen to me carefully." Her tone cooled. "If they get to you, there are two ways this goes: either they will keep you alive and torture you, sending the video to your mother; or they will kill you and send her your eyes as a keepsake. Either way, you lose. Your parents lose. Everyone loses. Unless you come with me now. Out here on your own, you will die. It's that simple."

For a split second, a new emotion flickered across his face—fear. But then the shutters went down again.

"God, you sound just like my mother. Did she send you out here to do this?" He didn't wait for her reply. "Well, you can tell her I'm a big boy now. She's safe and Dad's safe, and that's all that matters. But I'm not running away from anything."

She'd been warned to expect something like this. Michael had grown up steeped in his parents' stories of Russian violence and spies, but at some point he'd decided it had nothing to do with him. He didn't want to believe he was trapped in that world, but he was. He'd already lost the battle and he hadn't even started fighting yet.

Movement in the distance caught Emma's attention. Someone was running toward them. Seventy meters away. A man. She couldn't make out his features in the harsh morning light.

"Dr. Primalov." She spoke with new urgency. "Please believe me. Your life is in danger. Come with me now. Let us help you."

But Michael stepped back, holding up his hands. "Look, whoever you are, you did your best, but my answer hasn't changed. Tell your people I don't want what they're offering. I just want to be left in peace." He paused before adding, "Tell my mother not to worry. And, please. Leave me alone."

The runner was thirty meters away now. A man, dark hair, below average height, moving fast. He didn't look like a threat but then neither did she.

"Fine," she said, keeping her eyes on the runner. Twenty meters away now. "It's your decision. But do me a favor, would you?" She handed him a card with only a number written on it. "If you change your mind—if you find yourself in any trouble at all—call this number. Don't take any chances."

A look of surprise crossed Michael's face, as if he'd expected her to put up more of a fight. He slid the card into his pocket.

"I won't call," he warned.

"I wish you would," she said, stepping back from him. "I'm the only one who can save your life."

That seemed to jar him, and for a moment he hesitated. But then he shrugged as if physically shaking off her warning and began to jog away.

Emma stood at the crossroads as her target gradually disappeared in the distance. She had every intention of following him but she didn't want him to make a scene, so she let him get a good head start.

As she waited, two figures emerged from the morning haze. They were dressed in decent running clothes—new but otherwise unmemorable. They seemed ordinary enough. And yet something about them bothered her. At first, she couldn't figure out what it was. They were both beautiful runners. They worked incredibly well together, moving with an almost eerie smoothness. The man was tall and muscular. The woman had a straight, nearly breastless build, and long, slim legs.

They seemed perfectly at home in this park, moving fast, their eyes straight ahead. It took her a second to figure out what was wrong. It wasn't how they looked. It was how they *ran*. They moved with remarkable accuracy. Each stride the same length as the next. They were in perfect sync. That kind of precision is drilled into you in the military.

Emma dropped down into a crouch as if tying her shoelace as she surreptitiously watched the pair. Their earpieces looked like normal earbuds, but that meant nothing; she herself had used two-way radio earpieces that looked completely innocuous.

They were close now and moving fast. Emma lowered her gaze to her shoelaces, listening to the rhythmic thump of their feet in perfect sync as they ran by.

As soon as they passed, she jumped to her feet and fell in behind them.

They'd done nothing to raise suspicion aside from run well. It was all instinct. If she was wrong about them, she was wasting valuable time. Still, she stayed where she was.

Side by side, the pair ran past a wooded area and along a wide stretch of green, and soon Emma spotted Michael's dark hair and black T-shirt in the distance.

The two runners ahead of her exchanged a glance. The woman nodded as if acknowledging some silent message.

The man brushed his ear in a gesture that would have looked incidental to almost any casual observer, but Emma saw he was talking quietly. The woman kept her eyes on Michael, one hand hovering loosely above her jacket pocket.

Emma's ribs compressed around her lungs.

She'd been right. They were everything she'd feared.

And now, somewhere, someone was telling them what to do.

It took effort to keep her steps even. Her mind spun through the possibilities. Would they dare try to do it here, in a busy park, in broad daylight? It would be an international incident. Extremely damaging politically if it ever got out. But the old rules of espionage hadn't stopped Russia from murdering with impunity lately. They'd attacked in British parks before, after all. In bucolic country towns. On quiet streets.

Unlike the British Secret Service, the Russian spy agency, the GRU, is part of the military. Agents are handpicked, and said to be the most loyal, patriotic soldiers that country produces. They are chosen because they would willingly die in the process of completing an assignment. Within that group, a select few are trained as assassins. They are among the most feared operatives in the world.

Russia never forgets or forgives.

Yes, they would kill Michael Primalov in the middle of this park, if that was what they were ordered to do. And he would never hear them coming.

There was a new urgency in the way the two ran now, loping after him with feral intensity, like wolves who've sighted a wounded deer.

Instinctively Emma found herself speeding after them, and she had to force herself to slow down. Keep moving steadily.

She couldn't confront them openly—not unless she absolutely had to. She was outmanned and they were most likely armed. British intelligence officers did not routinely carry weapons. If she'd wanted to check out a gun for this operation, the paperwork would have taken all day and Ripley wouldn't have approved it anyway.

No, she needed a better plan. One that didn't involve a shoot-out in north London at seven in the morning.

She was still trying to decide what to do when the two runners suddenly stopped.

It happened so quickly there was no time for her to react. One minute they were jogging at top speed. The next, they were standing stone still and she was about to run straight into them.

Her feet skidded on the footpath as she tried to slow down. The man turned and looked straight at her, his blue gaze as flat and predatory as a shark's.

Thinking fast, Emma barked, "Watch it!" and veered around him, sharply.

As she sped ahead, her heart raced. The drop-back was a classic move—she'd used it many times herself to check if anyone was following her. She should have been ready for it. She'd been too close. Too distracted.

Now they'd seen her face. If they saw her again, they'd remember.

If she had any doubts left about who they were, that move banished them. It had been executed perfectly.

She ran stiffly, feeling their eyes on her back like ice against her skin. The place you want a GRU assassination squad is anywhere except right behind you.

Ahead, Michael was still racing across the park, oblivious to the drama playing out behind him. The sight of him helped her focus. He was her job. He was what mattered.

A little at a time, she began slowing her pace, as if she were running out of steam. Michael pulled farther and farther ahead. She could hear the pair behind closing in, impatient to keep up with him. Still, she stubbornly slowed, putting her hand on her ribs, and breathing heavily. Soon, Michael was almost out of sight.

A moment later, the two runners sprinted around her without a second glance.

Emma let them get a good distance ahead before running doggedly after them.

Adrenaline gave her new energy. With every step, she tried to anticipate their next move. Were they going to grab him when he left the park or would it be a public assassination? Would they make an example of him or shove him into a waiting car?

As they neared the park exit, Emma tensed, preparing herself for whatever was coming. The Russians were right behind him—close enough to slip a blade between his ribs.

But the two agents didn't grab him, or shoot him, or stab him. Instead, they turned smoothly onto a side path and jogged away.

Caught off guard for the second time in ten minutes, Emma stared at the retreating figures with bewilderment.

What the hell?

But there was no time to wonder what was going on. Michael was already out of the park.

Wiping the sweat from her face with her sleeve, Emma sprinted after him.

Traffic rumbled and growled around her, but she barely noticed. Five endless seconds passed before she spotted him, threading through the crowd as if he didn't have a care in the world.

Letting out an audible breath, she began to follow.

In her mind she went over what had just happened. The runners in the park had never intended to kidnap Michael; they were just gathering information. That drop-back move—they were trying to find out if anyone was protecting him.

She thought of the ice-cold moment when the man had turned to look at her. Had he had enough time in those brief seconds to figure out what she was?

She didn't think so. Her angry act had been good. And her own drop-back a few minutes later had clearly fooled them. They hadn't even glanced at her when they passed.

The realization sent an unexpected rush of exhilaration through her. She'd fooled a Russian assassination team. On her own. Now, though, she needed backup.

Keeping her gaze on Michael, who had finally slowed to a walk, she pulled her phone from her pocket and dialed a secure number.

A crisp female voice answered. "Vernon Institute."

"This is Makepeace. I need R."

There was a long moment of silence, like dropping into a well—the Agency doesn't go in for hold music—and then Ripley was on the line.

"Have you got him?"

"Negative. He passed on my offer. Also, we've got company. Some friends from the old country showed up. It's turning into quite a party."

"How many?" His voice was curt.

"Two so far, but there could be more."

"There will be more. Did they make you?"

"No. The ones I saw broke off early. There must be others waiting to pick up the surveillance. I could use some help out here."

"I can't offer you any assistance," he said flatly. "This is your case."

Emma was so surprised it took her a second to respond. "I'm already outnumbered two to one and I just got here. You said yourself there will be more of them. I can't do this alone."

The cool silence that followed lasted just long enough for a worried knot to form in the pit of her stomach.

When he did speak, there was a new urgency in his tone. "I wouldn't have chosen you for this job if I did not believe you were perfectly capable of handling it. You've trained for this your entire life. You've been ready for a long time. You have to handle this one on your own."

Emma wasn't sure how to take this. His faith in her was flattering, but she was going head-to-head with Moscow. She'd expect a team of four on the ground at least. She should have more equipment, more people—more everything.

Ahead, Michael was about to turn in to his street. She couldn't see anyone following him, but she knew, somehow, that they were there. She could sense it the way a cat senses the distant presence of a fox.

"I can handle it." Her voice was cautious but Ripley didn't seem to notice.

"Excellent. Now, pay attention. We knew it was likely he'd refuse. We also knew our Russian friends would show up. Nothing that's happening should surprise you." The reassuring tone had returned to his voice. "You are precisely where you need to be. For now, stay close. Approach him again when the time is right. We've left you supplies; Martha will message you the details. When you've got him, call for a pickup and we'll get you both out of there."

A large delivery truck rattled by and for a second Ripley's voice disappeared behind the noise. Emma cupped her hand around the phone in time to hear him say, "Do whatever you need to keep him safe. I'll have your back." The truck driver leaned on his horn, gesticulating furiously at a car stopped on a double-yellow line. Emma thought she heard Ripley say something else, but she couldn't make it out. But in the quiet that followed, she very clearly heard Ripley's final words.

"I'm counting on you."

The phone went dead.

4

THERE'D NEVER BEEN a time when Emma did not want to be a spy. As soon as she was old enough to understand what spies did, she wanted to be one.

Anyone who knew the truth about her family would have understood that obsession. After all, the first story she could remember was about one particular spy—her father.

From the time she was very small, her mother had told her about him. At night when she was tucked into bed, at a time when other little girls would hear tales of hungry caterpillars or bears that loved honey, Emma was told about her father.

This was how she learned he'd worked for the Russian government, but had betrayed his country by smuggling secrets to British agents in the chaotic years after the Cold War ended.

"He wanted to bring democracy and peace to Russia," her mother had explained. "He wanted good things to happen."

But good things hadn't happened.

For four years he'd shared valuable information with MI6. And then someone had grown suspicious. Exactly which secret had been the one to garner him attention, he never knew. All he knew was that one day everything changed. It hadn't been obvious, but suddenly he noticed he was being followed when he left work every day. Emma's mother, heavily pregnant with her first child, returned home from the supermarket one afternoon to find objects in the apartment had been moved, just a little. The changes were minor. If she hadn't been so fastidious about cleaning, she might never have noticed.

"It was tiny things. A paper on the table was turned upside down and I was sure it had been right side up when I left," she'd recalled in the velvety accent she'd never lost. "A drawer of clothing was fine—everything neatly folded. But in the wrong order." She'd held up her hands. "And I knew."

From that moment on her father had focused all his energy on getting his pregnant wife out of the country.

"He understood this was the end for us. There are no second chances in Russia," her mother would say.

"But why didn't he come with you?" Emma would always ask. "Why did he stay behind?"

And her mother would smooth her daughter's fine, straight hair, her eyes on some distant point Emma could not see. "Because if he ran, they would follow. Everyone would have been stopped at the border. He stayed behind to save his family. To save you."

"But why didn't he come *later?*" Emma had asked, a plaintive note in her voice. And her mother would reply with typical Russian bluntness.

"Because, little one, by then he was dead."

It was a tale her mother would tell her many times, repeating it as if she needed to say it aloud in order to understand it herself. By the time she was six years old, Emma could recite the story word for word.

This was how she knew that her father had come home one day from work agitated, talking fast, his skin pale and clammy, as if he had flu.

"You're going to visit your cousin in Paris," he'd told her mother. He'd grabbed a suitcase from a cupboard and thrown clothes into it as her mother followed him around their small Moscow flat, trying to understand what was happening. "You haven't seen her in too long. She knows you are coming. She's excited to see you before the baby arrives."

Her mother had tried to argue. "What are you talking about? I can't leave . . ."

Her husband had put his hand over her mouth and pointed at the ceiling, silently reminding her that he believed their apartment was bugged.

"You mustn't argue. There is a spa there that specializes in helping women with painful pregnancies," he'd said slowly, holding her gaze. "The treatment will help you."

Only when she'd nodded to show she understood did he drop his hand.

"But you will not come to Paris to see her?" she'd pleaded, clutching his jacket. "She misses you and I hate traveling alone."

He'd brushed his lips across her forehead and said, "I can't leave work. We are very busy just now."

"And I knew," Emma's mother would always say at this point, "that I would never see him again."

But there'd been little time to argue. Within an hour of his arrival home, the two of them were in a taxi. He'd kept up a cheerful conversation as the car rattled through the Moscow traffic, suspicious that even the driver might be a spy.

Only when they were out of the car and able to lose themselves in an airport crowd had he grown serious again. "Two British agents will meet you at the airport in France," he'd said, talking quickly. "They will take you to England."

"But what about you? When will you follow?" Her mother had stopped him, gripping his arm, searching his face for any sign of hope.

He'd held her gaze steadily. "I will come as soon as I can."

Before she could launch into another line of argument, he'd pulled her close, his long, familiar body warm against hers, and whispered, "Be brave. Always."

"And then he left us," her mother said simply. "Forever."

At the airport in Paris, French officers had met her at the gate, and taken her directly to a shadowy, empty room where two British officials "in nice suits" were waiting. They'd hurried her onto a private jet that whisked her to London.

"He was important to them," she would tell Emma with fierce pride. "They talked about your father like a hero. He *was* a hero."

As she'd feared, her husband had never made it out. Two days after that hurried flight to Paris, he'd been arrested. For weeks, Emma's mother waited for any sign that he was alive. The MI6 agents who looked out for her also heard nothing. As time passed, the silence grew ominous.

Her mother was still waiting when she went into labor. She gave birth to Emma alone in a London hospital where she barely understood the things the doctors said to her. She cried out her husband's name in fear and pain, but he did not come.

In the weeks that followed, she healed, took care of her baby daughter, studied English, and stared at the phone, which didn't ring.

Finally, one day, someone knocked on her door. When she opened it, holding baby Emma in her arms, she saw the same two agents who had escorted her from Paris to London three months earlier. She knew what had happened as soon as she saw their somber faces.

At this point in the story, she always gave her daughter the same order. "The Russian government murdered your father," she would say. "They killed a good man. You must never forgive them."

Emma listened. And she did not forgive them.

5

AFTER MICHAEL DISAPPEARED into his flat, Emma waited in a cold doorway down the street for half an hour. Hidden in the shadows, she studied every passing face but saw nobody who looked out of place. Just after eight o'clock, he re-emerged wearing chinos and a button-down shirt beneath a black jacket, a laptop bag over one shoulder. At a distance, she followed him down the street to a bus stop and lingered just out of view until a bus pulled in and he got in.

It would have been easy for him to notice her—all he had to do was look over his shoulder. But she was beginning to realize that Michael Primalov never looked back. He had the intense forward focus of a long-distance runner. And this made him vulnerable.

She waited for two others to board before getting on the bus herself, unnoticed in the crowd near the door but close enough to see the comb marks in Michael's wavy dark hair as he stared out of a window, his expression serious.

When he got off the bus, she followed, watching from a distance until he was safely inside the hospital. Then she followed the instructions the Agency had messaged to her phone, and retrieved a battered gym bag from a Ford Focus in the staff parking lot.

Twenty minutes later, she swept through the sliding glass doors into the hospital waiting room. The running clothes were gone, replaced by a crisp nurse's uniform. Her hair was concealed beneath a short, dark wig. An accurate replica of a hospital ID on her chest identified her as Jane Thurman.

As she crossed the hospital lobby, she moved like she belonged, her steps quick and steady. Half the game, when it comes to spy work, is confidence. People will accept anything as long as you give them enough reason to believe you are who you say you are.

When she spotted a nurse walking toward locked double doors marked "STAFF ONLY," she changed direction and fell in behind her, waiting as the other nurse pulled her ID from her pocket and tapped it against a reader.

Emma's fake ID had no chip: it wouldn't open anything.

"Hold the door, please," she called.

The nurse, a tall, angular woman with salt-and-pepper hair, barely glanced at her as she held the door ajar with one hand. "Thanks." Emma flashed a smile, but the woman was already speeding away, sturdy white shoes slapping impatiently against the linoleum floor.

Emma watched her body language with interest, making mental notes.

The hallway hummed with activity, but nobody spared her a second glance as she hustled by. There had been cutbacks in the health service for years. Everyone was used to temporary staff and a constant stream of new faces in uniform.

Emulating the nurse's disinterested haste, Emma strode to the elevators. As she waited, a trio of doctors ambled toward her, talking quietly. When the elevator door opened, the three walked in first, as if they hadn't seen her.

Emma got in behind them and pushed the button for the seventh floor. She kept her eyes on the door but the doctors barely glanced at her.

The three men got out on the fifth floor, and a slim woman, pushing a mop and a wheeled bucket sloshing soapy water, got in. Her blond hair was scraped back into a messy ponytail, and her face was angled away as she maneuvered the bucket into the lift.

"Which floor?" Emma asked, reaching for the buttons.

Lifting her head, the woman looked at her with ice-blue eyes. "Same as you," she said in a heavy Eastern European accent. "Seven."

The shock of recognition hit Emma at the precise moment the doors closed.

It was the woman from the park—half of the pair of runners who'd followed Michael. Like Emma, she'd changed out of her running clothes. Now she wore baggy scrubs, and the earbuds were gone. But it was unmistakably her—high cheekbones, muscular arms, predatory eyes.

Emma forced herself to breathe evenly as she dropped her hand to her side and stepped back.

The woman betrayed no signs of recognition. Still, Emma felt cold to her fingertips. It was entirely possible she was standing in an elevator with someone who had killed four people in Britain in the last month.

As she stared at her reflection in the mirrored door, Emma reminded herself that Ripley's rules in situations like this were always the same. Stay in character. Don't instigate a fight. Allow the danger to pass if at all possible.

Cautiously, she shifted her gaze to the other woman's image. Beneath the loose-fitting uniform, she was wiry, and a little older than Emma had thought that morning—late thirties. A fresh scar cut a thin red line across one cheek.

Maybe, Emma thought with some vindictiveness, one of her victims had fought back.

As the elevator climbed slowly, the woman sighed.

Emma gave her a glance. "Long morning?" She made her voice perky, only half-interested. A busy nurse, trying to be friendly.

"Very long." The woman had a disconcertingly direct gaze. "You must have long morning, as well." She gestured at Emma's nursing uniform.

Emma went still. Was there mockery in her voice? A glint of amusement behind the woman's even gaze? Did she recognize her after all?

She forced her face to adjust into a wry smile that felt tight on her lips. "Always."

As the word hung in the air between them, she was already assessing her chances.

Of the two of them, Emma was closest to the row of buttons that controlled the elevator. To stop it long enough to kill her, the woman would have to knock her out of the way first. It would be difficult, but not impossible. She could have any weapon tucked away inside her baggy clothes. A gun. A syringe.

Emma's nerves thrummed with anticipation. The moment had the fine edge of a sharpened blade. It felt like a hundred years before the elevator slowed.

"Seventh floor," the recorded voice announced as the elevator jolted to a stop.

The doors slid open. Neither woman moved.

"After you." Emma gestured at the bright hallway ahead of them.

Holding the mop handle like the hilt of a sword, the woman hesitated. Emma braced herself. But then the woman began dragging the bucket out of the elevator. It had one squeaky wheel; she could hear the sound fading as it rolled noisily down the hall.

Emma swallowed hard, trying to get the metallic taste of fear out of her mouth. The woman hadn't recognized her, she told herself. She'd have done something if she had.

All the same, the situation was worse than she'd thought.

She already knew how easy it was to get inside this hospital. She'd walked right in using only a stolen uniform and a fake ID. Half the cleaning staff here might be Eastern European. The Russians could have been in and out of here for days, watching Michael, finding his weaknesses. They must know the hospital inside out by now. Every back corridor. Every unlocked door.

She had to get Michael out of here.

Abandoning the calm nurse act, she dashed to an information desk at the junction of two long hallways and leaned across the counter to get the attention of a burly man staring at his screen.

"Sorry," she said when he looked up, giving her voice a helpless edge. "I'm new here. I'm supposed to meet with Dr. Michael Primalov and I'm unforgivably late. Could you point me in the right direction?"

The man had a broad, sympathetic face. "Don't worry. This place is a labyrinth; he'll understand. Especially Dr. Primalov. He's not the angry kind." He pushed his chair back and got to his feet, pointing to his right. "Head out that way. Take the first left you come across, and then right by the coffee machines. Pediatric oncology's his patch. You can't miss the wallpaper."

She thanked him and began hurrying in the direction he indicated, breaking into a run as soon as she was out of his line of sight.

She didn't understand what the man meant about the wallpaper until she saw the pale blue walls dotted with cartoon ducks, rabbits, and kittens. At the entrance to the ward, someone had painted the word "WELCOME!" on the wall in cheery daffodil yellow.

The ward centered on a large, curved desk with space for seven or eight staff to work at once. A nurse glanced up as Emma walked by, but, seeing her uniform, quickly looked back at her screen. Unwilling to draw more attention to herself by asking questions, she scoured the long hallway for any sign of Michael. But it seemed strangely subdued. The small wards, with their bright, childish decorations, and rumpled beds, piled with a jungle of stuffed animals, were all empty.

Despite all the cheerful touches, there was no way to miss the child-sized oxygen masks propped up on quiet machines. Seeing the tiny spaces the patients' bodies had occupied in the adult-sized beds was sobering, and Emma found her steps slowing. She'd known from his file that Michael specialized in children's cancer treatment, but she hadn't really thought through what that would look like.

About halfway down the corridor, the sound of a guitar and high-pitched laughter broke the hush. Emma followed the sounds until she reached a glass-walled room. On the other side of the window, fifteen children of various ages sat on the floor. Some wore little knitted caps to protect their hairless heads. Several sat next to IV stands, with clear tubes snaking down to their fragile arms. Some looked sturdy and strong, as if it was a mistake that they were here at all, but others were unnaturally frail, their skin translucent, their eyes huge and hollow. All of them were staring with rapt attention at a man in a black frock coat and top hat with a ukulele strapped across his chest. He was smiling broadly, in the middle of a story he'd been illustrating with a stuffed white rabbit. It took her a moment to realize the man was Michael.

"And so, the rabbit told the bear . . ." He motioned to the children and they all shouted eagerly, "I won't follow you *anywhere!*"

"I'm going to need your help on this next song," he warned them. "Ready?" He strummed the strings and the kids began singing in a discordant chorus so raucous it was difficult to make out the words.

"Isn't he great?" The voice came from Emma's elbow.

A nurse walked up beside her. She had wavy auburn hair and a scattering of freckles, and watched Michael with obvious affection.

"It's wonderful. The kids really seem to love him." Emma's eyes were still on his face; in none of the pictures provided by the Agency had he looked so happy.

"They know he's on their side," the other nurse confided. "It's incredibly tough for them here, surrounded by strangers while they're going through treatment. If they see him as a friend, it makes the whole thing less scary for them."

"Does he do this a lot?" Emma asked, glancing at her.

"Every week. We all look forward to it." The woman gave Emma a curious look. "I don't think I've seen you before." Her gaze flitted across the ID card on Emma's chest.

"Yes. I'm Jane. I started this week." Emma gestured vaguely behind them. "I shouldn't even be here. I was walking by and heard the laughter and wanted to see what was going on."

The woman smiled. "Well, you're very welcome. We need all the help we can get." She glanced at the watch pinned upside down on her uniform. "Speaking of which, I need to run. It was nice to meet you, Jane."

She headed away, her rubber-soled shoes silent on the linoleum floor. The movement must have caught Michael's attention, because as the song finished, he glanced up. When his eyes met hers through the glass, there was no recognition in his face.

The nurses had begun to shepherd the children toward a table with rows of juice boxes and bowls of fruit and tiny cakes. Emma motioned for him to come outside. He spoke to one of the nurses, who took the ukulele from him, and, stepping carefully past the crowd of small children, he walked out to join her.

"Can I help you?" he asked. He'd forgotten about the top hat, which was still perched incongruously atop his head.

Emma kept her voice low. "I'm sorry to come here like this, but you have to listen to me."

As soon as she spoke his face darkened. "Oh, for God's sake, don't you ever give up?"

"No." Emma kept her voice steady. "I can't give up because it is my job to get you somewhere safe. Please believe me: you are in real danger. Right now. This minute."

Her voice rose and an orderly pushing an empty stretcher glanced at them. Emma thought about the woman in the elevator. There could be others like her all over this ward.

"Can we go somewhere private to talk?" Seeing his mutinous expression, she said, "Please, Michael. Just give me five minutes."

"I already gave you five minutes," he snapped. But she held his eyes, unblinking and insistent until, at last, he gave a frustrated sigh. "Follow me."

He turned so suddenly that the top hat tumbled from his head and he snatched it from the air as she followed him to a windowless office barely big enough for a desk and chair. Michael leaned back against the desk, folding his arms across his chest. "This is a waste of time," he began. "I've given you my answer—"

"Did you know that while you were running in the park this morning, you were followed by two Russian agents?" Emma cut him off. "They've probably been following you for days. Maybe weeks."

His jaw dropped. "I don't . . . What are you saying?"

"We believe they are part of an assassination squad that has killed four people in the UK." Emma continued as if he hadn't spoken. "All the victims were close to your parents. Particularly your mother. There have been more murders in other countries. We think they've been saving you and your parents for last."

She could see the emotions flitting across his face—fear, worry—but when he spoke it was doubt that she heard.

"You're telling me you saw Russian agents?" he asked, incredulous. "In *Clissold Park?*"

"And ten minutes ago I saw one of them in this hospital. I'm willing to bet there are others. Watching you. Waiting for the right moment. We think they've been preparing for some time. Now they're going to act." She took a step forward, closing the space between them. "Michael, I need to take you somewhere safe. Just for a while, until our people can get this sorted. We're running out of time."

The look of determined disbelief faded slightly. "I can't do that," he said. But he didn't sound so certain anymore.

"They will kill you," she said simply. "And I think you know that. Please let me help."

He held her eyes for a long moment, before shifting his focus to the glossy black top hat in his hand. His shoulders slumped as he said, almost to himself, "I can't believe this is happening. My mother always said they'd come for us one day."

"And you didn't believe her?"

"I couldn't." He glanced up. "I've been British all my life. It's all I can remember. But my parents—they've always been Russian. I know they've been through things that I can't imagine. When they told me terrible things might happen, I thought they were just traumatized. Can you understand that?"

She could understand. Far more than she could say.

"I know this is hard," she began.

"Do you?" He flung a hand at the door behind her. "You saw those kids. I've dedicated my life to helping them. I'm good at what I do. You're asking me to walk away from them. From this life. To leave them to suffer."

"Not forever," she promised.

"For how long, then?" he challenged. "How long do I have to walk away from those sick children because of my parents' past?"

For some reason, she didn't want to lie to him. In truth, she had no idea if he'd ever be able to come back. But she could hardly say that.

"I don't know," she said. "Hopefully not very long."

"Hopefully." He made the word sound like an allegation. As if he knew everything she wasn't saying.

"I'm just trying to keep you alive. It might be that you can come back in a few weeks, after we've sorted this out, but I don't know." She paused, looking for words. "Michael, I saw you with those kids. I can see how good you are with them. But you must understand you can't help them if you're dead."

All the light left his face, and she was faced for a moment with the serious little boy with the dark, worried eyes from the photo Ripley had shown her.

Slowly, he shook his head. "I'm sorry. I won't walk away from my life because some spook tells me I should. I'm not leaving those kids. I don't intend to be a pawn in your twisted games." He threw the top hat on to the desk, where it spun before coming to rest at a jaunty angle on the keyboard.

Emma was bewildered. She'd had him. She could sense it. And then, just like that, she'd lost him again.

"Michael, please," she begged, "don't do this. Believe me, this is really happening. You can't wish it away. These people don't care how much you love those kids."

His face hardened. "Well, neither do you. So I guess I'll just have to take my chances." He pointed at the door. "Now, get out of here before I call security and have you thrown out."

6

ALL DAY LONG, Emma haunted the seventh floor, keeping an eye on Michael.

She made sure he never noticed her. There was no point in arguing with him further. She'd given him the information; now he needed time. But time was something they didn't have.

As the hours ticked by, she looked for the woman from the elevator but she never encountered her again. There was something ominous about her absence.

At eight o'clock that evening, Emma was waiting impatiently in a shadowy corner outside the Accident & Emergency wing, her eyes fixed on the staff exit.

She'd changed out of her disguise and back into her running clothes some time ago. The cool September breeze cut through the fleece jacket and she wished she'd worn something else as she jogged in place to keep warm.

According to his files, Michael usually left the hospital at around seven. He was running late but she didn't dare go back into the hospital to check on him. She'd be too noticeable.

By the time he finally walked out ten minutes later, her nerves were on edge. He wore the same dark coat he'd had on that morning, a laptop bag slung over one shoulder. He was talking to a tall woman Emma recognized as another doctor from his ward. They walked slowly, their heads tilted toward each other, talking quietly for so long Emma worried the woman would go home with him—that was a complication she didn't need.

Finally, though, they headed in opposite directions. Relieved, Emma followed Michael at a distance.

His normal routine was to catch the same bus home that he'd taken this morning, but he didn't do that today. Instead, he bypassed the bus stop and headed down the Holloway Road on foot. It struck her that his posture had changed since the morning. His head was down, his shoulders high around his ears. When a car honked, he twitched.

Good, Emma thought, with grim satisfaction. *You should be nervous.*

There was no way to truly protect him out here—any passing person could jab a needle into his arm and be gone before either of them realized what had happened.

At least he was headed in the direction of his flat. On foot, it would take him about half an hour to walk there. She didn't relish the idea of him being exposed and vulnerable for that long. But she knew the route he took every night, and she thought the risk was fairly low.

After about five minutes, though, he took an abrupt turn off the main road, and headed down a side street.

Emma's steps slowed. It would be harder to follow him on a quiet street without being noticed. She'd need to drop farther back.

She lingered at the corner pretending to look at her phone. Almost immediately, two figures melted out of the darkness to her right, moving with the swift silence of panthers.

As she watched them, Emma's breath caught. This was no casual walk. They were hunting.

To her relief, they hadn't spotted her. They must have believed she was just another commuter. So she had a chance.

Ahead, Michael passed under a streetlight; the glow illuminated his dark hair, and sent shadows across his face.

She saw the two men exchange a glance. One of them smiled.

They began to run toward him, their steps unnervingly silent.

Shoving her phone into her pocket, Emma followed.

The street was residential, middle-class; parked Audis and BMWs glittered beneath trees that were just beginning to turn autumn gold. The men wouldn't dare use guns here, she thought. It would be a knife or a syringe, or perhaps a single spray of nerve gas to the face.

Ahead, Michael walked on, utterly unaware that death ran toward him in cheap, Russian shoes.

"Hey!" The word burst out of her. A shocking roar in the silence.

Stumbling as if he'd been pushed, Michael spun around.

The two men faltered. One glanced back, and in the sulfurous glow of the streetlights she recognized him instantly. It was the male runner from the park that morning—tall and blond. Ice-cold eyes. The other man was stockier and older—maybe forty, with a nose that had been broken more than once.

Ignoring Michael, Emma ran toward the two men with a wide, apologetic smile. "I'm so lost. Do you know where Marsham Street is?"

They stared at her with threatening blankness, clearly trying to decide if she was a problem.

The older one first, she told herself.

Still smiling, she gave a last burst of speed and leaped, aiming a flying kick at the shorter man's chest.

It wouldn't have worked if he'd been even remotely expecting it. But every man everywhere, no matter how much you train him, underestimates a smiling young woman.

The blow caught him full force. His legs went out from under him and he flew back. His head connected with the wing mirror on the parked van behind him with a sickening crack. He slid down the side of the van and went still.

Expressionless, the younger man turned his attention from his partner to Emma. He took a moment to assess her, and then he lunged. Emma crouched, ready to spin away, but at the last instant she heard Michael say, "What . . . ?"

For a split second her attention wavered. The Russian's fist caught her right above her left eye.

She fell hard, her head hitting the curb with enough force that her vision blurred. She felt the air move above her head and, with effort, rolled to her left, avoiding a kick that had been aimed at her face.

She leaped to her feet, raising her fists. The night had blurred, and she swiped at her eyes trying to clear her vision. When she glanced down, there was blood on her hands.

The Russian's gaze shifted from her clenched hands to the blood she could feel trickling down her forehead. His lips twisted.

Emma had been hit harder than that before, though.

"Come on, then," she said.

But the Russian didn't run at her. Instead, he reached for the inside breast pocket of his jacket.

Whatever was in there, she couldn't let him get to it.

She rushed at him, aiming a lower version of the flying kick that had knocked out his partner. But he was ready for that, swatting her foot away with a quick chop of his hand.

She landed solidly and immediately threw herself at him again, aiming a kick at his stomach.

The Russian swung a punch at her ear and she ducked, aiming her knee at his crotch. It connected solidly. The man grunted and shoved her away with a sideways slam of his fist.

She spun around, watching him with cautious bewilderment. Any man should have been doubled over from that, but he didn't seem to feel it.

Again, she launched herself at him, swinging punches and kicks like it was graduation day at the training academy, but he took the blows with an air of disinterest. Even a kick that she was certain had cracked his ribs didn't slow him down.

He had to be on something. Some sort of drug that gave him energy and disguised pain, Emma thought.

She was aware that she was tiring, her movements were growing sluggish. Out of the corner of her eye, she saw Michael moving toward her, as if he thought he might help.

"Get out of here," she ordered between gritted teeth. "Run."

The Russian glanced at him hungrily. Spotting her chance, Emma swung a kick at his head. But she was worn out and her timing was off.

In the end, he made it look easy, grabbing her foot with one hand, twisting her around, letting go of her foot long enough to grip her throat with fingers like claws.

She struggled in his grasp, shoving the flat of her hand up against his nose, pulling fistfuls of hair out of his head, but nothing seemed to hurt him. Still she fought, clawing at his hands, elbows flying into his ribs.

And with every second she was growing more tired.

Everything she'd ever done—every bit of training she'd ever had—was all designed to prevent her from finding herself helpless like this.

She felt his thumb press against her carotid artery. Instantly, her air disappeared. She struggled, but there was nothing left in her. She was done.

Fear tightened its grip on her heart. She knew better than to be afraid. Fear was panic. Fear was death. But she was already letting go.

From the very beginning, surprise had been the only chance she'd had.

She could hear herself wheeze—a terrible, rattling sound.

The streetlights began to shrink until they were nothing more than pinpricks of light in a sea of black.

I'm sorry, Mama, she thought. *This shouldn't happen to you twice.*

From somewhere far away, she heard a thud. The Russian's body jerked. His hands gripped her convulsively, and then loosened and let go.

Released, Emma tumbled to the pavement, landing on her knees. She took a deep gulping breath of sweet night air. And another.

Slowly, painfully, she turned. Behind her, the Russian lay facedown on the pavement, his legs sprawled crookedly. Michael stood over him, still holding his laptop in both hands. His shoulder bag lay crumpled on the ground behind him. His eyes were wide, two spots of hectic color high on his cheeks.

"It was the only thing I had that was heavy," he explained shakily.

"It'll do." Her voice was hoarse.

Coughing, she stumbled to her feet, waving Michael away when he stepped forward to help.

"Jesus," she groaned, pressing a hand against the wound on her temple. "Now I know what it feels to be inside a cement mixer."

Michael was staring at the bodies sprawled on the pavement. "Who are those guys?"

"Who do you think?" She rubbed her throat gingerly.

"Those are Russian spies?"

"Unless you have a lot of enemies, I'd say that's a good guess." She wiped the blood off her cheek with the back of her hand. "Look, I know you have questions, but we have to get out of here before they wake up and kill us."

"You're hurt," Michael said. "We should go back to the hospital and get you checked out. We can call the police on the way."

"No police, no hospital." Her tone was abrupt.

"Are you insane?" He gestured at her face. "That guy nearly killed you. We have to tell the police."

"Michael, for God's sake. Look where you are." Grabbing his arm, she wheeled him around to face the bodies lying on the ground. "This is beyond the police. They can't help us. And I can't fight these guys again. I won't win. Please believe me: we have to run."

Maybe it was the brutal honesty in her voice, or her tight grip on his arm. Either way, he finally accepted the truth.

"OK, I get it." He reached for his bag, but she stopped him, pulling the computer from his hand and dropping it on the pavement.

"Leave it. Leave everything."

For a second she thought he'd argue again but then the older man shifted, his jacket making a sound like a snake sliding through grass. Startled, Michael jumped back.

"Come on," Emma whispered, grabbing his arm and pulling him with her. "Follow me."

They ran—slowly at first, but then faster as her head cleared—and soon they'd left the unconscious men behind them. At the intersection with the main road, she turned right, away from the hospital, and Michael went with her without question.

Emma kept trying to remember the route she'd planned for their escape, but her thoughts were muddy. She felt strangely distant from her own body, as if someone else were running for her. Nausea swirled in her stomach.

Barely slowing, she pulled her phone from her pocket and scrolled to the number she'd dialed earlier.

A man answered. "Vernon Institute."

It wasn't Ripley. It took her a second to place the clipped voice. It was Ed Masterson.

Emma's chest tightened. What was he doing answering the phone on this operation? Where was Ripley?

"This is Makepeace." Her voice was rough, like someone with a bad cold. "I need a location for pickup for myself and one other. Coming in hot."

"That's negative."

Emma's steps slowed. She was certain she'd heard him wrong. "Repeat please?"

"I said, that is negative," he said crisply. "You are not being picked up."

"You can't be serious." She half turned away from Michael, lowering her voice. "We're coming in hot—extremely hot. Get me R. Right now."

There was a pause. "R is unavailable."

Emma stopped walking. Michael slowed and looked back as she turned away, hissing into the phone. "What do you mean? He's running this operation."

"Not anymore." Masterson spoke deliberately. "R is not available at this time. Plans have changed."

Emma caught her breath. "Why is there no pickup? What the hell am I supposed to do now?"

"Things are extremely busy here. We are stretched very thin. R left instructions for you with the new arrangements. Everything will be explained."

Emma was beginning to wonder if she was losing her mind. Things were *busy*? What could be more important than this?

"I don't understand. Left them where?"

"He said to tell you they are with a contact named James Rogers. He did not tell us more than that." He paused before adding, "Actually, we'd like to know where this is, too. We can hardly offer assistance if we don't know where you're going. What's the location for this?"

Emma opened her mouth to answer but something stopped her. It was true the person running the operation would normally have this information, but if Ripley wanted Masterson to know, why hadn't he told him?

"Makepeace? The location," Masterson barked.

Still she wavered. Something wasn't right. But refusing to tell him would not go down well.

Finally, she said, "It's code for a dead drop we use in Islington."

"Copy that." She could hear someone speaking to him. A muffled sound as he replied. When he returned to the phone he spoke quickly. "Go directly to the drop. Follow the instructions there. And, Makepeace—you're to handle this on your own."

"But wait. Where is . . ."

Emma's voice trailed off. Masterson was already gone.

Slowly, she lowered the phone. Her feet seemed glued to the pavement.

Ripley would never leave her alone in a situation like this one. Something had to be wrong. He certainly wouldn't leave something as important as this case in Masterson's hands—his deputy had never run an operation. He was an office guy—he didn't get down in the dirt with the rest of them.

Still, why had she told him the drop was in Islington? She should have told him the truth. But for some reason she found she simply couldn't.

Michael was watching her, his eyes huge and nervous. "What's the matter?" he asked.

"It's nothing. They're just sending us somewhere I wasn't expecting." Her voice sounded stilted and unbelievable, but he accepted it.

He didn't know enough about how this was supposed to work to realize how wrong all of this was. Horribly wrong.

Directly ahead of them a bus waited at a stop, its interior lit up like a bonfire. A harsh beep sounded as the doors began to shut.

Leaving Michael where he was, Emma ran to the closing doors. Ducking down, she slid her phone inside just before the doors locked into place with a juddering thud. None of the bored passengers even glanced at her. The bus signaled and pulled out into the road. She stood at the edge of the street, watching as it grew smaller in the distance.

People pushing past gave her bloodied face a double take but kept moving. Londoners know when to mind their own business.

Michael walked over to join her. "Why did you do that?" he asked.

Emma didn't answer.

All she knew for certain right now was that the hammering behind her forehead was getting worse. Every part of her body ached. There was blood on her hands.

And this night was just getting started.

7

A T SCHOOL, EMMA had always felt somehow separate from the other children. None of them had mothers who drank bitter black tea and complained in Russian when the train was late.

None of their fathers had been spies.

She told no one the truth about her family. Her mother, she said, was a ballerina. Her father had died in a plane crash, or on a boat, or in a hunting accident, depending on her mood.

These weren't the only lies she told. She was honest about most things but found it easy to lie about her family.

She was practicing, she told herself, for the day when she could be like those agents who had rescued her mother, and tried to save her father.

Because, one day, she was determined to be one of them.

In her mind they were heroes. People who had risked their lives to save a Russian family they scarcely knew.

This was a secret she kept from her mother, who professed an absolute hatred for all spies.

"They would destroy the world to get their hands on one secret," she would say contemptuously. "They care nothing about the people they hurt."

Her mother felt betrayed by the loss of her husband, and traumatized by the months she'd spent alone in this strange country waiting for the man who would never join her. To her, spies were not heroes, but traitors who convinced others to betray their nations.

So Emma told her nothing of her plans as she raced through an international relations degree at university. When she graduated, she joined the army but did not mention that she'd requested an assignment to a military intelligence unit, which specialized in Russian surveillance, based near the German city of Bielefeld.

Once there, she made herself as useful as she could, polishing her already fluent Russian and German skills in night classes, working extra hours. Taking every language class she was offered.

That was as far as planning and hard work could take her. The rest was fate.

It was fate that made her commanding officer send word one day that he wanted her to "meet someone from HQ." When she walked into the utilitarian military office building shaking water from her raincoat, she found the CO chatting amiably with a man in a navy-blue suit. The two were about the same age, both physically fit and graying around the edges.

"Oh, excellent." The CO motioned for her to come in. The other man got to his feet slowly, his face watchful. "I need you to meet someone. This scoundrel is Charles Ripley. We go back years. Charles—this is the young woman I was telling you about."

Ripley shook her hand. His grip was steady, his fingers warm against her cold, rain-damp hand. He studied her face with an almost uncomfortably piercing gaze. In an instant she'd decided that he was not someone she'd ever want to lie to.

"Robert speaks very highly of you." His accent was cut glass—public school all the way, she decided. Eton or Harrow. Stepping back, he reached for a coffee mug he'd left sitting on the edge of the CO's desk. "I'm told you're the one to watch in his unit. Apparently, you're fearless."

"I'm not fearless," she replied without hesitation. "I'm just good at not showing how scared I am."

"To hell with that," her CO objected. "She's got the coolest head of anyone I've worked with. Well, since I last worked with you, at least, Rip. Never seen anyone so calm when it all goes to hell."

Ripley studied her with the ruthless interest of a cat observing a bird that had landed on the grass. "That," he said, "is an extremely underrated attribute."

"She'd be perfect for Six, with all her languages," the CO said.

"Perhaps," Ripley conceded. "But there are other options."

Only then did Emma realize what this meeting was really about. Ripley had to be Secret Service. Everyone knew some Army Intelligence officers moved straight to MI6, often at high levels. This was her chance.

Her heart began to race, but she kept her expression neutral as the CO lit a cigar, motioning for her to take a seat. "Her Majesty's Government would like an update on our operation in Poland," he explained, the words coming out in puffs of scented smoke. "I told Rip you know more about it than I do. Thought you might update him."

This was safe ground. Emma had been running the operation for the last few weeks. Shooting the CO a grateful look, she explained how she'd been helping Polish Intelligence eavesdrop on a Russian unit running military exercises near the Polish border. To do this, she'd personally placed listening devices in the temporary Russian base. She made it sound routine but, in truth, it had been her biggest job since joining the army, and Ripley saw straight through the false modesty.

"Wasn't that dangerous?" he asked.

"I suppose. But it was the only way we could figure out what they were planning. Until then they just kept surprising us." She glanced at the CO, whose lips curled up in a slight smile. "We don't like surprises."

The CO leaned toward Ripley. "Here's what she's not telling you." He tilted the cigar at her. "She waltzed across the Russian border disguised as a Polish worker. Cool as Cornish cream. No one looked at her twice. Got herself on the base, placed bugs where we needed them, and strolled home at four o'clock that afternoon, like it was a normal day at the office." He gave a slow headshake. "Those devices have been gold mines for us."

Ripley sat holding that coffee mug, watching Emma with unnerving steadiness. He had a curious ability to sit so still he barely seemed to breathe. Only when the CO finally fell silent did he speak, asking a few sharply focused questions about the operations. She answered as well as she could. And that was it. Fifteen minutes later, she was back out in the rain, wondering whether or not she'd passed the test.

In the days that followed, all the CO would say when she asked was that Ripley had enjoyed meeting her.

"But what happens now?" she'd prodded.

The CO's response was maddening. "If he wants you, he'll call."

Only he didn't.

Emma served out the last six months of her contract with the army without ever hearing from Charles Ripley or anyone else in the Secret Service. She was gutted. If she wanted to be a spy, she'd have to find another way. And it wouldn't be easy.

On the day she left the army for good, she flew from Germany to Farnborough airbase in England. There she collected her paperwork and caught a train for home from the local station, a civilian again at last.

It had been a long day. She was half asleep with her head against the train window, silvery green fields flying by unseen, when her phone rang.

The phone was brand new. She'd bought it in Germany a few days earlier after handing in the one the military had given her. When she picked it up, the screen was blank aside from the green symbol of an incoming call blinking insistently.

She hit answer. "Hello?"

A voice with a cut-glass accent said, "This is Charles Ripley. Have you got a job lined up?"

Emma was so shocked it took her a second to reply. "No. Not yet."

"Excellent. I've got an opening, and I think you'd be perfect for it. You're on the train now, aren't you?" He didn't pause to explain how he could possibly know that. "Come into London on Monday and I'll tell you all about it. My assistant will send you the location. Ten o'clock."

And just like that, she was tapped to be part of the Secret Service. Working for an agency with no name, in a job with no description.

It was everything she'd dreamed of.

8

"WHAT ARE WE going to do?" Michael's voice was unsteady. He was shivering, his face pale in the shadows.

Emma's head throbbed viciously. She was dizzy, and her thoughts kept slipping away. She might actually have a concussion.

She'd lied to Masterson about what Ripley's message meant. If he ever found out, she'd be written up for insubordination, or worse, but Ripley's absence in the middle of an operation, and his message—both were warnings she could read as clearly as the writing on an illuminated billboard.

Something had gone very wrong. And Masterson could not be trusted.

Spotting a cab with its yellow light on, she made an instant decision and stepped into traffic to flag it down. "We need to get away from here," she told Michael, forcing confidence into her voice, as if everything happening now had always been part of a plan. "I'll explain on the way."

When the cabbie rolled down his window, she leaned in, trying to look steadier on her feet than she felt. "Gospel Oak, please."

The driver scanned her face with concern. "You OK, luv? Looks like you hurt yourself." He shot Michael a suspicious glance.

Emma stifled a curse. The call to Masterson had distracted her so much she'd forgotten about the blood on her face.

Thinking fast, she touched her forehead, adding a quiver to her voice. "It's so stupid. I tripped on the curb and went flying. I don't think I broke anything, but I need to get home and clean myself up." She gestured at Michael. "My friend is a doctor."

The sad act worked. "Looks like you really gave your head a whack," the driver said sympathetically as he unlocked the door. "Sit yourself down."

In most cities when it all goes to hell, you want a cop. In London, it's a cabdriver you look for.

Inside, it was warm and dry, and Emma resisted the urge to lean back against the headrest until the pain passed. Instead, she turned to the window to check her reflection in the darkened glass. A bruise shadowed her temple and a streak of blood ran down the side of her face, smeared across her cheek where she'd rubbed it. She tried to wipe it off with her sleeve, but it clung stubbornly to her skin.

"Use this." Michael, who'd been silently watching, held out a slim packet of alcohol wipes. Seeing her expression, he shrugged. "I always have them on me. Professional hazard."

"Thanks." She swiped at the blood, welcoming the cleansing sting, turning when she'd finished so he could see. "Is that better?"

He gave her a look that was part bafflement, part disapproval. But all he said was, "Let me try." Taking the wipe from her, he dabbed her cheek with it, his hands gentle but assured. There was a pause in which the only sound was the cab's engine as it growled down the road. "Look, I know you don't want to hear this, but that was a hell of a beating. You could have serious injuries. Does your head hurt?"

After a quick glance at the cabbie to ensure he was listening to the radio and not to them, she said, "Of course it does. I just had the shit kicked out of me."

Ignoring her tone, he said, "Any dizziness? Flashes of light at the fringes of your vision? Nausea?"

"None."

She got the feeling he knew she was lying.

"Look at me." She shifted her gaze to meet his. A slight frown creased his forehead as he studied her as if he might be able to see the damage written on her face. "Follow my fingers." He held up his left hand with two fingers raised, moving them slowly up and down, back and forth.

He was left-handed. Had she known that? It must have been in his file.

She wondered what he'd say if she told him how slow and confused her thoughts really were right now. How her head seemed to be beating her up from the inside.

She batted his hand away. "Michael, come on," she said. "I'm going to be fine. I promise I'll get checked out." With a glance at the cabdriver, she lowered her voice to a whisper. "But first, I need to get you to safety, OK?"

He clearly wanted to argue but seemed to recognize the futility of trying. He gave a slight shrug. "Fine. Just try not to die on me."

"That's my plan." Wincing, Emma shifted in her seat, angling her body so she could watch the street behind them. The roads were busy, but as they turned corner after corner, she could see no indication they were being followed. That was something, at least.

Michael moved to the opposite side of the taxi, putting distance between them. She could feel his cool gaze. When she looked up, his arms were crossed.

"So, are you going to tell me what's happening now? Or am I just supposed to follow blindly?"

Emma knew him well enough by now to realize that if she didn't give him some sort of explanation, he'd make this all much harder.

"There's been a complication," she said after a pause.

His eyebrows drew together. "What kind of complication?"

"They've changed the place where I need to bring you." Emma

kept her voice low. "I have to pick something up that will . . . give me more information. It won't take long."

She'd chosen her words carefully and he seemed to know this. He studied her for a long moment, his eyes unnervingly piercing.

"I don't like being lied to," he said, finally. "I don't like any of this. What proof do I have that you are who you say you are? For all I know you could be working for the people who want to hurt my mother. This could all be some fucking double-bluff, or whatever you call it in spy language." He rubbed his forehead. "Christ. How did I get into this mess?"

"Come on, Michael." Emma made her voice calming. "You saw those men back there. That's all the proof you need."

He turned his hands over on his lap—a small gesture of concession.

"Listen, I just need to pick up some information so I can take you somewhere safe. Then I'll put myself in a nice quiet hospital room for a few hours, I promise."

It was unnerving how steady his eyes were. As if he could see through her to the mountain of things she wasn't telling him.

He's smart, Ripley had told her. *And he's stubborn.*

He exhaled. "Fine. But if you keep lying to me, this isn't going to work."

The cab slowed. The driver looked back at them in the mirror. "Gospel Oak Station is just ahead. Where do you want to stop?"

Relieved to have an excuse not to answer more of Michael's questions, Emma leaned forward and gave him quick directions. A minute later, he pulled up in front of a restored Victorian pub at the end of a row of trendy shops. The shops were all closed at this hour, but the pub was heaving. Smokers clustered outside, balancing pints on the edges of flower boxes bursting with blooms. Nobody noticed them standing at the curb as the cab pulled away.

"I take it we're not going in there." Michael pointed at the pub.

Shaking her head, Emma began walking toward a long stretch of darkness in the distance, motioning for him to follow.

"Pity." He trudged beside her, hands shoved into his pockets. "I can honestly say I've never wanted a drink more than I do right now."

Emma didn't respond. She was thinking about Masterson and Ripley and what might be happening back at the Agency. She hoped Ripley's message held some answers.

Because the Russian agents she'd fought would be back on their feet by now.

And they would be furious.

9

WITHIN A MINUTE, the lights of the street vanished, and a long expanse of green opened up. Emma turned right onto a wide, paved path.

"The thing you need to pick up—it's in here?" Mark surveyed the park with a puzzled air.

"It better be," Emma said.

They were on the edge of Hampstead Heath—a sprawling, wooded area of parkland. In the distance, Parliament Hill rose steeply to a rounded point from which views of the London skyline were famously spectacular, but Emma didn't head in that direction. Instead, she took the first left onto a narrower, unlit path, moving cautiously through the darkness.

Her first undercover assignment had involved working in a bar frequented by Russian business executives in nearby Highgate. Ripley, who didn't trust technology, would leave her messages here when there was something he wanted her to know. There were no CCTV cameras inside this end of the Heath, and very few lights.

She knew precisely where to go: she'd been here dozens of times.

All the same, the bench seemed to creep up on her, and she almost tripped over it.

"Hey, wait," she called softly to Michael, who hadn't noticed her sudden stop.

In the quiet of the park, she could hear voices from the streets in the distance, and the restive sound of birds rustling in the trees overhead as her fingers ran across the wooden seat, finding the brass plaque on the back. She knew without being able to see it what it would say. "To James Rogers from Anne: his favorite view."

Crouching down, she felt along the ground beneath the bench until she located a stone, about the size of her fist. When she moved it aside, she felt the circular hole dug out beneath it. Carefully, she reached inside. Her fingers brushed dirt and pebbles. Nothing else.

Swearing under her breath, she angled her body lower, trying to get her hand deeper. She identified rocks, something slimy and cold— a rotting leaf, maybe. But nothing useful.

Despite the chill in the air, a trickle of sweat ran down her back. It *had* to be here. Ripley wouldn't send her here for nothing.

She'd almost given up when her fingers brushed something. It was small but felt out of place. Not a pebble. Something softer.

Grasping it carefully between her index finger and thumb, she sat up, resting it in the palm of her hand.

It was a square of tissue-thin cigarette paper, folded until it was no bigger than her smallest fingernail. On one side, she could see an "E." Even in that one letter she recognized Ripley's distinctive, almost typographic handwriting.

Some of the tension in her chest eased. He had been here, sometime in the last few hours. He'd been fine then.

Setting it down for a second, she rubbed her hands hard against her legs to get the dust off her fingertips before carefully unfolding the paper. The only thing inside was a tiny piece of plastic—a data card.

She turned to look up at Michael, who stood watching her with quiet befuddlement. "I need to borrow your phone."

In the profound quiet of the park, she heard the rustle of clothing as he pulled it from his pocket. She turned the phone over until she found the right opening and slid the tiny card in. The phone churned for so long, she thought for an awful moment it wasn't going to be able to read it. Kneeling on the cold, damp earth, she whispered a prayer under her breath.

Just as she'd begun to despair, the screen lit up, white letters against black. She scoured them eagerly.

Ripley had encrypted the text using an old code, one they hadn't used since she first started working with him. Emma knew instantly that she'd been right to lie to Masterson. He wouldn't have done this if everything was fine.

The message was brief and blunt.

Change of plans. I think I know who's behind the attacks. If I'm right, this is more dangerous than we feared. Don't bring the guest home. Take him to the neighbors. Avoid all cameras, they're not ours right now. Be careful with M. No calls. No tech. Move fast. Stay dark.

After that, there was only one line. "I chose you for a reason. This is why."

As Emma read her mentor's words, her body tightened into a coiled spring.

For the second time that night, all the air left her lungs.

They should be running as fast and as far as they could, and yet she remained crouched in the dark as cold spread through her to her fingertips, reading his words again, trying to get her brain to accept what he was telling her.

The "guest" was Michael. The "neighbors"—this was what Ripley called MI6. He wanted her to take Michael to their headquarters across the river at Vauxhall Cross rather than to the Agency. Almost inconceivably, this meant that Ripley feared the Russians might know that the Vernon Institute was their cover. Or that he didn't trust someone on his own side.

The worst part, though, was "Avoid all cameras." The city's massive CCTV network—London's famed ring of steel—was not "ours."

It had been hacked. If the Russians had the cameras, they could hunt her and Michael down like animals.

"Be careful with M." Ripley must have known Masterson would be put in charge of the operation. Either he didn't trust him or he didn't want him involved in this operation at all. He was telling her to handle this alone.

Now she understood why there hadn't been a pickup. And why no one was free to help. There was a silent war going on right now—one nobody in London could see. But it was real. And she was right in the middle of it.

Emma yanked the card from the phone with more force than necessary and dropped it onto the pavement before grinding it under her heel with a vicious twist of her ankle until it was reduced to powder. Then she kicked the shattered pieces into the dirt with barely contained fury.

Michael watched this with trepidation. "What's going on?"

Emma kept her face turned away from him. She couldn't think of a believable lie. But she could hardly tell him the truth. Because the truth was, they were screwed. And, whatever Ripley thought, she didn't have the knowledge or the skills to do what he was asking of her.

How the hell was she going to get Michael across London without being seen by any camera with a GRU assassination squad hunting her?

She couldn't do it. No one could. Not alone. She needed six other people. No. Ten, actually. She needed ten to do this. In a carefully planned operation. Alone, she was dead.

"Dammit, Ripley," she whispered. "Where are you?"

Squaring her shoulders, she turned to face Michael. "Right. I know where to go." Somehow, she imbued her voice with all the confidence she didn't feel.

Those intelligent dark eyes searched her face for any sign of deception.

"So," he said cautiously, "everything's OK?"

"Everything is *not* OK," Emma told him. "But it will be."

With that, she turned and began to jog back across the dark park. A few seconds later, she heard his footsteps following.

She was glad he wasn't asking more questions—she needed a few minutes to think this through. She couldn't take him straight into the heart of the city without a plan in place. And they couldn't stay still. They were too findable.

Findable. She looked down at her hand, still holding his phone.

Without breaking stride, she threw it hard. It sailed into the line of shrubs bordering the path.

"What the hell did you do that for? That was mine!" Behind her, she heard Michael slow, as if he might try to retrieve it.

"Leave it. It's bugged," she told him over her shoulder. "I'll get you a new one."

There was a pause as this information sank in. Then she heard the steady thump of his footsteps as he hurried after her.

"How do you know that?" he demanded.

"It's my job to know."

"My whole life was on that phone," he said, sorrowfully.

"I'll get you a new one of those, too."

The street appeared ahead, the streetlights bright after the darkness of the park, and she motioned for him to follow as she slanted off the path onto the grass, skirting the main entrance to the park and then dashing across the road. They'd just reached the shadows on the other side when she spotted three quick-moving figures heading toward the park entrance. Grabbing Michael's arm, she dragged him out of sight behind a parked van. For once, he had the good sense not to speak but gave her a silent, quizzical look.

She held her finger against her lips, and then pointed at the group on the other side of the street.

The three moved with animal smoothness as they turned in to the park. She couldn't make out their faces, but one of them was tall enough to be the man who'd tried to kill her. Emma was willing to bet the other two were the older man with the uneven nose, and the thin blond woman from the hospital.

As they disappeared into the park, the short one dropped back and swept the street with a look, as if he'd sensed their presence. Emma held her breath, digging her fingers into Michael's arm. Willing him not to move.

Finally, the man turned to follow the others. Emma sagged back against the metal of the van, her heart pounding.

Either she'd been right about Michael's phone or they'd been caught on CCTV on the way here. It didn't matter which—the speed with which the assassins had arrived told her everything she needed to know about how serious they were.

As soon as the three disappeared from sight, she jumped to her feet. "Hurry," she hissed, pulling Michael with her.

He was still staring at where the figures had disappeared. "You think they're looking for us?"

Emma, scanning the nearby buildings for CCTV cameras, responded without glancing at him. "I think they're looking for you."

He flinched, shoulders hunching as if he'd taken a blow.

Cursing her own glibness, Emma slowed. "Hey," she said.

Despite every fiber in her body calling her to run, she waited until he lifted his eyes to meet hers.

"I know you're scared," she told him. "I am, too. But I promise I'm going to keep you safe. You asked me to tell you the truth, and I will as much as I can. In return, I need you to trust me. And right now, I'm telling you we need to run like hell."

He searched her face—for what, she didn't know. Honesty? Trustworthiness? Whatever it was he was looking for, he must have found it.

He nodded. "OK." His voice was tight, but resolute. "Let's go."

10

TEN MINUTES LATER, Emma and Michael stopped to catch their breath in a dark, narrow alleyway behind a row of shops.

She stayed near the entrance, watching the street, looking for signs that they were being followed. Her head still hurt but her thoughts felt clearer now.

Michael had barely spoken since that exchange outside the park. Now, though, he glanced at her.

"Is someone picking us up here?" he asked.

"Not exactly." She waited as a van turned a corner and disappeared from view. "I'm going to bring you to the office personally. I just need to make a couple of stops first. It won't take long."

He craned his neck to see what she was looking at. "You think those guys are still trying to find us?"

"I know they are." She paused, turning to face him. "Look, there's something I need to tell you. The message from my office—it said the CCTV network has been hacked. We have to avoid cameras. *All* cameras."

"I don't understand." His frown deepened. "Who hacked it?"

"Let's just say your mother's friends in Moscow have been busy."

He pressed his hands to his forehead. "How can this be happening?"

"I wish I knew the answer to that," Emma said. "Trust me when I say this was not how today was supposed to go."

"But this is *London,*" he reminded her. "There are cameras everywhere. There are cameras all over the tube. And on buses and trains. On the streets." His voice took on an edge of panic as the realization set in. "How can we get across the city without being seen?"

"We walk." Motioning for him to follow, Emma headed out of the alleyway and toward the well-lit street around the corner. "Carefully."

She kept her tone light but the truth was, he was right. Not only was London the most filmed city on earth, the camera system was equipped with state-of-the-art facial-recognition software. The interconnected citywide CCTV system was how criminals were caught. If that was being deployed against the two of them, evasion was almost impossible. The only thing in their favor right now was the fact that face-recognition technology is less accurate in the dark. She had to get Michael across the city before the sun came up or they were finished. Even then, the odds were against them. They were completely alone. Up against the best spy network in the world.

It was nearly eleven o'clock by now, and the city was beginning to quiet. Few people walked down the brightly lit main street, and most of the shops were shuttered. Emma could see no obvious cameras but she knew they were there—tucked under eaves or high beneath gutters. Most weren't connected to the central network that had been compromised. But some would be.

She was about to say something when a group of three men turned a corner and headed toward them, talking loudly, laughing louder. Drunk, she decided. Probably not a problem. But best avoided. Anything that attracted attention was bad right now.

"Keep your head down," she whispered to Michael, tilting her face at the pavement.

Out of the corner of her eye, she saw him notice the men and look away. Neither of them spoke as the three neared. She felt their eyes on the two of them, and she stepped closer to Michael but kept her face turned away.

She heard one of the men say too loudly, "What's the matter with them?" And sniggering replies she couldn't quite make out.

But they kept going, and that was all she wanted.

When the men had passed out of sight, Michael asked, "Can I at least know where we're going? Or is that secret, too?"

"We need to make a short stop in Camden." Emma kept her tone easy.

"And after that?"

"Vauxhall."

He gave her an incredulous look. "You know those two places are on opposite sides of the city, right?"

"Yeah, well." She shrugged. "Buckle up. It's going to be a long walk."

Twenty minutes later, the two of them stopped on a deserted north London street. A grimy sign above their heads read ALL THE TIME INTERNET CAFÉ in bright yellow letters.

"We're going in *there*?" Michael's voice held quiet disbelief. Clearly this was not the smoothly planned government rescue he'd expected.

Emma could have explained that she'd come in here regularly while she'd been undercover with the activists. Or that she knew the owners deleted data from the computers several times a day.

But all she said was "They don't have CCTV. And the coffee's good."

Inside, the narrow room held rows of computer terminals on long tables with privacy barriers between each screen, only two of which were occupied. The place smelled of coffee and dust.

A tired-looking young man in a T-shirt that had a clock and "ATT" on the front stood up as they approached the front desk. She didn't recognize him. He must be new. She didn't like new people.

"An hour, please." She wouldn't need that long, but she'd been here often enough to know it was the minimum.

He typed something into his computer and then wrote a code down on a slip of paper and handed it to her. "Booth seventeen," he said. "You want some coffee?"

"Yeah." She grabbed a couple of chocolate bars off the stack by the register, and two bottles of water from the cooler. She added a small pack of ibuprofen to the stack and then pointed at the burner phones hanging on the wall behind him. "One of those, too."

"This one?" He reached back for a black, basic model.

She nodded without looking at it. "How much?"

When he rang it all up, it took the last of her cash. She was going to have to get more money soon. But that meant another stop, and she was already worried about time.

Despite what she'd told Michael, getting across the city without being seen would be neither fast nor easy. They needed every minute. But first, she needed to plan.

Booth 17 was at the far end of the second row; nobody was sitting nearby. Emma broke the burner phone out of its packaging and plugged it in to charge. While Michael dragged a chair over, she swallowed two painkillers and half a bottle of water, then waited until the guy from the front desk brought over steaming mugs of coffee and walked away again before getting started.

"OK," she said, sliding Michael a chocolate bar and tearing one open for herself. "Let's figure this out."

They ate, staring at the glow of the monitor while she traced a winding, crooked path across the city. It was only six miles from Camden to MI6's brutalist glass-and-concrete headquarters south of the river, but they couldn't walk a straight line if they wanted to keep out of sight. Parks were good. They had very few cameras and limited lights. Also canals and residential streets.

Someone had left a scrap of paper and a pencil on a nearby desk and she grabbed it to scribble a few directions. By the time she'd finished, the clock on the computer told her it was nearly midnight. The walk across the city would take several hours by the route she'd outlined. The sun would come up at around 7 a.m.

For the first time, hope began to kindle in her heart. Even if everything took longer than she anticipated, they could do this.

Her headache was finally receding, but the fight had taken a toll. She felt weary and sore. She wrapped her hands around the mug of coffee, absorbing the heat, wishing she had a whole pot.

Michael set his cup down. "This is probably a stupid question, but can't we just take a taxi?"

She shook her head. "Taxis have cameras mounted in the rearview mirrors and they're easily traced. Besides, if a street camera caught us getting into one, they'd be on us in a minute. I don't want to put an innocent person in danger."

"Uber?" he suggested with little hope.

She gave him an incredulous look. "No."

Ripley had told her to "stay dark." That meant cash only, no tech, no apps, nothing that could be traced now or later. They had to be off the grid.

Michael crumpled his chocolate wrapper into a tiny ball. "You really think we can get away from them on foot?"

"I know we can." Her voice was steady but she knew the more questions he asked, the more worried he was going to get. She shoved her chair back and unplugged the phone, sliding it into her pocket. "I need the loo. Give me two minutes and we'll hit the pavement."

A narrow flight of stairs at the back led down to a dimly lit corridor with a storage room and a closet-sized utilitarian toilet lit by a single fluorescent bulb. She closed the door behind her and slid the lock into place.

The quiet—the aloneness—felt like having the weight of a car lifted off her body. She stood still, her back to the door, and breathed.

She could do this. She *would* do this. Ripley didn't make mistakes.

I chose you for a reason.

In the mirror, her face looked pale. Her hair was tangled and lank. The bruise on her temple was turning purple.

She stared into her reflected blue eyes, searching for doubt. Doubt was a killer. It crept up your spine to muddle your thoughts and slow your reflexes.

She believed she could this. It wasn't going to be easy. But she was determined. She was fast. And she had a plan.

She turned on the tap and splashed cold water on her face, scrubbing her hands to remove the last traces of blood from around her nails. When she was done, she pulled her hair back with an elastic band. The face in the mirror stared back at her with measured calm.

She looked normal again. She looked ready.

As she ran back up the stairs, she went over the map in her mind. The first leg of the journey was the easiest. It would get harder when they reached the city center—it was impossible to avoid cameras there. But if they made it that far, she'd find a way.

As she reached the top step, her feet stopped of their own accord. She stared at booth 17, struggling to take in what was right in front of her.

The seat where Michael should have been waiting was empty. He wasn't anywhere in sight.

He was gone.

11

Emma hurtled across to the computer where they'd sat together minutes ago. The chairs had been pushed back into place. Both mugs had been cleared away. Even the scrap of paper and pencil had disappeared. It was as if they'd never been there at all.

For a fleeting second, the floor seemed to sway beneath her feet. The shadows at the edges of the room swelled, darkening her vision as the reality rose to meet her. Someone must have followed them here. If that was the case, it was over. Michael was dead.

Forcing herself to stay calm, she scanned the room. There had been two people at computers when they came in, now there was only one—a skinny twenty-something in a faded denim jacket. His attention was laser focused on the scantily clad body on the screen in front of him. He didn't look up as she ran over and grabbed his chair.

Startled brown eyes peered up at her as she knocked the headphones off his head.

"The man who was sitting right there." She pointed at the booth across the room. "Where did he go?"

He shook his head, eyes wide, pointing at the woman on-screen as if she were an alibi. "No English," he pleaded. "No English."

The other man (she searched her memory, finding an image of him—older, thinning hair, plaid button-down shirt with a threadbare collar, reading what looked like email) was gone. And there was no sign of the smooth-faced worker who'd brought them coffee.

Her mind worked through every detail. How long had she been out of the room? No more than five minutes. There was no sign of a fight. Even if someone had him, they could only have a two-minute head start.

Moving fast, she threaded her way past the computers to the front, searching for the guy who'd checked them in. The desk at the front was empty. Was it him? Was he the one? Maybe he'd helped the older man, and they were in it together.

She was about to turn away when she heard a shuffling sound from behind a narrow door half-hidden by a jacket left hanging from a hook.

Without a second's hesitation, she ran around the desk, kicked the chair out of the way, and threw the door open.

On the other side was a small, crowded cupboard, barely big enough to hold a coffeemaker and a sink. Standing in front of it, the guy in the ATT T-shirt was washing the coffee cups she and Michael had used. He looked up at her with an expression of almost comic surprise.

"The guy I came in with—did you see where he went?" she demanded.

Regaining composure, he gestured with the mug, sending soapy water slopping onto a floor that looked like it was used to it. "Outside. He said you were finished."

"Was he alone?"

The question seemed to bewilder him. He stared at her.

"Answer me." Her voice rose: *"Was he alone?"*

"I didn't notice." He sounded scared. "I think so?"

Whirling away from him, she crossed to the front door in three steps and yanked it open.

Michael stood on the pavement by himself, hands shoved into the pockets of his jacket, looking up at a night sky turned velvet gray by the city lights.

Emma sagged back against the wall. He was fine.

She transitioned from relieved to furious at rocket speed. "What the hell are you doing out here?"

Startled, he spun around and eyed her warily. "Nothing. I just wanted some air."

"Jesus Christ, Michael." She was so angry she could hardly speak. "Are you actually trying to get yourself killed? Do you want to die?"

"Of course not." Color rose to his face. "I just wanted air."

"They have air *inside*."

"I didn't think it was a big deal. Why are you so angry?" He held out his hands. "Everything is fine. I'm fine."

"Oh, for fuck's sake," she snapped, turning away. "Let's go."

For a long time after that neither of them spoke. Emma fumed as she set a pace just slightly faster than a harried London commuter's normal speed. Running would attract notice if they passed a camera. She took a series of turns—first left, then right, then right again— sticking to quiet streets she trusted. This part of the journey, at least, was familiar. Threading through the narrow, twisting back lanes gradually calmed her. After spending months undercover with Raven's group, she knew Camden well. It was an odd neighborhood—one that had long been cheap to live in and popular with musicians and artists drawn by the huge flea market, funky coffee shops, and music bars. Now, though, like most of London, it was ruined by a seemingly endless influx of billionaires and property speculators.

On the main streets the all-night bars and clubs would still be jammed, but these streets were where the bankers slept, and they were quiet as a vault.

Michael hadn't looked at her since they left the internet café. With his shoulders slumped and his head down, it was hard to see him as the same bright young doctor she'd met this morning. He looked defeated. She wasn't making this easy for him.

Of course he hadn't thought twice about going outside alone—this wasn't his world. He was a brilliant doctor and she'd talked to him like he was a toddler.

That was a fail, Emma.

She cleared her throat. "I'm sorry I shouted at you."

His head jerked up. Those dark eyes met hers.

"I was scared," she told him frankly. "When I came upstairs and found you gone, I was afraid something had happened to you. But I shouldn't have lost it like that. We're in this together."

There was a pause before he said, "Thank you for that."

The polite words hung in the air between them, too sparse for comfort.

Ahead, the lights of Camden High Street loomed, but before they reached it, Emma motioned for Michael to stop. "In here." She headed to a concrete ramp leading down into darkness.

An hour ago he would have asked for an explanation, but now he followed in silence as she walked down the steep ramp. Motion-detector lights blinked on one at a time, revealing in pieces, like an ugly jigsaw puzzle coming together, a stained cement floor, rough industrial walls, and rows of parked cars. Somewhere nearby, water dripped with slow insistence.

Emma had noticed when she was living in the neighborhood that this parking garage had no cameras and wasn't manned overnight. Even during the day, a service came by only intermittently to check on it.

"This way," she said, motioning for Michael to follow her to a battered locker door marked "FIRE EXTINGUISHER" in lettering so faded it was barely legible.

Crouching down, she pulled off the fake lock she'd put on three months ago. Despite the rusted exterior, the door opened silently on hinges she'd oiled carefully back then. She pulled out a heavy antique fire extinguisher and set it to one side. Behind it was a worn gym bag she'd placed here the first week she went undercover with the activists.

She unzipped it and began pulling out items with swift efficiency and setting them on the oil-stained floor—a thick stack of twenty-pound notes, a set of lockpicks in a black pouch, a small flashlight, a short knife that fit neatly into her hand. Next came clothes—a dark jacket and a long-sleeved black top.

She emptied the pockets of her dirty fleece before stuffing it without ceremony into the empty bag. Her top swiftly followed. It was cold in the garage and goose pimples rose on her shoulders during the seconds it took her to yank the new top over her head.

"What is all this stuff doing here?" Michael's voice echoed off the concrete walls.

"I put it here a while ago, just in case." She pulled on the jacket, grateful for its clean, dry warmth.

She began filling her pockets with the cash and supplies. When she picked up the knife, he stopped her. "What's that for?"

"Emergencies," she said, sliding it into her boot.

She rummaged through the bag until she found a blond wig at the bottom. Tucking her own hair back behind her ears, she pulled it on and straightened it as best she could without a mirror.

"Is it crooked?" she asked, turning so he could see.

He studied her face, his eyes unreadable. "It looks fine."

Hurrying now, she zipped the bag closed. Only when she'd picked it up and turned to go did she hear him say quietly, "How bad is it?"

He was so smart. He'd seen how she'd reacted back at the Internet café, and now he was looking at her supplies and figuring out what it all meant. If she lied right now, he'd know. If he knew, he wouldn't trust her. She needed to give him the truth.

"Quite bad," said Emma.

He let this information sit for a moment, and then said, "Do you think we can make it?"

"We're going to make it," she told him, with such firmness she almost believed it herself. "It's a big city. We won't be easy to find. All we have to do is keep our heads down and keep moving." Before he could ask more questions, she took a step back, studying him critically. "But we need to do something about your clothes."

"What's wrong with my clothes?"

"They'll be looking for a man with dark hair, with your build, wearing what you're wearing. The software will find you faster if you don't change." As she spoke, she shoved the bag back into the wall cavity, and put the ancient fire extinguisher in front of it.

As they began walking back to the ramp, he looked around curiously. "Why did you choose this place to hide your things?" he asked. "It's so empty."

For the first time in hours, she smiled. "That's why."

Something had changed in the last few minutes. Some unspoken agreement had been made between them. When they reached the top of the ramp, they were moving in sync. Like a team.

Michael glanced at her. "So, if you hid your bag here, you must have been working nearby?"

"I was investigating a group of environmental activists," she told him.

His jaw dropped. "You're joking."

"It was a complete waste of time," she said. "They sent me in because the group was getting funding from Russia, but I'm pretty sure they never had a clue where the donations were coming from. They just thought they'd lucked out and a bunch of rich millionaires had embraced their cause. Besides, they weren't a danger to anything except a block of tofu. Christ, if I never eat tofu again, it will be too soon. It's like eating wet air."

They were near the exit now; she motioned for him to hang back while she stepped out to check the street. Nothing stirred.

They began walking quickly back the way they'd come.

Michael was still puzzling over her revelation. "If they weren't a threat, why were you there?"

"The guys who run the intelligence agencies in this country are a bit old-fashioned," she told him. "Vegans are their kryptonite."

He laughed, and it occurred to her she hadn't heard that sound since he'd stood in front of a group of children that morning, wearing a top hat. "I shouldn't be telling you any of this, of course. It's all top secret."

"Apparently I'm going into protective custody in a few hours. Who am I going to tell? My mother?" His tone was light, but Emma didn't miss the sting in his words.

"You know," she said, "I really am sorry this is happening to you."

He gave her a direct look. "Thanks. That means a lot."

"I'll talk to my people," she said. "Maybe there's a way that you could—" She never finished the sentence.

A black Range Rover careered around the corner. The headlights were blinding as it bore down on them, engine roaring. Emma threw up one hand to shield her eyes, grabbing Michael's sleeve with the other.

"Who is it?" he shouted to be heard over the noise as she began pulling him away.

"No one good."

The two of them broke into a sprint, but the powerful vehicle roared behind them. They couldn't outrun it. They needed to go somewhere it couldn't.

At the corner she turned left, running hard. Michael matched her stride for stride.

"Down here." She darted into a small dark alley. It was cluttered with detritus, lined on both sides by huge retail rubbish bins. They vaulted discarded plastic boxes and veered around large metal containers. There was no way for the SUV to get through.

But as they rounded a bend a solid brick wall loomed ahead of them. Skidding to a stop, Emma spun around—on all sides they were hemmed in.

"It's a dead end." Michael was panting, his hands on his knees.

Behind them, the SUV waited, its engine revving. With slow deliberation it backed across the entrance to the alley and stopped, blocking the only way out.

They were trapped.

12

THREE DAYS AFTER the phone call from Ripley offering her a
job at the Agency, Emma walked into the Vernon Institute for the
first time. The instructions she'd been given were very clear.

"Don't come inside," the woman on the phone told her. "Just stand
on the front step and we'll come to you." Emma was so eager she arrived by tube half an hour early and paced around the neighborhood
until the appointed time arrived. When she returned to the front steps
of the Institute building, Ripley was waiting.

"We meet again," he said, holding out his hand.

He led her through the security system. It surprised her how normal things seemed inside. It could have been any office building in
London, were it not for all the biometric locks.

Ripley led her up the stairs to his office and closed the door.

"What I'm about to tell you is covered by the Official Secrets Act,
as I'm sure you're aware," he began when they were both seated. Over
the course of three hours, he quietly and dispassionately told her
about the Agency and its role in stopping Russian infiltration into
the UK.

"Some in government still believe in a benign, post-Soviet Republic of Russia," he explained in a bone-dry tone. "Those people are either remarkably gullible or impressively ignorant." Then, in a few short sentences, he described three recent examples of Russian espionage within the country so audacious it took her breath away.

When he finished, he lit a Dunhill and leaned back in his chair. "This is what we're here to stop. Now, I've followed your progress in the military, and I know about your history. You come highly recommended. If you agree to work with me, I'll train you myself. I will teach you everything you need to know to succeed in British Intelligence. But the most valuable gift I will give you is this: I will never lie to you." He paused, watching her with an inscrutable expression. "I ask one thing in return. I need you to tell me the truth: are you joining because of what happened to your father?"

"No!"

It came out too sharply, and Emma made herself soften her tone. "It's really not because of my dad. This is for me. It's what I want to do."

Later, she would come to realize it was the only time she had ever lied to him.

"Good." He watched her closely. "If you make this job personal it will kill you, and I cannot allow that. Do you understand?"

Her mouth had gone dry. "Yes, sir."

Then, to her surprise, he smiled. All the fierceness evaporated from his expression. "Never call me 'sir' again." He balanced the cigarette on the edge of a glass ashtray. "Now, there are three things that will keep you alive in this business and you might as well learn them today." He ticked them off on his fingers. "One: Paranoia will protect you. Two: What you don't know will kill you. Three: You must always have an escape plan. By the time I've finished training you, you will be ready for anything the Russians throw at you." He stood up and held out his hand. "Welcome to the Agency."

As the Range Rover pulled into place, blocking any escape, Emma stared at the walls around her. Each held a row of tightly closed doors. These were staff entrances, used for taking out the rubbish and bringing in stock. All the shops were closed now. There were no windows. Nothing but blank walls and locked doors.

She ran to the nearest and tried to open it, but the handle wouldn't budge. It felt sturdy. Michael, seeing what she was doing, began trying the other doors. "Try them all," she told him, racing to the next. "Find one we can kick in."

Behind them, three figures emerged from the Range Rover. It was too dark to make out their features, but she would have bet any money it was the three from the park. Their movements were leisurely, as if they knew there was no need to rush; their victims weren't going anywhere. This was like shooting rats in a cage.

The next door was also locked. Emma swore under her breath as she scrambled to the next one and grabbed the handle, willing it to turn. But it wouldn't budge.

With every step she berated herself. They must have passed in front of a camera. But where? She'd been so careful. And how had they found them so quickly?

A few meters away, Michael tried a battered-looking door, shaking the handle hard. "It's loose," he hissed. "But locked."

The figures were moving closer. Lethal shadows in the darkness.

Emma ran to his side. "Step back," she ordered.

Bracing herself, she kicked the door hard, right next to the handle. It wobbled. She could feel how loose the lock was.

"Come on," she whispered through gritted teeth, and kicked it again, aiming the heel of her boot right at it.

This time the door splintered and gave, swinging in with such force it crashed against the interior wall.

Sensing the shadows behind them beginning to run, she shoved Michael inside and ran in after him, slamming the door behind them. Her breath came in short bursts as she looked around the windowless space—it was as dark as a cave.

"Keep it shut," she told him, shoving him against the door. "Don't let them in, no matter what you do. If they get in, we're dead."

He pressed his back against the door, bracing himself with his hands against the doorframe as she yanked the flashlight from her pocket and switched it on. The white beam swung wildly, illuminating a crowded storeroom in its hectic glow. Cardboard boxes and wooden crates were everywhere—stacked on the floor, piled on metal shelving.

Something crashed against the door with such force the whole wall seemed to shake.

Michael struggled to keep the door closed, air hissing between his teeth. "Hurry," he urged, but she was already speeding through the stacks, swinging the light back and forth, looking for anything she could use. She was halfway across the room when the beam glinted against something inky black propped against a large wooden crate.

A crowbar.

Grabbing the heavy pole, she sped back to where Michael stood, just as another crash caused the door to bow in its frame, nearly knocking him off his feet. In the harsh beam of the flashlight, she could see the tendons bulging in his neck as he pressed back against it.

"Give me space," she whispered. "On three. One. Two . . ."

He leaped aside as Emma jammed the bar under the door handle, pushing the other end so violently into the rough wooden floor that it carved a deep gouge.

The crash came again. The door shuddered, but the bar held. Emma thought it might buy them a few minutes. No more than that.

"Come on," she urged, grabbing Michael's hand and pulling him with her.

They crossed the storage room, passing through the only other door. Immediately they found themselves in an elegant living room, surrounded by plush sofas, low marble tables, and what looked like statues of tall, skinny cats. On the other side of the room, street lighting filtered through the blinds covering a glass front door.

"What the hell?" Michael asked as he dodged a long heavy coffee table and skirted a fussy low chair.

"Fancy furniture shop." Emma vaulted over a velvet ottoman to reach the front door. Unlike the back door, this one had a decent lock.

"Hold this." She shoved the flashlight into Michael's hand and knelt in front of the door, pulling the lock picks from her pocket.

They both heard a crashing *thud* from the back door. The force of it was enough to make the blinds shiver. Next to Emma, Michael was breathing fast; the light shook restlessly as he twisted around to look over his shoulder.

"Hey." She kept her voice easy, trying to calm him down. "Keep the flashlight as steady as you can, OK?" Meeting his eyes, she added, "The crowbar will hold."

The light steadied, and she carefully inserted two slim metal tools into the lock.

You can't rush picking a lock—the whole process hinges on a calm mind. Blowing out a long breath, she focused on her work, using sheer will to ignore the sounds from the back room. The picks slid across metal, skidding into tiny, unseen grooves, catching nothing, catching nothing, and then *clicked* into place. The tumblers shifted with a low clunk, and the door swung loose.

"That was remarkable." Michael stared at her with new respect as she pocketed the picks and stood up.

"All in a day's—" Before she could complete the thought, another violent crash from the back room cut her off. "Talk and walk," she told him, running through the door.

"I thought you said it would hold." Michael followed her out.

"The crowbar will be fine. But that door's going to collapse."

Outside, Emma slowed long enough to close the front door behind them—if the Russians had to search the shop, it could buy them a few minutes.

"This way." With Michael on her heels, she darted to the left, past a row of closed stores and businesses. She could hear the sound of a noisy bar nearby, and she gravitated toward that cacophony. A bar meant people. And if they could lose themselves in a crowd, even briefly, it would help.

After a minute, the sound of music and conversation grew louder. Soon, people began to appear—young women in short skirts and tight jeans, guys in T-shirts and loose jackets. Emma guessed a music bar was just closing for the night and everyone was heading home.

"Slow down," she told Michael quietly, adjusting her own pace to a leisurely stroll. "Join the crowd. Blend in."

He tried to do as she suggested, but she could sense the effort it required for him not to keep running. His muscles twitched as she sauntered up to a group of clearly tipsy young women, who were shouting at each other as if the music was still turned up.

"That guitarist, though," a dark-haired girl in a skin-tight mini-dress sighed. "I totally would, you know."

The girl next to her threw her head back and laughed with such force she lost her balance and reeled into a lamp post. "Sorry, darlin'," she told it blearily, before turning back to her friend. "Everyone in the bar knew you would, Amy. You were creaming your drawers every time he touched the strings."

"The strings were my body," Amy told her, taking no offense.

They were too drunk or stoned to notice Emma and Michael had basically joined their group and were moving with them as they walked in the general direction of the tube station.

On a nearby corner, she spotted three cameras, mounted high on a post.

Nudging Michael, she motioned for him to lower his head, tilting her own face down. There were cameras everywhere in Camden.

They needed to get off the main streets. The two assassins must have broken into the shop by now. They would already be out looking for them.

She tried to imagine what she'd do in their place. She envisioned them figuring out they weren't hiding inside, then discovering the door was unlocked. Bursting out onto the quiet road, and finding it empty.

They'd get back in their car, she thought. They could move very fast in that thing at this hour. There were still taxis and buses on the main roads—London was never truly still—but the traffic was light. Given time, they'd find them. This crowd wouldn't save them for long.

Also, how *had* they found them in the first place? Maybe they were caught on camera, but that didn't explain how they'd traced them to the parking garage. They were only inside for five minutes, and there were no cameras on that street.

No, it had to be something else.

Glancing down a side street to the right, she saw a familiar shop-front. She couldn't make out the sign from where she was, but she knew it had a red star and, around it, the words "Vegan Tees." She used to joke about it with Ripley, calling it "Marx & Spencer."

Touching Michael's arm, Emma tilted her head. "This way." The drunk girls didn't notice as the two of them turned down the narrow lane.

When they reached the small shop with its array of T-shirts in the window bearing leftist slogans and red stars, she paused to check the street in both directions. Everything was quiet.

She took the flashlight from her pocket and pulled the sleeve of her jacket down around her hand, then bashed it against the window next to the lock. The glass splintered into a thousand tiny shards with barely a sound.

I always told Raven he should get an alarm, she thought, reaching in to turn the old-fashioned lock.

Michael followed her into the dark, dusty shop where, even at this hour, everything—every shirt, every candle, even the walls around them—carried the musky, heady-sweet smell of patchouli.

"Do I even want to know what we're doing here?" he asked.

"We're getting you a new look," Emma told him, and closed the door.

13

AFTER THAT FIRST meeting with Charles Ripley at the Vernon Institute, Emma spent the entire journey back home deciding how much to tell her mother. It was a delicate balancing act—she had to tell her something, but it couldn't be the truth.

Her mother always claimed she could spot a spy without saying a word. "It is a power I have," she insisted, in the soft accent of her birth country, her beautiful, heart-shaped face serious. "I learned it when I was young."

Once, when Emma was fourteen and they were in a coffee shop, her mother had pointed at a man who stood talking to the barista. "He is a spy," she whispered, emphatically, her eyes narrowing.

The man was average height, generally uninteresting, in khaki trousers and a button-down shirt, a light jacket draped over his arm. He'd been looking around the room as he waited for his coffee, his gaze skating across the two of them without seeming to notice them.

"He just looks like a man," Emma said, doubtfully, but her mother tutted in disgust.

"I know he is a spy. Don't talk to him." She leaned back, staring at the man so hard he finally noticed and gave her a nervous glance before turning away. Emma had been mortified.

"Mum," she hissed. "Stop staring at strangers. It's embarrassing."

"Embarrassing." Her mother sniffed and picked up her cup of black tea with its vivid slice of golden lemon. "You know nothing."

But Emma knew enough. She knew her mother's obsession had everything to do with her past and, most of all, with what happened to her father.

Although he had died months before she was born and thousands of miles away, her father's life and death had always been at the very center of Emma's childhood. She knew before she could speak that he'd been a great man. A brave man. One who tried always to do the right thing. And she knew as soon as she was old enough to comprehend such things that her mother was traumatized by his death.

She knew her mother would never trust anyone who worked in any Intelligence Service. To her it meant only one thing: betrayal.

"Guess what?" she'd said, when she walked into the modest suburban house where her mother had lived for more than twenty years. "I got a job!"

Her mother looked up from her computer and gave her one of her rare, meaningful smiles. "What? This is wonderful! I thought you'd take a few days before you even started interviewing. How did this happen?"

"It was my CO. He recommended me to a friend of his who works for the government." Emma grabbed an apple from the bowl on the counter and ran it under the tap as she talked, her voice light with excitement. "I interviewed today. I didn't want to tell you because I didn't think they were going to offer me anything."

"For the government." The faintest hint of suspicion entered her mother's voice. "What is this job? Is it the Army again?"

Emma bit the apple, shaking her head as she chewed. "No way," she said with her mouth full. "I'm done with the Army. It's a civil service job. Regular pay, office in London, desk of my own, huge bureaucracy making sure nothing ever gets done . . . I can't wait."

If you want to lie well, give your words a kernel of truth. It's easier to defend something if you believe it yourself.

Her mother leaned back in her chair, watching her closely. "The government is big. Which department is this?" Her tone told Emma not to dodge the question.

"Foreign Office," Emma said brightly. "I think my languages did it for me. Being fluent in German and Russian comes in handy." She tilted the apple at her mother. "You were right to make me study."

There was a long pause as her mother considered this information, but when she spoke again the tension had left her voice. "Foreign Office. Maybe you can do some good. Make this government see sense."

She believed her. Somehow that made it worse.

"Oh God. I'm going upstairs to change before you talk politics at me." Emma headed across the room, pausing only to brush a kiss against her mother's hair. "Love you, Mama."

Her mother smiled after her. "A Civil Servant. My daughter is a true English girl now."

"English *woman*, thank you," Emma called back as she ran up the stairs to her room, her own smile fading as soon as she was out of sight.

She'd never wanted to lie to her mother, but she had no choice. Her mother would never forgive her for working in Intelligence, so she must never know.

This job was the only chance she had to pay back the government that had murdered her father and ruined her mother's life.

And she intended to make them suffer.

*   *   *

THEY HADN'T PUT the lights on inside the T-shirt shop, but a streetlight in front sent enough of a glow through the windows for Emma to see what she was doing as she ran down the aisle, scanning the stacks of clothes. "What size are you?"

"I don't know. Large?" Michael stood near the door, watching as she rifled through the T-shirts until she found one with an L on the collar and tossed it across to him. He held it up, looking disbelievingly at the picture of Che Guevara on the front. "Is this a joke?"

"No. Find some trousers you can wear—they're over there," Emma instructed, gesturing at a rack next to his elbow. "Take everything off, even your boxers. And your socks."

Her tone was brusque. If she was right, they'd be found, and soon. They had to get what they needed and get out of here.

But Michael still hadn't moved; his brow was creased with suspicion. "What's going on?" he demanded. "Why am I changing everything?"

Emma, who was digging through a stack of khaki boxers, stopped. "I think they put a tracker in your clothes."

He stared at her. "What? I don't . . . How would they do that?"

"By breaking into your house. Your office. Your gym locker . . ." She ripped the price tags off a pair of briefs and held them out to him. "Trackers can be very small. It would be easy."

"They've been in my apartment?" Stunned, Michael stared down at Che's face, that famously angular jaw sharply outlined against the gray fabric.

"Definitely," Emma said. "But they could have done it anywhere."

"And you think that's how they found us earlier?"

"It's the only thing that makes sense. It's how they work."

He stood still, staring at the clothing in his hand. The tendons in his neck stood out sharply. A muscle worked in his jaw.

All this time, he'd stayed so calm she'd begun to suspect he hadn't fully accepted what was happening around him. He'd disassociated from it. At last, though, he seemed to realize there was no error. This was all really happening.

In one swift, furious move, he tore off his jacket and hurled it to the floor.

"Those *fuckers*." He yanked at the collar of his shirt until the buttons popped loose and flew across the room, pinging off the shelves. "They were in my *house*." His shirt followed the jacket. Underneath it, his body was athletic and pale, the long muscles in his shoulders taut with rage and pain and loss.

Emma knew better than to try to make this better. Anger was good right now. It was cleansing. Besides, it was time for him to stop pretending this didn't matter.

And anyway, he wasn't wrong.

As he threw off the rest of his clothes, she headed to the back of the shop.

The one remaining problem was shoes. Raven didn't stock any. And if she were the GRU, she'd have put a tracker there.

By the time she'd located a pair of Raven's shoes and a jacket—khaki green and made in China—Michael had calmed down again. In a Che T-shirt and jeans, he looked years younger—less a doctor and more a grad student on his way home from the bar.

Emma pressed a pair of well-worn Dr. Martens boots into his hands. Raven could live without them. "I hope you can wear a size nine. These are all I can find."

He took them from her without a word, and pulled them on in grim silence, tying the frayed laces angrily.

She walked over to the register and, pulling the roll of banknotes from her pocket, counted five twenty-pound notes and put them inside, before wiping her fingerprints off the keys.

"We should go," she called over to Michael. He shrugged the jacket on and reached down to pick up his wallet, which he'd set on the table next to him.

Emma stopped him. "You need to leave anything behind that was in your pockets," she told him. "Anything could be tagged."

He looked down at the small set of keys and the plain leather wallet, his expression blank.

Emma knew what those two small items symbolized. With them went his flat, his money, his credit, his identity . . . They were the last pieces of life as he knew it.

There was no time for him to get used to all he was losing. If there really was a tracker among his things, then that door was about to come crashing in.

She put her hand on his arm, holding it there until he looked up. "You'll get it back someday, Michael. I swear it. You'll get it all back."

"Well, they won't have tagged this." He pulled his medical ID out and held it up. Seeing her dubious expression, he grew stubborn. "It's proof of who I am. Of what I've worked for. I'm not giving it up. They can't have everything."

She held out her hand. "Let me see it."

For a second, she thought he'd refuse, but then, reluctantly, he handed it over.

She held it up to the streetlight, rubbing her thumb across the smooth plastic. Finding no unexpected bulges or telltale cracks, she handed it back. "Keep it. Now, let's get going."

Leaving his clothes in a pile on the shop floor, they slipped out the way they'd come in.

They ran to the first corner and turned right, then left again. Along the way, Emma paused long enough to drop his keys and wallet into a gutter.

It was getting late now. There was no traffic on the street—no sign of a black Range Rover speeding toward them, and yet her nerves were still on edge.

In a few minutes, they found themselves on a slender strip of a street that wound between an eclectic mix of flats and office buildings. She was keeping them off the main roads as much as possible, turning down any thoroughfare the Russians were unlikely to consider. They were moving at a dead run when an explosion split the night. It was close enough that the ground beneath their feet seemed to shiver.

"What the hell was that?" she asked, scanning the street.

"There." Michael pointed.

It took a second before she saw it. A column of smoke, pale gray against the dark sky, soaring straight above the rooftops. Sparks, glowing and dancing amidst the darkness, began to rise.

Emma's stomach dropped.

She knew with chilling clarity—as if the smoke had written it on the sky—what had happened.

The Russian team had found the clothes containing their tracker, and they were sending her a message. They'd had enough of the chase. They wanted their kill.

14

MICHAEL LOOKED BACK to the smoke, sudden awareness darkening his face. "Was that the *shop*?"

"It doesn't matter; we have to keep going." Grabbing his hand, Emma pulled him with her as she sprinted away. She knew people, drawn to their windows by the explosion, might tell the police about a blond woman and a dark-haired man spotted running away right afterward, and cameras might capture them fleeing, but she had no decent choices left. It was run or die.

Leaving the backstreets behind, she made a straight dash for the busy main road. They paused at a red light, catching their breath, dazed by the bright lights and crowds of people. It was nearly two in the morning but Camden's nightlife was kicking. In all the noise, it seemed nobody had noticed the explosion. When a trio of fire engines roared past, lights flashing blue, sirens howling, the exuberant crowd barely even glanced at them.

When the light turned green, she and Michael joined the drunk and happy throng flowing across the street in the direction of the tube station. Emma moved on autopilot.

She was still trying to process the escalation of violence. Blowing up a building in a crowded London neighborhood out of pique was insane. She was bewildered by the risks the Russians were taking. One miscalculation and they could have killed dozens of innocent people, triggering an international crisis.

Why would they take that chance? And where the *hell* was the Agency? Where was Ripley?

She was so lost in the tangle of her worried thoughts she almost missed the worn sign peering out from behind a thick hedge: RE-GENT'S CANAL.

Skidding to a stop, she touched Michael's sleeve. "This way," she said, pointing at steps leading down.

"We're going down there?" Since the explosion a new edge of fear had entered Michael's voice.

"Just stay close," she told him. "I've got a plan." But the words left a bad taste in her mouth. Tonight, all her plans had a habit of crumbling to dust.

The canal had been at the center of the route she'd come up with in the internet café hours earlier. On the map, it had been a clean blue slash across the northern half of the city. She'd envisioned it as a quiet shortcut, one with no cars, no people. When they reached the bottom of the steps, though, Camden Lock was anything but empty. A bar backing onto the water was still in full swing—bass pumped out of the windows; voices shouted to be heard. Draped lights lit up the canal-side path where a stylish crowd danced to the music. A sickly-sweet cloud of pot smoke filled the air.

"Jesus," Emma muttered. "Don't people ever go home?"

A group of stylish young women teetering on high heels turned to stare as they pushed their way through the crowd.

Emma knew they must look odd. She was sweating and she wasn't entirely certain her wig was still straight. Michael's Che T-shirt and worn boots were out of place among the expensive striped shirts that surrounded them.

Smoothing her wig and forcing herself to glance around brightly, she turned to Michael and whispered, "Smile. You're at a party."

An unnaturally tight smile forced up the corners of his mouth. It was more a grimace than a smile.

"This is madness," he said.

When Emma looked over her shoulder the crowd had filled in behind them. In seconds, they'd passed through it and were out the other side. It only took ten minutes of walking down the towpath to leave Camden's twenty-four-hour party atmosphere entirely behind. One moment, they were surrounded by music and laughter. The next, there was nothing but silence and velvet darkness.

It was the magic of the canals. Built to move goods quickly from the docks on the Thames across the crowded city, London's waterways no longer serve any industrial purpose, but they are still the best way to cut across town in a hurry—dipping under crowded roads and rolling by twenty-first-century skyscrapers without a second glance.

There were no cameras down here, but also no streetlights. Emma pulled the flashlight from her pocket and switched it on. The bright beam bounced off the smooth path ahead, the slow-flowing water beside them, and the small forest of trees that fringed the pathway, hiding London from view.

Michael was keeping a steady pace jogging alongside her, but when the light caught his face she thought he looked utterly exhausted. His skin seemed stretched too thin across his cheeks, and his eyes stared nervously into the shadows.

They were both worn out. Her entire body ached. If they didn't get some rest soon, they'd collapse.

Gradually, she slowed to a walk.

Michael noticed the change of pace instantly and gave her an inquiring glance as he adjusted his steps to match hers.

"I think we need a rest," she explained. She glanced over her shoulder again—nothing but emptiness lay behind them. "We should be safe down here long enough to catch our breath."

Wiping the perspiration off his forehead with his jacket sleeve, Michael asked, "How the hell did they find that shop? Was it the tracker you told me about?"

"Probably," she said.

"Surely the police will get involved now," he said. "That explosion was huge. The press will ask questions."

Emma made a vague gesture. "Everything can be explained away," she said. "Old building. Gas explosion. Poor maintenance."

"They wouldn't do that." He sounded shocked.

"They do it all the time."

For some reason, this made him angry. "You sound so jaded. You know that, right? I mean, you talk about the government covering up an attack by a foreign power like it's a normal day at the office. You people—it's like you're beyond the law. Why shouldn't the law apply to you?"

"I'm sorry if I sound like I don't care," she said evenly. "But earlier you asked for the truth. And the truth is, no one will ever know what happened back there except you, me, and a small group of people in a few government offices."

After that they walked in silence for a few minutes.

Something stirred in the bushes across the canal and Emma swung the flashlight at it in time to spot a fat rat scuttling along the edge of the waterway, its tail swishing fallen leaves in the dirt. She turned the light away. Best not to know what was hiding around them.

The quiet seemed to defuse Michael's irritation because after a while he spoke more calmly. "Can you tell me one thing? How did you know all this was going to happen? When you stopped me in the park this morning, you knew they were coming. How could you be so certain?"

"A lot of people close to your mother have been murdered recently," she said. "A man was killed this week. His name was Semenov. He worked with your mother back in Russia. Did you know him?"

"Semenov." He said the name slowly. "I don't think so."

"Were your parents in close contact with their old friends from Russia?" she asked.

"Some. But my mum is careful about what she tells me. And whom I meet."

Emma gave him a curious look. "Why would she be careful about that?"

"I think she doesn't trust anyone. She never got over the things that happened back in Russia. She always thought Russia would want revenge." He kept his eyes on the path ahead. "I guess she was right."

"Russia never forgets or forgives," said Emma automatically. It was one of Ripley's favorite sayings.

Michael shot her a look of surprise. "My mother says that all the time. I've never heard it anywhere else."

"Oh, really?" Emma said. "It's something my boss says a lot."

Somehow, she wasn't surprised Ripley and Elena Primalov shared favorite sayings. It seemed the two of them had a lot in common.

All night long she'd been trying to figure out what Ripley was up to. His secretiveness, his tension, his abrupt disappearance—it was all out of character. But there was one obvious factor that could explain everything. What if this case was personal for him? What if Ripley had known Elena Primalov back when he was working in Russia? What if he knew her *well*?

The timing worked—Ripley had been working for MI6 in Russia at the same time the Primalovs were secretly providing information to the British government. Elena would have been a hugely important operative, and Ripley was one of the best handlers in the business—it would have made sense to assign him to that case. And if they'd worked together over several years, they might have grown very close.

The pictures in Michael's file made it clear that Elena Primalov was an attractive woman. With that strong jaw and those dark eyes, she'd been even more striking when she was younger. But it was her intellect that would have proven irresistible to Ripley.

Of course, she'd been married at the time, with a young son, but Emma knew there was no aphrodisiac like danger.

What if Michael is Ripley's son?

The thought came to her from nowhere, but she didn't brush it away immediately. Instead, she rolled it around in her mind to test it, glancing at Michael curiously. Maybe there was something of Ripley in the sharp line of his jaw, and his long legs. But his father was tall as well. And his eyes—those were pure Elena.

Michael glanced up and caught her watching him. "What?" he said.

"Nothing." Emma turned away. "I just thought you looked pale."

"I'm thirsty as hell," he told her. "I was just wondering how bad canal water really is."

"You might as well drink battery acid," she said tartly, pushing thoughts of Ripley and Michael's mother from her mind.

Every few seconds she glanced over her shoulder again—but the path remained empty. With each step she felt a little more confident that taking a Londoner's shortcut had been a good idea. She didn't think they'd passed a single CCTV camera since they left Camden. Still, she didn't want to let her guard down. She had no idea how many Russian agents were out there looking for them.

"I've been wondering what happens next," Michael said. "I mean, assuming we don't get killed tonight. What happens to me? What happens to my flat? My job?"

This wasn't a subject Emma wanted to get into—there was no happiness for him in it. But she owed him as much truth as she dared to give.

"When we reach MI6, a team will be waiting to take you to a secure location," she said. "You might change cars along the way once or twice, but it's a very efficient process. They're good at this sort of thing." She tried not to think about Semenov, hunted down at his safe house and murdered. "Your belongings will be packed up and put into storage. Your employers will be given an excuse. Either a family emergency, a health emergency—something they'll believe. It will all be taken care of. Once you're settled, you'll work with an adviser getting new employment."

Something seemed to drain out of him in that moment. It was as if he'd visibly shrunk.

Emma stopped walking. "I'm sorry. Are you OK?"

He shook his head, covering his mouth with the back of his hand. "It's just . . . My whole life, gone. I . . ." His voice thickened. "I think I'm going to be sick." Retching, he turned away, half running to the canal's edge, where he stood with his back to her.

Emma stayed where she was, uncertain of how to react.

How had Ripley done this sort of thing for thirty years? He'd convinced dozens of people to walk away from their families, their homes, sometimes taking nothing with them but the clothes on their backs. But she'd never done it before. It felt like stealing. Stealing a life.

She watched Michael put his hands on his knees and breathe deeply.

"Michael," she said hesitantly. "Can I help?"

"I'm fine." He didn't look back as he spoke, but a minute later he straightened slowly and began walking back to her. "It's nothing. Sorry about that."

She held up a hand. "Please, don't apologize. I honestly don't understand how you're not going insane with everything that's happened today."

She was relieved to see a faint smile cross his face. "I'm a doctor, remember? Every day is insane."

She grasped this new topic with both hands, desperate to pull him back from the danger zone. "Yeah, I don't know how you do that, either," she said. "Those little kids. How can you stand it? How does it not break your heart?"

"It does break my heart. Every single day." There was a sudden passion in his voice that verged on rage. "Those kids are what I live for. Being there for them. That's why I said no to you at first. I'm not stupid. I understood what you were telling me about the danger. But you were making me choose—my life or theirs. And I want to choose theirs. But I also don't want to die. Can you understand that?"

"Of course I do." She gave him a long look. "If I could change any of this, I would. I hope you believe that."

To her own surprise, she meant it. At some point on this journey, she'd come to respect Michael Primalov far more than she'd expected to.

His grave, dark eyes met hers. "I know you would."

Around them, the city seemed heavily silent, as if they'd accidentally left it and were now somehow many miles away.

Michael stretched his arms up and groaned wearily. "God, I'm so tired. I'd kill someone for a cup of coffee."

"I'd kill them for a sandwich," Emma agreed. "And I could do it, too. I'm trained."

He gave a short, startled laugh. "I know. I saw you take on two men back there. Bare-handed. That was something else."

"Yeah, and by the way, did I thank you for that?" she said. "I might not have made it through if you hadn't sacrificed your laptop for me. I guess I owe you a computer."

"It was the least I could do." He glanced at her bruised face. "How's your head?"

"Oh, I think I'll survive this one."

"This one." His tone was pensive. "There'll be another one tomorrow, I suppose? Another stranger to save."

"Actually, you're my first rescue," she said. "To be honest, usually this job is a lot less dramatic."

"Is it? I'd imagined you running around the world, swooping up men in distress every day."

"Yeah, well." She glanced down at her knuckles, pale blue with bruises, skin torn from the fight. "Not quite."

He fell silent for a moment before saying, "This might be an unacceptable thing to say and please don't take it the wrong way, but aren't you a little young to be a . . . whatever you are?"

"I'm an intelligence officer. And I'm about the same age as you," she said.

"But why do you do it?" he persisted. "It's dangerous. It's exhausting. Frankly . . . it's terrifying. You're smart. You could do anything. Why this?"

"Would you ask a man that?" Emma gave him a direct look.

"Ouch." He winced. "That's valid. I withdraw the question."

He looked so gratifyingly contrite she took pity on him. "Look, it's not a huge mystery. I did this sort of work in the military and I was good at it. When I got out, it was natural to keep doing it. Now, here I am. Living a life of international mystery and glamour."

She hoped her ironic tone would put an end to this conversation, but Michael wasn't done yet.

"Are you MI5? Or MI6?" he asked.

"You know I can't answer that, right?"

"You can't even say which one you work for? Come on," he pleaded, "you can tell me. I swear I won't tell anyone."

Emma laughed. "I can't tell you, Michael. Give up."

As she spoke, she cast an automatic glance behind them—the long, curving path was empty. But ahead, the canal passed under a roadway. There was no lighting on the towpath—the shadows were thick. It would be a good place to attack. And an obvious place for a camera.

The concern must have shown on her face because his smile faded. "What's the matter?"

"Underpasses are good hiding places. I'm going to drop back a bit. Keep your head down."

She slowed her pace, allowing him to get a good length ahead. She had two motives for this—to be ready to help if anyone jumped him and also so a camera, if there was one, wouldn't see two people together who fit their description.

It was cooler in the darkness of the tunnel, and damp. It smelled of green water and mud and the things that lived in it. The road above them was quiet as a tomb. Their footsteps sounded hollow, and their breathing seemed suddenly loud. Even though she was certain no one was behind them, Emma's muscles tensed. They were so vulnerable here. So cut off. It would be easy to kill them both.

Instinctively, she moved closer to Michael.

But nothing stirred. No cameras glowed on the dark metal ribs of the arched underpass roof.

Seconds later they emerged on the other side, and the canal path again became nothing more than an unthreatening walkway. No shadows slunk from beneath the bridge to greet them.

Of course not, Emma thought. *How could they know we're here? I'm getting paranoid.*

As long as they were on the canals, they were safe. But it was nearly time to go back on the street, where the Russians would be waiting.

15

"So, does your family like what you do?" Michael asked when the underpass was well behind them. "They must worry about you."

Emma thought of her mother, blond hair pulled back, sitting at the kitchen table holding a cup of black tea fragrant with herbs, watching her with worried gray-blue eyes framed by an intricate pattern of delicate lines carved from loss and time.

"My mother doesn't know." The words came out before she'd realized she was going to say them.

He blinked. Absorbing, no doubt, not only what she'd said but what she hadn't—she hadn't mentioned any other family. But all he said was, "What does she think you do?"

"I told her I work for the government. That's all she knows."

He considered this. "Why don't you tell her the truth?"

"Your parents must be very proud of what *you* do, at least," Emma said, sidestepping his question. "I mean, you're basically a saint."

"Not exactly." There was an unexpected hint of bitterness beneath his tone, and she gave him a puzzled look.

"Why not? What's wrong with them?"

"It's just their history, I guess. You must know my mother was the top nuclear physicist in Russia. For her, being a doctor is aiming low." He adopted a condemning Russian accent. "Mikhail, you are smarter than this. Why do you not want more from science? Where is your ambition?"

Emma found herself smiling. "That is so familiar."

"Really?" He gave her an interested look. "Is your mother like that, too?"

It was far too easy to talk to him. Too easy to say too much.

"Oh, you know," she replied lightly. "Like you said. Nothing is ever enough." She checked her watch. It was nearly three o'clock. "Hey, are you rested enough to run for a bit?"

After that, they didn't talk for a while. They ran silently past the brightly painted houseboats of Little Venice, all quiet and dark at this hour. Occasionally a dog barked at the thudding of their footsteps, but no one came out to check, and the barking soon faded to silence.

Gradually, they began encountering grand houses with lush gardens backing onto the canal, and apartment buildings lit up, even in the middle of the night.

Emma knew if they stayed on the canal much longer, they'd end up moving in the wrong direction. She hadn't told Michael that what came next was the most dangerous part of their journey. She didn't want to scare him. But there were more cameras on the streets above them right now than anywhere else in the city.

This was the part she'd worried about from the start. She had to assume that most of the rest of their journey would be captured on camera. Facial-recognition software would constantly be searching for them. And sooner or later it would find them.

But they had no choice.

When they reached a path heading up from the water's edge to street level, she turned onto it without a word, and he followed.

They jogged up a steep, slanted path, Emma's trepidation growing with every step, until they emerged on a wide, busy road.

After an hour in the canal's shadows, the streetlights seemed blinding. The cars whizzing by on the half-empty streets made them both twitch. Even the homeless men, sleeping under dirty blankets in the doorways of shuttered office buildings, appeared sinister, their faces hidden by hats pulled low.

"Christ, I don't like this," Michael muttered after a motorcycle roared past them at high speed, its headlight dazzling.

"It's fine," she assured him. "We're so close now. Just a few miles to go. An hour and we're there."

That was technically true. If they ran the whole way, they'd make it to MI6's hulking headquarters on the Thames that quickly. But with the pavements empty of pedestrians they couldn't run—that would make them too obvious. Not running was also filled with danger as it gave the Russians more time to find them.

Emma knew exactly how camera tracking worked. And she knew anyone skilled at their job would spot them. And the Russians were very good at this game.

So they had to move quickly, but not too quickly. And they had to hope that they'd get lucky.

She steered Michael across Marylebone Road and onto a side street, but even in the shadows cameras were unavoidable. She could see them everywhere she looked—on tall posts and tucked into the wide doorways of the office buildings.

In her mind, Emma was visualizing the map from the Internet café, and the line zigzagging from canal to park to tiny backstreet. It appeared they'd stayed on the canal too long and they were about a quarter of a mile off track. She needed to get them back on that safer route heading south.

They paused in the shadows near a corner, while two vehicles passed by. Automatically, Emma noted the make and license plates. The first was a white van, number plate beginning VL5. The next was a blue Mercedes, registration HN1. As soon as the vehicles were gone, they hurried on.

Almost immediately, though, she heard the purr of an expensive car in the distance.

"Another one," she warned Michael, pulling him away from a streetlight.

"They're getting more frequent," he said as they pressed back into the protective darkness near a house with an arched brick gate.

"I know."

That rare, breathless quiet that comes only very late at night in a metropolis was already waning. Delivery vans rattled by on their way to collect their first loads of the day. Travelers wanting to get an early start were getting up.

They stood close together, her hand on his arm. They were whispering despite the fact that nobody in the vehicle sweeping down the street toward them could possibly hear them. Neither of them said it aloud, but they felt exposed. Some animal instinct had awakened in both of them and it sensed danger. The freedom and safety of the canal seemed far away. On the streets, they were prey.

A black Land Rover with a license plate beginning DN7 rolled by without pausing. They waited until it was out of sight before resuming their journey. As Emma worked out which side street they should take, something about the hulking SUV nagged at her, but she couldn't identify what it was. The plate number seemed uncomfortably familiar, but where had she seen it before?

One of the first things Ripley had taught her was the skill of reflexively memorizing license plates, car colors, bumper stickers. Being aware of seemingly insignificant minutiae could help you notice if you were being followed. She'd always been good at it. Right now, though, she couldn't place that SUV. It wasn't the same one from earlier in the alley, she was certain of that at least. The make was different, and the plate number.

Had it driven by them while they were walking away from the canal? Or even back in Camden? It bothered her that she couldn't place it. She'd been too distracted to memorize the small details. And it's the small details that kill you.

Feeling suddenly uneasy, she hurried her pace. Michael followed wordlessly as she turned right at the corner, half running down the street. The offices were gone now, replaced by rows of silent houses and flats. The road was empty and unthreatening and yet with every step her trepidation grew.

If she could just remember where she'd seen that Land Rover.

Giving up on her plan to find her way back to the route she'd sketched out, she turned left at the next corner, barely noticing the street name, and then right at the intersection after that. Unlike the main roads, the backstreets were still wrapped in late-night stillness.

By the time they reached the next corner, she'd begun to breathe again. The Land Rover was nothing. Maybe her memory had transposed digits, or caught a letter here and a number there. They were fine.

When they reached the junction, they turned left. The street was lined with imposing, five-story houses built of creamy white stone. Any one of them would set you back ten million pounds. Best of all, there wasn't a camera in sight.

She was just about to mention that to Michael, when a car turned the corner. It happened too fast for them to dive for cover—they were pinioned in the headlights.

Emma shielded her eyes against the blinding lights, but she knew before her vision even cleared what she would see: a black SUV with tinted windows, and a license plate beginning with DN7.

They'd been found.

16

A S THE LAND Rover rolled toward them without urgency, its headlights lit the two of them up like actors on a stage. There was no way to hide from the revealing glare, but it was just possible that whoever was inside still wasn't certain the two of them were who they thought they were. There was still a chance.

Michael squinted at the car, his brow furrowing. Grabbing his hand, Emma pulled him close, tilting her head toward his. He gave her a startled look. Up close she could see the shadows underlining his eyes like bruises.

She lifted her lips toward his cheek—his skin smelled of cold city air. "Get ready to run," she whispered. Without turning her head, she shot a telling glance in the direction of the SUV. There was a brief pause before he lowered his head a fraction to show he understood.

"Keep walking," she breathed, her lips brushing his skin, like a tipsy girlfriend whispering promises of filthy things to come. "Act drunk. And, whatever you do, don't look at that car."

The SUV's engine purred as it approached, neither speeding up nor slowing down, closing in on them.

Ignoring it, she stayed close, angling her face to Michael's and away from the street, nudging him to keep looking at her. But he was too nervous to remember everything she'd told him. He kept half turning to glance at the Rover. Any second, he was going to look up at it face on, and then they really would be finished.

Without warning, she reached up, wrapping a hand around his neck, and pulling his head down to hers. "Kiss me," she whispered against the side of his mouth.

For a second, he pulled back, but then he realized she meant it. Hesitantly, he leaned closer. She could feel his breath warm against her skin. When their lips met, his mouth was firm, his lips pleasantly rough from cold and stress. He tasted of salt and cold night air. She pressed herself against him, pulling him closer until she was enveloped in his arms, the soft cotton of the cheap jacket around her shoulders. She heard his breath catch in his throat, felt his arms tighten around her.

She was aware that the SUV had slowed so those inside could get a good look. If Michael looked up now, he'd give it all away. She needed him to keep kissing her. Sliding her hands down his back, she teased his lips with her tongue. She felt his body react. They were making their own heat—for the first time in hours she wasn't cold. His arms tightened around her, hands pressing against her back. It felt as if they were poised on the edge of an abyss—the growl of the engine blocked out all other sounds, the headlights creating a blinding halo around them.

If this was the end, it was a hell of a way to go.

Then, to her astonishment, the Land Rover passed by.

Emma lifted her head, pressing her chin against Michael's shoulder and peering past him to the Land Rover. It was nearly at the corner.

Michael's face was flushed from the kiss, his eyes bright.

"Did they see us?" he asked eagerly. Before she could stop him, he twisted to look over his shoulder.

"Don't—" she said. But it was too late.

They both heard the hiss of brakes as someone hit them hard.

The color drained from Michael's face as he realized what he'd done.

Grabbing his hand, Emma pulled him with her as she began to walk slowly away from the car.

"I'm sorry," he whispered, stumbling after her. "I just . . ."

His voice trailed off, and in the silence that followed, Emma heard very clearly the click as the driver shifted into reverse.

"Run," she ordered, already in motion. *"Now."*

They took off, hurtling past the imposing white mansions. Behind them, the SUV's engine whined angrily as the driver reversed hard.

"Don't look back!" she shouted at Michael, keeping pace with him step for step. "Just stay with me."

The Land Rover was close now, but they were nearly at the intersection. They had to get there before the driver or they didn't stand a chance. But where could they run? Ahead was Oxford Circus. Behind was Regent's Park. This was a densely crowded part of the city with cameras on every corner, but somehow they had to lose that car.

"Follow me," she called to Michael, increasing her speed, and vaulting across a pile of bin bags before veering across the street, swinging around a postbox. The city was so quiet, it was as if they were completely alone. All Emma could hear was the tense rasp of Michael's breathing just behind her, the thudding of their feet, the frustrated revving of the engine as it gained on them.

They rounded the corner at speed. Behind them, the Land Rover's engine screamed as the driver swung it around, thudding over the curb. Emma didn't break pace, hurtling across the street and turning again at the corner. Michael matched her stride for stride.

A deafening crack split the night. Instinctively, both of them ducked. Michael tripped and nearly fell, catching himself at the last second.

Gunshot, Emma realized.

"Are they shooting at us?" Michael shouted, disbelief in his voice. She didn't reply—she didn't need to.

It was a warning shot. The shooter was sending a message: they didn't want to shoot an agent of the British government in the middle of London, but they would if they had to.

Knowing how the GRU operated, she suspected, if they couldn't catch up to them, they'd shoot her, anticipating that Michael would stop to help. That's when they'd get him.

But they wanted to keep him alive. And she could use that.

She darted into the street, just ahead of the Land Rover.

Adrenaline flooded her body, heightening her senses. She could hear Michael's quick intake of breath, and sense his sudden turn in her direction. Feel the heat of the engine as she passed far too close.

Then the shrill shriek of brakes drowned out everything as the driver struggled to avoid hitting Michael, who was right behind her.

Never looking back, trusting him to go with her, she hurtled between parked cars, using all her remaining energy on this gamble. They were moving so fast the next intersection was already in front of them. Breath burning her lungs, Emma took the corner hard, fists pumping at her sides.

What she saw in the distance gave her a rare burst of hope—an ambulance blocked the narrow strip of road, its engine running, blue lights silently flashing. Two paramedics in green jumpsuits were getting into the front seats. It looked as if it was about to leave.

The SUV had reached the corner behind them, its engine roaring. Using the last air left in her lungs, Emma screamed.

"Hey!"

A female paramedic glanced out the window at the two of them hurtling down the street.

"Help us!" Emma shouted.

"Help!" Michael waved his arms.

Behind them, the Land Rover stopped.

She could hear the unhappy growl of its engine as the driver hesitated.

Emma thought she could feel the people inside the SUV watching her—sense the gun pointed at her back. Imagine them calculating the odds, eyeing the paramedics.

In the end, though, it was no contest. Even for the GRU, there are limits. With a petulant roar, the vehicle turned and wheeled away, tires squealing.

Emma and Michael stumbled to a stop.

"Is it . . . over . . . ?" he asked, clutching his side.

Emma bent double, her hands on her knees, droplets of sweat falling from her face to the cement at her feet. She couldn't get enough air in her lungs to allow her to reply so she nodded.

Michael collapsed on to the pavement and lay beside her, breathing heavily, staring up at the sky.

He was so still, Emma had a sudden, horrible thought. Dropping to her knees, she grabbed his arm. "Are you hit?"

He gulped air like water, trying to force it into his lungs. "I . . . don't . . . know."

Panting, she ran her hands down his back, across his stomach, under his legs—no blood. She sagged back as the fear ebbed, along with what remained of her energy.

"You're OK," she said, as much to calm herself as him. "We're OK."

In the distance she heard an eerie howl of sirens and wondered if someone had called the police.

The paramedics, who had watched all this unfold, abandoned the ambulance and walked cautiously toward them. It was a woman, blond hair pulled back, and a man, olive skin, worried eyes.

"What was that about?" The female paramedic gestured in the direction of the Land Rover's taillights.

They looked concerned but not as worried as Emma would have expected if they'd heard the shots. She guessed the noise of the ambulance engine and the canyon of buildings around them had drowned it out enough that they hadn't realized what was going on just a few streets away.

"I don't know," Emma lied. She pointed at Michael, who still sat on the pavement, hands loose on his knees, his head bent. "Check him, would you please? He might be hurt."

The woman's lips tightened as her eyes swept across the bruise on Emma's face. "Looked to me like you both got hurt." But she knelt beside him and began asking questions, her gloved hands holding his wrist with cool professionalism.

A sudden cold breeze shifted the strands of Emma's wig and cooled the sweat on her back, making her shiver. She climbed stiffly to her feet.

The male paramedic eyed her with cool suspicion. "Why were they chasing you?"

"I don't know. We were just walking home from a party, and they started following us." Emma wiped the sweat from her face with the back of her hand, keeping her expression innocent.

"That was an expensive car," he pointed out.

"Look," Emma said, "I don't know what's going on. We didn't ask why they were trying to mess with us. We just ran. Thank you for scaring them away."

His eyes narrowed, and she could see he was considering the likelihood of her story.

His partner stood up and dusted off her knees. "I think you're fine," she told Michael, reaching out a hand to help him to his feet. "Bit bruised, but you'll live."

"Thanks." He stood next to Emma, who was already backing away.

If he was fine, they needed to get going.

"Right, well, thanks for everything," she said, tugging at the hem of Michael's shirt until he followed her. "Sorry to bother you. We know you're busy."

Still doubtful, the male paramedic said, "You should call the cops. Those guys might come back."

"We will," Emma promised. "Thanks again." She hurried away, gesturing for Michael to follow.

They fast-walked around a corner, breaking into a run as soon as they were out of sight.

"He's right, you know," Michael said. "They'll come back for us."

Emma didn't reply, but he was right. Their one chance had been to slip unobserved through the city, and that was lost now. She had to *think*.

Without slowing, she tugged the blond wig off and dropped it in the gutter. The disguise was finished now that the Russians had seen it. Everything was finished. They couldn't escape. They'd been found too quickly. The Russians must have a huge team searching for them. And her own office had abandoned her to her fate.

She couldn't win this one. Not on her own. They were trapped.

"What the hell do we do?" Michael asked, without slowing down. "We can't outrun them."

"I'm working on it," she snapped.

But the map she'd memorized so carefully earlier was now a chaotic cat's cradle of tangled streets. And those guys would find them. It might take a while, but they had all the advantages.

Her eyes were drawn to a white metal camera mounted on a tall post. As she watched, it turned slowly in their direction until it pointed directly at them.

An unexpected flame of fury flared inside her. None of this should be happening. This was *her* country. London was her city. She would not be hunted in it like an animal.

In that moment, she made a decision. One way or another she and Michael were going to get through this night alive. Just to piss those bastards off.

Keeping her eyes on the watching camera, she raised her middle finger at it.

"Fuck you," she said slowly, enunciating each word so whoever was monitoring the footage could read her lips. "Fuck all of you. I'm going to *win*."

17

MOST OF WHAT Emma knew about hand-to-hand combat she'd learned in the military. The Secret Service trains agents in surveillance, evasion, and observation. But the army turns soldiers into blunt instruments—kill or be killed. Fight or die.

Within days of joining the Agency, she'd learned that Ripley had his own unique training methods, and that he was determined his agents should not rely on computers. Training for new agents went on for months at numerous locations, including unmarked government-owned buildings and disused military bases. So when, eight months into her training, Emma received a message ordering her to a neglected Second World War airstrip about an hour south of London, she wasn't surprised.

She arrived to find Ripley waiting for her alone in an old hangar. The training simulations had been growing more intense, and his forbidding expression told her this one might be tougher still.

"Your job today is to survive." He thrust his thumb at the rusted door behind him. "When you walk out there, you're going to be in the middle of an attack. You have to figure out how to get out of it alive. That's all I'm going to tell you." He turned his wrist to glance at his watch. "It's nearly time. Stay here and wait for the call. Good luck."

He walked away without further explanation.

For nearly half an hour, Emma waited alone in the huge, empty hangar, trying to imagine what lay ahead, and endeavoring not to look nervous in case someone was watching.

A lot of the Agency's training had involved dropping her in the middle of complex simulations, leaving her to figure her own way out. But this one felt bigger than the others. She could hear cars and voices behind the decaying building—see flashes of activity through a half-covered window.

It was a hot July afternoon, and by the time an open-topped Land Rover roared in through doors big enough to admit a Lancaster bomber, Emma was sweating.

The soldier at the wheel motioned for her to get in. His face was hidden behind mirrored aviator sunglasses, and he didn't say a word while they crossed the crumbling runway, veering around potholes, toward a cluster of buildings that gradually materialized into a town, shimmering in the heat like a mirage. Surrounded by the ruins of a World War II airfield, it looked, for all the world, like a town in the middle of an apocalypse.

Only when they grew closer could she see that it was all fake, built like a film set. The streets were lined with banks and shops, houses and flats, but the veneer of normality was paper thin. Emma was certain that on the other side of the walls there would be nothing but battered concrete and bare boards. Still, that was easy to forget when the stop lights cycled through the colors—red, amber, green—and the traffic stopped on cue. It was bewilderingly elaborate. Cars honked at slow-moving vehicles, and drivers waved at friends. Women pushed babies in carriages and lingered outside shops to chat, but, when the driver pulled up to the curb and waited for her to get out, she could see bullet holes as big as her fist in the walls of the bank.

"I guess this is my stop," Emma joked nervously.

The driver stared straight ahead as if she hadn't spoken.

"OK, then," she whispered and climbed down to the street. As soon as she closed the door, he sped away.

The worst part of these simulations was not knowing where the danger would come from. In previous tests she'd faced a sniper, an attempted assassination with a nerve agent, and multiple physical fights.

Each time her job had been to dodge the attack and restrain the attacker. On those occasions, it had been just her and a few other people. This time the pavements were thronged. It was like a Saturday afternoon in south London.

It was hard to get her bearings as a group of muscular young men rushed toward her, calling insults to one another. She tensed, ready to fight, but none of them so much as glanced at her as they passed.

Not them, then.

A prickle of sweat ran down her spine and she moved cautiously down the street. She knew Ripley would be somewhere watching, and she scanned the people around her, consigning faces to memory for when he asked about them later. Red hair, white T-shirt. Blond woman in a black dress with black flats. Balding man with a scar above his eye.

She walked all the way to the end of the block, passing people and cars, offices and shops, ready at every stage for a fight—but nothing happened. When she reached a pedestrian crossing, the light turned red, and she paused automatically to wait for it to change.

Across the street, she watched a woman in a burka pushing a carriage that couldn't possibly have a real baby in it, alongside a muscular dark-haired man who was talking and gesturing at something in the distance. Instinctively, Emma turned to see what he was indicating. Perhaps because of this, she got only a glimpse of the man walking from the other direction. He was in his thirties, and thickly built—wiry dark hair in need of a cut, khaki shorts, and a black T-shirt. There was nothing memorable about him at all, until he whipped a gun from behind his waist and thrust the barrel against her ribs.

"Come with me right now or I'll shoot every person you can see. Then I'll shoot you." His voice was quiet and conversational, and somehow that was the most menacing part. "I'll shoot the baby first and then the mother."

Emma could feel the cold metal of the gun through the thin material of her top like a shard of ice against her hot skin.

A kidnapping. That's what this operation was. Only instead of protecting someone else, she was to be the victim. They hadn't practiced this before or planned for it. There'd been only the briefest of time spent on agent abduction in all of her training up until now.

I can't do this, she thought, panic rising in her throat like bile. *I'm not ready.*

It took all her strength to push back against the fear that threatened to immobilize her.

She made herself think of her army hostage-negotiation training. *Listen. Engage.* Then the three Ds: *Distract. Dissemble. Disarm.*

Turning slightly to see him better, she held her hands out, palms open and empty. "It's fine. I'll come with you. Just put the gun down and tell me what you want. Please, don't hurt anyone else. I'll do exactly what you want."

"I won't hurt anyone if you cooperate." Keeping his eyes on hers, he twitched the gun to the right, a movement she felt rather than saw. "Blue Vauxhall, parked in front of the bank."

She looked where he indicated and saw the car, incongruously clean and gleaming in the sun. "I see it," she said.

"Good." His patronizing approval made her skin crawl. "You're going to walk there, open the passenger door, and get in. See the kid standing next to it?"

Emma's eyes darted to a tall, skinny young man with light-brown skin. He couldn't have been more than seventeen. He had a mop of curly hair and was smiling crookedly at the woman next to him, who looked so like him she had to be his mother. They couldn't be agents. They had to be civilians.

What are they doing here? she thought with rising horror.

But the man hadn't finished his thought. "If you don't do everything I ask, I'm going to blow his pretty face off."

The relish with which he said this sickened Emma.

A cold calm descended on her. She walked toward the car, her steps slow and deliberate. She felt as if she could see everything more clearly: the young man standing by the car, the buildings shining in the sun, the man with the gun pressed against her back. He was five inches taller than her. But that didn't mean anything.

His right hand gripped the gun, his left hand held her shoulder, propelling her to the car. She did as he told her.

They were nearly to the blue car when someone ran by them. Instinctively, the man turned to look.

Emma dropped to the ground, sliding from his grip. She rolled hard to the left and came up with her right leg already rising and kicked his gun hand.

She'd practiced this move day after day after day. It was one of the hardest self-defense moves but, done right, it could catch an attacker completely off guard.

She did it right. The gun went flying.

There was a split second when she clocked the satisfying look of surprise in his eyes before he lunged for her. He had fifty pounds of pure muscle on her and half a foot in height. But she was fast. She dodged to the left, and immediately spun right again, kicking his knees with every bit of strength she had. He wobbled but caught himself.

His face purpling, he swung a punch at her head so hard she felt the air move as it approached. She ducked, but he caught a handful of her hair with the ends of his fingers and wrenched her backward.

The burning pain of it filled her eyes with tears. Gritting her teeth, she swung her right arm above her head and punched up. The flat of her hand connected full force with his nose.

"Fucking *hell*." He let go, reeling away from her.

Emma turned to see blood flooding down his face, staining the front of his shirt.

Over the hands that clutched his nose, his small blue eyes were furious. "What are you doing? You're not supposed to fucking kill me. It's a bloody simulation. *Jesus*."

"Sorry." Emma was mortified. "I didn't mean to hit you that hard."

"Christ, look at Adam," a male voice said. "She broke his nose."

A ripple of laughter spread down the street as everyone broke character and turned to watch the action.

"It's not funny." The man held the bridge of his nose gingerly. "I'm going to have to go to the hospital. Rip, what the hell?" He raised his voice, looking down the street.

Ripley, smiling broadly, stepped through the door of the fake bank building where he must have been watching the action the whole time. "I'd call that a pass," he said cheerfully. "Although Adam's right. You aren't actually supposed to hurt anyone. This isn't the army, you know."

"I know. I'm so sorry. I got carried away." Emma had held out her hand to the wounded officer. "No hard feelings?"

With some reluctance, he wrapped her fingers in his thick, bloodied hand and gave them a perfunctory shake before turning his attention back to Ripley.

"I'm glad she's on our side. That's all I've got to say. But get someone else to test her next time."

Ripley waved over the young curly-haired man standing by the car. "Take Adam to the infirmary," Ripley ordered, resting a hand on his shoulder. "Get him patched up."

Across the street, the woman pulled the burka over her head and tossed it carelessly into the baby carriage. Beneath it she wore athletic shorts and a T-shirt that said "BORN TO RUN."

Ripley turned to Emma, still looking pleased. "Congratulations. You just passed your final test." Raising his voice to be heard over the increasingly relaxed crowd on the street, he said, "Well done, everyone. That's all for today."

As they began to mill in the general direction of the hangar, he turned back to Emma, his face growing serious. "Welcome to the team. It only gets harder from here."

18

MICHAEL AND EMMA ran blindly, hurtling down one side street and then another. When Emma spotted a quiet mews lane, she headed straight for it.

"This way," she called to Michael, and they darted in.

In the sheltering darkness, she stopped and bent over to try and catch her breath. Her lungs ached from running. Her legs were numb.

The dead-end street was neat and tiny—no more than fifty meters long and lined on both sides with small carriage houses, each fronted with perfectly clipped topiary and expensive cars. Emma counted two Lamborghinis and a canary-yellow Bugatti, and no visible cameras. Still, there could be smaller cameras, tucked tastefully out of sight, so she drew Michael into the shadows near the entrance where they leaned against the cold stone wall. Both of them were exhausted. They'd had no water in hours. The muscles in Emma's calves had begun to spasm. She knew they couldn't keep this pace up. They needed help if they were going to get through this alive.

Michael wiped the sweat from his face with his sleeve and watched with a slight frown as she pulled her phone from her pocket and began to dial.

The phone in the Agency rang six times before anyone picked up.

"Vernon Institute." The voice was female, unfamiliar, and cool. Emma didn't recognize it but that wasn't a surprise. Night calls were sometimes transferred to MI5 when things were busy.

"This is Makepeace 1075." Emma kept her voice low and urgent. "I need a lifeline."

In the silence that followed she could hear the woman typing. When she spoke again Emma heard a subtle change in her voice—a new caution beneath the cool efficiency.

"What is your current location?"

"Queen Anne Street."

"We can't give you a pickup," the woman told her. It was the wrong thing to say.

"I don't care about your *problems*," Emma exploded. "We are being shot at in Oxford bloody Circus. We are running hot from multiple units. Find R. Tell him I've had enough. I need a sodding lifeline or there will be blood in the street."

There was a long pause before the night operator replied crisply, "Understood. I'll request your lifeline."

The phone went dead.

Swearing furiously under her breath, Emma shoved the device back into her pocket.

Michael, who had heard enough to gather it hadn't gone well, searched her face. "What'd they say?"

"They're going to help us," Emma said, hoping it was true. "We just need to wait."

Pressing her back against the creamy limestone wall, she peered out from the sheltered mews into the dark street. It was quiet as a tomb. The sirens she'd heard earlier had fallen silent. There was only the faint rumble of distant traffic.

She kept imagining what was happening back at the office. If Ripley was still unreachable, the operator would go to the next person on the list. That was Masterson. He had told her not to call for help, and

Ripley had specifically warned her not to trust him. So, she had little hope.

The simple truth was, nobody could help her except the one person who apparently wasn't there. And with this whole operation spinning out of control on his watch, Masterson was going to need someone to blame.

With a silent groan she pressed her fingertips against her temples.

To get to Vauxhall from here on foot they had to cross Mayfair, with all of its cameras, Piccadilly, which was basically a street-level film studio, and then the river, all while roving bands of GRU agents pursued them.

Of course, she could try to involve the police, but that held problems of its own. When agents worked undercover they carried no government identification. There was no way for her to prove who she was. It had never occurred to her to worry about it before. After all, the Agency had a system for everything. Phone calls were made. Very brief conversations were had at high levels. Problems were quickly smoothed over.

For the first time she allowed herself to wonder what would happen if nobody made those calls.

She checked her phone, which had not made a sound since the operator hung up. Its screen stayed stubbornly dark.

"Come on," she whispered.

Just then, the quiet was broken by the sound of a car driving slowly down Queen Anne Street outside the mews. Instinctively, Michael stepped forward to look.

"Get back." She pushed him into the shadows, and leaned forward enough to see the main road, ready to dive back to safety if necessary.

Instead of a Land Rover, though, what she saw was a London taxi, gliding down the street like a mirage, its yellow roof light cheerfully aglow. It was a picture of such abject normality, for a moment she couldn't accept what her eyes were showing her.

"Bloody hell," she breathed. "You can't get a taxi around here in the middle of the *day*."

Even as she said it, though, an idea took shape in her mind.

"Michael," she said. "Follow me."

A second later, he stood beside her on the street watching as the taxi cruised toward them.

"I thought we weren't supposed to take taxis," he said.

"I'm making an exception," said Emma. Then she stepped forward and thrust her hand into the air.

The cab's headlights dazzled her, and for a moment she couldn't see what was happening. Until, with a creak of old brakes, it stopped in front of them.

The passenger window rolled down and the driver leaned over to peer at them. He was tough-looking, muscular, about fifty, with a head so clean-shaven it glistened. His narrowed eyes considered them with the open suspicion of long experience.

"Where to?"

"Victoria Station," she said.

He didn't move to unlock the door. "It's closed."

"We're catching an early train. We might as well wait there." She kept her eyes wide and steady. "No point in getting a hotel room this late."

Victoria Station wasn't far. If they were lucky, they'd get there before anyone watching them had the chance to catch up. Once there, they could dive out and lose themselves in the confusing maze of streets and find another way to get across the river.

His gaze swung from her torn jacket and bruised face to linger on Michael's Che T-shirt. "You got cash? I don't take cards."

Emma pulled a twenty-pound note from the bankroll in her pocket and held it out to him. "Payment in advance. Keep the change."

He plucked the note from her fingers and rolled up the window. The door unlocked with a *clunk*.

Emma jumped inside. Michael was right behind her, not even trying to hide his relief. She didn't have the heart to tell him that he shouldn't look so hopeful. If anything, she was putting them in more danger. But they couldn't sit in an alley waiting to get caught.

Inside, she ran a quick scan of the car. It was an older model of the traditional London cab. There was no credit-card reader, and a worrying tubercular rattle shook the floor under her feet. Nonetheless, a steady red light above the rearview mirror made it clear where the camera was mounted.

"What's the plan?" Michael asked, as they rattled toward Bond Street. "Why Victoria? Why can't we go all the way?"

In the mirror, the driver was watching them with mistrust. Emma leaned her head toward Michael's, talking quietly: "We'd never make it across the river. They'll be looking for us. We need to lose them first, at least for a little while."

This close, he smelled of salty sweat and the cool, green cologne he used, and she was unexpectedly reminded of the kiss. It had been a long time since she'd kissed anyone like that. She found herself wondering, irrationally, what he'd thought of it.

"Do you think we can?" he asked. "Lose them, I mean?"

No, Emma thought.

"With a little luck," she said.

Outside, the city flashed by, bright in the dark night. A police car sped past, blue lights swirling, siren off. Delivery trucks rattled by. Everything looked normal.

"By the way, I wanted to tell you I was sorry," Michael said. When she gave him a puzzled look, he explained, "Back there—they figured out it was us because I turned around to look at them. We might have made it if I hadn't done that."

With his shoulders hunched and his elbows resting on his knees, he looked endearingly humble. It tugged at her heart.

Christ, what was wrong with her?

"That was absolutely not your fault. You couldn't have known." Her voice was firm. "The only people responsible for shooting at us are the ones with the guns."

He lifted his head and gave her a long look, as if there was something he wanted to say. But before he could speak, Emma's phone buzzed and she snatched it from her pocket.

It was a message from a blocked number. All it said was: "51:51928 -0:09863. Go under."

She opened a map on her phone, punched the coordinates in, and stared at the screen as it zoomed in on the junction of two narrow, winding streets.

"What is it?" Michael asked.

"I'm not sure," she said slowly. "It might be a rescue plan. There's only one way to find out."

Leaning forward, she tapped the plexiglass divider behind the driver, holding up another twenty.

"Change of plans, mate. We need to go to Farringdon instead."

The cab dropped them off on a curving dark street between two hulking, nearly windowless buildings that once must have been warehouses, but that had been, along with most of the area around them, converted into sprawling modern office space.

There were no cameras in view, and Emma doubted this was a coincidence.

As the two of them stood on the pavement, the driver looked out the window at the desolate streetscape, his brow furrowing. "You sure this is the right place?"

"This is it." Emma pulled three twenties from her pocket and held them out to him. "Look, I need to ask you a favor. Before you go home, could you make two more stops?" He eyed the money but didn't take it. "I don't want you to pick anyone else up," she continued. "Just drive to London Bridge Station and stop there for as long as you would normally wait for someone to get out. And then go on to Waterloo Station and do the same thing."

He studied her with eyes that had seen everything. She could see him weighing up her bruises, her determination, her level of need.

"Someone after you?" he asked, still not reaching for the money.

"Yes, they are."

"Bad guys?"

"The worst," Emma said. "And I would like to make it harder for them to catch us."

He considered her face a moment longer and then made up his mind. "I don't want your money. I'll do it for nothing."

For some reason, amid all the awfulness, that lifted her heart. The way Londoners looked out for one another when it all went to hell was one of the best things about this overpriced, overcrowded city.

"You're a good person," she told him. "But take the cash. It's government money, not mine."

"Oh, in that case . . ." With a wicked grin, he took the notes from her hand and slid them into his breast pocket.

"Thank you for doing this," she told him as he shifted into gear.

"No worries." His last words came as he pulled away: "Don't get caught."

When the cab was gone, the street felt utterly abandoned. Michael looked at the converted warehouse office in front of them with its sleek, modern windows. "Are we going in there?"

Emma turned a slow circle, taking in the impassive structures around them. In every direction she could see nothing but trendy buildings in glass and stone. "All I was told was that we should go under."

"Go under?" His eyebrows rose. "What does that mean?"

"No idea." Emma scanned the blank walls around them. "I thought it could be an abandoned tube station or a cellar. But I'm not seeing one of those."

It was the kind of street where two Londons seemed to meet—the old warehouses converted into office buildings stood on either side of them; beyond, vast skyscrapers towered, windows glittering like squares of gold.

"Maybe they meant a basement?" he suggested doubtfully.

The problem was that Emma didn't see how they could even get into the buildings. They all had modern, triple-glazed windows. Next to every door, state-of-the-art security panels gleamed.

She walked out into the middle of the street, staring at the stone walls around her, trying to identify what she was missing. "No manhole covers," she muttered, dragging her toe across the tarmac. "Come on, Emma. Figure this out."

If it hadn't been so quiet, she might never have noticed the sound. It was soft but persistent.

She began to pace the street, searching the gutters, hovering over storm drains. But she couldn't find what she was looking for.

Her attention settled on a low metal door worked into the stone wall of a converted warehouse across the street.

She crouched next to it, motioning for Michael to stay quiet. The sound of rushing water was much clearer here.

He stood next to her, cocking his head. "What is that?"

A slow smile spread across her face, and she tapped the low door with her fingertip. "This is where we're going."

He looked at the unpromising entrance doubtfully. "What's down there?"

"If I'm right, it's a river."

By then, she was already pulling the lockpicks from her pocket and examining the old padlock holding the double doors in place. It looked as if it hadn't been opened in years.

"Of *course*," Michael said, realization dawning. "It must be the Fleet."

Emma nodded, her focus on the lock. It was old and uncomplicated, but rust had made the mechanism tough to manipulate. She gritted her teeth as she pressed the delicate tools against problems she couldn't see.

Michael watched her hands with interest. "Did they teach you how to do that?"

"Nope. This is not a government-sanctioned method of entry." She kept her focus on the lock. "I taught myself."

The pick slipped against the rusty lock, and she let out a breath and tried again, holding the tools steady, willing herself to be patient. Her heart rate slowed. This time, when she felt the pick take hold, the lock moved more easily. A second later, it opened with a click they could both hear in the quiet. She glanced back with a smile. "There are videos on YouTube."

"Honestly," he said, "are you a spy or a burglar? Tell me the truth."

"A little of both, I guess." She stood and shoved the lockpicks back in her pocket. "Just trying to keep the Russians on their toes."

The doors opened with a complaint of old metal. The air on the other side smelled dank and damp.

Emma pulled the small flashlight from her pocket. The glow illuminated a rust-speckled metal staircase, leading down into absolute darkness. From below, they could hear the ghostly, crystalline sound of water rushing against stone.

Emma suppressed a laugh of pure relief.

There was no way this idea had come from Masterson. This was classic Ripley. He studied the city like a chessboard, thinking always of what the enemy knew and what it didn't. Only *he* would think of the city's hidden rivers.

Maybe he was out of communication, but he still had her back.

Feeling suddenly buoyant, she stepped inside and motioned for Michael to follow.

"Come on," she said, her confident voice echoing off the rough stone walls. "Let's go swimming."

19

RIPLEY HAD JOINED the Secret Service at the end of the Cold War and he never stopped using the skills he'd learned in those early days. He spent months training Emma in methods of covert surveillance, and how to notice when she was being followed. He did this, he said, because the Russians still used the same methods they always had.

"We got high tech, but they didn't change," he liked to say. "We stopped noticing because we were too busy staring at our computers. All the while, they stood behind us and watched us make that mistake."

But Emma already knew that. During her time in Army Intelligence in Germany, she had seen it in action.

Most members of her unit had been eager young tech-heads— deep into cyber surveillance. Their territory covered all of the Russian border region. When the Russian military set up a large training camp on the border between Belarus and Poland, Emma's team worked for weeks trying to hack the computers on the temporary Russian base, only to come up against a wall of elaborate security software so invincible it felt as if the Russians were laughing at them. Time after time they failed to break through.

When Emma first suggested physically placing the bugs inside the Russian camp, though, everyone had stared at her as if she'd lost her mind.

"You'll get caught," her captain told her. "There's absolutely no way we could ever try that. It would be a violation of international law."

His logic baffled her. "Why is it OK to hack them but not OK to place the hearing devices by hand?"

"Hacking is deniable," he'd explained. "If they actually find a living, breathing member of the British armed forces on their base, it's a little hard to say we didn't do it."

His inability to conceive of success galled her. She was fluent in Russian, German, and Polish, among other languages. She could find a way to blend in.

"What if I don't get caught?" she'd argued. "Think of the information we'd get. It would be incredible."

But his mind was made up. "Sure, or you could end up being tortured in prison and my career would be over."

That put an end to the conversation, but Emma wasn't ready to give up on the idea. She began to conduct research into how she might get inside the Russian training camp. There was no shortage of information—the Polish government had been concerned enough about what the Russians were up to just across the border that they'd collected reams of data. The borders were porous, and the Russians had placed their base on unoccupied territory in the bleak countryside. In strategic terms, this made sense—they were close enough to intimidate the Polish military and irritate its allies in Europe and America.

All the same, the camp's location was problematic for the Russians. For one thing, it was in neighboring Belarus, and so not on their normal supply route. It had no airstrip, so everything they needed on the base had to be trucked in. There were few civilians in the sparsely inhabited borderlands to work on site, forcing them to bus people in from the few villages in the area. This meant that most of the civilians who worked on the base were of Polish heritage or had Polish families and were not sympathetic to the Russian soldiers.

This was the part that interested Emma the most.

Her contacts in Polish Intelligence informed her that three Polish women crossed the border into Belarus five mornings a week and were picked up by a van that drove them to the base to work as cleaners. They had been doing this for months, and their journey was now routine. They had been providing information to the Polish government about the base from the start.

The day she made this discovery, she was so excited she asked for a meeting with the commanding officer.

When she walked into his office, he waved her to a seat. There were stacks of papers on his desk, and he looked distracted.

"What's this about?" His tone wasn't promising.

She didn't know him well back then. She wasn't ranked high enough to have regular meetings. But she knew the captain wouldn't listen, so he was her only hope.

"I know how to get on the Russian base," she began. Instantly, he held up a hand to stop her.

"I thought we'd already rejected this idea. Too risky."

"Yes, but just hear me out." Talking fast, she told him about her plan. At first, he endured this with clear impatience. Gradually though, his demeanor changed. He leaned forward, making notes, occasionally asking for more details.

When she finished, he leaned back in his chair and fixed her with a steady look. "You really want to end up in a Russian prison, don't you?"

Heat climbed up her neck. "No. I just think it will work."

There was a long pause. And then a smile spread across his face. "Well, as it happens, so do I. We must both be mad."

With that, he picked up the phone and called the captain in. When he arrived, the CO made her explain her plan again.

The captain combusted. "We can't send a military officer across the bloody border. What if she gets arrested?"

"I hear you, Mike." The CO rocked back in his chair. "There is certainly risk in this. So, tell me this: how much progress has the digital team made?"

"That's not the point."

"It *is* the point, actually." The CO's tone hardened. "We've been trying to get access to their computers for three months, while they're merrily rolling Russian tanks to the edge of the Polish border. Poland is one of our allies, remember, so they might as well be rolling their tanks into bloody *Bristol*. We have to try something different. This"—he thrust a finger in Emma's direction—"is different. She's done her research. She speaks fluent Polish and Russian. It could work. Now you and I need to make sure the plan is watertight. If it blows up in our faces, I want to be able to tell the court martial hearing I crossed all the Ts."

A few days later, Emma moved onto a Polish military base near the border with Belarus. Nobody knew she was there except for a handful of Polish intelligence agents. With their help, she spent three weeks cultivating the young women who worked in the Russian camp. Finding one willing to let her do her work for one day in exchange for four hundred pounds cash was unexpectedly easy. It turned out they all hated the Russians.

"Will it hurt them?" a woman named Monika asked.

"Yes, it will," Emma told her.

"Good," Monika said with satisfaction. "Then we will do whatever you need."

The Polish team chose her as the one Emma could replace. She and Emma were roughly the same age, with vaguely similar features. They were almost the same size, although Monika's hair was darker and shorter. A box of hair dye and a pair of scissors could take care of that. The main problem was Monika's deep brown eyes—they were so obviously different from Emma's blue eyes. She told herself it was unlikely anyone would notice if she kept her gaze lowered, but she knew that wasn't true.

When she informed him, the captain was visibly relieved. "Well, that's it, then. You'll have to call it off if you can't find someone else," he said. "This risk is too high to take chances like that."

Emma had been devastated, but he knew he was right. Security at the base was thorough, and all the guards knew Monika well. She couldn't replace one of the other women, because they were all physically wrong—too tall or too short or too fair.

A few days later, though, the CO showed up unexpectedly at the Polish base. She had snapped to attention, staring at him in surprise.

"At ease," he said with a slight smile. "I'm just bringing your mission a good-luck present."

He dropped a small box on Emma's desk.

Puzzled, she picked it up to examine it. It was a pair of contact lenses. Dark brown.

Before she could find the words to thank him, the CO headed for the door, his words floating back over his shoulder. "Can't let a good mission fail just because of blue eyes."

The plan was simple. All the women would cross the border together as usual, only Emma would take Monika's place. The other women would distract the guards enough that they didn't notice the switch. Emma would place the hearing devices on the base while she worked as a cleaner. If she didn't get caught, she'd be a hero.

Monika loaned Emma the dark blue uniform all the women wore when working on the site, along with the pass she used to access the base, her passport, and the blue quilted jacket she wore every day.

Monika and the other women, Tanya and Julia, helped her work on her Polish accent, teasing her when she said words the Russian way instead of the Polish way. "You sound like our enemy," Tanya would say, a smile softening her words.

After weeks of work, the day finally came. They'd chosen a Friday for the operation, as it was the quietest day on the Russian base. Many officers went away for the weekend, desperate to get back to civilization. Only a skeleton crew stayed behind.

At five in the morning, Emma stood in her small room, looking at herself in the frameless mirror that hung above the battered table she used as a desk. Her brown hair was dyed ebony, and cut so that it just brushed the tops of her shoulders. Her deep brown eyes confused her—it was as if someone else's eyes were gazing out of her face. The changes made her skin look paler, her cheekbones more pronounced—more like Monika's bone structure than her own. When she pulled it on, the warm coat smelled of Monika's smoky, vetiver perfume.

"I'm Monika," she whispered, challenging herself to believe it. But her stomach churned.

Now that the moment had come, she was certain it was all a terrible mistake. The captain had warned her over and over about what would happen if she was caught. His words circulated in her brain sickeningly. "You'll be interrogated for days. Put in the worst prison they can find. Paraded in front of state-owned media. The British government may deny you work for us. Or they'll say you're a rogue agent—that you operated without permission. They'll disown you . . ."

Covering her mouth, she ran to the tiny bathroom and threw up her breakfast in the metal toilet.

Then she rinsed her face, brushed her teeth, and went downstairs to meet her team.

She was going without any wire or earpiece; there would be no communication with the British base once she crossed the border. All she had was Monika's phone, which had been given a secure SIM card. With that she could call the British embassy if the Russians arrested her.

In the freezing pre-dawn darkness, she met the other women just outside the border crossing. They were all pale and quiet as they walked together into the wooden building.

From the start, everyone had assured her crossing the border would be the easy part and, as she joined the weary queue, shuffling across the unheated room to where the border guards waited, she could see why. The same guards worked the crossing every day, and they barely glanced at her passport, waving her through seconds later and motioning for the next in line to step up.

There was no time to celebrate this success, though. On the Belarus side of the border, a battered white van sat waiting, its engine sputtering irritably. The vehicle was so spattered with mud its registration plate was illegible. The driver, a doughy man who smelled of cheap cigarettes and acrid sweat, watched the three of them as they crowded in, his eyes flat and unfriendly. As they'd planned, Emma got in first, taking a seat at the back. She kept her head down, but she didn't like the way his gaze lingered on her. Tanya, tiny and red-haired, elbowed her, grinning. "You're so hungover this morning, Monika. I told you not to drink that much. You always regret it."

Julia, a vivacious, leggy blonde, gave a throaty laugh. "She can't hold her booze, but still she tries."

Emma forced her lips to curl into a pained smile. "I can't learn if I don't practice," she said.

The women roared with laughter.

"I thought drinking was something all Poles did well," the driver muttered. But the distraction worked, and soon the van was thumping down the unevenly paved road.

The other women were remarkable that day. They chattered non-stop, distracting and annoying the driver as they crossed the flat, empty border wasteland.

It was just before seven when the van pulled up on a featureless stretch of muddy land beneath a January sky that was still as black as night. The base was little more than a cluster of low, utilitarian buildings on a field that looked as if it might once have been part of a large farm. Four guards in wool coats, dark green hats pulled low, stood at the main entrance holding machine guns.

Stiffly, Emma stepped out of the van into air so frozen and dry it pinched her face. As the women joined a queue of workers entering the base, they immediately began grumbling.

"It's too cold to make us stay out here for so long," Tanya said, just loud enough to be heard by the others in line.

"They do it just to make a point," a worker ahead of them agreed.

"They need to realize if we get frostbite, we won't be able to clean their shit from the toilets," Julia said, setting off a dark rumble of supportive laughter.

The women stomped their feet for warmth, and blew on the tips of their gloved fingers, all the while surrounding Emma in a way that would have appeared, to any casual witness, completely natural, but which also served to shield her from view.

Even through the cloud of fear that enveloped her, she had admired them. They had taken to their roles like naturals. It was as if they spent every day protecting British spies.

As they neared the guard post, the women grew more restive, jostling each other as the guards examined their passes. When it was time for Emma to hand over her ID for review, Julia abruptly demanded, "Why is our pay so late this month? Don't they know we have children to feed?"

The young guard who'd bent over the card bearing Monika's name glanced up at her, his brow knitting. "I know nothing about that," he said curtly. He couldn't have been more than nineteen. He had eyes the color of a Siberian sky and baby fat on his ruddy cheeks.

He tried to turn his attention to Emma, but the women were now besieging him.

"We can't keep coming here if they don't pay us," Tanya interjected. "You should tell them." The others in line chimed in their solidarity.

An older guard leaned over the young guard's shoulder to shout at them. "Why don't you shut up and do your jobs, you lazy bitches? We don't have time to listen to you." He glared at Emma, who was waiting for her ID. "Why are you standing there?" He swung his rifle in the direction of the door. "Get moving."

The young guard was so flustered he handed the identification back without another glance.

"Why aren't you polite to women?" Julia demanded. "I feel sorry for your mother." Taking Emma's hand, she marched her past the guards with her head held high, their insults bouncing off her strong shoulders like arrows off armor. When they were out of sight, she turned to Emma and gripped her hands fiercely. "Whatever you're here to do, I hope it brings those bastards down."

The base was lightly occupied, and no one spoke to Emma as she emptied rubbish bins in empty offices and carefully placed listening devices in telephones and on desks. Julia and Tanya stayed nearby always.

The quiet on the base gave Emma the courage to go further than she'd thought possible. She enlisted the two women to stand watch outside the door as she connected a USB reader that she'd hidden inside her watchband into computers left unattended and downloaded software that would give them access to the system they'd been unable to crack before now.

When they crossed the border back into Poland Emma thought her legs might buckle, but they held. The three of them walked away from the border, talking with adrenaline-fueled excitement, to the chosen meeting spot, where a taxi waited. The CO stood beside it in civilian clothes, his face hard until he saw them walking arm in arm. Then his wide grin reached his eyes.

"It went well?" he said.

"Like a dream." Emma turned to the women. "Thanks to these heroes."

Before she left, Tanya pulled her into a rough hug. Julia wrapped her arms around the two of them. When they let her go, their eyes were damp.

"I owe you so much," Emma said, squeezing their hands. "How can I thank you?"

Julia looked at her, a fine vengeance in her eyes. "Keep making them pay."

20

T HE SOUND OF the flowing water grew louder as Emma and Michael descended. The air, which seemed heavier with every step, held a dank sour-sweet river smell that belonged in the countryside, rather than under a city street. They had to take it slowly—the old staircase was unsteady, and some steps were all but rusted away, making their descent treacherous. After a few minutes, the staircase ended without warning, depositing them on a narrow brick embankment. They stood with their backs pressed against the damp wall as Emma swung the flashlight across a wide, shallow waterway.

"Wow," Michael whispered, awestruck. "Look at it."

In the cool white light the waterway was extraordinary. The Victorians hadn't just buried the river—they'd built a cathedral over it. In absolute darkness, and complete isolation, the river flowed beneath a high, vaulted brick ceiling. On either side, narrow brick banks in perfect condition rested, unused for over a century. In a few places, sturdy iron rings still waited for boats that would never need to be moored again.

More than twenty rivers flow underground in London—their

paths got in the way of progress starting in the fifteenth century, and pushing them underground meant the city could rise unhindered above them. The Fleet was one of the last to go. That legendary river, once believed to have healing powers, was paved over in the 1870s.

Ever since, its waters have flowed in darkness.

There were no cameras down here. No attacking Land Rovers to run them down. The people searching for them would never think to look here.

At the edge of the river Emma paused, letting the light beam balance on the slow-moving current. It revealed only the top of the water; everything that lay beneath remained hidden.

"What is it?" Michael asked.

"Nothing," she said. "I'm just trying to figure out which way to go."

Michael pointed to where the water gurgled around a cluster of fallen bricks. "The river flows in the direction of the Thames." He gestured to the right. "We should go that way."

He was useful, this doctor.

They set off down the brick walkway at the side of the water. It was unnervingly dark. Everything outside the flashlight's beam disappeared in shadow. More unsettling was the noise. Every sound echoed back at them—the thud of their shoes against the slippery bricks, the faint sound of their breathing. It all bounced off the walls, the bricks. Sometimes the sound seemed to come from behind them, as if someone was following just out of sight in the dark, breathing over their shoulders.

Goosebumps rose on Emma's back. More than once she spun around sharply to look behind them, certain she'd heard someone whisper, the hiss of a voice bouncing off the stone and brick.

"What is it?" Michael asked, the second time she did this.

The light slid across an empty river.

"It's nothing," Emma said, and her voice echoed around them. *Nothing . . . Nothing . . .* "Just thought I heard . . ." *Heard . . . Heard . . .*

They began walking again, both of them listening intently for any sign that they weren't alone, and finding only ghosts.

"It's beautiful down here." Michael's voice echoed around her. He glanced at her. "It was very smart of your people to think of it."

"They're good like that." She raised the light to see farther ahead. "My boss knows everything there is to know about London."

"I guess he's . . . R, then?" Michael asked. "I heard you mention him on the phone."

There was no harm in him knowing an initial, Emma decided. "That's him."

He picked his way along the slick embankment as he considered this.

"Can I ask you a personal question?"

Her eyebrows rose. "Go for it."

"Emma's not your real name, is it?"

She thought for a long moment. Ordinarily she would have dodged this. But there was something about being underground that lowered her defenses. The night had a conspiratorial feel. They seemed miles from the circumstances that made names secrets.

"No. It isn't my name."

"I thought not." He looked pleased. "I mean, of course it isn't your real name. They wouldn't have you running around using a name someone could look up on Facebook."

"I'll tell you something nobody knows," Emma said, emboldened by the darkness around them. "Most agencies pick their agents' names for them. They get assigned. But we choose our own."

"And you chose Emma Makepeace." He looked thoughtful. "That is so interesting."

"Is it?"

"Well, it's a bit of a statement, isn't it?" He gestured vaguely. "Makepeace, I mean. It's a name that says something."

Aside from Ripley, Michael was the first person ever to notice her name, or to ask about it.

"I chose Emma because I thought it was the most English name there is," she confessed. "It sounds like Jane Austen and pink roses. And Makepeace . . . Well, I guess that was a statement of purpose." She gave a short laugh. "God, I was so naïve back then."

"It's a good name," he said firmly. "No apologies."

They walked for a while in silence, and then Emma said, "If you could choose your own name, what would you pick?"

It was a light question—just something to fill the time. But when she glanced over at him, she saw he was looking down, his lips pursed with thought.

"Well," he said, "I chose Michael. My parents named me Mikhail, but I wanted a British name. I wanted to fit in. And I felt like this was my country. Mikhail . . . that came from their country. From Russia. And that wasn't who I was."

"How old were you when you made that decision?" Emma asked curiously.

"I was eight, I think," he said. "We'd moved to a new house, and I was enrolling in a new school. The head teacher asked if I had a nickname, and I told him I wanted to be called Michael. I think it was the first adult decision I'd ever made. I was giddy with the power of it. My parents didn't find out for half a year."

Emma slowed to navigate around a chunk of fallen masonry, holding the light so he could see his way. A few seconds passed before she asked, "What did they say when they did find out?"

His smile faded. "It was Christmas. I was in the nativity play and they saw my name in the program. 'Michael Primalov.' My mother said, 'Misha, they have spelled your name wrong!' She wanted to complain to my teacher. But I told her, 'I chose that name. That's who I am now.'" He pressed his hand against his chest in an unconscious gesture. "'I'm not Mikhail. I'm Michael.'" The emotions of that long-ago night were written on his face, in the worried crook of his eyebrows. "She said, 'You break my heart, Misha.'"

He said it quietly, but the last word echoed around them mournfully. *Misha . . . sha . . . sh . . .*

"She didn't mean it," Emma told him.

His dark eyes gleamed in the shadows as he looked up at her. "How could you know that?"

"Because my mother would have said the same thing," she said. "Choosing a British name, that's your right. And even if you did hurt her briefly, remember what she was going through back then. Her whole life had been upended. She was probably afraid of losing you, along with everything else." She stepped over a small tributary that cut across the brick and poured into the river in a silvery tumble. "I'll bet she doesn't even remember that night."

"Maybe not." He didn't sound convinced, but he also didn't look melancholy anymore. And for some reason that mattered to her.

"I suppose there's no point in asking what your real name is," he said.

There was a pause punctuated only by their footsteps.

He was right. There was no point. She wasn't allowed to tell anyone. She'd never even considered it.

"It's Alex."

She didn't know she was going to tell him until she'd done it. The second she said it, she wanted it back—this secret, protected part of her.

Michael, though, was intrigued. "Alex." He tried it out. "That's a good name, too. It suits you more than Emma. Emma's too soft. There's something spiky about Alex."

"It is a good name," she said. "But I shouldn't have told you."

Their steps stopped. In the quiet that followed, they exchanged a long look.

"Thank you for trusting me," he said. "I would never tell anyone."

"I know."

The moment seemed to stretch too long. Feeling suddenly awkward, Emma turned away, focusing on the uneven bricks underfoot. The embankment had narrowed farther, so walking side by side was increasingly unsafe. She pulled ahead, grateful for the distance this provided.

This operation was messing with her judgment. Maybe she still had a concussion. Maybe she had actual brain damage.

Unaware of her inner turmoil and clearly emboldened by her sudden willingness to confide, Michael tried more questions. "What did you mean earlier when you talked about your family? You said my family sounded familiar."

Emma thought for another long moment.

"My mother came from Russia," she said finally.

He looked at her with real surprise. "You're joking."

But she could tell he knew she wasn't.

"What you said about your mother reminded me of her," she said. "She wants the best for me and that can make her very critical. Nothing I do is good enough. But I know, or at least I tell myself, that's only because she loves me."

His steps slowed as he stared at her. "That is so familiar. My parents are just the same. I know they were incredibly brave. They took huge chances to protect the world, as they saw it, from nuclear disaster. They risked their lives over and over again. I understand why they wanted me to follow in their footsteps. But I'm a different person. And it's hard for them to let me just . . . be."

"It's hard for them to understand that you're the one who knows what's best in your own life," Emma said. "But you are."

"You should tell my mother that." His voice grew dark. "In fact, if you see her, please bring it up."

Emma's chuckle echoed.

As they picked their way across the increasingly unsteady walkway, Michael asked, "Does your mother still live in Russia?"

Emma focused on the torchlight on the dirty bricks. "She moved to England when she was pregnant with me," she said. "My father stayed behind. He worked quite high up in the Russian government. He was helping the British understand the new leaders so they could work with them. He thought it was the right thing to do." She paused. "He got caught. Arrested. Jailed."

She thought of the picture her mother kept on the dresser. Her father was a stranger to her: a lanky man with a wide smile that lit up his angular face. In the picture, he wore a brown suit and a bad tie, and he was leaning against the side of a car. He had blond hair and blue eyes—he was only a little older than she was now.

In her mind, he had no other clothes. His hair never grew or was cut. And he was always smiling.

"Your father was a spy and you're a spy?" said Michael. "That's something else."

"Yeah, you could say that."

"What happened to him after that? Did he get out?" Michael reached for her arm, trying to slow her down. She hadn't realized she was walking so fast.

She stopped, looking back to where he stood in the dark. "He's dead. They shot him."

His sharp intake of breath echoed, turning into a gasp that swirled around her.

"I'm sorry," he said.

Emma couldn't understand what on earth had compelled her to tell him the truth. She'd never told anyone. Not as a child. Not as an angry teen. Never as an adult. Ripley, of course, had known from the start. He knew everything. But no one else ever knew.

Michael was still talking, saying all the right things, but she turned away. She *had* to stop telling him things about herself. This was why it's a bad idea to open the door to truth—it's so hard to shut it again.

The flashlight beam highlighted a sudden drop-off right ahead, where the embankment seemed to disappear.

"Hold on," she said, lifting a hand. "The path runs out."

The river itself was narrower here, and there was no walkway within the beam of the flashlight, which she noticed for the first time was beginning to fade.

"Let me try it first," she told Michael, although he'd made no move to bypass her. She stepped down, her feet instantly soaked in freezing water. She could feel the tug of the current, but it was gentle enough. Nothing they couldn't handle.

"OK, the current's not bad but it's bloody cold," she called back. Behind her, she heard the splash as Michael followed her down.

As the icy water hit him, he gasped and said, "I have no idea why I thought underground water would be warmer, but I already can't feel my feet."

"It gets better once you start moving," she lied. "Sort of."

They were both acting as if the previous conversation had never happened and Emma was grateful to him for going along with it. The last thing she'd wanted to do tonight was think about her father. But there was something about Michael that summoned confidences.

He would have made a good spy.

Walking in the water took more effort and they stopped talking. They'd been wading for about twenty minutes, picking their way cautiously around unseen obstacles, when Emma began to hear an odd sound. It seemed to come from the bend just ahead of them. The water had been getting deeper for some time—it was now up to their knees.

"Hold up," she called, raising her voice to be heard above the roar. "Wait here."

She moved carefully, holding out her arms for balance. With every step, the roar grew louder, until she could hear nothing else. When she reached the bend, she held the flashlight up to get a better view. About fifty meters ahead, the sleepy river changed—two new waterways seemed to converge into it, and the river became deep and agitated. As she watched, a tree branch flew atop the surface as if propelled by an invisible hand, and smashed into the wall, disappearing underwater, and then bobbing up some distance downstream.

Turning, she motioned for Michael to join her. "I don't like this," she said, raising her voice to be heard above the roar. "It gets pretty deep ahead, and that current looks vicious."

He waded to her side and frowned at the rushing water. "Looks like other rivers joining this one. We must be getting close to the Thames."

Emma swung the fading light along the round walls beside them. Ripley had told her how to get down here, but not how to get out. She'd hoped it would be obvious. But there were no exit signs down here.

Her heart sank.

"We have to backtrack," she told Michael above the roar of the water. "We must have missed something. There has to be a way out." She stared into the darkness behind them, as the water rushed around her frozen ankles, the current pulling at her like hands trying to drag her away. "Or else we're trapped."

21

IT WAS HARDER work wading back against the current. There seemed to be more hazards under the dark water than they'd noticed earlier and, with their feet so numb, each of them stumbled and fell more than once, splashing clumsily. Emma shone the flashlight at the edges of the tunnel, searching for an opening, but all she saw were solid walls curving up over her head, like a brick sky. Condensation formed on the ceiling and fell on them in a cold, constant rain, soaking them to the skin.

Although she said nothing, with every step her apprehension deepened. What if the only way out was the way they'd come in? The whole thing would have been a pointless waste of time and energy. They could end up right where they'd started. Only more exhausted now, and with miles still to go.

Michael, who had been scouring the ceiling as they walked, stopped abruptly.

"Hey, come over here. Hold the flashlight up," he called to her. "I think I see a door."

Sloshing through the water, she lifted the light to the round walls and curved ceiling above them. But there was nothing there—just a broken section where the bricks had fallen into the river.

He forged ahead, undaunted. Emma swung the light to the other side of the river.

There had to be a way out. Ripley wouldn't send her down here if there wasn't.

But they didn't have much time. The batteries in her flashlight were growing steadily weaker. It might last another ten minutes. She hadn't said anything about it to Michael yet—she couldn't bear to. The thought of being down here without light made her stomach curdle.

She moved back to the middle of the water, searching the walls again. They had to be missing something.

"Look—there." Michael stumbled toward her, pointing in the direction of the wall to their left. "What's that?"

Emma shook the flashlight to try and get more from the batteries. The fading glow illuminated what looked like a narrow ledge about five feet up. At first, she could see nothing else, but then, in the shadows, she thought she could just make out a passage of some kind.

"You think that's a way out?" she asked, squinting to get a better look.

"I don't know. But it's worth a try." Michael sloshed to the crumbling wall. "I think there used to be a ladder of some sort mounted here." He pointed at rusted holes about as big as a fist. "It must have rotted away." He reached up to the ledge. "I think I can get up here, though. Give me a boost, would you?"

Holding the flashlight between her teeth, Emma reached down and knitted her fingers, bracing herself as he placed a cold booted foot in her hands. He swung up with surprising ease, climbing carefully to his feet on the narrow outcropping of brick, which she could now see was barely wider than his shoes. Balancing cautiously, his arms outstretched, he inched across until he could peer into the opening.

"There's a ladder up here!" he called back excitedly. "This has to be a way out. Come on, I'll help you up."

Turning back, he crouched down and held his hand out to her.

Emma reached up without hesitation, wrapping her fingers around his wrist. His skin was cold and damp, but his grip was strong, and he pulled her up to the brick ledge in one smooth movement, holding her arm until she caught her balance. Five feet wasn't that high, but it wouldn't make for a pleasant fall. Bricks and stones waited below.

"Thanks," she said.

He motioned for her to follow him to an opening in the wall. "Come look at this. The ladder is old but useable."

Emma stepped carefully along the ledge until she reached the opening. From here she could see it was original to the tunnel, with the same clever brickwork she'd noticed around the staircase they'd come down at the start. Behind it, an ancient metal ladder was fixed to the bricks with bolts. The flashlight was too weak to show her where the rungs led, but odds were it had probably once been a worker-access point. Which meant there had, at least back then, been a way out at the top.

Not a single trace of light came down from above. There was no way to know if the original opening was still up there and hadn't been paved or built over at some point in the last 150 years.

"It doesn't look that stable." Emma grabbed the nearest rung, pulling it hard. It shifted beneath her hand.

She glanced back at Michael. "I don't like this. The whole thing could come down."

He held out his hands. "Do we have a choice?"

They both stared at the rusted metal ladder.

Emma let out a long breath. "I'll go first. If it holds me, you come after."

She switched off the flashlight and shoved it in her pocket. Instantly, the cavern was plunged into total darkness. She could see nothing—not the ladder, not her hand on it, not Michael, even though he stood so close she could feel his breath warm on her shoulder.

"Good thing we don't need to see to climb." She could hear nervousness beneath his bravado.

Gingerly, she put her foot on the first rung. The ladder quivered but held beneath her weight. Moving slowly, trying not to jar the worn bolts more than she had to, she began to make her way up. Her fingers found gritty metal, cold as a tomb and rough with rust that was so thick, she could smell its coppery, blood-like scent every time she moved.

At first, the structure seemed almost sturdy. The higher she went, though, the more she felt it quiver beneath her.

"I'm coming up now," Michael called.

"OK, but take it easy," she shouted down.

The second he began to climb, the ladder shuddered with every step. Emma stopped moving as it swung sickeningly.

"Slow down," she called back. "It may not hold—"

Even as she said it, she heard a splintering sound of metal giving. Michael gave a short, panicked cry that cut off almost instantly. The ladder shook violently beneath her hands, nearly knocking her off.

Her breath hitched in her throat and she wrapped her arms around the nearest rungs, clinging to the fragile structure. Dirt and rocks rained down on the river below.

When the ladder stopped swinging, she could hear nothing at all but the river beneath them.

"Michael!" she shouted.

Frantically she reached for the flashlight, but as she pulled it from her pocket it slipped from her cold fingers. She heard it thud off the metal, and then nothing.

She cursed under her breath, and called again, "Are you OK?"

There was a pause, and then the ladder quivered.

"Well, I'm going to need a tetanus jab," he said between gritted teeth. "But I'll live. If this thing doesn't kill us both."

Emma closed her eyes, steadying her panicked breathing before replying. "What happened?"

"A rung broke, and almost took me with it," he said. "I've got a cut but I'm OK."

"Take it slow," she ordered. "Let me get further ahead so we can balance out the pressure. Parts of this ladder are stronger than others."

"Lesson learned."

Now desperate to get above ground, she began to climb again, using the same deliberate technique—feeling the rung above, testing its strength, taking the step. Repeat. She could sense the ladder quivering when Michael began to climb, but he was moving more cautiously now, staying well behind her.

She didn't know how long they'd been climbing when she bumped her head against an unseen ceiling.

"I'm at the top," she called back, reaching above her. Relief coursed through her as she identified what she was touching. "Feels like metal."

He stopped a few rungs down. "Is there any light?"

"Nothing." She traced the edges of the metal with her fingertips. "It's round, though. It has to be a manhole cover."

"Can you lift it?"

Bracing her feet on the ladder, Emma raised both arms to push the unseen cover with her hands. It didn't budge.

"I'm trying." Her voice was strained. "It won't move."

"You want me to have a go?"

Emma shifted her weight to look down and heard something fall from where the ladder connected to the wall. It clanked against a rung and then thudded below.

"I'm not sure it can hold us both in the same place."

Again, she pushed hard on the unseen metal cover, groaning from the effort.

Nothing.

She let out a frustrated breath. "But I can't lift it. We're going to have to try to do this together."

"I'm coming up."

The ladder trembled as Michael climbed. She felt his hand brush her shin as he pulled himself toward her, and she shifted aside to make space, until he stood on the same narrow rung. They were squeezed in together; she could feel the warmth of his skin through her soaked clothing. She could just make out the shape of his face as he tilted it up to look at the heavy metal cover above.

He pressed his hands against it, testing it. "Do you think it's sealed in some way?"

"I bloody hope not."

He shoved against it experimentally, straining to lift it. She could feel his biceps bulging, hear his tightening breath. The ladder shivered from the pressure, sending more rubble tumbling down.

He sagged back, wiping a hand across his face. "It gave a little. I think we can move it. It might just be rusted into place. Can you take that side, and I'll push on this side?"

"Sure." When Emma shifted into position, the ladder gave a warning creak.

She stopped instantly. "I don't like the sound of that at all."

"Me neither. We may not have too many shots at this." She could hear him feeling around the back of the ladder. "I think the top bolts are going. Let's do this fast."

It was harder to brace herself with him on the same rung—their feet tangled together. Emma leaned forward to balance her weight and cautiously lifted her hands, praying the ladder would hold for a few more minutes.

"On three," Michael said. "Push as hard as you can. One . . . Two . . . *Three*."

Emma pushed with all her strength. She could feel Michael's body tense against hers. The manhole cover shifted, but only a little.

"Come on," he grunted. Emma tried harder.

The ladder juddered beneath them. "Don't stop," he told her, his voice tight. "It's moving."

Emma hung on, trying to keep her balance and push at the same time.

Suddenly, with a scrape of metal, the manhole cover gave way. Rust and dirt showered down over Emma's face, but she held on to the heavy lid, straining as they shoved it aside.

She drew in a breath of cool, fresh air. A golden, electric glow that had to be a streetlight washed across them. After so long in the dark, it seemed painfully bright, and she had to squint against the glare.

"Quick," she told Michael, brushing dirt from her eyes. "Get out. I'll follow right behind."

Eagerly, he scrambled up. Just as he began to move, the ladder began to shake as if a monstrous unseen hand below them were twisting it like a toy. A bolt near her hand burst loose, sending rubble down into the darkness.

"Go!" she ordered.

He grabbed the edges of the manhole and pulled himself up, springing out and spinning around to reach for her. Emma scrambled after him.

Just as she reached the top, the ladder shuddered and began to sink beneath her.

With a startled cry, she released the rung she was holding and grabbed the edge of the manhole. In seconds, the ladder had disappeared, and her feet dangled in thin air as the old metal construction crashed down to the river.

Before she could even scream, Michael was there, reaching into the hole to grab her arm in a bruising grip, dragging her to the surface, and depositing her on the street. There, they both collapsed, and lay on their backs, panting.

"Dammit," Emma said, between breaths. "Who's rescuing who here?"

His only reply was a brief, exhausted laugh.

Emma knew they should get moving, but she felt as if she'd used up everything.

And yet, somehow they had to get across the river before the sun came up. And she had no idea how she was going to do that.

22

I T WAS RIPLEY who told Emma that her father was famous among spies. The information he'd provided, as tensions rose during the troubled years after the fall of the Berlin Wall, had kept the West from making dangerous mistakes while Russia literally tore itself apart. Both MI6 and the CIA had tried to get him out of the country toward the end, when the new Russian government grew more paranoid and vindictive, but they hadn't managed it in time.

"Your father's death is one of our great failures," he said in a meeting in his office soon after she joined the Agency. "He was shot along with four other government officials. All of them knew it was possible, but we'd promised to do our best . . ." He turned his unopened cigarette case over in his hand, his long face shadowed by the memory of that time. "But it wasn't enough. The Russians wanted to make a point. To demonstrate their strength."

He said the last word with bitter contempt.

"Did you know him?" she asked.

Ripley glanced up. "Your father? No. He wasn't one of mine. I knew *of* him. I was part of the group trying to get everyone out. We knew how much danger they were in. But the Russians moved more quickly than we'd expected." He set the black case down on his desk and said quietly, "That was a very bad week."

"Do you know who ordered the execution?" She kept her voice easy, just a casual question, but Ripley fixed her with a steady look.

"I do not," he said. "That sort of information is never findable." He added, pointedly, "Nor should you try to find it."

Her expression didn't waver but still he studied her, his eyes both inscrutable and somehow knowing.

"If I were in your shoes," he said, "I would want to know everything you want to know. And I would want to do everything you want to do. But I have decades of experience in this world so I'm going to impart a piece of advice to you that I hope you will take to heart." He leaned forward, holding her gaze. "Hurting the person who killed your father will do nothing to change the past. But mark my words— you can still have revenge. I've been taking revenge for thirty years. I do it every single day." He thumped his finger against the desk, punctuating his words. "Those listening devices you planted while you were in the army? That was your first act of revenge. Every day you work with this agency you will be taking your revenge. Work with us and the men who killed your father will learn to *fear you*."

He held her gaze. "Can I count on you? Will you take your revenge my way?"

Emma drew a breath. All her life she'd wanted to find the man who'd pulled the trigger. Find him, and pull a trigger of her own. But Ripley was offering her something more valuable—a payback that never ended.

"It's a deal," she said.

He gave her a thin smile of approval. "Excellent. Then I have an assignment for you."

"An assignment?" Emma sat up straighter. "Does that mean they finished the review?"

Her security clearance had been under review for months. She'd filled out endless forms, giving the government her full family history and access to her bank accounts. She'd endured an excruciating interview with an elderly civil servant who, over a cup of tea, had asked her to identify every person she'd ever had sex with.

The fact that her family came from Russia was obviously the main problem. Until her distant relatives had been investigated to the government's satisfaction, she was stuck on desk duty.

Ripley seemed to find this more offensive than she did, bridling at the insinuation that he would choose an agent who might betray her country.

"Not yet," he said. "This assignment is outside the reach of the review. You will be working for me directly, under my authority. There's someone in town I don't like. And I want you to watch him."

He handed her a picture of a fleshy, dark-haired man, and told her the basics. He was an oligarch who worked as a fixer for senior officials of the Russian government. "He travels the globe having meetings with other very wealthy despots," Ripley said. "And suddenly he's in London, apparently on a shopping trip."

"And you don't think he really needs a new outfit?" Emma guessed.

"Let's just say"—Ripley stood up, straightening his cuffs—"I have questions."

The assignment called for disguise and surveillance. For the first part, he sent her downstairs to see Martha, the Agency's legendary disguise guru, whose office in the basement of the Institute proved to hold enough wigs, clothing, and fake glasses to suit any West End theater. There might have been some order to her collection; if so, Emma couldn't see it. Shoes spilled out of open boxes and battered shopping bags, wigs sat on top of briefcases, fabric overflowed from beneath racks of clothing in endless colors and sizes.

The subterranean room smelled strongly of dry-cleaning chemicals, and jazz poured quietly from unseen speakers. It was so different from the offices upstairs Emma felt as if she'd somehow wandered into a vintage clothing shop.

"Hello?" she called tentatively.

Almost instantly, a woman appeared from behind a rack of suits, multiple ties streaming from her hands.

"You must be Emma," she said, smiling. "Ripley told me you'd be coming."

In her early thirties, Martha Davies was tall and pencil thin, with short black hair, bright red glasses, and a matching slash of scarlet lipstick. She had a disarmingly blunt manner, and a tendency to get straight to the point.

After she'd dropped the ties into a basket overflowing with more, she stood Emma in front of a full-length mirror and stepped to one side, looking her up and down with her head cocked to one side, like a bird eyeing a vulnerable insect.

"At last they send me someone fun to dress. I get so bored of putting middle-aged men in plain suits." Her accent spoke of Manchester and Liverpool, and Emma liked her instantly.

"Give me the brief," Martha said. "What kind of person are you following?"

"All I know is he's Russian," Emma told her.

Martha's expression told her they were always Russian. "Oligarch or drug dealer? And where are you going to be?"

"Oligarch. And Bond Street, I think."

"Oh goody." The woman brightened. "I have just the thing." She disappeared behind the racks of clothes. For a moment, the clicking of her heels against the polished concrete floor was the only evidence of her presence, but then she emerged holding a knee-length Chanel suit in an odd shade of pink Emma couldn't define, and a caramel-colored wig that, tucked in the crook of her arm, looked not unlike a Pekinese.

"You're a size twelve, aren't you?" she asked, studying Emma's hips with a critical look that made her instantly defensive.

"Ish."

"This should fit." Thrusting the outfit into her hands, Martha directed her to a curtained corner. "Try it on. I'll find shoes."

The suit fit like a glove. When Emma emerged, Martha clapped delightedly. "Perfect. You look like all the money."

Emma shifted her weight, resisting the urge to scratch. "It itches."

"It's wool, dahling." Adopting a startlingly accurate cut-glass accent, Martha held out a pair of taupe low-heeled shoes. "One must suffer for perfection."

After fussing over Emma's makeup and giving her a small Mulberry bag with the throwaway warning, "Lose this and you'll owe me six months' pay," Martha placed her in front of a mirror and stepped back to study the final product.

The person in the mirror was a confusing blend of glossy legs and a prim, high-necked blouse. The suit both emphasized and hid her figure.

"I look like an expensive prostitute," Emma announced.

"You look like a trophy wife," Martha corrected her. She tilted her head, eyes bright behind the vivid glasses. "Have you done disguise work before?"

Emma thought of Monika, and cutting her hair in a Polish bathroom, the cheap dye that had turned her pillows black for a week.

"A little," she said, before adding, "*very* little."

"Well." Martha began putting the makeup back in a series of neatly organized rectangular containers. "It's all about belief. Believe you are who you're meant to be. A trophy wife never hurries and never worries. Most of all, she never apologizes. She accepts that she deserves everything she has because she works very hard at being a good wife to her powerful husband. Channel just a little bit of that Stepford Wife vibe and you'll blend in perfectly."

The phone on her desk rang. As she turned away to answer it, Emma stared at herself in the mirror, fascinated by the transformation. Her own mother would have walked right by her on the street without a second glance.

Ripley had told her Martha was a genius—now she believed it.

The call was brief. When it ended, Martha turned to her.

"A car is waiting outside. The target is currently in the Gucci shop on Bond Street. You're to take over for the person who's been following him all morning." Her tone was suddenly pure business. "Ripley says you should look out for a brush pass. If you see it, don't interfere. Just get a picture of the person he's contacted, then head straight back." She handed her a pair of black sunglasses. "Take these." She turned them over. "The camera is in the lens. Press here"—she tapped the top outer corner on the right side—"to take a picture."

Emma slipped the sunglasses into the bag.

"Those cost more than the bag, by the way," Martha told her as she headed for the stairs. "Be a love and bring them back in one piece so we can still be friends."

Outside, a black four-door Jaguar with windows tinted an illegal hue purred at the curb.

Emma climbed into the backseat. The driver, a man in a dark suit with military build, shifted into gear. In the mirror, his face was chiseled and expressionless. Emma was certain she'd seen him before. But it wasn't until she noticed the bump on the bridge of his nose that she figured it out.

It was the man who'd tried to kidnap her during the training at the airbase.

"Wait a minute. You're Adam, aren't you?"

For the first time he met her eyes. He didn't look thrilled to be having this conversation. "That's me."

"How's the nose?"

"I think it adds to my rugged good looks," he growled, unsmiling, as he steered the car into busy Westminster traffic.

There was a pause as Emma tried to decide how to respond to that. "Did I apologize for that? I really hope I did."

The look he gave her in the mirror was withering. "I have no idea."

After that, Emma stared out at London on a busy afternoon, barely seeing the red double-decker buses or the crowds of tourists queuing outside Westminster Abbey. The tall curved fences protecting Buckingham Palace went by in a golden blur. She kept her expression neutral, but her heart was skittering wildly—after weeks of waiting, she was doing something at last. But now that the moment was here, she wasn't sure she was ready.

Doubt still swirled in her mind as Adam pulled up in front of an art gallery where a canary-yellow statue of a bearded goat inexplicably dominated the front window. He turned to face her.

"Your man's left Gucci now, but he's on a bit of a spree—you'll find him in Louis Vuitton." He tilted his head in the direction of the designer shop just in front of the car, its door framed by two elegant topiaries.

"Thanks." Emma reached for the door handle.

"My number will be messaged to you," he continued patiently, answering the questions she'd forgotten to ask. "If you need a pickup, text the address to me. I'll be nearby. Remember, all we want is a picture of the person he's meeting. Don't talk to him. Don't interfere with anything that happens. For God's sake, don't go hurting anyone—we don't want to have to do any cleanup today. This is bim bam." He swung his hand. "In and out. Got it?"

Bristling at the implication that she might do otherwise, Emma responded with a terse, "Got it," and opened the door. Remembering Martha's advice at the last second, she climbed out primly but with casual insouciance, as if wearing overpriced clothes and getting out of chauffeur-driven cars was an ordinary part of her day.

Outside Louis Vuitton, she paused to look in the broad window, ostensibly considering the glossy, espresso-brown luggage while actually taking in the reflection of the street behind her. It was still office lunchtime and the street was busy with pedestrians and taxis. She could see nothing that worried her. The doorways opposite the store were empty; nobody in view was watching the shop, or her.

After fixing the already smooth hair of her wig, she walked to the door and reached for the handle. Before she'd even touched it, it unlocked with a click. Emma suppressed a smile. Her costume had passed muster with the shop workers watching her on CCTV from inside. They didn't let just everyone in that easily.

"Welcome! Can I assist you, madam?" A skeletal young man, with pale skin and a suit that looked more expensive than hers, wafted over, holding out his hands as if he might pick her up and carry her wherever she wanted to go.

"Oh, thank you." She gave her voice boarding school vowels, slowing her natural verbal cadence to a leisurely drawl. "I'm actually looking for a new suitcase for a trip I'm taking to Dubai next week." He opened his mouth to offer to help and she continued, pretending not to notice. "And I'd prefer to look on my own, if that's not a problem."

It wasn't a question, and he didn't miss that—he probably spent most of every day dealing with irritable rich people. His expression remained pleasantly bland as he gave a half-bow and stepped back. "Absolutely. I'll be just over here if you have any questions at all."

This quiet exchange passed unnoticed by the other shoppers around them. These included a chic American couple in their sixties, dressed in pale linen as if on their way to a regatta, and the tall man in his forties whose picture Ripley had shown her earlier that morning.

Moving with no particular hurry, she strolled slowly in his direction, stopping to touch the handle of a bright red suitcase and managing to look at the four-figure price tag without flinching. A laptop bag caught her eye, and she paused to lift it as if considering carrying it onto a private jet. All the while, her target stood in front of a mirror as a slim young woman tied a silk scarf around his neck and laughed prettily at something he said. The mirror was well chosen—he could see the entire room reflected in it.

Emma became deeply interested in a display of bulky handbags as she watched him out of the corner of her eye. He was studying himself in the mirror, a half-smile playing around his full lips. There was no question he was enjoying the shop assistant's attention.

"I do not know," he mused in a heavy Russian accent. "The color is . . . how do you say? Drab."

That, at least, was true.

"I think it's quite elegant." The girl stepped back to study it with apparent seriousness. "That color would go with so much. It would go with blue, with charcoal . . . It really suits you." The girl kept a professional distance, turning to pick up a scarf with a hint of blue in it. "This one would match your eyes."

The man took it from her and held it up. As he did, his phone vibrated. He checked the screen and put it away. Whatever the message had been, it hadn't made him happy. His demeanor changed from self-indulgence to impatience. "I'll take this one. Can you wrap it for me?"

Startled by this abrupt decision, but clearly delighted, the young woman led him over to the cash register, chattering eagerly. He handed over his credit card but Emma could see he was distracted; his fingers drummed against the edge of the counter as the rectangle of silk was painstakingly folded and enrobed in tissue before being slipped into a thin box.

Emma moved closer to the door, readying herself to follow when he left. Spotting this, the young man who had approached her earlier wafted back. "Are you sure I couldn't interest you in one of our new line? The magenta is particularly charming."

"I don't think so." Emma gave a tight smile as the Russian man passed them and went out of the door, a bag in his hand. "I'm just not seeing what I'm looking for. I'll come back when I'm feeling inspired."

Without waiting to hear what he said in response, she followed the man out. It was just after one o'clock, and New Bond Street was thronged with tourists and office workers. It took a moment to find her target, and by then he was already losing himself in the crowd.

Emma sped after him as quickly as the tasteful taupe heels would allow, but she was still a good distance behind when he turned a corner and disappeared.

"Oh, sodding hell." She said it loud enough that a pair of shoppers turned to gawk at her as she broke into a run, shoes clunking hard on the pavement, shoving past a cluster of Italian tourists, the designer bag flapping from its delicate gold chain as she hurtled to the intersection.

By the time she reached the corner, he was halfway down the street. A woman in running clothes was just passing him. As Emma watched, she bumped into him, and then hurried on without apologizing. The man didn't seem to notice, but as she stared at him, she saw his hand dip into his pocket.

The glasses. In the rush, she'd forgotten all about taking a picture.

The woman, glossy brown hair pulled back, dark blue leggings and a skin-tight top, was jogging straight toward her.

Sweating now, Emma ripped the small bag open and scrambled for the sunglasses, yanking them on hastily, then staring at the woman and touching the top right corner repeatedly with her finger.

As the woman neared, Emma turned away, busying herself by pulling the phone from her bag, as if this was why she'd paused in her journey.

She waited until the woman had jogged by before texting Adam for a pickup.

Only then did she allow herself to feel relieved.

It hadn't been pretty but she'd done it. She had the picture.

The feeling of success lasted until she got back to the office to find Ripley in his office, drinking coffee with the female jogger and the "Russian" target. Her heart sank.

"Right." Ripley closed the door behind her and motioned for her to take a seat. "So that was a test, and it seems to have gone rather impressively wrong."

Heat rose to her face. On the one hand, she was glad she hadn't embarrassed the Agency on a real assignment. On the other, everyone would know she'd failed. But Ripley was already motioning for the two agents to speak. "Tell Emma what she could improve."

"I didn't spot her in the shop," the man explained, his Russian accent gone now, replaced by flat Yorkshire vowels. "But she was right obvious as soon as we got on the street. She didn't try to blend in. She just come gallopin' after me like a horse comin' up from behind at Cheltenham."

Ripley motioned at the jogger, who said, "I spotted her the second she came around the corner. Running like that and in that dress." She gave Emma an apologetic glance. "It wasn't very subtle."

When he turned to Emma, Ripley's expression was veiled. All he said was, "From your perspective, what happened out there?"

Emma swallowed hard. It had been her chance to prove herself and she'd blown it. She had to take responsibility for that.

With effort she said, "I had it under control inside the shop. But he moved too fast on the street and I wasn't ready for that. I had no choice but to blow my cover."

To her surprise, Ripley looked almost pleased. "One of the hardest things for new agents to learn is to how to stay in character when the target does something you don't expect. Adapting to obstacles—that's at the heart of what you have to do." He gestured at her pink suit, rumpled from running, and the wig, which sat slightly askew. "We can make you invisible, but only you can figure out how to stay that way. So. Tomorrow we try again."

Seeing her unhappy expression, he added, "Don't worry. By the time we're done, you'll be ready for whatever this job throws at you."

23

EMMA AND MICHAEL limped down the street, trying to get their bearings. Under the streetlights she could see that Michael's left arm was covered in blood from a jagged five-inch gash where he'd sliced it on the broken rung. Both of them were filthy, their faces and clothing caked in dirt and blood. It was just after four in the morning and the streets were still quiet, but early workers would be waking soon and their odd appearance would attract notice, even in jaded London.

She walked a little ahead as they neared the junction with a wide avenue. A few early delivery vans rumbled by as she looked cautiously around for street signs. As soon as she realized where they were, relief spread through her.

To the left was Fleet Street, with its tall modern office buildings. A short distance beyond was Blackfriars Bridge. Beneath it, the wide, slow River Thames gleamed black in the darkness. MI6 was just over a mile away.

Emma had never been happier to see anything than that cold, muddy water.

Turning to Michael, she pointed to the river. "We're at Blackfriars. We came out in just the right place. We're nearly there."

He stared at the bridge with its distinctive blunt red and cream arches. "Nearly there . . ." He repeated her words as if trying to accept them.

A lone van approached from the bridge, and she pulled him into the shadows in front of a closed shop until it passed.

Glancing down at his bloodied arm she asked, "How bad is it?"

He looked at the wound dispassionately. "It's stopped bleeding. I'll clean it up when we get there."

When we get there.

They hadn't used words like that before now. They hadn't had any faith they'd actually make it. Suddenly, they were starting to believe.

They began walking again, and this time the pain didn't seem as bad as it had a few minutes ago. They moved with new energy.

In the glow of the streetlight, Emma glanced at Michael. He moved with jerky, tired steps. He looked nothing like the man she'd talked to in the hospital the previous day.

This night had changed him. Perhaps it had changed both of them.

Eight hours ago, she'd just wanted to do her job and get him into custody. Back then, she'd seen him as spoiled and irrational—a problem she had to fix. Now she saw him as intelligent, resilient, and loyal. He'd saved her life and risked his own.

She wasn't easily surprised. But Michael Primalov had surprised her over and over again.

Sensing her gaze, he gave her a questioning look. She stretched her sore muscles. "When we get there, all I want is a huge cup of tea."

"Don't say things like that," he groaned as they jogged down the street. "It's torture."

"Maybe they'll have sandwiches at MI6," she said, warming to this fantasy. "And cake."

She felt giddy from the sudden and unexpected onset of hope. With a bit of luck, they could make it to MI6 in forty minutes. It would all be over.

They were nearly at the river when she spotted the Range Rover.

The driver had parked away from the streetlights, just far enough back from the road to be out of sight, but with a good view of the bridge. The sight of it sent ice into her veins.

Maybe it's a coincidence, she told herself. *Lots of people have cars like that.*

But even as she thought it, she could see the ghost of exhaust rising behind it. The engine was idling. And she knew. They were waiting.

It was the same model and color as the one that had chased them earlier. Nothing was open around here at this hour. There was nothing for anyone to sit and wait for.

Nothing, except them.

With cold clarity she pieced it all together. There was no way for the Russian team to know in advance that she and Michael would walk down this specific street. Putting a car here—it had to be strategic. And if that was the case, she was certain they'd find another car just like this one at the foot of Waterloo Bridge. And the Hungerford. Every bridge nearby would be covered.

She had to give the Russian agents credit. It was perfect: a simple solution to looking for two needles in a sprawling city of hay. They were keeping them on the north side of the river, corralling them into the section with the most cameras, and the fewest places to hide.

Emma felt as if someone had kicked the backs of her knees. All her hopes faded away, leaving a hollow sense of despair. The river lay between them and safety. And now there was no way across it.

Wordlessly, she touched Michael's arm, and motioned for him to follow as she branched off the main road onto a dark, narrow lane that curved behind two towering office buildings and stopped in the darkness.

Leaning against the wall next to her, Michael shot her a puzzled glance. She stepped back so he could see and pointed at the dark vehicle idling near the bridge. "They're here already. Waiting for us."

"No, it can't be." Aghast, he stared past her. He looked as if she'd punched him. "How could they find us so fast?"

"I don't think they have found us," she said. "I think they're making sure we don't cross the river."

"Are you sure it's them? It could be anyone."

Emma ran a tired hand across her face. "It's them. Believe me, I wish more than anything it wasn't." She paused, but then decided to give him all the bad news. "It's worse than it looks. I have a feeling they control the whole river. It's exactly what we would do in their place."

"But how can you know that?" he demanded, suddenly tense. "Shouldn't we check the other bridges?"

"Yes." She dropped her hand to her side. "We should walk to each one and see how thorough they've been, but there are five cameras on every city block around here and I honestly don't think we'd make it very far."

Silence fell as he realized what she already knew.

"We're trapped," he said.

She gave a slow nod. "When they lost us—when we went underground—this must have been their backup plan. Stop us from getting across the river. Hem us into a small area of the city and it won't matter that they don't know where we are: we can't get to safety."

A thought came to her then. How did they know she wanted to cross the river? The Agency was on this side of the water. So was MI5. And the Home Office. Lots of places they could have gone. The only Intelligence building south of the river was the MI6 headquarters. How on earth did the Russians know that was where they were headed?

She thought again of Ripley's message. "Be careful with M."

But surely he hadn't meant *this*. Masterson was a technocrat, not a traitor. And yet . . . how had they known?

Beside her, Michael still stared at the car, every muscle in his neck taut as a wire, before slapping his hand against the wall. "Those *bastards*." The words carried the full weight of his rage and fear and exhaustion.

Keeping her eyes on the car, Emma put Masterson out of her mind. All of that was for another time. Right now she had to get them out of this.

She wondered who was in the car. Was it the three agents from earlier or someone completely new? Someone rested, who hadn't spent hours slogging through sewers and dodging bullets and running for their life. Someone who'd had water and food. Someone who could pick them off with ease.

Either way it didn't matter. If they were spotted, they were dead.

But there had to be a way out of this. They just needed to be smart. Silently, she worked through the possibilities. The tube didn't open for another hour—they could wait for that and try to lose themselves in a crowd. Maybe they'd outrun them that way. The Russians wouldn't think that they'd put the public at risk.

And they were right. She couldn't risk other people getting hurt.

That ruled out buses, trains, all public transport. The busier the city became, the fewer chances they could take. People would be everywhere soon. Each one a human shield for the Russians, who had already proven they were willing to risk innocent lives.

"What we need is a helicopter," Michael said, melancholy in his voice. "Or a boat."

Emma nodded, still staring at the river in the distance. It took a minute for his words to sink in. Then she turned to him, her eyes wide, excitement flaring inside her. "We need a boat!"

He gave her a doubtful look. "Yeah but . . . we don't have one."

"No, we don't," she said. "But I know where we can steal one."

24

THE THAMES RIVERFRONT, always thronged with traffic and pedestrians during the day, was completely empty. Nothing seemed to be moving at all. No planes crossed the sky. No police cars prowled the streets. It was as if the city held its breath, waiting to see what would happen next.

Emma and Michael clung to the shadows and studied the river across the street from them.

The twisting old lanes they'd followed to get here had been silent, dark, and absolutely littered with CCTV cameras—on every corner, on the backs of buildings, in doorways, and higher up, getting a bird's-eye view. They were everywhere. The Ring of Steel was a tool Emma had used many times in her work, but she'd never really considered what it meant. After all, the system had always been on her side. Suddenly, though, she saw the red glow of the night-vision lenses as sinister.

Already, their images would have been captured and absorbed into a hard drive somewhere. Facial-recognition software was looking for them and, when it found them, this stretch of road would be filled with Russian agents.

"It looks safe," Michael whispered, squinting into the distance. "What do you think?"

Emma pointed out the ever-watching electronic eyes. "Cameras there, there, and there. Keep your head down." She straightened. "Now, let's go get ourselves a boat."

They sprinted across the road to the walkway on the bank of the Thames. They had an easy rhythm now—Emma taking the lead, Michael staying close, reacting to hand signals or a quick warning look. It was as if they'd worked together for months, rather than just one long night.

Emma's earlier fatigue had passed as soon as they began running. By the time she reached the entrance and leaped over the barricade in front of it, all her nerves were singing. Michael followed a second later, his feet thumping hard but steady when he hit the ground.

On the other side of the low barricade, a ramp angled down toward the water. Waves rocked the boats moored below, sending metal jangling as they ran down to where a chain-link gate blocked the way. Beyond it, illuminated by the low glow of security bulbs, Emma could see a row of black-and-yellow rigid inflatable boats secured to the dock. Each RIB could hold about ten people, she reckoned. The company used them for entertainment, speeding tourists past the Tower of London and out to Canary Wharf.

It was just what they needed.

"I'm going over," she told Michael. Gripping the cold metal, she began to climb up. Michael followed. This time, when he hit the ground, he grunted with pain.

"Are you hurt?" she whispered, giving him a quick look.

"I'm fine," he insisted, although he was clutching his wounded arm.

Taking him at his word, she ducked low as they ran down the ramp to the dock, where five bright yellow plastic-hulled RIBs were chained to the decking. Each one was individually locked in place with a sturdy padlock.

Choosing the last boat in the line, she motioned Michael toward it. "Check the engine: make sure there's fuel. I'll get it unlocked."

He gripped the rubber side of the vessel, but then paused. "Is this a good time to tell you I've never actually driven a boat?"

Emma, busy pulling her lockpicks out, didn't look up. "Me neither. But I think we'll figure it out."

The boat rose and fell as he jumped aboard and headed unsteadily toward the rear of the boat.

As she worked the lock, Emma tried not to give in to the doubts that plagued her. They needed to be moving faster. She didn't believe the Russians had overlooked anything. They would have thought of boats.

But no one jumped over the fence after them. Or popped out from the shadows.

She knew she was tired and paranoid. This really might work. If they could get a boat started, they could go down the river straight to MI6's offices. It would be an unorthodox way to arrive, but that was the whole point.

Driven by urgency, she moved too quickly, and her pick jabbed the back of the lock and bounced off it. Biting back her frustration, she pulled the slim metal picks out, drew in a long breath, and tried again. This time, the pick found the tumbler instantly. Closing her eyes, she slid in the second needle-thin tool entirely by feel and pressed it home.

The lock clicked open.

Shoving her picks back into her pocket, Emma stood and released the speedboat from the chains before jumping aboard, steadying herself as it swung beneath her. When she'd found her balance, she headed to where Michael was crouched over the central steering console.

"Half a tank of fuel," he said when she walked up. "That should get us there. But there's a problem." He tapped the spot where a keyhole sat empty.

Emma sighed. "Bollocks."

"I've been looking everywhere," he said.

Without much hope, she felt around the edges of the steering column. This company took care of its equipment. It wasn't going to make it easy. But a spare key would be useful—especially with a lot of employees sharing responsibility for so many boats.

"Check there." She pointed at a small storage space, much like a glove compartment, in front of Michael. "Feel around the top. They might tape it in place so it doesn't get lost."

As he searched, she felt under the backseats, looking in every opening, fingers moving with professional speed and efficiency.

"Come on," she whispered. "Give me one thing."

Michael pulled a rumpled stack of papers and a small can of oil from the glove box and set them aside. "There's nothing else in here," he said, reaching deeper into the opening. "It's empty." Then he stopped, his expression changing. "Hang on. I think . . ."

She glanced up just as he turned to her, his hand outstretched. A silver key, still fixed to a sticky piece of tape, glittered in his palm. "Got it."

Her fingers brushed his as she took it from him and ripped the tape off. "Say a prayer," she told him. "Because I am out of Plan Bs."

He stood close, watching as the key slid into place. She could hear him whispering, but it took her a second to catch the words. "Отче наш, сущий на небесах. Да святится имя Твое . . ."

It was the Lord's prayer. The sound of it gave her the strangest feeling—cold and warm. Safe and dangerous. As if she were home and far from home, all in the same moment.

"That's my mother's favorite prayer," she told him, and turned the key. The engine burst to life with a powerful roar that split the quiet like a blade. The whole boat felt alive—she could feel the vibration of it beneath her feet, as if it were as eager as she was to get out of here.

Well, if prayer worked, Emma thought, who was she to argue?

Cautiously, she tried shifting into gear. The boat jumped away from the dock with such force Michael lost his balance and nearly fell, grabbing the back of the driver's seat for support as Emma clung to the steering wheel.

"Hang on," she called, and moved the throttle up. The boat shot out across the water.

Michael whooped, thrusting his fist into the air.

"I told you we could figure it out," Emma said as she steered them toward the middle of the wide river.

The vessel was responsive and fast. Soon they were speeding across the black water, skimming the top like a bird. The cold breeze blew Emma's hair back as she spun the steering wheel to the right, turning the boat upriver in the direction of MI6.

Part of her wanted to laugh from the sheer excitement of it, but the rational part of her brain nagged at her. This was too easy. Something wasn't right.

"Why weren't they watching the boats?" she asked, raising her voice to be heard above the engine.

Standing next to her, Michael angled his body so he could see the shore behind them. "I don't know. No one's following. Maybe they didn't think about it."

Emma said nothing, but she couldn't believe this was true. The Russians had left nothing to chance. Clearly, they'd been planning this operation for weeks. They'd had time to study how the Agency reacted. To watch Ripley's team.

She wouldn't let herself think about Masterson again, and whether he could be a reason the Russians knew so much.

They didn't know about me, though.

The thought came to her from nowhere, but it was absolutely true. The whole time the Russians had been murdering scientists in towns and cities across Britain, she'd been on assignment in Camden, hidden away with a group of harmless hippies. So the Russian agents had never seen her. Had no idea how she operated.

Maybe this was why Ripley had chosen her—she was completely clean. She'd never been on a major assignment before. No one knew what she looked like, or how she worked. It might even be why he'd sent her to Camden in the first place. He'd wanted to hide her.

If that was the case, then he'd seen this coming for months. And he'd kept her out of sight until now—training and preparing her, getting her ready, so that when the moment came she could appear, completely anonymous, utterly unpredictable.

I chose you for a reason . . .

Well, she wasn't about to let him down. With fresh resolve, she pushed the throttle up farther. The speed lifted the nose from the water, sending a fine mist of icy spray over them as she navigated to the middle of the Thames. The silvery cold of it against her skin made her shiver as the gray hulk of Waterloo Bridge loomed just ahead of them, streetlights highlighting its blunt shape clearly in the dark.

So far, they were completely alone on the water. Not a barge or boat in sight.

Next to her, Michael leaned back, looking up at the sky.

"What is that thing?" he asked.

Emma, focused on controlling the powerful boat, didn't look. "What thing?"

"Above us. That red light."

She eased back on the speed long enough to glance where he indicated. The noise of the engine drowned out every sound, but Michael was right—above them, maybe fifty feet, a red light hovered steadily. There was nothing to secure it. It was in midair. And it was keeping up with them.

Emma stared at it, her stomach plummeting. "It's a drone. Hold on."

She thrust the throttle forward, white-knuckling the steering wheel as the boat shot under the middle span of Waterloo Bridge like a bullet. They were in darkness for a second, and then out the other side.

Both of them looked up. The red light was still there.

"Is it them?" Michael shouted to be heard above the roar of the engine, craning his neck to look at it.

"Who bloody else?" Emma kept her focus on the river ahead.

"What are they going to do with it?" he asked.

The first gunshot came before Emma could reply. They both ducked so abruptly the RIB jerked hard to the right, and she fought to control it as she twisted around to look over her shoulder. In the glow of the streetlights, she saw the black outline of a speedboat tearing out from underneath Waterloo Bridge. It moved with remarkable speed, skimming toward them.

"*That's* what they're going to do," she shouted. "Get down."

She pushed the throttle up. The boat bounded forward, the nose so high as they passed beneath the soaring white spans of Hungerford Bridge that she couldn't see in front of them. She had to ease off the speed to get sight of the river again. It was too dark to make out how many people were on the speedboat or how many guns they had, but it didn't matter. One was too many.

A second gunshot cracked across the water.

Crouching behind the wheel, Emma steered the boat in a zigzag evasion pattern. The night became a blur. The river was suddenly hard and unfriendly; the RIB flew up and landed with a violent thud that jolted her spine. Icy spray soaked them. Her fingers were frozen and slippery on the wheel. They were moving too fast for her to make out obstacles ahead. The lights of Westminster Bridge seemed to rear up in front of them out of nowhere.

Another shot rang out, and another. She noted distantly the circles in the water where the bullets hit like skimmed stones.

Swearing under her breath, she pushed the throttle to the limit and the boat flew into the air, coming down with such force it knocked the breath from her lungs. They were going too fast now; she was losing control.

"Help me," she called to Michael, who crouched next to her.

He pulled himself up and grabbed the other side of the wheel, trying to keep it steady. Still, the vessel swung beneath them, tilting perilously on one side, the engine screaming a protest in the air. Even with both of them holding on, the wheel pulled away. Emma's cold, wet fingers slipped from it. Unable to stop it, she watched it spin. Felt the boat hit the water again and then rise far too high. Heard the *thudthudthud* of gunfire all around them.

A sharp stab of fear threatened to stop her heart.

Then the sky became the river, and the river became the sky.

And the cold water took her down.

25

I N ALL HER time at the Agency, Emma never went out on a single operation with Charles Ripley. He trained her, mentored her, shepherded her through the government's labyrinthine regulations, but never went on actual assignment with her. She used to tease him about it, but he always told her he was too old for street work. Until four months ago when, one cloudy May afternoon, he called her into his office.

The air had been heavy with cigarette smoke. There was a folder open on his desk. She read the words "EYES ONLY" upside down before he closed it and looked up at her.

"A Russian government official arrived in town yesterday on a commercial flight. I'm putting together a team to follow him and I want you to be part of it. We're heading out shortly. Go see Martha. Tell her I want you to be unmemorable and unrecognizable." He stood with quick impatience, as if even this short conversation was taking too long.

He was already walking into the corridor when she called after him, "Where am I going? Martha will need to know."

His words sailed over his shoulder as he headed toward Ed Masterson's office next door. "I've spoken to her. She's going to dress you for Knightsbridge. Meet me downstairs in thirty minutes."

All the way down to Martha's basement room, Emma puzzled over what had just happened. Normally, a briefing before any operation could last an hour or more, but he'd told her almost nothing. He'd seemed distracted and anxious. Ripley never got anxious.

When she found Martha in her basement office, the disguise specialist was already deep in the racks of clothing. She wore a 1940s dress and sturdy heels that clunked against the polished concrete as she rushed around the cavernous room gathering items.

Emma sometimes thought Martha was the one person at the Agency who truly understood Ripley's moods. She'd asked her once how she'd ended up here. "I worked at Shepperton Film Studios for a costume and makeup company," Martha had confided. "One day Ripley came to our office—he wanted to buy some clothes and wigs. Really random stuff. I just assumed he was a filmmaker. He asked a thousand questions, and never accepted an easy answer. Still, it was only when he offered me a job that I understood what was going on. That was seven years ago."

It was classic Ripley, Emma thought. He found people for the Agency in unusual places. She and Adam were both ex-military. He'd found others when they were actors or bartenders. His instincts about people were virtually unerring.

Martha decoded his instructions into dark trousers, flat-heeled boots, and a black leather jacket. Emma's real hair was hidden beneath an ash-brown shoulder-length wig. A prominent prosthetic nose utterly changed her face.

It was a much more thorough disguise than Emma had expected.

"Glasses or no?" Martha stepped back, eyes narrowing as she tapped her chin with one blood-red nail. "I think glasses." Grabbing a basket filled with assorted spectacles, she dug through it quickly and handed her a trendy framed pair. "These'll do."

Emma ran up the stairs to find Ripley already waiting by the door, his expression dark. "You're late," he snapped, and turned away without waiting for a reply. Thinking it best to stay silent, she followed him through the security doors. Outside, a black BMW purred at the curb; she saw Adam's distinctive blunt features behind the wheel.

In the car, Ripley handed her a picture of a trim man wearing a well-cut suit. He had neatly styled gray hair and high Slavic cheekbones. "The target is Grigory Chernov, sixty-two years old. Former KGB, now GRU. He's deputy director of the European division, based in Moscow. His specialty is defectors. He's known to have personally tracked down at least twenty people suspected of cooperating with the West. Some of them are now in jail. Some are dead." His face was hard. "He likes to get his hands dirty."

He told her they would be following Chernov but not engaging with him. "We just want to know why he's here."

It all sounded reasonable, and yet none of it explained Ripley's presence on this operation. Or the fact that he was so visibly fuming.

Normally, Emma would have pushed for more information, but he clearly wasn't in the mood to be questioned.

Twenty minutes later, she, Adam, and Ripley were walking through affluent Knightsbridge, beneath a leaden sky. In designer jeans, an expensive jacket, and sunglasses, Adam looked like a hedge fund manager on a day off. Unlike the two of them, Ripley hadn't attempted to change his appearance at all. His familiar face was tense as he moved with swift impatience through the throngs of tourists and shoppers on the pavements around Harrods department store.

A doorman in a vivid green waistcoat held the heavy glass door open as they approached. "Sirs, Madam." His tone was deferential, though his eyes had already moved beyond them to a rowdy group of schoolchildren.

None of them spoke. As soon as they were inside, they separated. It was easy to lose themselves in Harrods—local shoppers and international tour groups packed the aisles, gathering around the expensive merchandise as if they were in some sort of retail museum.

As Ripley worked his way across the ground floor, Emma headed through a perfume section bigger than her flat, working her way toward the staircase behind it. She knew Ripley was taking the escalator, and Adam was to use the elevator.

They were to work from the top down, each of them taking a separate floor. Emma ran straight up to the fifth floor, where she walked through the eye-wateringly expensive array of shoes, pretending to browse the glossy stiletto heels while scanning the faces she passed for any sign of the man in the photograph. She moved quickly, but not fast enough to attract attention. Harrods had excellent security, and their goal was to not be noticed.

"Fifth floor clear," she said quietly into the microphone attached to her collar.

"Sixth floor clear." Adam's voice came through the earpiece hidden behind her hair.

"Roger that." Even through the microphone she could hear the chill in Ripley's voice as she hurried down the stairs to the first floor, her next assignment.

She'd just begun to make her way through a lingerie section when Ripley spoke again, fast and low. "Subject spotted. Second floor."

A jolt of electric anticipation ran through her.

"En route," Adam said quietly. "Taking the stairs."

In case the cameras were on her, Emma glanced at her watch and tutted before heading to the escalator, restraining herself from running past the other shoppers as it glided down with an ethereal lack of urgency.

"On the escalator," Emma said into her microphone as a group of stunningly beautiful Italian teenagers chattered around her, oblivious.

It seemed to take an hour for the escalator to finally reach the second floor, where she stepped into an artfully decorated menswear section.

She moved slowly, stopping at the first rack of button-down shirts and surveying the room beyond it until she saw Ripley near a table of folded sweaters. Emma walked over to stand near him, picking up a black cashmere sweater and holding it up as if examining the cut. It cost more than she made in a week. Adam was a short distance away, browsing a display of jackets. She still hadn't seen the target anywhere.

"To your left." Ripley's voice was low.

Emma glanced over to see a man in a charcoal-gray suit waiting at the counter as his purchases were wrapped. His face was turned down as he studied his phone, but, when the shop worker said something, he looked up and she recognized the high cheekbones and thin mouth from the image she'd studied in the car.

His hair was steel gray and so freshly cut that the skin on his neck was still red. His hands were loose at his sides, and he betrayed no signs of awareness that he was being watched, waiting patiently as the young man at the counter put tissue-wrapped packages in a green, square bag with the store's name on the side in gold.

"Thank you for shopping at Harrods," the young man said, presenting the bag to him with a flourish.

"Yes, of course. Always a pleasure." Grigory Chernov had a thick Russian accent but seemed comfortable with English. He also seemed comfortable buying expensive things—he already carried another Harrods bag, much larger than the new one.

He strolled in the direction of the escalator without ever glancing in their direction.

Ripley stood still, watching the man go. Tension seemed to vibrate from him, like a wire with electricity singing through it.

"I'll follow him." Adam's voice came through Emma's earpiece. She saw him turn in Chernov's direction.

"No." Ripley's command was quiet but firm. "Stand down. This one's mine. Both of you watch the exits from this floor."

Adam turned abruptly toward the elevator. He said nothing, but Emma saw him shoot Ripley a quick, puzzled glance.

Trying not to look as worried as she felt, she headed toward the top of the staircase.

Ripley prowled through the rows of elegant clothing like a cat, as Chernov stopped to look at a row of jeans with languid curiosity.

Near the entrance to the stairs, Emma paused at a rack of Hugo Boss ties. This section of the store was surprisingly quiet. Only she, Adam, Ripley, and Chernov were within view.

Ripley was still heading straight toward Chernov. Emma waited for him to stop and take up a position near the target and stay out of sight. But that wasn't what happened.

"Grigory!" Ripley made his voice jovial, a surprise meeting between friends. "Good heavens. It's been years!" He reached out, capturing the surprised Russian's hand before he could pull back and pumping it enthusiastically. "My God. You look healthy. What on earth are you doing in London?"

Ripley had said "no contact." This was *all* the contact.

Adam's dismayed voice came through her earpiece. "Ripley, what the hell are you doing?" But their boss didn't seem to hear.

A series of emotions flickered across Chernov's face. Shock, followed by a brief and quickly suppressed flash of fear. All replaced in an instant by smooth politeness.

"Charles," he said. "This is . . . unexpected."

They know each other, Emma realized with a thrill of shock.

"My goodness, what a surprise to see you here." Ripley still held his hand: his other hand rested on Chernov's shoulder. His smile was poisonous. They began to move in step and Emma realized Ripley was propelling Chernov, against his will, to a quiet corner behind the racks. "We must catch up."

Soon, they were out of sight.

Emma hesitated. Ripley's instructions had been clear—she was to watch the exit. But what if he got into trouble?

Adam must have come to the same conclusion—he was moving slowly in the direction the men had gone.

Emma began to do the same, staying just out of sight, and stopping when she spotted the men in a shadowed corner near a staff exit.

"What the hell are you doing in London?" Ripley demanded, just loudly enough for her to hear. "You have no business here: no diplomatic pass was applied for. If you came in under a false name, I will find out and have you ejected."

By now, Chernov had recovered from his surprise. "Is it necessary to be so dramatic, Charles?" He wrenched his fingers free of Ripley's grip, and straightened his jacket, brushing invisible dust from the lapels. "I am here on a shopping trip. Just a tourist. I've broken no laws.

My embassy will have filed all the necessary paperwork. I am not on a blacklist, as far as I know. Tell me if I am wrong about that."

The air between them crackled with mutual dislike.

There's history here, Emma thought. *Bad history.*

She glanced over her shoulder to check the shop floor, but the young man at the counter was the only assistant in the department right now and he was busy with a cluster of shoppers who'd arrived all at once. None of them had noticed the drama playing out in a quiet corner across the cavernous room.

"Come on." Ripley sounded impatient. "You don't come to London on vacation and I don't have time to play games. What are you planning?"

Chernov held up his shopping bags. "I'm planning to buy a bottle of perfume for my wife. Chanel Gabrielle: her favorite. Then I'm going to get something for my daughter. Perhaps I will eat at a wonderful British restaurant tonight. And enjoy your beautiful weather." His expression was innocent, but the sarcasm under his words was palpable.

Ripley must have noticed that too, because he tensed. He was only an inch or two taller than the Russian man, but, when he drew himself up, he seemed to tower over him.

"That's fine. You pretend to be a tourist, but know this." Ripley lowered his voice to a threatening whisper, his eyes fixed on Chernov's cold blue gaze. "I will have you followed every minute of every day you are here. I will know every single thing you do. You won't take a piss without me getting a report about the vitamins in your diet. Every conversation you have while you're in the city will be recorded and played back for me. Whatever you think you're planning—whoever you think you're meeting—we will know. Do you understand me? This is *my* city. And you have no business here."

Emma had never seen him so furious—every muscle in his body was taut with suppressed emotion.

Chernov didn't flinch away; their faces were inches apart and still he held Ripley's gaze. "You do that, Charles. You follow me around and sniff my piss. But you need to understand one thing, too—I have a right to go anywhere I want. This is a free country. You cannot stop me."

Something in his tone sent prickles down Emma's spine. It wasn't what he was saying—it was what lay beneath those words. It sounded like a threat.

His face darkening, Ripley said, "Let me worry about my country. You worry about getting home in one piece. I suggest you do it tomorrow. You're not welcome here."

Turning, he strode across the room toward the stairs, passing Emma without seeming to notice her. Chernov watched him go with a look of pure malice.

Through her earpiece she heard Ripley growl, "Adam, follow him. Don't let him out of your sight. Makepeace, back to the office."

She wanted to argue that she should help Adam with the surveillance, but his tone brooked no opposition. That had been an order.

By the time she made it downstairs and out past the liveried doormen, there was no sign of Ripley anywhere. She caught a taxi back to Westminster, getting out several streets away from the office and then backtracking on foot. Just in case.

In the basement, Martha removed Emma's disguise. She seemed to know the operation hadn't gone well, and she asked no questions.

As she dressed in her own clothes, Emma went over the operation in her mind. It wasn't like Ripley to lose control the way he had today. Something else had to be going on. Something he hadn't told her.

When she climbed the steps to his office a few minutes later, she found Ripley sitting with his back to the door, a cigarette in his hand. The room had taken on the gloomy gray wash of the sky outside the arched window where it had just begun to rain.

"Can I come in?" she asked.

He turned around in his chair. In the fading light she saw some indefinable emotion cross his face, but, by the time he motioned for her to enter, his expression was smooth.

She perched on the chair across from him. "I don't want to question your judgment but . . . what happened back there? I thought you said no engagement."

"I changed my mind." His tone was clipped. "I decided to challenge him. See where that took us."

"Where did it take you?"

He gave her a sharp look. "I don't know yet. But if he leaves town that tells me something. And if he doesn't that tells me something else. Either way, I'll be a step closer to understanding what he's up to."

"You know him, don't you? Personally, I mean."

"Oh, we're old friends." Ripley tamped out the cigarette. His long face was preoccupied. "He was assigned to watch me when I was an agent in Moscow. He bugged my flat and had me followed. I was very careful, but he was very good at what he did. He identified one of my Russian operatives. A very thoughtful young woman who trusted me completely when I said we would keep her family safe. Someone I cared about." He picked up the cigarette case and turned it over in his hands. "Chernov came to me and said he would have her arrested and her son taken away. He told me I could save her if I betrayed my country by working for him." His voice tightened. "I don't like being blackmailed. It's insulting. It assumes that I'm blackmailable."

"What happened to her? The woman, I mean," Emma asked.

"We got her whole family out. Right under Chernov's nose." He gave a thin smile and dropped the cigarette case back on the desk. "But I had to leave as well. Chernov's vindictiveness made it impossible for me to work in Moscow. As soon as he realized I was gone, he hunted down five more of my operatives and had them arrested. Some are still in prison. Some are dead." He met her eyes, and she saw cold fury in his gaze. "So, if you thought today was personal . . . trust me, it was."

"Why do you think Chernov's really in London?" she asked. "What's he working on?"

"I don't know. But if he came here, he has a reason. And I don't like him running operations in my city."

"If that's the case, why didn't you let me stay out there and help Adam?" she asked.

Ripley gave her a long look she couldn't read.

"Adam doesn't need help. And I wanted you here because I've got a new assignment for you." He leaned over to pull a folder from the briefcase resting at his feet. "There's a group of climate activists we want to know more about. They're being manipulated by a Russian propaganda agency. I suspect they're harmless, but we need to be sure. They're based up in Camden." He slid a file across to her. The picture on top was of a thin, angry-looking man, his arms covered in tattoos. He was wearing a T-shirt bearing a Russian red star and the slogan "CLIMATE FAILURE IS DEATH."

"That's your target. Bit of a hothead, I gather. We need to know everything about him." He gave her an apologetic look. "I'm afraid we've chosen you because you're the right age; it has nothing to do with your language skills this time. We think he's more likely to trust someone under thirty."

Emma reached for the file but then drew back. It was a good assignment—she'd never gone deep undercover before. But the Chernov case was a big deal, and she couldn't help feeling disappointed that he didn't want her to be part of it.

"What about Chernov? I can't help at all with that?"

"We have it covered." He must have seen her expression because he gave a slight sigh. "Look, I brought you with me today because I wanted you to get a good look at Chernov. I have a feeling we're going to have trouble from him. He's planning something. He won't do it now. He knows he's being watched. Sometime soon, though; I can sense it. Whenever that happens, I promise I'll bring you in on it. You'll get your chance."

26

EMMA BROKE THE surface of the icy river and drew a deep, gasping breath, blinking water from her eyes. She stared into the cold darkness around her with blank incomprehension—the river and the sky seemed to join together in a sheet of glossy black, and it took a second for her to understand where she was. The stolen yellow and black RIB was a few meters away, floating upside down. Its engine had fallen silent, and all she could hear was the low whine of the Russian speedboat in the distance.

Other than that, though, she was alone. There was no sign of Michael.

"Michael!" she called, pausing to cough river water from her lungs. "Where are you?"

There was no reply. The water rocked her from side to side as she turned a slow circle.

She raised her voice, trying not to panic. *"Michael!"*

"Over here."

The weak voice came from the inverted plastic hull of the stolen boat.

Relief rushed through her like heat, and Emma kicked hard to propel herself toward the sound. It was difficult to swim properly. Her hands and feet had gone numb. Her boots were full of water, which made her movements unwieldy. Her shoulder ached, probably from the way she'd struck the surface.

She found Michael clinging to the boat, shivering violently, his face white as milk in the darkness.

"Thank Christ," he said as she neared. "I thought you were dead."

She reached out to hold on to the edge of the boat. "Are you OK?"

"I think so. What did we hit?"

"I don't know. It happened too fast." The high noise of a speedboat engine was growing louder, and, when she pulled herself up to see over the hull, she made out a dark shape cutting across the water toward them. "They're getting closer."

A powerful beam of light swept the river, stopping when it reached the upturned vessel.

They ducked down behind the stranded boat. Emma looked over her shoulder for an escape route. They were too far from shore. They'd never reach it without being spotted.

"We have to hide. They'll pick us off if we stay here," she told him. "Can you swim?"

Again, the spotlight swung over the top of the RIB, turning the black water white.

Michael gave a tense nod.

"Then follow me." The light was nearly on them. *"Quick."* She dived into the dark water, kicking hard until she was beneath the upturned boat. When she rose to the surface in the pitch black, she took a cautious breath. The air was fresh. She grabbed the edge of an upside-down seat to hold herself afloat just as Michael splashed up next to her, sputtering. She could barely make out his features in the gloom as he scrabbled for something to hold on to. The ominous growl of the Russian boat was louder now, echoing off the thin plastic dome surrounding them.

"Is it safe here?" he whispered.

Emma didn't know the answer to that.

Outside, the speedboat was circling, the sound of the engine growing louder. She imagined the light shining down on the water and shifted closer to the center of the boat, hoping the murky Thames hid their dangling legs from view.

It was unbearably cold, and she could feel the river's strong current tugging at her feet. Michael's teeth were chattering and he was trembling so hard she could hear the water shifting around him. She whispered, "We only have to stay here until they leave. We'll get out of the water soon." He nodded, his lips tight.

She calculated there was enough air under here to sustain them for at least an hour, but the cold would kill them before then. It was September, so the water wasn't yet winter-frigid, but it was cold enough.

"Talk to me about exposure," she whispered to distract him. "How long have we got?"

He tried to think. "I d-don't know." His voice shook. "F-f-forty m-minutes? Less? I'd need to know the t-t-temperature of the w-w-water."

"They won't stay that long," she promised him. "Their little gunshow will have attracted attention, and they're not going to want to get caught out there."

It was all she could do not to shiver as hard as he did. Her body ached from the effort of staying still.

Right then, the speedboat's engine cut out. The sudden silence was deafening. Emma could hear her own ragged breathing, the soft splash as Michael tried to adjust his position. In the quiet, every sound was amplified.

She knew what the Russians were up to: they couldn't see them so they were going to try to *hear* them.

Giving Michael a warning look, she touched her finger to her lips.

Outside, she heard voices—male, speaking Russian. One of them called out, "Nothing on this side." Another one replied, "Nothing over here, either." There was a pause.

A third Russian voice, whom she took to be the boss, swore, "Where the fuck are they? Find them."

It was a distinctive smooth baritone. Oddly familiar.

Emma stopped breathing to listen.

"Search again," the man ordered. "They have to be there."

She knew that voice. But in the cold darkness she couldn't place it.

The water around her shivered as if it was vibrating. For a second, she wondered if it was the Russian boat causing the disturbance. Then she realized that the movement was coming from Michael, who was trembling so violently he was shaking the RIB like a tiny earthquake. He had to stop. If they were looking hard enough, the men would notice.

She put her arm around his cold, wet shoulders, drawing him closer. He blinked at her. "Try to stay still." She whispered the words in his ear.

She could feel his muscles tense as he fought to stop trembling.

Outside, the men had fallen silent. A knot formed in Emma's stomach.

She held Michael tightly, ignoring the pain in her shoulder. His skin was clammy against hers, but where they touched something like warmth rose between them. She could feel his pulse, rapid and uneven—or was it her own heart beating? The cold seemed to be thinning her skin, making it hard to tell.

A *thud* shook the hull and Emma almost lost her grip on the upside-down seat. Michael's breath hissed between his teeth as they fought to hang on. The Russian boat must have run into them. It had to be intentional. They were trying to shake whatever was underneath loose.

Voices above them spoke in Russian. Emma heard again that frustratingly familiar voice.

It wasn't one of Ripley's contacts, or anyone she'd met often. But she had heard it before. It was distinctive—smooth and deep.

Suddenly, on the other side of the hull, the speedboat engine roared to life, so close and loud Emma flinched. The Russians began to talk again, and she heard the man say, "We don't have time. Get us back, *now*."

And suddenly she had an image of a man with steel-gray hair facing Ripley and snarling, "You cannot stop me."

Grigory Chernov? she thought, bewildered. *What's he doing here?*

Clinging to Michael, she tried to remember everything she could about that day four months ago. She recalled the venom in Chernov's face as he and Ripley glared at each other. Ripley's uncontainable fury.

What had Ripley told her later? He'd said Chernov threatened to arrest an operative who'd worked with him in Moscow.

In her mind, she heard Ripley's voice in the shadowed office heavy with cigarette smoke. *He said he would have her arrested, and her son taken away.*

It had to be Elena Primalov.

Ripley must have been the one who got Elena and her family out of Russia. Chernov had been in charge of watching Ripley in Moscow so he could well have known that Ripley had had a relationship with Elena. That he cared about her.

And if Michael really was Ripley's son, as Emma suspected, then all of this, at last, would make sense.

This night—everything she'd been through—this was Chernov's revenge for Ripley humiliating him.

The Russian boat had begun pulling away, the engine's rumble receding gradually until it faded in the distance.

Michael let out an unsteady breath and shifted his weight, but Emma shook her head. "It could be a trick." She breathed the words against the cold flesh of his ear. "Stay still."

They stayed in the cold water, shaking in the dark, for what felt like forever, but must have been no more than four minutes. Emma counted the seconds in her mind—up to sixty, and start again. The whole time, she strained to hear anything from the surface—a splash, a thud against the hull. Any sign that someone was up there, waiting to pick them off. But there was nothing.

She couldn't feel her feet. Her shoulder hurt. It was getting harder to think clearly. Forty minutes, he'd said. They must have been in the water for half that already.

"Stay here," she whispered. "I'm going out to check. I'll tap three times if it's safe for you to follow."

As she turned away, he gripped her hand. "Be careful."

The water was pure ice as she dived down, kicking hard. The ache in her shoulder was worse now—a burning pain ran down her entire left side.

With one final kick, she reached the surface, hands raised to fight.

The upturned hull of the stolen boat glistened in the lights from nearby Westminster Bridge. She could see the current shifting the waves; feel it tugging at her, dragging her with it. There was no sign of the speedboat. They were alone.

Far away, though, she could hear what sounded like another vessel. Maybe the Russians. Maybe the police.

She rapped the hull three times. Seconds later, Michael splashed to the surface next to her. She could see the effort it took for him to kick his legs and stay afloat. Things that would have been easy ten minutes ago now took all of his strength. They were both too cold and too tired.

"The current's getting stronger," she told him, shivering so hard her voice shook. "We need to get to shore."

Leaving the upturned boat, they struck out toward the south bank of the river. Michael swam well, and soon pulled ahead. Emma had to favor her left arm, which wouldn't lift above her head or extend at the shoulder. She tried to balance that out by powering with her right. But the current was too strong. No matter how hard she kicked, the lights on shore didn't get closer.

"The current's worse where its deeper," Michael called back to her. "Get to the shallows."

She didn't tell him that she couldn't get to the shallows, no matter how hard she tried—she was too exhausted to speak. Her clothes seemed to be dragging her down. Everything felt heavy: her legs, her arms. Her lungs burned from the effort. Still she fought on, kicking doggedly. But the current had her.

She didn't know how long she'd been struggling when hands grabbed her, lifting her up.

"Hang on." Michael stretched one arm across her chest, as he powered to the shore.

"I'm fine," she protested, through numb lips. "You don't need to . . ."

"I know," he said. "But let me help."

He had to be as tired as she was but he swam steadily, his strong legs moving them through the current until, only minutes later, her sodden boots hit the river bottom. It took the last of their energy to drag themselves out onto the muddy shore.

Emma lay on her back, trying to catch her breath. Even though she could no longer feel the cold, she still shivered violently. She'd never been this exhausted in her life. Not in army training, when they had to run for hours. Not when Ripley kept her up for three days, making her practice functioning on no sleep. Not in the bad old days when she was small and her mother had insomnia and spent night after night pacing their tiny flat, clutching a glass of clear vodka, and talking to her father's ghost in Russian.

"We can't . . . stay . . . here," she said between gasps. "They'll be . . . looking for us."

"Need . . . a minute," Michael replied without turning his head to look at her. "Just . . . to . . . breathe."

Emma knew she should argue—should make him get up—but she was so tired. At least they'd ended up on the south bank of the Thames. They were across the river from Parliament. MI6's fortified building was on this side. They were so close. They could do this. She just needed a minute to rest.

Her eyes drifted shut, and instantly she was floating somewhere warm and dry. It was blessedly safe . . .

She jerked to awareness with a start, and the cold air hit her like a fist.

Next to her, Michael lay still, his breathing slow and even. When she rolled over to wake him, the movement sent a stab of burning pain through her shoulder so vicious her breath caught and she had to stay still until it passed. Slowly, she drew herself up until she was sitting and gingerly reached over to shake his shoulder. "Wake up."

He shifted, and then sat up with effort, wiping a hand across his face, grimacing when he felt the mud under his fingers. "Christ. How long was I out?"

As he straightened, his gaze fixed on her shoulder and sharpened. "Is that blood?" Suddenly alert, he pushed himself to his knees and leaned forward to see better.

Puzzled, Emma glanced down. Her top was soaked and sticking to her skin, but not just from water. A bloom of a dark red had opened across her left shoulder.

She must have hit something in the water.

"We don't have time for this," she told him, struggling to get up. "We have to go."

"Sit still." It was worryingly easy for him to push her back down. "I need to take a look at the wound."

There was no point in arguing. Reluctantly, she stayed where she was as Michael delicately lifted the fabric of her top and peeled it up to see the skin on the other side. She was so cold she couldn't feel his fingers against her shoulder. Couldn't feel much of anything at all. But she heard his breath catch.

He looked up at her. "Shit, Emma. You've been shot."

27

THEY STUMBLED ACROSS the uneven riverbank, their feet sliding on the mud as they made their way to a set of stone steps leading up to street level. Across the river, Emma could see the Houses of Parliament and Big Ben lit up against the black sky like a tourist postcard.

"Are you sure you're OK to walk?" Michael asked, worry hanging heavy in his voice.

"It's nothing," Emma answered shortly. "I'm fine."

"It's not nothing," he fired back. "It's a gunshot wound. You've been floating in filthy water for half an hour. You could have sepsis. We have got to get you to a doctor."

"Luckily for me, I already have one of those." She tried to make her tone light, but his expression told her he didn't see any humor in the situation. Her arm ached enough that she didn't find it very funny, either.

"Look," she said. "As soon as you're safely in custody I'll go straight to A & E."

"No." Michael stopped abruptly, a new tension in his voice.

Emma, who had been walking ahead of him, paused mid-step and turned back. "No?"

"No," he said again, his voice hardening. "This isn't a concussion or a bruised neck, Emma. This is a *gunshot wound*." He emphasized each syllable, as if he was talking to a child. "I cannot allow you to pretend you are not slowly bleeding out through a potentially deadly wound while we wander through south London in the *freezing cold*." His voice rose. "We are going to hospital and we're doing it now. St. Thomas's is right there." He gestured up at a long, modern building overlooking the river. "I'm not going one step farther until some-one has taken care of that wound. If you refuse to get help, then I'm done."

"Michael . . ." she began, but he wouldn't let her talk.

"It's not funny, Emma. None of this is funny. It's a nightmare I can't wake up from." His voice broke and he paused before continu-ing, "I'm not going to let you kill yourself. For me or anyone else."

Emma looked back at the river where the yellow RIB was drifting slowly with the current. The hospital was very close. They were virtu-ally beside it.

A thin haze of pain had settled over everything, making it hard to think clearly, but she knew they couldn't have much more than an hour left before sunrise. And yet he had a point. Her arm felt as if it had been set on fire. She wouldn't be much use to him if it got worse.

"Fine," she said. "We'll go to the hospital, but not to A & E: they'll ask too many questions."

He watched her narrowly. "What do you propose instead?"

"I want you to handle it."

Before the words were even out of her mouth, he'd begun shaking his head. "I'm not an emergency doctor. This isn't my area. You need a trauma surgeon."

"Oh, come on," she said. "Most A & E doctors got out of medical school two days ago and haven't slept in six weeks. I'd rather have you any day."

She could see that he was bracing himself for an argument so she cut him off. "It's the only way I'm going in that building, Michael.

And please don't think for a second that a gunshot wound means you can make me do anything I don't want to."

They glared at each other across the wet dirt until, finally, he held up his hands. "Fine. You win. I'll do it. But I want you to know it's a bad idea."

"Understood." Emma tilted her head, looking up at the sprawling building twelve feet above the waterline. "Now, the only question is: how do we get in there without being seen?"

He was already walking up the steps toward the street. "I trained at St. Thomas's. If you ever want to know how to sneak in or out of a hospital, ask a medical student."

The back of the hospital was protected by a forbidding, ten-foot brick wall. Michael moved quickly along it, never looking up until they reached a stretch where two sections of wall joined. At the meeting was a rusting metal gate.

When he lifted the latch the gate swung open with a screech of protest. On the other side lay an old courtyard. It had an abandoned feel, as if it had been accidentally left behind. Stained cigarette butts sticking out of dirt-filled plant pots betrayed what it was mostly used for these days. At the center stood the moss-dappled statue of a man who might have been a saint, his hands outstretched as if to say, "Just *look* at this mess."

Michael had scarcely spoken since their argument on the beach. Her injury seemed to have shocked him into an intense new focus. His dark eyes looked straight ahead, and he moved swiftly toward a door Emma could just make out in the gloom.

As she hurried to follow she tripped over a broken paving stone. The jolt sent a fresh stab of pain through the left side of her body, and she cried out involuntarily.

Michael spun around. "What happened?"

"It's nothing. I'm fine." Her strained voice betrayed the lie, but, when he hesitated, she motioned impatiently with her good arm. "I'm *fine*."

She had to be fine.

As Michael expected, the door leading to the smoking patio was unlocked. Inside, it was blessedly warm. Emma inhaled the dry, astringent hospital air hungrily, as if it alone might heal her.

In the bright fluorescent light, she could see how battered they both looked. Michael's hair was plastered to his skull. Mud was smeared on his face and hands. Their clothes were filthy and soaking.

Their shoes squelched as they hurried down a quiet empty hallway. The rooms in this wing appeared unoccupied. Still Emma felt exposed. As they sped down the corridor, she clocked the hospital's comprehensive security system, counting the CCTV cameras with increasing despair.

. . . Seven . . . Eight . . . Nine . . .

After a few minutes of silence, they began to hear signs of life. The plaintive *ding ding ding* of an alarm on some unseen electronic monitoring device. The shuffling of equipment being moved. The low, quick cadence of urgent voices on the other side of a wall.

Even as the sounds grew nearer, Michael moved steadily down the corridor. Suspicion began to tighten its grip around Emma's chest. It would be just like him to take her straight to A & E. He was such a do-gooder. Even though it would be an act of suicide on his part, he'd do it if he thought it would save her. That was the most ludicrous part. He kept trying to be the hero. He wouldn't let himself be saved.

She was trying to decide what to do when he suddenly darted into a darkened room on the right and motioned hastily for her to follow. Emma's wet shoes skidded on the polished linoleum floor as she made the sharp turn after him. As soon as she was inside, he closed the door and locked it.

The space was small and plain with an examining table in the middle. Michael went straight to the sink mounted on the wall, turning the water on hot and pumping soap onto his hands with clear relief.

"Sit down," he ordered without looking at her. "Take off your top."

"I want to wash my hands, too," she objected.

"Sit. I'll bring a cloth." He scrubbed his fingers with a kind of fixed determination, scrubbing up over his wrists nearly as far as his elbow until the water ran brown against the white porcelain.

Emma lifted herself onto the table and sat with her feet dangling. Just being in this position made her feel like a child, helpless and vulnerable.

It took effort to lift the hem of the soaking-wet top and pull it awkwardly over her head. Her left arm was too painful to move, so her right did all the work; she didn't so much take off the top as peel it. Underneath, her bra was filthy, but she couldn't reach behind her back to unhook it, so she lowered the strap from her shoulder gingerly past the bleeding wound.

"Here." Michael took the bloodied top from her hands and threw it into a bin, returning seconds later with a clean white towel. He'd washed the mud off his face and suddenly looked more like himself. Color was returning to his skin.

"I'm going to use this to clean the wound." He held up the towel, hesitating before adding, "It'll hurt."

"Do it," she said, bracing herself.

He'd soaked the towel in hot water and she felt the welcome heat of it in the instant before it touched her, and then a searing pain.

She closed her eyes, biting her lip hard.

"I'm sorry," Michael said.

Carefully, he pressed her body slightly forward so he could see the back of her shoulder. He cleaned her with the towel, leaning forward to examine the wound, so close she could feel his breath against her skin, soft as the brush of a feather.

"Looks like it went straight through." She could hear relief in his voice. "You could have bone damage, and you certainly will have tendon and muscle damage. But at least we won't have to extract a bullet."

After a second, he straightened. "Right," he said, throwing the towel in the bin. "I can patch you up enough to keep you going for a few hours, but you'll need a surgeon to take a look at it later."

He began rummaging through the boxes and bottles on the shelves in the cupboard, pulling a few down and stacking them by the sink.

"I need to get more supplies," he said. "Will you be OK to wait here?"

"If I keep telling you I'm fine, will you eventually start to believe it?" Emma slid off the table and looked around. "I need to wash. I'll do it while you're gone. Are there more cloths?"

He pointed at a tall cabinet. "In there. Don't touch the wound if you can help it."

When he'd gone, she rifled through the cabinet, pulling out a stack of worn, but clean, towels.

In the small mirror above the sink, the face that looked back at her was worse than she'd feared—wild-eyed, with dirt streaked across her cheeks and hair matted with mud and river water.

Grimacing, she kicked off her soggy boots, and emptied her pockets before peeling out of her filthy trousers. She'd lost her lockpicks along with her jacket in the water. The burner phone was still there but ruined. The roll of money was soaked but fine, and somehow the small knife in her sock had survived the swim. She took everything off, wriggling her bra down until she could step out of it. By the time she had everything off leaving only her socks, the white linoleum floor was streaked with dirt.

She was shivering hard, and all the motion had made her feel quite sick. She had to stay still for a few seconds until the room stopped swinging.

As soon as her stomach settled, though, she grabbed a bottle of disinfectant soap from the sink and used it liberally, rinsing off the mud, moving carefully to avoid jarring her shoulder, which had begun to ache in a low but threatening way.

The closest thing to clothing she could locate in the cupboard was a pale gray paper hospital gown. She was trying to figure out how to tie it behind her with only one good arm when she heard footsteps. She spun around just as the door opened and Michael walked in, his arms filled with boxes and bags.

Like her, he'd cleaned up while he was out, and changed into blue medical scrubs. She could see a bandage on his arm where he'd covered the cut he'd received on the ladder. He gave her an approving look as he closed the door behind him.

"You look better." He set the packages down on the examining table and handed her a large bottle of water. "Drink all of that," he ordered. The command wasn't necessary; she was already tearing the top off and upending the bottle, swallowing it greedily. It was sweet and clean and it washed away the metallic taste of river mud. The bottle was halfway empty before she stopped to breathe.

"Take the rest of it slow," he advised. "I've got another bottle for you when that one's done." He bent over his stack of supplies, pulling out squares of neatly folded blue fabric. "I got you some scrubs, too."

"Oh perfect."

Emma shook out the trousers eagerly and pulled them on beneath the paper gown. They were a little big on her, but she could run in them. Gingerly, favoring her left arm, she managed to tie the waist strings in a double knot.

She started to unfold the top as well, but he stopped her. "You don't want to get blood on that. Hold off until I've stitched you up." He directed her back to the examining table and began bustling around, putting syringes on trays. He talked briskly as he worked. "Your wound doesn't look infected, so I think we can clean it up and put in a couple of stitches," he said. "That should get you through the night, and then someone else can look at it properly."

His voice was steady, confident. All the nervousness and hesitation the night had brought with it had evaporated the second he walked through the doors of the hospital. He organized his supplies with the relish of a banker counting money.

"It doesn't hurt as much as it did earlier," she told him. "Maybe it's not as bad as we thought."

"It's bad enough." When he had his instruments together, he stopped in front of her and pointed at the top of the bulky paper gown. "I'm going to need to pull this down. Is that OK?"

Reaching up, Emma pulled the gown down without ceremony, exposing the bullet hole in her shoulder. She glanced down at it curi-

198 · AVA GLASS

ously. It didn't look like much: about the size of a ten-pence coin, it was the color and texture of raw meat. Blood oozed from it, running red down her chest, leaving rust-colored stains on the pale paper.

Michael draped a towel across her good shoulder, tucking it carefully under her wounded arm, like a toga. Then he snapped on a pair of surgical gloves and began filling a syringe from a small vial.

Emma observed this doubtfully. "What's that?"

"Antibiotics." He held the vial up so she could see. The name on the label meant nothing to her but she let him inject it, barely feeling the sting of the needle. He dropped the used syringe into a tray and began to fill another, slightly bigger than the last.

"This is anesthetic," he explained, before she could ask. "To help with the pain."

As he turned toward her, though, her hand shot up, grabbing his wrist. "It won't make me woozy, will it?" she demanded. "I need to keep my head clear."

He looked from her hand to her face, his brow creasing. "It's a local anesthetic. It will only numb the wound. It won't affect your thinking." When she still didn't let go, he gave her a measured look. "Let me work, Emma."

She wasn't sure he'd ever said her name before. Even though it wasn't truly hers, she still liked the way it sounded. And the fact was she did trust him. She believed he understood how dangerous things would get for both of them if he drugged her, even with the best of intentions. Even for her own good.

She let go of his wrist.

"I have a high threshold for pain," she informed him loftily.

A wry smile lit up his face. "I have absolutely no doubt of that."

She turned away as the needle pierced her skin with a sharp sting, staring at a poster above the sink that made hand washing sound as complicated as nuclear science.

"There," he said a few seconds later, dropping the syringe in the cardboard tray. "Done."

The throbbing pain had already begun to dissipate. Her body, which had been tensed against the ache for more than half an hour, slowly began to relax. She hadn't realized until the pain stopped how much it had hurt.

She sat still as he flushed the wound with antiseptic and fixed the edges together with butterfly stitches. His hands were confident and gentle. He never hurt her once as he covered the wounds in bandages, securing them in place with surgical tape.

"You're really good at this," she said. His head, bent close to her shoulder, tilted up as he looked at her. His face was only inches from hers.

"Thanks. I haven't worked on a bullet wound in years."

There was something bittersweet about seeing him like this. Knowing it could be a long, long time before he ever worked in a hospital again.

Their eyes held. She felt the connection between them like warmth in the air, and realized, with a kind of shock, that she cared about him. He was a good person. And if they both survived the next few hours, she was going to hate to watch him walk away when it was all over.

She reached out to touch his hand. "Michael . . ."

His fingers wrapped around hers, warm and strong. He gave her a look of pure understanding. "It's not your fault. It's just the way things are."

They both heard voices at the same time. Someone was in the corridor on the other side of the wall, talking loudly. There was no time to turn off the light. No time to hide.

They froze, staring at the door as the voice approached. It was a man, with a strong European accent. "I don't know what time it's likely to be ready," he was saying as he neared the door to the examination room. "He keeps calling and asking me this."

Without moving, Emma looked around the room for anything that could be used as a weapon. The syringes Michael had used lay on a cardboard tray within reach. It wouldn't kill anyone, she thought, but it might slow them down.

The seconds stretched as the man reached their door and then, moments later, passed by, his voice gradually receding in the long corridor.

As soon as he was gone, Emma jumped down off the table. "Are we done here?"

There was a brief pause before Michael pulled the gloves from his hands with a snap. "We are."

The air between them felt suddenly uncomfortable. Emma busied herself unfolding the top he'd brought her and carefully navigating it over her wounded left shoulder.

"Did you find me any shoes when you were gathering supplies?"

"Oh, yeah. I'm afraid these were the best I could do." He handed her a pair of white thick-soled shoes—the kind nurses wore on the wards. "I hope they fit."

She hopped up on the table to try them out over her filthy socks. Like the scrubs, they were a little too big, but that was better than too small. "They'll do," she said, lacing them tightly.

Her left arm felt strange. The burning pain was gone, but it was stiff, and she couldn't move it far in any direction. It wouldn't be much use in a fight.

Across the room, Michael was cleaning up the used medical supplies.

"I meant to ask you—how'd you get all this stuff?" she asked as he threw the used needles into a red bin. "Do they just leave it lying out?"

"Of course not," he said. "It's kept locked up. Only doctors can access it."

Emma went still, a cold realization settling on her.

"Michael, how did they know you're a doctor?"

For a moment, he didn't move. Then he pulled a card from the breast pocket of his scrubs with slow reluctance. She knew it was his medical ID before she even saw his face on it, looking back up at her.

"I showed them this."

Emma's heart stopped. He must have known what using it would mean, but there was no time for recriminations now. If the Russians had any sense at all, they would think to hack the computers at the hospital near where the boat had capsized. Michael's ID would set every alarm ringing. The hospital's CCTV cameras would give them a map to their door.

She stared at him, her mind retracing their path through the hospital corridor. All those cameras.

"They're coming. We have to go *now*."

28

Emma opened the door and checked the long, brightly lit corridor. Above the tense rasp of her own breathing she could hear the faint sounds of hospital life. Everything looked perfectly normal, but she thought she could sense trouble coming. Feel it the way a deer senses an oncoming storm.

"We can't go out the way we came in," she said. "Is there a staff entrance? An underground car park?"

She kept her voice urgent but calm: she didn't want to panic him. She hadn't explained anything—she didn't have to. He'd instantly understood how serious the situation was.

"There's an exit through basement level one. That's probably the best way out. Only doctors can use it. It's always quiet."

"Perfect," she said. "Show me the way."

They turned right in the hallway. Michael's movements were steady. All night long, he'd been getting better at bouncing back from the body blows, she thought. It was a valuable skill. Half the trick of survival is knowing how to let go of each failure and start over.

"We have to go through A & E to get there," he warned. "I don't know any other way, and we'd waste time looking."

She didn't argue. There wasn't time.

Within seconds, they were in the heart of the medical center. Even in the predawn hours, the place was a hub of activity. Nurses hustled in the corridors, machines buzzed and hummed. But their scrubs acted as a kind of anonymity filter, and, as Emma had hoped, nobody looked at them twice.

When they reached the Emergency wing, she searched the faces around her but saw no sign of the blond pair or the man with the broken nose or Chernov. Still, that no longer meant anything. There could be many Russian agents looking for them right now. There was no way to know who the enemy was by sight alone. No way to recognize them before they pulled a gun. Any crowd was dangerous.

Her sense of foreboding grew stronger. "We need to hurry," she said, angling her head so Michael could hear. "I've got a bad feeling about this."

They weaved their way quickly past stretchers. Several had people on them, frail and listless, their eyes closed against the bright fluorescent light.

"Are you a doctor?" one woman asked as Emma squeezed past, reaching out a thin hand to pluck at her sleeve.

She must have been in her late seventies, with huge blue eyes and a cloud of gray hair.

"No, I'm not," Emma said, keeping her voice soft. "But one will come by soon for you."

As she sped down the hall, she heard the woman's reedy voice say, "I do hope so."

Moments later, they hurried around the edge of the sprawling Emergency waiting area where a crowd of at least thirty people slouched on blue plastic chairs, staring into the distance, half-asleep as they waited their turn.

Emma's gaze settled on two men standing at the front counter, talking to the admission nurses. They were thickly built, both wearing dark jackets. Their backs were to her but, even without seeing their faces, she sensed they didn't belong here. There was something arrogant about the way they spoke to the women at the counter. The one on the right was leaning an elbow on the high front desk. The one next to him turned to stare at the other patients with his shoulders tense, hands shoved aggressively into his pockets.

As if he felt her eyes on him, he swung a look in her direction. Emma turned away, keeping her feet moving forward even as her stomach curdled.

"Hey, you! Hold up." The authoritative voice came from just to the right. A doctor, her stethoscope draped around her neck and a sheaf of papers in her hand, motioned them over.

Emma exchanged a brief, helpless glance with Michael.

"Are you free?" The doctor's gaze skated over their uniforms, pausing briefly when it reached the bruise on Emma's face, and the tangled hair she'd tried to smooth with her fingers. "I've got a patient here who's been admitted. I need to get him upstairs." Glancing around the crowded corridor, she shook her head. "They just keep coming. God, it's been a hell of a night."

"We're supposed to be picking someone up right now and taking him down to imaging." Michael put just the right note of apology in his voice. "But we don't want to leave you in the lurch . . ."

The doctor sighed and looked past them, as if help might magically appear. "No, I can't pull you off that. It's just that I called for someone an hour ago and the patient's still sitting here."

Emma grabbed on to Michael's story. "When we finish with this job, we'll come straight back and see if you still need someone. If you do, we'll take him up then."

The woman flashed a tired smile. "You're a star."

They walked away at a brisk pace. As soon as they were out of the woman's view, she turned to Michael, "How much farther is it?"

"Stairs on the right." He pointed to a door ahead.

Half running now, Emma raced to the door and yanked it open. Her shoulder twinged its objections.

In the utilitarian stairwell, their footsteps echoed off the worn lino-leum. One level down, they reached a dark landing. Motion-detector lights flickered on as they approached.

Sensing her urgency, Michael passed her and headed for the near-est door, running through it with Emma on his heels.

He pointed to the right. "Down there."

They raced in that direction, their borrowed shoes slapping against the polished floor. There were rows of doors on both sides, but he didn't slow until they reached a room marked "STAFF ONLY." Skid-ding to a stop, he reached for the handle, but it wouldn't open. He jiggled it again, but it stubbornly refused to turn.

"Locked." They both noticed the swipe pad next to the door at the same time, and the pale red light glowing beside it.

"Shit." Michael pressed his forehead against the thick wood, his eyes closing. "This wasn't locked when I was here before. It's new. We need a hospital pass."

"Is there another way into the parking garage?" Emma asked. "A back door? Anything?"

Without lifting his head, he shook it, rolling his forehead against the door. "This is the only way."

Emma examined the swipe pad, her frustration rising. They couldn't go back. Those two men she'd seen wouldn't be alone. They were undoubtedly searching the hospital floor by floor. They'd make it down here eventually.

"Let me try your card." She said it abruptly, holding out her hand.

"Try what?" Michael stared at her.

"Your medical ID."

He seemed to think this ridiculous. "I'm not on staff here."

She kept her hand out. "It's an NHS hospital. You're an NHS doc-tor. I'm willing to bet the system is inefficient enough that it's not about the hospital name. Besides, it can't hurt to try."

He handed her the card. She held it to the reader and, murmuring a prayer, swiped it.

The light blinked but stayed red.

"Try it again." Michael leaned forward. "You did it too fast."

Once more, she lifted the card to the top of the reader. This time she swiped it steadily. The red light flickered. And turned green.

When she grabbed the handle, the door swung open.

"Remember how bad you felt about using that card to get supplies?" She glanced over her shoulder at Michael. "Now you get to feel good again."

The doctors' lounge was small and crowded with cheap, worn furniture. A spotlessly clean kitchenette sat on one side of it. The room was deserted.

"This way." Michael walked away from the kitchen to a narrow hallway at the far end. "I think the door to the garage is down here."

Behind him, Emma paused as they passed a row of hooks where a dozen coats hung haphazardly. She grabbed two at random as she followed him. Ahead of her, Michael had already reached another door.

When he opened it, a wave of cold air poured in. Shooting her a triumphant look, he stepped out into a parking garage.

Emma ran to catch up to him, handing him a dark gray jacket as she passed. He gave it a puzzled glance.

"No time for questions," she said, striding past him toward the entrance ramp. "Let's get the hell out of here."

29

THE SKY WAS still dark when they emerged onto the street in front of the hospital, but Emma thought she detected the first gray hints of dawn above the tall, curved walls of the nearby Park Plaza Hotel. There were more cars around now, and she could hear the rattle and hum of trains clattering on the rails behind Waterloo Station, getting into position for the morning rush hour.

They were two miles from MI6. Just two miles. They could run it in twenty minutes if someone wasn't trying to kill them. But everything in her told her that the men she'd seen in the hospital would not be alone. They would have friends out here, hunting.

"We need a car," she said, thinking aloud.

Bewildered, Michael gestured back at the car park behind them. "There are cars in there."

"Doctors drive new cars. We need an old car." She turned right and strode down the road. "Old and cheap."

"Should I ask why?" Michael asked, keeping pace with her.

"It'll make sense in a minute. Just help me find a crap car."

Finding a cheap car in central London is not as easy as it used to be. It's the capital city of Audis and BMWs. But pockets of old London stubbornly persist, even in the most expensive areas. And, after five minutes, Emma spotted a narrow side street between two anonymous modern buildings. It was lined on both sides by parked cars; most were modern, but a council tower block loomed at the end of the cul-de-sac, and the cars back there were older.

Muttering under her breath, she ran from one car to the next, peering in the windows. When she reached a battered red Ford, she stopped.

"This one," she said, blocking the light reflecting off the window with her hands so she could see inside. "It should work." She glanced up at Michael. "Now find me a brick."

"Oh, come on . . ." He backed away, horrified.

"Michael, there's no *time*." Her voice rose. "You asked me to let you work in the hospital. Well, let me work out here." She began scouring the area for anything heavy and portable, but it was clean in the way of modern metropolises: everything useful or abandoned was hauled away as soon as it touched the ground.

"Where do they keep their rubbish?" she muttered as she searched the street, conscious of a trio of cameras mounted on a pole directly above her. If those cameras didn't bring the Russians, they would absolutely bring the cops and right now she wasn't sure which would be worse.

Rounding the corner, she spotted five industrial rubbish bins lined up behind the high-rise like a row of small tanks, surrounded by decorative masonry stones.

"Over here." Emma motioned for Michael, who was halfheartedly searching behind her. "Let's take one of these."

The crease in his forehead told her what he thought of all of this. "We're stealing a rock?"

"We're *borrowing* a rock to save two lives," she corrected him, crouching down to tug at a stone the size of a loaf of bread. The action sent a slice of pain through her shoulder, but she ignored it, pulling until it came loose from the sealant that held it in place.

Lifting it was another thing, though. She seemed to have left much of her strength in the hospital and her arm was starting to throb. "Jesus, rocks are heavy."

"You'll start bleeding again—let me have it." Clearly still not on board with this development, Michael nonetheless reached out to take the stone from her. "You're sure there's no better way?" he asked.

"This is the only plan I've got."

When they reached the car, she pointed at the driver's side window. "That one."

Michael hesitated.

"Do it," she ordered.

With open reluctance he raised the rock above his head and threw it. The glass shattered into a million crystalline pieces. The sound seemed deafening in the quiet little street.

Michael stood back from the damage, watching as she reached inside and unlocked the car door.

It might have surprised her that someone who'd survived being chased, shot at, attacked, and nearly drowned would be squeamish about breaking into a car, but she was getting to know Michael Primalov pretty well. And it didn't surprise her at all. In his entire life he'd probably never so much as dropped a piece of chewing gum on the pavement, much less committed an act of petty larceny.

With her good hand, she dragged the rock off the seat and threw it onto the pavement behind them. "There. They can have their rock back." Pulling her jacket down over her fingers, she swept the shards of broken glass off the seat.

Glancing over her shoulder to where Michael still stood, she snapped impatiently, "Get in." As he walked around the car she pushed the driver's seat all the way back and slid down into the wheel well. Using the knife from her sock, she began to prize open the plastic cover on the steering column. By then Michael was in the passenger seat.

"We needed an old car," she explained, "because they don't have ignition-override systems or high-tech modern security." The cover popped loose and she moved it to one side. Gingerly, she reached into the dark inner space behind the steering column and loosened the wires she found there, drawing them out with delicate tugs of her fingertips.

"Why am I not surprised that you know how to hotwire a car?" said Michael.

"Believe it or not," she said, "it's an incredibly handy skill."

She'd have killed to have her flashlight back for just five minutes. In the shadows of the footwell, it was too dark to easily make out the colors of the wires, and, if she chose wrong, not only would the car not start, it wouldn't start again until a mechanic fixed the damage she'd done.

She chose one wire, and then searched until she found the other she wanted. Using the knife, she stripped the colored coating down to the bare metal.

She shoved the knife back into her shoe and pushed herself up into the driver's seat.

"OK." She glanced at Michael, who was sitting uncomfortably next to her. "Here goes."

She touched the metal wires together. The car gave a brief growl and fell silent.

At least she knew she had the right wires.

Letting out a breath to steady herself, she tapped the wires together again, and pressed the clutch to the floor. She felt a sharp spark of electricity beneath her fingers, like an insect sting. The car roared to life.

"Yes!" Michael whispered, despite himself.

Dropping the wires, Emma shot him a wicked smile. "I'll make a burglar out of you yet."

Shifting into gear, she pulled out of the cramped parking space and switched on the headlights. In the quiet, she could hear the tires crunching over the broken window glass. "It's not far," she explained as she turned the car around. "So they'll be expecting us to walk. Hopefully, this will take them by . . ." Her voice trailed off and she finished the sentence softly, ". . . surprise."

Michael followed her gaze and made a low sound of shock.

A man stood in the middle of the narrow road ahead of them, legs spread, unmoving. He was holding a gun.

30

EMMA SLAMMED ON the brakes. The car screeched to a halt, throwing them both forward. Michael slapped his hand on the dash to steady himself.

The car's headlights gave the man an unhealthy pallor, but Emma recognized his muscular build and thick jaw. It was one of the two men she'd seen inside the hospital. His cold eyes narrowed as he squinted into the glare, pointing the gun straight at her head.

Silently, Emma raced through the options. There were precious few of them. The street behind them was a dead end. The only way out was past the gunman. She could try to run him over, but he would have plenty of time to fire, and Michael might be killed. She couldn't take that risk.

She wanted to kick something. They were *so close*. They had the car. Was this really how it was going to end? After everything they'd survived?

"What do we do?" There was panic in Michael's voice. His fingers gripped the door handle so tightly his knuckles paled.

He was relying on her. Ripley believed in her. She *had* to handle this.

Taking a breath, she spoke quickly. "I'm going out there. I need you to stay here and get ready. I might need you to drive."

His eyes widened. "Emma, *no*. He's got a gun. I'm no expert at what you do, but I know bad odds when I see them."

She could see fear like sparks in his dark eyes, and she reached for his hand, continuing calmly: "Listen closely. I'm going to leave the car running. If for some reason I don't come back, you need to get in the driver's seat and drive this thing." She pointed ahead, beyond the man with the gun. "Go to the end of this street and turn left: stay on that road until you see MI6. It couldn't be easier. I know you know the building—everybody does. When you're close, get out of the car and run like hell to the door. Leave the car in the road. Leave it running—it doesn't matter. Hold your hands up as you run. Tell the guards your name. Scream it at them. They will protect you."

"Emma, *no*." He gripped her hand. His skin felt so warm and alive against hers that it hurt. His dark eyes pleaded with her. "Please don't do this. There has to be another way. We can run. We can get away."

"We won't make it. There is no other way." Her words were blunt but her tone was gentle. "This is all we've got." She glanced back at the man, who squinted into the headlights, his gun steady. "Besides, I'll be fine. I can take this guy."

She could see in Michael's face that he knew this wasn't necessarily true. She was wounded. The man was half a foot taller and about twice her weight. And none of that really mattered because he had a gun.

"Just let me help," Michael begged. "I can distract him. Something. Anything."

The man advanced toward them.

Emma's voice sharpened. "Michael, *listen to me*. I need to know that you will do what I've said." Unexpectedly, tears burned the backs of her eyes and she blinked hard, horrified at this sign of weakness. "If you sacrifice yourself in a crazy attempt to save me, then everything we've done tonight was for nothing." She held his hand tighter. "It has to mean something—can't you see that? I saved you for a reason. I'm saving you now because you matter. You need to live and do good things with your life. If you die here . . . What was the point?"

She could see everything in his transparent face: all the things he wanted to tell her. Everything she wanted to hear. She'd been wrong, earlier—he would have made a terrible spy. And she liked him so much for that.

"I'll do it," he said, holding her hand tightly. "Just don't die on me."

"It's a deal." She leaned forward and brushed her lips against his, quick and hard, and let go of his hand.

"Be ready for anything that happens now." She threw the door open and jumped out in a smooth movement.

The man stopped in his tracks. Without hesitating, she strode toward him, positioning herself in front of the Ford, in the full glare of the lights, knowing he wouldn't be able to see her well.

"What the hell do you want?" she demanded.

"You know the answer to that." He tilted his head in the direction of the car, squinting into the glare of the lights. "Give him to me and you can walk away. We don't want anything to do with you. He is all I'm here for."

His English was very good. He might have lived in the country for years: long enough to soften the guttural Russian edges.

Behind her, she heard Michael's door open, and her heart sank.

"Sure," she said quickly, raising her voice and shifting her position, hoping the man hadn't heard the metallic click. "That's fine. Obviously, I trust you completely. After all, your people have tried to kill me repeatedly over the last twelve hours. But it's nice to know we can be friends now."

In the cold white glow of the headlights, he raised the gun.

"It is an offer." His voice was flat. "You can take it or leave it."

"I'll leave it." She stepped closer, moving boldly, letting him know he didn't scare her. "Tell me something—why do you want him so badly? You've risked so much tonight, and for what? Whatever it is you're after, his mother will never give it to you."

"So you say." He shrugged, the gun swinging vaguely. "We don't agree. Let's find out who is right."

"Actually, I've got a better offer," she said. "Let's trade. Five minutes ago I called my people and asked them to send help. It'll be here any second. If they find you here, threatening me, do you have any idea what they'll do to you?"

He tilted his head, squinting into the lights as if trying to make out her features. "I think they'll put me on a plane home and never tell anybody this happened."

"I wouldn't count on that. Not after tonight. But you can walk away. Just turn around and go. Disappear into the city. This is your chance."

Cocking his head, he stared hard at her. Then he gave a cold smile. "I could do that. Or I could shoot you and take him." He'd been holding the gun loosely, but now he raised it in a swift, practiced movement, holding it absolutely steady and pointing it directly at her face.

"How about you catch me first?" Emma dropped down to the pavement and rolled to the right, coming up just outside of the headlights, and began to run, leading him away from Michael, and gambling that he wouldn't fire at someone he couldn't see.

Behind her, she heard the thud of his feet as he ran after her. He was fast for a big man, crossing the space much more quickly than she'd hoped. He caught her near the back of the car, grabbing the edge of her jacket, and yanking her toward him with enough force to send pain shooting down her arm from her wounded shoulder.

Twisting her body, she shrugged out of the too-big jacket. She had just enough time to drop down and pull the knife from her shoe with her good hand before he grabbed her, lifting her bodily and throwing her hard against the car. There, he leaned his weight against her, pushing her back, holding the gun up to her face.

"Why do you have to make this so hard?" he demanded, his face close enough to hers that she could smell the cigarette smoke on his skin. "Now I'll get your blood on my new jacket."

His weight compressed her lungs and sent pain shooting through her injured shoulder.

"Not if you don't shoot me," she said, her words coming out in short gasps.

He pushed the cold barrel so it dug into her cheek. His pale blue eyes slowly took in the outlines of her face as a thin smile curved his mouth.

He spoke in Russian. "You're so stupid, you know." He moved the gun barrel against her lips. "You think you can fight the whole Russian government?"

Emma's right arm swung up, thrusting the knife into his ear in one smooth move. The finely honed German blade slid in to the hilt.

The man stared past her. His gaze went horribly blank, as if she'd switched him off.

She answered him in his own language. "Just watch me."

The gun slipped from his fingers, clattering against the trunk of the car before falling to the ground. Blood, black in the dark, ran down the side of his thick face. He began to fall onto her, and she grabbed his shoulders, pushing him away. His body crumpled at her feet.

She stood over him, her fists clenched as if he might get up and go for her again. But that was never going to happen. A puddle of blood had already formed under his head.

He'd got blood on his jacket after all.

Although she'd been trained to do it by two government agencies, she'd never killed anyone until now. She'd always thought it would feel like the end of the world—a violation of everything in her soul. But it felt like nothing. Nothing at all.

31

EMMA LOOKED UP to find Michael standing beside her. He looked down at the body on the pavement.

"What do we do with him?" he asked.

She had to clear her throat before she could speak. "We leave him." She straightened, the fog of shock clearing from her mind. Behind them, the Ford's engine still rumbled. The headlights glowed in the empty street.

"Get in," she told him. She didn't have to say more—the urgency in her voice was enough. She bent down long enough to snatch the man's gun from the ground and ran to the driver's side of the car.

"Hold this." As she jumped into the car, she threw the gun to Michael. He caught it instinctively and held it at arm's length as she slammed the Ford into gear and floored it, only remembering to close her door when the car was already in motion.

Michael stared at the gun with blank distaste before setting it down between his feet.

Emma would rather have held on to it herself, but she needed both hands on the wheel as they careered around the corner without slowing, tires squealing.

Michael clung to the handle above his window, watching her. "Are you OK?" he asked, shouting to be heard above the engine and the cold wind whipping through the broken window.

"Yes." She didn't look at him. *Couldn't* look at him. What if she saw condemnation in his face? This man who wouldn't so much as park illegally. He'd admired her earlier. What must he think of her now? A murderer. A cold-blooded psychopath.

She kept her eyes fixed on the road. To her right, the Houses of Parliament floated at the periphery of her vision, golden and glowing, surreal in the dark. The city was still the same as it had always been. But *she* was different.

Suddenly she saw the man in front of her again. His eyes emptying. The way his body had teetered awkwardly. Only seconds earlier he'd moved with the speed and grace of a great cat. Bile rose in her throat and she forced it back, tightening her grip on the wheel. The car swerved.

"Don't think about it."

Michael's words startled her, and she shot him a surprised glance. His face held no judgment.

"You did what you had to do. He would have killed you. I saw it. You saved our lives." He put a hand on her shoulder. "Take a deep breath."

Obediently, she drew in air, forcing the image from her mind. Her heart rate began to steady. Her vision of the road cleared.

"That's better." Michael looked ahead, one hand still on her arm, a steady presence warm enough to take the chill from her blood.

Emma swerved around a rubbish truck; then slammed on her brakes behind cars stopped at a red light. There were far more people and too much traffic around now. It wasn't rush hour, but that was coming.

The black sky was gilded with the first rays of pale orange and gold as the light ahead turned green. It seemed to take forever for the cars in front of her to go.

"Move," she growled. "Just *move*."

Finally, they were in motion again. Emma changed lanes, pushing the accelerator pedal to the floor. The old engine rattled unhappily, but their speed rose and they flew past the other early-morning cars.

As soon as they were clear, she fixed her eyes on the rearview mirror. At first glance, it all looked normal. Then, in the faint dawn light, she saw three black SUVs in the distance, swooping in like hawks looking for prey.

Her throat tightened. "They've found us," she said.

Michael twisted around to see.

At that precise moment, with exquisite bad timing, the light at the next intersection turned red.

Emma swore under her breath.

"Hold on," she warned. "This is about to get bumpy."

She pushed the pedal to the floor and swerved hard to the right, steering the old Ford over the low concrete curb that divided the lanes, and pulled into oncoming traffic.

A taxi veered around them, blaring its horn as they sped past the cars waiting at the light and careered onto the roundabout. A gleaming silver Mercedes swerved hard to avoid them and lost control, skidding into a concrete barrier with a crunch of metal. Emma kept her eyes fixed on the road ahead. They were flying down the wrong lane, cars pulling over to avoid them. Tall office buildings blurred on their left; the Thames flowed cold and impassive on the right.

Spotting a clear stretch of road ahead, she swung back into her own lane. The Ford's engine emitted an unmistakable scent of hot metal and oil.

"They're getting closer." Michael was twisted in his seat watching the Russian vehicles behind them. Another red light loomed ahead, but there were no cars between them and the intersection.

Emma sped toward it, leaning on the horn and shouting through the broken window, "Coming through! Get out of the way!" As they flew across the junction, she heard the screeching of brakes and the sickening crunch of metal against metal behind them. When she looked back, though, she saw the black trio of SUVs, weaving through the chaos of smashed cars.

She gripped the wheel tight, trying to control the old car as they took a sharp bend. The Ford felt out of control beneath them, as if the steering was about to go. As soon as the road straightened, one of the black vehicles swung into the oncoming lane, trying to pull up alongside them.

"Go faster," Michael urged, clinging to the handle above the door as they swung wildly around a slow-moving van. But the engine was already rattling its protest. Faster wasn't an option.

Ahead, a bus lumbered to a stop. Swearing, Emma swerved hard. Two of the chasing vehicles dropped back, but the closest one kept pace, pulling up alongside them.

Suddenly, it lurched toward them.

"Look out!" Michael shouted.

Emma veered hard left, only narrowly avoiding slamming into a small car beside her. For a split second she had a clear view of the driver—he wore a suit with a crisp white shirt. His eyes were wide, his mouth a perfect "O" of shock, and then he was out of sight and they were shooting toward the next red light.

Emma kept her foot down, ready to run it, until she noticed a woman making her way slowly across the intersection. She wore sandals, even though it was cold, and a baggy dress. Her ankles were thick and every step seemed painful.

"Oh my God," Emma whispered, gripping the wheel as she slammed on the brakes. The worn tires shrieked in protest. The acrid smell of rubber filled the car as the Ford skidded toward the crossing. The woman looked up at them, her face blank. She should have run, anyone would have run in those circumstances, but she stopped and stared, as if she couldn't believe what she was seeing.

They were going to hit her.

"*Nonono* . . ." Emma whispered. "Why doesn't she move?"

Michael threw up his hands to cover his face.

Emma jerked the wheel hard to the right, avoiding the woman and driving directly at the Range Rover next to them. Caught off guard, the driver swerved away with too much force and the big vehicle spun out of control as they raced by. In the mirror, Emma saw it whirling drunkenly across the road before slamming into a concrete barrier, and then reeling over the top of it and sliding with slow dignity into the Thames.

"Did you see that?" Michael asked, turning to watch it hit the water.

"One down." Emma spoke through gritted teeth as she tried to keep the Ford on the road.

Now only two SUVs were behind them, engines roaring furiously, as if the loss of the third had made them angrier. Emma pressed the accelerator to the floor. For a fleeting instant, she caught a glimpse of the opaque green-glass walls of the MI6 building in the distance, its roof bristling with antennae. They were still a good half-mile from it.

"There." She pointed, raising her voice to be heard above the scream of the engines and the rush of wind pouring through the broken window next to her. "Not far now."

Michael never got the chance to reply. A deafening bang split the air. The Ford's rear window shattered. Silvery shards of broken glass showered over them.

"Get down!" Emma shouted, too late. In the mirror, she could see a passenger hanging out of one of the SUVs, a pistol in his hand.

Michael was doubled over in his seat.

"Are you OK?" she demanded. The roar of wind through the broken window and the screaming of the engine made it hard to hear anything as she steered the car in a zigzag pattern back and forth across two lanes, holding the wheel in an iron grip that sent stabbing pain through her shoulder. "Michael, *are you hit?*"

"I'm OK, I think." His voice was thin but he straightened slowly, brushing glass from his hair. "Are you hurt?"

"I'm good. Stay down," she ordered, steering right, then left, then right again, gripping the wheel with all her strength, barely in control while the tires spun as if the tarmac had turned to ice.

The wound in her shoulder burned, and, when she glanced down, she saw a growing bloodstain on the blue of the scrubs. She'd torn her stitches, but that was the least of their problems.

The car carrying the gunman was trying to pull up alongside, where they'd have a perfect shot. Emma tried to push the accelerator farther, but her foot punched futilely on the floor: the car had no extra power to offer.

Her heart hammered against her ribs as she slalomed across the lanes, trying to keep in front. Trying to make them harder to hit.

Ahead, the road curved around a new office building on the left, and abruptly the view opened up. She could see the whole of the MI6 building, the sturdy glass and concrete tower seemed to glow in the dawn light. They were nearly there.

Despite what she'd told Michael earlier, now that they were here, she could see there was no way to stop the car and run to safety. The men behind them would shoot them in the back. The only option was to drive directly into the underground parking garage, protected by multiple layers of blast-proof concrete and razor wire. But the heavy steel garage door was shut.

Michael had risen up into his seat to see what was happening. He scanned the building ahead eagerly. "Where do we go?" he asked.

"We need to go in there." She pointed.

His brow creased. "It's closed."

"It'll open." Her voice sounded more confident than she felt.

They were a hundred yards away now and closing fast. She didn't dare slow down.

The door didn't budge.

A sick emptiness began to churn in the pit of Emma's stomach. Her worst fear through all of this was that Six wouldn't be ready for them. That the right people didn't know they were coming. If that was the case, she and Michael would be seen as a threat as dangerous as the people behind them. They could face fire from both sides. That couldn't happen. She had to believe someone was there, waiting for them. The alternative was certain death.

Locking her jaw resolutely, she kept the accelerator pedal on the floor. The building was so close she could see the reflection of the Ford in the glass.

"It's not opening . . ." There was fear in Michael's voice.

The SUV on her right swerved toward them, but she cut past it. The Russians hadn't fired again. They must know armed police units were based nearby. But if Six didn't know who the good guys were, the officers inside would take them all out.

Fifty yards. The door had to open. It had to.

"Let me in, you bastards," she whispered to the huge, sprawling building. "Let me *in*."

"Why aren't they opening it?" Michael was sweating, his hands gripping the dashboard.

"They will," she insisted, staring at the unyielding door. "They have to."

Twenty-five yards.

The door remained sealed.

Emma peered into the rearview mirror, trying to see the faces in the black vehicles behind her, but the sun was rising behind them, blinding her.

It didn't matter what she saw. She was trapped between them and the cold steel door ahead, which would not budge.

After all they'd been through, was this night going to end in complete defeat? Wasn't there one person in there she could trust? One human heart in all that glass and steel?

"Look!" Michael leaned forward, pointing.

In the glare of the early-morning sun, the heavy door began to move.

It was lifting faster than she'd thought possible, as if this moment had always been planned. As if there'd never been any doubt.

The knot that had twisted itself tight inside Emma's chest released. She felt as though she could breathe again for the first time in hours.

When she glanced in the mirror, she saw the Russian vehicles had begun to drop back.

"They're giving up," Michael said, staring through the broken back window. "They're turning around."

Emma gave a laugh that was almost a sob.

As the wind blew her hair into her eyes, she stuck her hand out of the broken window and shot her middle finger at the cars behind her.

"I told you I'd win!" she shouted into the breeze.

Then she turned the steering wheel to the right and, without touching the brakes, shot through the open door into the heavily guarded, underground sanctuary.

They were safe.

32

SMOKE POURED FROM beneath the hood of the Ford as it sput-
tered down the concrete ramp into the dimly lit underground
parking garage. Still clinging to the wheel, Emma felt breathless with
exhilaration. Stunned by their own survival, neither she nor Michael
spoke as she navigated through silent rows of parked cars toward a set
of glass double doors. The moment had a dream-like sense to it. But
that feeling didn't last long.

As if from nowhere, black-clad security officers melted out of the
shadows, their faces hidden behind dark masks that left only cold eyes
and machine guns exposed.

Emma slammed on the brakes. The old Ford stopped with a shudder and died.

"What's happening?" Michael sank back in his seat. "Who are
they?"

"I don't bloody know." Emma's voice was tense. This wasn't the
welcome she'd expected.

"Get out of the car." Five male voices began shouting the command,

almost in unison. A barrage of noise. *"Get out of the car now. Show us your hands."*

Emma, who'd had just about enough of being threatened, leaned over and snatched the Russian gun from the footwell.

Michael stared at her. "What are you doing? Aren't they on our side?"

"That's what I'm going to find out."

There wasn't time to explain her thinking. Maybe this display of weaponry was just an abundance of caution. Perhaps they wanted to make sure nobody aside from Emma and Michael was in the car. But there were other possibilities, with Masterson still a question mark in her mind and Ripley nowhere to be found. She had no idea what had been happening behind the scenes while she'd been dodging Russians for hours. And she wasn't taking any chances.

Her eyes on the armed men, she said, "I'm about to get out of the car. I want you to slide over to my seat and get out behind me. Stay *right* behind me at all times."

Blessedly, he trusted her enough not to ask questions. He gave a tense nod, and braced himself.

Emma unlatched the door and kicked it open with all her strength, vaulting out of the Ford in the same instant and landing on her feet with the gun raised.

She could hear Michael climbing out behind her.

Pressing him back so that he was shielded by the car on one side and her gun on the other, she spoke clearly, "My name is Emma Makepeace. This is Michael Primalov. I work for Charles Ripley. You should be expecting us."

"I don't care who you are. Drop your fucking weapon!" The command came from the officer at the front. His rough voice had a northern accent. He was six feet tall and his gun was aimed directly at Emma's forehead.

"I will not drop this gun until I know who I'm dealing with." Emma's gun didn't waver, her finger was steady on the trigger. "What the hell is going on here? You're supposed to be expecting us."

From somewhere she heard a new voice. "We are indeed expecting you."

A portly man in a charcoal-gray suit stepped between two of the security officers. His round face was smooth and pleasant. His hands were empty.

"I would very much like you to put down that gun," he told her. "So that we can talk."

"Who the hell are you?" Emma demanded.

Her tone didn't seem to bother him. "My name is Andrew Field. I'm here to take Michael Primalov to safety." He looked over her shoulder to where Michael stood pressed between her and the car. "Dr. Primalov, are you injured?"

"Don't talk to him." Emma shifted her position to block Michael from view. "Talk to the person holding the gun."

Field met her gaze with small, observant eyes. "Miss Makepeace, please believe me: we're on your side. I really need you to put down that weapon. These gentlemen will not put down theirs until you do."

"Then we have a problem." Emma's voice was tense but steady. Through the haze of exhaustion and stress, she wondered fleetingly if she was being unreasonable. They *should* be safe here. But after everything that had happened, she needed to be convinced. "Where's Charles Ripley? I want to see him."

"Ripley is looking for the man who tried to kill you tonight." Field's tone was measured, and he looked from her face to the gun with more disapproval than fear.

"Well, tell him to get over here," she snapped. "He's the only one who can take Michael. This was his operation."

"Come now, let's be reasonable. You don't get to choose these things," Field said. "He's asked me to step in—"

"I don't know you." Emma cut him off. "I will only hand Michael over to someone I know."

For the first time she detected a hint of frustration in Field's expression. "That isn't your decision to make."

Emma raised the barrel until it pointed at his chin. "Oh, I think it *is*."

The two stared at each other across the cold concrete, taking the measure of each other.

But then Field's expression changed. His voice grew low and urgent. "I know about Grigory Chernov, Emma. Ripley is trying to find him now. That's why he's not here. He sent you to me because he trusts me. I need you to do the same."

At the mention of the Russian's name, Emma's breath caught. All this time she'd thought she was alone with the knowledge of who was behind the attack. But they knew. And she wasn't alone at all.

Field stepped closer, holding out his hand. "I swear we'll take care of Michael. We'll keep him safe. Please. Put down that gun and let us do our jobs."

His hand remained raised between them, palm up, fingers open.

Exhaling slowly, Emma flipped the gun over until the barrel pointed at the floor, and held it out. Betraying no relief, as if he'd always known the moment would end like this, Field took the pistol from her, examining it swiftly before sliding it into his pocket and turning to the armed guards.

"You can stand down. Thank you very much for your assistance."

A clatter of metal echoed off the cement walls as machine guns lowered around them.

As swiftly as they'd arrived, the armed officers turned and disappeared into the depths of the building.

"Thank Christ for that," Michael said, sagging back against the car.

Field's attention switched to him. "Dr. Primalov, I'm very glad to meet you. Are you hurt?"

Michael shook his head stiffly, the motion sending tiny fragments of glass showering from his clothes and hair. There was no warmth in his expression, and he spoke curtly.

"I'm fine. Emma's the one who's hurt."

"It's nothing," Emma said, although blood was trickling down her arm and dripping onto the rough cement floor.

"She was shot." Michael raised his voice very slightly. "She's had basic treatment, but she needs a surgeon."

His fierce loyalty hurt Emma's heart.

Field pulled his phone from his pocket, pressed a button and spoke without waiting. "I need medical in Location D. Right away, please." Still holding the phone, he turned to Michael. "Are you certain you're uninjured?"

"Just a cut." He held out his arm revealing the bloodstained bandage covering the cut he'd received climbing the ladder.

Field spoke into the phone: "Two injured."

When he'd finished the call, he turned back to Emma. "Where did you get the gun?"

"It's Russian," she said.

His expression didn't change. "I see."

"Oh, and there's a body. On Blair Lane, across from St. Thomas's Hospital," Emma told him. "Also Russian."

Field dialed again, watching her from beneath thick brows as he spoke. "Black Unit to Blair Lane, across from St. Thomas's. There's a job for them there."

Black Unit was a top secret, almost mythical group whose job was said to be clearing up evidence of Secret Service activity when operations went wrong. Until that moment, Emma hadn't been entirely convinced they existed.

When Field put the phone down again, Michael stepped forward. "You need to know we stole this car. We don't know whose it is."

Field's small blue eyes alighted on him with interest. Emma found that she wanted to throw herself in between them. To somehow protect Michael from Field's cool, emotionless appraisal. "Please don't worry about that, Dr. Primalov," he said. "We'll ensure the owner is appropriately compensated. We're just glad you both made it safely. It sounds like it was quite a night."

Michael looked at Emma, his jaw tight. "I would say that doesn't even begin to cover it."

"We're very glad you're safe. You've had a lot of people very worried," Field said, his tone as mild as if Michael and Emma had shown up late for a dinner party. He reminded Emma of Ripley, who had the same ability to make an international crisis appear as mundane as burned toast.

At that moment, the double doors swung open and a team carrying black medical bags strode toward them. Field motioned them over. "Check these two. She has a gunshot wound in her left shoulder. He has a deep cut to the right arm."

The paramedics moved toward Emma, but she waved them to where Michael stood near the battered Ford. "Treat him first."

Michael protested but Field gave the medics a nod and they quickly surrounded him, asking questions, opening bags.

Taking advantage of the distraction, Emma pulled Field to one side. "How do you know about Chernov?"

"Ripley figured it out last night," he said. "But by then it was too late to stop everything unraveling."

He betrayed no apparent resentment for having been held at gunpoint only minutes earlier, and Emma admired his sangfroid. She had the distinct impression she wasn't the first to point a gun at Andrew Field.

"Do the Russians still have the cameras?" she asked.

"We got eyes back twenty minutes ago," he told her. "We still don't know how they did it. We were all expecting something to happen, but nothing on this scale." He glanced back to where the medics were examining Michael's arm. "They really wanted him."

"Do you know what's happening at the Agency?" She lowered her voice. "Why did Ripley send me here instead of a safe house?"

Field's expression hardened. "The situation is a bit unstable, as the minister would say. Or, as I would put it, it's all completely fucked. A number of people in charge are pointing fingers to protect themselves. Someone must be responsible for losing the cameras. Someone else has to explain how our good friends in Moscow could blow up a T-shirt shop in Camden and walk away without being caught. That's why Ripley sent you to me. He knows he can trust me." He fixed her with a steady look. "Frankly, if you walked straight into Ed Masterson's greedy hands right now, you might well end up blamed for this entire mess."

His tone when he mentioned Ripley's deputy was ice cold. All of Emma's suspicions about Ed Masterson came flooding back to her.

She searched Field's face. "Is Ripley in trouble?"

"Yes, he is," Field said without hesitation. "His security clearance has been revoked and he's been placed on immediate leave. Masterson is now acting leader of the Agency."

"They've *fired* Ripley? They can't do that."

"They can," he said. "And they did."

Emma was horrified. As far as she was concerned, there was no Agency without Ripley. He handled every operation. Oversaw every detail.

This all had to be Masterson's doing. Masterson was the one who'd left her out there alone. Masterson had been in charge when things went very badly wrong. And now Masterson had Ripley's job.

"Where is Ripley now?" she said quickly. "I have to talk to him."

"Now isn't a good time." Field glanced around to make sure no one could overhear and spoke quickly. "There may be something you can do to help him but not right away. Wait for him to get in touch with you. In the meantime, you'll need to play your cards right with the debrief. Tell them the truth—you just did your job out there. Stick to the facts and you'll be fine. They've got nothing to hang on you."

The medics had finished with Michael and were now heading purposefully toward Emma. Field's last words were spoken so quietly she could barely hear them. "And be careful—everyone has knives out right now."

After that, the medics surrounded her, asking questions, checking the bullet wound. By the time they were done, an ambulance had been called. It seemed Michael was right after all, and she did need to go to a hospital.

He was still talking with Field near the remains of the battered old car. As the paramedics re-bandaged her shoulder, Emma watched their body language, wondering what they were saying. Whatever it was, it couldn't have been welcome news. When Field stepped away to take a call, Michael slumped back against the old car, his head down.

The two of them had been anchored to each other ever since that run in the park twenty-four hours ago. Already, she could sense her connection to him slipping. She didn't like how much that bothered her.

Shaking the paramedics off, she stood up. "I need five minutes."

She walked over to where Michael stood and leaned against the car next to him.

"How are you holding up?" she asked, searching his face.

"Well, I finally got that tetanus jab." He'd forced a light note into his voice, but Emma wasn't fooled.

"No lockjaw for you, then." She waited for him to say more, but he was still staring into the distance. "So . . . what did Andrew Field tell you?"

Michael exhaled slowly, his hands clenching. "He said I'll go to meet my parents first. In a week or two, they'll send us someplace more permanent. They don't know where yet." His voice was flat and empty. He sounded utterly defeated. "They'll find something for me to do. They don't want me to worry about that."

Emma leaned against him, close enough that she could feel the warmth of his arm against hers.

"You're alive. That's a victory," she told him quietly. "You'll make something happen wherever they take you. You'll always make good things happen."

He rubbed his eyes and nodded, his jaw tight.

"Your life isn't over," she continued. "It's just taken an unexpected turn. And really, after last night, you should be used to that. Unexpected turns can bring good surprises."

He turned to look at her, his gaze sweeping across her face, as if committing her to memory. "You've been a good surprise, Emma Makepeace. I owe you my life."

"And I owe you mine," she said simply. "You know, I think you're an extraordinary man, Michael Primalov."

"Coming from you, that means something." He smiled at her.

Against the warm metal of the car, she found his hand and laced her fingers through his.

"Look," he said, with a sheepish smile, "I know all about transference and trauma, and all of that. But—will I ever see you again?"

She thought for a moment before replying. "My bosses would say no. It wouldn't be safe for you. The rules strictly forbid it."

He held her gaze steadily. "What would *you* say?"

"I'd say . . . Nothing is impossible."

"I like your answer better."

She studied his face. The sharp jaw, the long, fine line of his nose, and those extraordinary eyes.

If things were different . . . she thought regretfully.

"You'll be OK, won't you?" she asked. "It will make me feel better if I know you'll be fine."

A melancholy smile lifted the corners of his lips. "I'll be fine, if you swear to me you'll take fewer risks on the next rescue. No rusty ladders."

"No ladders," she said, lifting her hand to her heart. "That's a promise."

"Emma . . ." he began, but before he could finish the thought the door to the garage began to lift with a metallic clank. Daylight flooded in, and the flashing blue lights of an ambulance filled the shadows.

Her heart kicked. This was the end. Whatever she'd told him, the truth was, as soon as she got in that ambulance, she'd never see him again.

Spontaneously, she turned and, ignoring the pain in her shoulder, wrapped her arms around him. She felt his surprised intake of breath, and then his arms tightened around her waist, pulling her close.

"Thank you," he whispered.

She knew they were being watched. That everything that happened would be analyzed and considered during the investigation to come. But right now, she didn't care.

"Wherever they take you, please be happy," she said.

"I'll try."

He pressed his lips to her hair and whispered something else. Emma nodded against his shoulder and then, with reluctance, let him go and walked toward the ambulance, where the crew stood waiting for her.

The last she saw of Michael, he was leaning against the car. Andrew Field was walking out of the double doors followed by a phalanx of undercover agents, ready to take him to his new life.

And as the ambulance pulled out of the darkness into the morning light, Emma kept hearing his voice, whispering, "You are remarkable."

33

THE SUN WAS high as Emma closed the door of her flat and headed out. It was a perfect October day—crisp and clear, the sky an almost painfully intense shade of blue. She wasn't due at rehab for an hour yet, but she wanted to be outside. Her shoulder had improved steadily over the last few weeks, so it was less of a chore now to exercise it. The surgeon who'd operated on it had told her recovery would be unpredictable—there was a chance she might never get all the movement back. But it was already returning to normal, a little at a time. Even the scar had begun to fade.

She'd been on medical leave for three weeks, but had the feeling that was less about her health and more about the internal investigation into the Primalov rescue. She'd been interviewed by investigators three times now. Each time they'd asked the same questions in different ways.

That was probably why she'd seen almost nobody from the Agency. The only two she'd heard from had been Martha and then, weeks later, Ed Masterson.

Martha had showed up at the hospital while Emma was recovering. She'd appeared wearing a 1940s dress and deep red lipstick, and bearing an array of pastel macarons in a box tied with a vivid pink ribbon.

"R sends his love," she'd said quietly as she set the box down on the table next to the bed.

Emma had sat up eagerly. "Is he OK? Where is he?"

"I don't know. It's best that way." Martha slid a plastic chair closer and sat down. "That toad Ed Masterson is drooling all over Ripley's office and everyone is furious. Ed's been angling for that job since he walked in the door. This"—she gestured at the bandages wrapping around Emma's arm—"is just the ammunition he's been waiting for."

Emma was horrified. "How could they promote him? The whole mission fell apart under Masterson's watch. He refused to help me. He left me out there to die."

"You know that and I know that. But Ed's making bloody certain the investigators believe Ripley's responsible for all of it. Ripley was out in the field looking for you all night. But Ed's trying to convince them he abandoned his post." She paused. "He's also telling them you weren't ready. That Ripley sent you out too soon."

"That bastard. Half the GRU was out there running roughshod across sodding *Knightsbridge* and I brought him in safely." Emma was furious. "Masterson can't do this."

The heart monitor next to her bed beeped a warning.

Emma took a breath, forcing herself to calm down before she voiced the suspicions that had plagued her since the ambulance deposited her at the hospital. "I don't trust Masterson. Not just because he's a liar and he's trying to get rid of Ripley. There's something wrong with him. The way he acted that night. It was like he didn't want Michael to survive."

She'd expected Martha to tell her she was crazy. That it had just been a bad night. Instead, the other woman cast a glance at the closed door, before saying, "I have doubts of my own. Adam told me he wanted to go out to help you but Ed flatly refused." Her wide-set eyes darkened. "He said everyone was needed in the office but there was nothing for us to do—the tech team was handling the hack."

Emma's jaw dropped. "He told me no one was free to help."

"It's a lie," Martha said flatly. "He *chose* not to send anyone."

There was a noise in the hallway and the two women fell silent until a team of nurses passed outside the door.

"Have you told Ripley this?" Emma lowered her voice. "What does he think?"

Martha said, "I think he's blind when it comes to people on his own team. Ripley personally chose Ed to be his deputy. He thinks he's ambitious, but he doesn't think he's corrupt." She paused. "I just think, when ambition goes too far, it becomes something else. Something dangerous."

Emma wondered if it was just corruption, or if Ed's greed had taken him to even darker places.

"I need to talk to Ripley," she said. "Can you find him?"

Martha shook her head. "No one knows where he is. He called a few days ago and asked me for some supplies. It looked to me like he was planning to conduct surveillance on someone. I left them for him in a dead drop. He told me he'd get in touch when it was safe, but none of us should try to find him." She drew in a breath. "It looks bad for him."

That conversation had been three weeks ago. Emma and Martha had spoken several times since, but the disguise specialist had had no news for her. Ripley was staying out of sight.

Then, two days ago, Ed Masterson had rung and asked Emma to come into the Institute for a meeting "about your return to work."

When she'd walked into the building—pleasantly surprised to find the security door still recognized her biometrics—he'd greeted her like an old friend.

"Makepeace," he said jovially. "Good to see you. How's the shoulder?"

"Getting better." She grinned back, because two could play that game.

She hid her outrage when he ushered her into Ripley's office as if it were his own. The oak-paneled room remained determinedly empty, but she could sense Ripley's absence in the very air of it. The faint, sweet smell of Dunhill cigarettes was gone, but his personality had somehow filled that room so thoroughly no belongings were necessary. Ripley owned this room; Masterson was squatting in it. And she got the sense that Masterson knew that and resented it.

"Come in. Have a seat." He took the chair behind Ripley's desk and rocked back comfortably. "Glad to hear you're feeling better. I wanted us to have a little chat about next steps."

"Yes." Emma moved her left arm. "As you can see, it's in pretty good shape. The doctors put it all back together."

"Well, that's what I wanted to go over with you. HR have sent down some paperwork for you to fill out." He opened the black folder that lay on the desk. "There will need to be a full physical assessment before we can let you back to work." He slid a stack of pages across to her.

"Sure." She kept her voice light. "There's always bureaucracy, right? How long do you think it will be before I can come back?"

"I don't know the answer to that." His expression filled with sympathy. "It depends on you. They'll want you to take a psych exam as well, of course. After all, you've been through a great deal. We don't want you coming back before you're ready. Take your time. Let yourself heal."

His false concern set her teeth on edge. She didn't want to play games. And she didn't want to come back to the Institute and work for Ed Masterson. But she said nothing. She knew Ripley would have told her to stay quiet and observe.

"Still, we're really looking forward to getting things back to normal." Masterson paused, and then asked casually, "Oh, by the way, have you heard from Ripley?"

A subtle but unmistakable new tension rose between them.

"I haven't heard from him at all." Emma blinked. "Isn't he here?"

"He's on leave. I'm surprised Martha didn't tell you."

So he knew about that hospital visit.

A chill ran down Emma's spine. Ripley had been right to stay away. They were watching her.

She remembered Andrew Field's warning: "Knives are out."

"Bit of kerfuffle here, as you can imagine," Masterson continued when she didn't say anything. "The ministers want to make an example of someone, and it seems they've chosen Rip. Obviously, we're fighting his corner."

"Obviously." Emma's tone was dry. "Have you spoken with him?"

"No, no. Of course not." He frowned. "That would be inappropriate. Nobody's allowed to talk to him. I just thought you might have. I know you two are close."

There was something unpleasant in the way he said it.

Emma forced her expression to stay neutral. "Well, I haven't heard a thing from him," she said.

There was a long. tense pause. "If you do hear from him," Masterson said finally, "it's your duty to inform us. The allegations against him are quite serious."

The meeting had left her fuming, and increasingly worried for Ripley. She knew better than to try to find him, but with every passing day she was more tempted to at least try.

She went over all of this in her mind as her feet carried her down Gipsy Hill. The south London neighborhood was so familiar she didn't really notice the noise of the traffic or the buses lumbering by. In the distance, the London skyline was beautiful enough to catch her attention, the towering skyscrapers dwarfing Parliament into insignificance. This was a path she walked every day, down to her favorite coffee shop, just outside the Gipsy Hill train station. During the weeks when she hadn't been able to work, this and her physio's office had become her regular haunts.

When she walked in, the woman at the till lifted a hand. "Hey, Anna," she said in a light Irish lilt. "How's it going?"

"All good, Maria, thanks. Enjoying the sunshine."

Emma hadn't intentionally lied to Maria about her name. The coffee shop owner had misheard her at the beginning and Emma never corrected her. It was useful for people not to know things. Emma, on the other hand, knew her full name was Maria O'Donnell. That she was from County Cork. Divorced, with one grown child. That she'd poured her life savings into this business ten years ago and was just getting by. She had no criminal record. No dodgy contacts.

Emma leaned against the counter, watching her froth the milk. "Any gossip? And can I have one of those blueberry muffins?"

"Those came in from the baker this morning. They are *deadly*. I've had two already." Maria's smile was rueful as she slid a plate across holding a fat muffin studded with berries. She chatted away until the coffee had brewed, then filled a mug to the brim.

Emma took a bite from the muffin as she walked toward the back of the L-shaped café, savoring the buttery sweetness.

As she rounded the corner, her steps slowed. The whole room was empty, except for her favorite table, which nestled in a quiet nook, and was currently occupied by a tall man.

Isn't it always the bloody way?

With a sigh, she began to turn back. Just as she did, though, the man glanced up and she met his eyes.

"Ripley!" she breathed.

34

H E S M I L E D . "I T ' S good to see you." When she just stood there staring, still clutching her muffin and a huge mug of coffee, his smile broadened and he gestured at the seat across from him. "You may as well sit down before you spill that."

Emma looked from him to the chair, then shook herself into action, setting down the mug and plate and sliding hastily into the seat.

She couldn't take her eyes off him, as if he might disappear if she turned away. He looked good. Undamaged. He wore one of his forgettable suits and a white shirt, but no tie. All the same, he seemed out of place in a coffee shop. Like finding a panther in a living room.

"I know I'm staring," she told him. "It's just . . . I've been worried."

"I'm sorry about that," he said. "I'd have called, but calling isn't a very good idea right now."

His tone was mild, but his words hit her like a hammer.

My phone is bugged.

"Is it us or them listening?" she asked.

He cocked an eyebrow. "Us, as far as I know."

Christ, she'd missed his wry, unruffled steadiness.

She searched his craggy features. "Are you really OK? Where have you been?"

"It's been an unusual few weeks, but it's not me I'm worried about." His eyes grazed her shoulder. "What's the prognosis?"

She swung her arm. "It moves fine. I think I'll get full use of it. I've got a few more weeks of physio to go." After a brief hesitation she asked, "I wanted to ask—do you know how Michael is? Were there any problems getting him to the safe house?"

Ripley looked at her shrewdly, but all he said was, "According to Andrew, everything went well. He and his parents have been moved to a new location. They're settling in fine."

Emma had thought about Michael a lot over the last few weeks. It was hard to let go of him, although logically she knew she must.

There was much more she wanted to ask but she knew how it would look, so instead she took a sip of her coffee and changed the subject.

"What about Chernov? He got away, didn't he?"

"Yes, and I still don't know how. We had people watching every flight out." His jaw tightened. "It was a neat job; I'll grant him that."

Some part of Emma had hoped Ripley's silence had been because Chernov was in a prison somewhere, being interrogated, but she'd known from the start that was wishful thinking. Chernov was a pro. He would have had an exit plan.

"It was because of you, wasn't it?" she asked. "The whole thing was because of what happened that day at Harrods."

"Not that day. Another day. Twenty years ago." He paused. "I can't remember what you know. Did I tell you he threatened an operative of mine—a woman I'd been working with for some time?"

Emma nodded.

"Well, that woman was Elena Primalov."

So, it was just as Emma had suspected during that long, dark night.

"I should have told you sooner," he said, "but it never occurred to me that Chernov would take things so far. I thought the Russians were murdering the scientists the same way they killed the ex-spies who betrayed them. I should have seen that this was different. It was a classic case of seeing what seemed most obvious, rather than looking for a deeper motive. By the time I figured out what was going on, it was far too late. The wheels were in motion."

"But why would he do all of this now, after so many years?"

With a sigh, Ripley turned over his hands. "To understand Chernov you need to understand that Elena's betrayal was complete. The revelation that she'd been providing information to the West was a huge scandal. But it went beyond that for him. He was personally responsible for controlling British spying efforts in Russia at that time. When he figured out Elena was working for me, he was incandescent. He should have arrested her immediately. That would have been the smart move. Instead, he decided to make an example of her. And of me."

Across the room, Maria was humming to herself as she wiped down tables. He watched her without seeming to see her.

"I think that's why he offered me the opportunity to betray my country." An edge of contempt entered his voice. "He needed to punish me, and that would have been the perfect way to do it. He could have tortured me for years that way. He should have known me well enough by then to understand I'd never do it. But, like many despots, he projects his own lack of morality onto everyone around him. So he made that offer, I said I'd consider it, and then I got Elena, her family, and myself out of Russia as quickly as I could."

Cautiously, Emma said, "Was there more to it than just Elena giving you information? Chernov must have believed you cared for her a great deal. After all, he basically asked you to choose your country or her."

Something flickered in his impassive eyes. A long moment passed before he replied. "It would make me uncomfortable to talk about Elena without her permission. Her marriage is not unhappy. And she has a right to privacy."

His forbidding expression told her to drop it. Still, hidden among those carefully chosen words, she thought, was the truth: he and Elena had had an affair. She might never know more than that.

"So, how did you get the Primalovs out?" she asked, returning to safer ground. "It can't have been easy."

"Back then I had a huge underground network of Russians in place. They smuggled the family on a container ship." He gave a thin smile. "We snatched them from beneath Chernov's nose. So yes, I believe this was revenge. For that escape, for my role in Elena's betrayal, and for what it did to him. You see, after Elena escaped, Chernov's career went up in flames. Until then, he was on track to be head of Russian security. Her betrayal put an end to that. He knows the job he has now is the highest he'll ever rise." This fact clearly gave him grim satisfaction. "It's fair to say we've been at war, Grigory Chernov and I, ever since. That day at Harrods, I suspected he was planning something—I could smell it on him, the pleasure he was taking in it. That's why I had you go in disguise. It's why I sent you to Camden later: I needed one of my agents to be unknown to him. Just in case."

He pulled his cigarette case out of his pocket and opened it before remembering. He snapped it shut with an irritated gesture. "What a bloody nuisance that smoking is treated like homicide these days." He dropped the case on the table. "Where was I? Oh yes. I knew he was planning something but not what. When the Russians began murdering the scientists, I didn't immediately connect it to Chernov, but we began watching the borders very closely. When we noticed six GRU agents arrive in the country on separate flights, we brought the Primalovs in immediately, but Michael refused. Which is when I sent you to get him." He paused. "Chernov arrived in the UK at six o'clock that night. By the time word got to me, he'd disappeared. The CCTV system was hacked a short time later. By then the mission to bring in Michael was under way and it was too late to call you back. You wouldn't have come anyway."

This all made sense. Emma could see all of it in her mind—Ripley getting the call about Chernov, the cameras going dark. His decision to strike out and find Chernov himself.

But there was one puzzle piece that still didn't fit.

"What about Ed Masterson?" she asked. "His behavior that night was bizarre. He left me out there alone. Refused to offer any help, even when he knew how bad it was. And now he's trying to push you out."

Ripley's face hardened. "Ed's a fool. His only benefit to the Agency is that he went to Eton with half the government, and he speaks their language. He's not capable of running the Agency, and his behavior that night proves it. As soon as the internal investigation is over, he can go back to taking ministers to lunch."

The bell above the door jangled, and a woman carrying a baby in a sling walked in. "Just a latte to go, please," she told Maria, leaning against the front counter. "I've got to catch the train."

Emma and Ripley fell silent until the woman paid for her coffee and hurried out.

As soon as she'd gone, Emma said quietly, "You don't think there's any chance Ed is more than stupid, do you?"

Ripley went very still.

"What do you mean by that?" He looked disbelieving. Almost angry.

"I don't know." She felt suddenly uncertain. What she was suggesting was hugely damaging. But she had to voice her suspicions. "The Russians kept finding us that night. They seemed to know more than they should."

"For instance?" He watched her intently.

"They seemed to know I was heading across the river instead of straight to a safe house, or MI5, or the Institute. I couldn't figure out how they could know to guard the river crossings. At the time I thought it was just good planning. Since then, though . . ." She took a breath. "I keep wondering if someone at the Agency helped them. I know it's probably not true but—"

"You think Ed betrayed us to *Chernov*?"

It was unnerving the way he looked at her. She felt pinioned to the wooden chairback. Unable to move.

Finally, he shook his head and it was as if he'd released her. "No. I don't see it. He's not competent enough to be a double agent." His voice was firm. "Never attribute to malice what can be explained by incompetence. Ed's ambition exceeds his ability by a considerable margin, but he's no traitor."

He pushed his coffee cup aside with a controlled flick of his finger-tips, signaling an end to that conversation.

Emma hoped he was right. She trusted Ripley above everyone. If he didn't see it, it probably wasn't there. But then she remembered Martha saying she thought he was blind about the people he chose for his team.

She changed the subject. "What's going to happen now? Masterson seems to think they're going to fire you."

A smile as cold as winter crossed his face. "Oh, they're going to try. But I have a lot of friends—people I've worked with for years. They know what's happening, and I feel confident reason will triumph. Please don't worry about my future. That's not why I wanted to talk to you today." He paused. "Andrew Field is working with me on the Chernov situation." He turned, checking the room around them. It remained empty. Maria was washing dishes behind the counter, her back to them.

He continued quietly. "We're going to track Chernov down. He can't get away with what he did that night. Andrew has already assigned a unit to work on it. I'm being allowed to bring in a team of my own. I want Adam. And I want you."

"But—you're under investigation," she reminded him. "They'll be watching you. Both of us, actually."

He waved that away. "I worked at MI6 for twenty years. They can see what's going on at the Agency and they've offered to keep me busy while Masterson digs a grave for his career. Andrew's handling all of it through his office. I am, shall we say, a silent partner. You would be too, given that you're technically still on medical leave. Officially, Andrew is just bringing Adam in to help him on a project related to Chernov. That's all Ed will be told."

A flame of excitement ignited in Emma's chest.

"And you're really going after Chernov?" she asked.

"Andrew and I have been working on a plan ever since you and Michael Primalov roared into MI6." Ripley leaned back in his chair, watching her. "Now, all I want to know is: are you in or out?"

35

Two days later, Emma stood in the oddly stylish Eurostar terminal at St. Pancras Station, waiting impatiently for her train to be called. The passport in her pocket identified her as Sarah Laine, aged twenty-eight. It had ostensibly been issued three years ago and appeared well thumbed, but she'd received it only yesterday. In theory she was traveling by herself but, from where she stood, she could see Adam leaning against a wall near the coffee kiosk, his eyes on his phone.

She hadn't yet spotted Ripley, but she had no doubt he was here somewhere. He'd arranged every step of the plan.

At the coffee shop on Gipsy Hill, he'd filled her in on the details.

It turned out that Grigory Chernov had left London the morning after the attack but, instead of going back to Moscow, he'd traveled to Brussels. Then, two weeks later, to Paris.

"He's been in Paris ever since," Ripley had told her that day. "He should have gone home long ago. There's no reason for him to stay in the city unless he's planning something else."

"Another attack here?" she asked. "Or in Paris?"

"We don't know." His face betrayed no emotion. "He's had meetings with a number of known or suspected Russian agents, but he's given us little to go on. He must suspect he's being watched."

"But surely he can't come back here." The thought that Chernov might ever put one foot in the city again burned.

"He has a diplomatic passport," Ripley said. "Stopping him would be difficult. This is why we need to take care of him before he has the chance to do whatever it is he's planning."

Emma's breath caught.

"When you say 'take care of him,' what does that mean?"

"We want to make sure that he never dares to try this sort of thing again. This time I intend to destroy him."

His slow, deliberate words sent a chill through her. This was a new side of Ripley—more ruthless and dangerous. It struck her that this must have been what he'd been like back in the days when he was based in Russia. Harder. More vindictive.

But then, nobody was angrier at Chernov than she was. She was the one who'd faced death at his hands. And watched him ruin a good man's life.

"I'm in," she said. "What do you need me to do?"

Talking quickly, he laid out the basics. Emma listened, asking only occasional questions. When he finished outlining the plan, she leaned back in her chair. "It could work."

"It *will* work," he corrected her. "The only hard part, as I see it, is getting him away from his bodyguards. They're always with him, and they're all ex-military. We don't want a battle on the streets of Paris. But the only time he leaves them behind is when he visits his mistress."

Emma's lip curled. "He's married?"

"Married with five children, all living in luxury in Moscow," he said. "In Paris, however, he spends his time with Valerie Merrett, an ex-model, twenty-seven years old, very pretty." He let a beat pass. "It appears she is deeply, passionately in love with Grigory's enormous bank accounts."

"So, we're going to use her to get to him," she guessed.

"Precisely," Ripley said with relish. "It appears he trusts her completely."

He'd looked at her directly then. "There's little role for you in this plan. Andrew's team will handle most of the work. But I want you to be there all the same. After what he did to you that night, you've earned the right to see him take his punishment."

The call came to board the train to Paris, pulling Emma back to the moment. She straightened. Adam had already begun to stroll over to join the crowd heading for the platform. Emma was about to do the same when someone touched her arm. She turned to see a tall, elderly man peering at her anxiously. He had a walking cane, and watery blue eyes. He was hunched over, as if his back hurt.

"Could you help me please? Which is platform six?" His voice was shaky and thin.

Emma hesitated. She wanted to keep Adam in sight.

"It's right there." She pointed impatiently to where the crowd was disappearing through glass doors.

"Thank you." The man bobbed his head. "That's very kind." Instead of moving on, though, he stood watching her as if he expected something more. In the end, it was the amused twinkle in his eye that made her take a second look.

"Ripley?" She stared at him. His disguise had completely fooled her. Martha had outdone herself this time.

"You really should pay closer attention," he told her in his own voice. "Everything is so rarely what it seems." He reverted to the thin, old-man voice. "Would you be so kind as to assist me to the platform. I hate to ask but . . ."

"Jesus Christ," she muttered, but she let him take her arm. They joined the last of the crowd threading through the doors and up to the platform. Ripley walked slowly, as if each step took effort.

"Facial-recognition software is really very good, you know," he told her cheerfully. "One can't be too careful. I presume you took all the necessary precautions?"

"I took a train to Victoria Station, put on the wig there, then changed taxis three times. Nobody followed me."

"Excellent. Then we are all ready." They reached the top of the ramp and turned onto the long train platform. Most passengers were already on board. "Ah, here we are. This is my carriage." He turned to her and bowed, that twinkle back in his eyes. He was enjoying this. "Thank you for your assistance, my dear. Have a lovely trip to Paris."

36

A T NOON ON a Saturday, the Gare du Nord station in Paris is packed and noisy. Constant announcements echo from loudspeakers as crowds rush to and from the trains, pouring into the Métro entrance.

Emma allowed herself to be carried along to the west exit, stepping out into a cool Parisian afternoon. The air had the sweet smell of an autumn rainstorm, but the skies had cleared and blue was beginning to fight the gray.

She walked with confidence straight to the street, scanning the cars until she found a blue Audi with a license plate beginning JF-723. When she approached it, the driver—tall, early thirties, with a shock of strawberry-blond hair exactly like the picture she'd been shown—climbed out and opened the back door for her. "Welcome to Paris, Miss Makepeace."

His tone was light, but his eyes scanned her face, making the same assessment that she'd just made of his.

"Merci." She got in and he closed the door behind her.

"Not a problem." He had a thick Scottish accent. All she knew about him was that his name was Jon and he worked with Andrew Field. As soon as she was in, he jumped behind the wheel and pulled away from the curb.

"Package collected." He spoke quietly into a lapel mic. She could see him listening for a second, then he glanced at her in the mirror. "Did everyone get through fine?"

"Yes. No issues."

"That's affirmative," he told the microphone.

"Is everything in place?" she asked.

He glanced at her in the mirror. "Oh, aye. Old Grigory's having a lavish lunch at the moment with some mates. He's got no idea what's coming."

He paused to hear something from his earpiece and then caught her eye. "The others are all collected now. They tell me Ripley's doing his old-man impression again."

His chuckle sounded affectionate, and Emma thought about what Ripley had said about his "friends" at MI6. Everyone she'd met from Six held him in very high regard. It made sense—MI6 oversaw Russia, and their work overlapped with what the Agency was doing. Still, she wondered if Ed Masterson had ever considered, as he plotted to replace Ripley, just how well connected his boss actually was.

As he navigated through the crowded streets, Jon filled her in on the current situation. Chernov was under constant surveillance; so far today he'd done precisely what they'd expected. Now he was in a restaurant with a group of known Russian agents, having what looked like a celebratory meal. After that, he was scheduled to go to the gym, and then to meet his girlfriend in the evening.

Emma didn't ask how they knew what his plans were. It was their job to know.

"Here we go." They pulled up to the curb on a narrow lane lined with elegant limestone buildings just off the Boulevard Saint-Germain.

"Right, then," Jon said. "Let's go get our guy."

Once out of the car, they quickly joined the flow of tourists walking along the fashionable street. Emma let Jon take the lead, matching him stride for stride as he turned right, then pausing with him in front of a large shop window filled with vivid women's clothing draped across skeletal mannequins.

"Do you see the restaurant behind us? Les Deux Magots?"

Emma studied the scene reflected in the glass. She could see herself and Jon—she was stylish but unmemorable in black, her own hair hidden beneath a shoulder-length honey-blond wig. He wore a dark gray jacket that looked just expensive enough, with a scarf tied Parisian-style around his neck. Across the street behind them was an elegant building—classic Parisian cream stone with delicate wrought iron balconies. The restaurant's famous name was written in gold on the green awning. Through its large windows, she could just make out a round table at which men in suits had taken every seat.

"Is that them at the front?" she asked.

Jon nodded. "Doesn't mind advertising his presence, does he?"

Chernov's audacity was astounding. He must know every person in British Intelligence was out for revenge, but he hadn't taken even the basic precaution of choosing a table hidden from the street. He was showing off; demonstrating how little regard he held for his enemies.

She squinted at the reflection of the group in the silvery glass: she couldn't make out the details of their faces from here, but she could see the bottles of champagne on the table.

"What does he have to celebrate?" she wondered.

"That's the question we have, too. We've got someone inside, keeping an eye. He says it's all extremely jolly. Could be they're putting the finishing touches on another operation. Either way, they're all happy and that's no bad thing. We need our guy nicely trolleyed before we drop the bait." Jon watched the group for a second before stepping back. "We'd better move. Down here."

She followed him to a spot tucked away in the shadow of a little wooden kiosk selling hot chocolate and *vin chaud*. From there they had a good view of the restaurant but were unlikely to be noticed by those inside.

"Do you want a hot chocolate?" he asked, reaching into his pocket.

Seeing the doubtful look on her face, he chuckled. "We're tourists, remember? We need a reason to stand here."

Emma felt idiotic.

"Sure," she said. "Hot chocolate would be great."

As she waited, Emma kept her focus on the restaurant.

The idea that Chernov was in there, so close she could cross the street and in seconds be standing in front of him, was hard to process. If Ripley's plan worked, today she would pay Chernov back for everything. For the raised red scar on her shoulder. The bruises that had taken two weeks to heal. The moment on the icy cold river when she'd thought she would die. The sense of loss she still felt when she thought about Michael Primalov.

Grigory Chernov was going to pay for all of it.

Jon was gone longer than she'd expected. When she turned to look for him, though, she found he wasn't alone. He and Andrew Field walked up to her, smiling like old friends.

For some reason, seeing Field's sharp, clever face again made her feel better.

"Emma." Holding lightly to her upper arms, he kissed both her cheeks like a local. "It's lovely to see you looking so well. Much better than when last we met." As he spoke, he placed a piece of soft dark fabric in her hands. She turned it over blankly before realizing it was a knitted cap.

"You should wear that," he said, still smiling. "All the Parisian women are wearing them today because of the damp. It will make you less memorable."

She slid it on without hesitation, then accepted the cardboard cup of hot chocolate Jon held out to her, taking a casual sip, like any tourist.

"They're nearly finished inside," Andrew told her. "They've asked for the bill. I think it's time to make the call."

Jon glanced at his watch. "Timing's perfect. The others should be nearly ready."

Andrew pulled a phone from his pocket and looked up at her. "You know the whole plan?"

She nodded. Andrew's team had cloned Valerie Merrett's phone. The plan was to text Chernov from her number, inviting him to an afternoon assignation at the Four Seasons: their favorite five-star hotel. The suite the two of them regularly used had been booked.

"You're sure the real Valerie won't interrupt our plans?"

"Oh, she's very busy today," Jon assured her. "She received an invite to an exclusive fashion event on the other side of the city. Her phone is also currently not working. It must be broken, although no one's certain how it was damaged."

They really had thought of everything.

"Well, then. Would you like to do the honors?" Andrew said, holding the phone out to Emma. "I understand you have a special friendship with our Grigory."

Emma, who hadn't expected this, took it gingerly. "Do they speak English with each other?"

Andrew nodded. "Chernov speaks several languages, but not French."

The phone was a basic Samsung: a mirror in every way for the one Merrett used. When she clicked on the icon for messages, "GC" was at the top of the list.

Jon took her cup and threw it into a nearby bin so that both her hands were free. "She calls him 'darling,'" he told her, his tone contemptuous. "She'll say something like, 'Darling, come to our suite.'"

"Yes," Andrew agreed. "But add some enticement. 'Hurry. I miss you.'"

"Sign it 'Bisous,'" Jon added. "With lots of Xs, like a teenager."

Emma typed quickly, her chest tight with anticipation. She could imagine Chernov getting this message: the excitement of an unexpected afternoon tryst with his hot girlfriend. Irresistible after so many glasses of expensive wine.

She finished typing and turned the phone around so the other two could see.

My darling, I have a surprise! Come and see me in our suite. I'm waiting for you. Hurry. I need you. Bisous xxxxxxxx.

"Ah now, that's perfect," Jon said admiringly.

Andrew gave Emma a nod.

She pressed send.

The three of them looked up at the restaurant across the street.

"Now," Andrew said with malicious patience, "we wait."

37

I N T H E E N D , the wait wasn't long. Chernov's reply came within minutes.

I'm on my way. Order champagne. I want to find you naked and soaking wet. xxx.

Jon rubbed his hands together. "Now things get interesting."

His eyes were bright and bloodthirsty. Emma recognized that look—it perfectly reflected the fire in her own chest. The rage she still felt for Chernov and everything he'd done.

Jon stepped away to speak into his microphone. When he returned, he told Andrew, "The others are set."

All business now, Andrew gave a tense nod. "Get the car."

Jon disappeared around the corner, moving fast. Emma and Andrew stood in the shade of the kiosk, watching the restaurant. Andrew spoke so quietly she had to lean closer to hear him.

"The last time I saw you, you were in shock and covered with blood because of this man. I believe you have just begun to pay him back for that."

She glanced at him, surprised. Slightly plump and with thinning hair, Andrew gave every appearance of being almost preternaturally calm and rational. But she heard real fury simmering beneath his words.

"You hate him, too," she said.

"Oh yes. Chernov has arrested several of my operatives over the years. Two of them never made it out of prison. All were people I considered friends."

Across the street, the restaurant door opened and five men in suits walked out, red-faced and roaring with laughter, patting each other on the back with too much force.

Chernov was in the middle of the group, his gray hair distinctive. The others seemed to be teasing him.

Andrew watched them, expressionless. "It is time someone put Grigory to bed," he said as Jon pulled the car up in front of them. "It might as well be us."

Emma climbed in the back. Jon pulled into an illegal space with a view of the men. The three of them watched as a chauffeur-driven black Range Rover pulled up in front of the restaurant.

The men cheered drunkenly as Chernov vaulted into the backseat and slammed the door.

"He's eager," Jon observed.

"From the sound of that message, he's desperate," Andrew replied with distaste. "I imagine he'll break a few speed limits on the way."

When the Range Rover took off, Jon pulled in behind but kept a good distance. Andrew never looked up from his phone. Neither of them seemed bothered when the Range Rover raced through a red light, leaving them behind.

"Are we losing him?" Emma asked.

Andrew held up his phone. "We placed a tracker on his car earlier. His driver is skilled at spotting surveillance so we're keeping our distance." Turning to Jon, he added, "Looks like he's going straight there. Take a shortcut. Let's get in before him."

Jon took a left off the main road and wheeled expertly through the confusion of Paris streets, pulling up ten minutes later in the curved drive of a sleek hotel.

As they jumped out, Jon tossed the keys to a parking attendant, who snatched them from the air with admirable ease. Jon paused to speak to him briefly in fluent French, slipping him what looked to Emma like a fifty-euro note before they hurried together through the wide opaque glass door into the cool, refined air of the five-star hotel.

There was barely time to notice the marble floors, the six-foot-tall vases of exotic flowers arranged in artistic circles at the center of the room. The elegant black-clad staff behind the desk. The heady scent that filled the room.

"I'm going straight up," Andrew said. "You two stake out the lobby and wait for him. Pretend to be a couple and come up with him in the elevator." As if he'd just thought of something, he turned to Emma. "Does he know your face?"

"I don't think so," she said.

"Well, be careful all the same." He gestured at her head. "And you can take off the hat now."

Emma snatched it from her head as he walked to the elevators and stuffed it into the pocket of her black leather jacket. She was still smoothing her hair when Chernov's Range Rover pulled up outside the row of arched glass doors.

"Showtime," Jon said.

He hooked his arm around Emma's waist, moving her closer. She leaned her body against his and looked up into his eyes. He was so tall, well over six feet, she had to angle herself back to see his face.

"Should we be closer to the elevators?" she whispered.

He smiled down at her. "Probably."

They strolled without hurrying toward the elevators, arms still around each other. He paused to nuzzle her shoulder and she gave a low, sexy laugh, looking past him as Chernov burst through the doors into the lobby.

"Jesus, he's all but running," she said. "Push the up button."

Still holding her close, Jon reached over and hit the elevator button. The doors opened with a subtle swish as sophisticated as the room itself. The two of them stepped in, clinging to each other as if oblivious to everything around them.

Too soon, the doors began to close. Emma feared they'd mistimed it. But then a hand caught the sliding door from outside and Chernov muscled his way inside.

"I'm sorry," he said, barely glancing at them as he punched the number 14.

"Pas grave," Jon replied. Emma was impressed. Pretending to be local was the perfect move. Chernov, uncomfortable with his inability to speak the language, would find this intimidating and ignore them.

The Russian turned away, his eyes on the dark glass door as the elevator rose swiftly.

Jon pulled Emma closer and trailed kisses along the edge of her neck. She allowed herself to melt into his arms, her attention on Chernov.

It was odd being so close to the man who'd spent twelve hours trying to kill her only a few weeks ago. The man who would have been content to leave her body floating in the Thames.

The thought filled Emma with pure hate.

As the elevator neared the fourteenth floor, Chernov twitched with impatience, straightening his jacket, flexing his fingers. He strode off while the doors were still sliding open, and powered down the hushed, tastefully decorated corridor.

Emma and Jon followed, their steps soundless. Their target was too excited to look back. Too eager. Too drunk.

The door to suite 1407 had been left slightly ajar. The lights were out.

Perhaps surprised by the darkness, Chernov paused outside, but then he smoothed his hair with the flat of his hand and pushed the door open.

"Darling, I'm—"

Emma and Jon were on him before he even knew they were there, grabbing him from behind and manhandling him into the room. He never stood a chance.

As they tumbled inside, someone closed the door behind them and locked it.

Someone else hit a switch and the room flooded with light. Emma and Jon released their hold on him and stepped back as Chernov stared wild-eyed around him.

"Hello, darling." Ripley sat on a cushioned chair upholstered in cream silk, watching Chernov with a look of pure triumph. "I thought you'd never get here."

Chernov whirled toward the door, but Jon and Adam were ready for this. Before he could even take a step, they pounced on him.

Emma stayed back as the three struggled. Another person wasn't necessary. It took Chernov only a minute to recognize that as well, and give in.

"Here you go, mate." Grabbing him by the shoulders, Adam turned him back to face Ripley. Jon frisked him with quick efficiency.

"No weapons. I've got his phone." Jon held it up.

"Excellent. Thank you." Andrew held out his hand and Adam tossed the device to him.

Chernov breathed heavily, his face turning an unhealthy shade of purple as he straightened his rumpled suit.

They were in the sitting room of a two-room suite. Ripley's chair had been placed facing the door. A matching sofa had been moved back against the walls. Only a low table stood between him and Chernov. Even though the room was large, the presence of so many people made it feel claustrophobic.

Emma took a position in front of the curtains. Nearby, Andrew plugged a reader into Chernov's phone to download his data.

"What the fuck is this?" Chernov demanded. Fury twisted his face.

Ripley lifted one hand in a vague gesture. "Let's call it an intervention."

"You're out of your mind." Chernov's breath came in short, furious gasps, his hands clenched at his sides. "You're interfering with an agent of the Russian government in international territory. I will report this."

He looked around the room, including them all in his threat. "Every one of you will be included in my report."

"Must we play these games, Grigory?" sighed Ripley. "You must have known we couldn't let what happened in London go without response."

Chernov made an ugly attempt at a laugh. "Oh, please. It's not as if you did nothing in Moscow. You're no angel."

"True. But I never bombed Russian shops, risking hundreds of lives." Ripley's voice was a razor. "I didn't open fire on civilian streets. I didn't shoot at Russian agents going about their duties in their homeland. I followed the *rules*." For the first time he showed his fury, eyes blazing.

"The rules have changed." Chernov's tone was dismissive. "You're living in the past, Charles. I have no choice but to live in the present."

He seemed to be finding his equilibrium now, keeping his focus on Ripley, and ignoring everyone else.

"You really think the actions you took in London that night were acceptable?" Ripley rose in his seat. "Grigory, it was an act of war."

"Was it?" Chernov held out his hands, mockingly. "Then where is your army? Tell me, does your government even know you're here right now?"

"I think you'll find," Andrew Field interjected mildly, "they do know. But please do carry on."

Keeping his gaze on Ripley, Chernov tried a different tactic. "Why are you so angry? Your agent did not die. You did not lose Mikhail Primalov. Why not take your victory and be happy?"

Ripley leaned forward, his face tightening. "You threatened my people. I will not accept that sort of activity in my city from you or anyone else."

"*Your* city," Chernov scoffed. "I keep telling you—you do not own London."

Ripley made a short, sharp gesture. "Here's what's going to happen. You are never coming to London again. You're going to keep out of the country altogether from now on. You will run your operations from elsewhere. As you always have."

Chernov looked amused. "And tell me, please—how are you going to prevent a man with a diplomatic passport from going wherever he wants to? You haven't that kind of power. From what I understand, you have no power at all anymore."

Ripley's expression didn't change, but Emma's breath caught. Chernov knew that Ripley's deputy had replaced him, and that his job was in peril. How could he possibly know that?

It was Andrew who responded. "Don't think for one moment that you understand the British Intelligence Service. It makes you look like a fool." He stepped forward. "Besides. You have trouble of your own." Reaching into his jacket pocket, he pulled out a stack of papers. One by one he began to lay them out on the tasteful low table between Ripley and Chernov. The first was a picture of a gated French mansion, built of creamy-white stone. The second was a blurry shot of Valerie Merrett, nude, with Chernov standing behind her, his hands on her waist. The third was a photo of a computer screen, covered with numbers. The fourth was a body, lying on the street, blood staining the gray concrete around it.

As he looked at the images, Chernov's arrogance evaporated. He stared at the pictures hard, as if trying to see through them.

He recognized all of it, Emma realized. He knew what was coming.

"Here's what we know." Andrew pointed at the first picture. "We know where you got the money to pay for this house, and we know that your office has no idea that you own it." His hand moved to the second picture. "We know your wife knows nothing about her. And we know what your wife's father would think of your . . . indiscretion. We also know he has a reputation for killing those who betray him." The third picture. "We found the bank account where you keep the money you're laundering in the Cayman Islands. We believe you stole some of it from your father-in-law." The fourth picture. "This is how your government punished the last man who did some of the things you've done."

He stepped back, leaving the pictures lying there. Chernov couldn't seem to take his eyes off them. The color had drained from his face.

"You've betrayed your country, Grigory. That is not something your people are quick to forgive." Ripley's voice was soft and filled with malice.

Chernov looked up, his expression stricken. "What have you done, Charles?"

"Only precisely what you would do in my shoes." Ripley shook his head sorrowfully. "You went too far, Grigory. You invented new rules and then you broke them. And now you must pay the price."

He rose from the silk-upholstered chair and towered over his Russian counterpart, his face devoid of sympathy.

"I'm going to let your own people decide what becomes of you. As we both know, there is no justice like Russian justice. We have given them everything. They know you are here. There's no point in running. It's time to face the punishment that's coming to you."

He glanced at Andrew, who touched his earpiece and then nodded a response to the unspoken inquiry.

Ripley made a quick gesture with his right hand and everyone moved to the door. He alone remained standing beside Chernov. The Russian man appeared hunched, as if crumpling beneath the force of the blow he'd just been dealt.

"If you survive this," Ripley said, "don't ever come back to London."

Chernov lifted his head and gave him a look of pure loathing. "I will survive, Charles. And I will *remember*."

But by then, Ripley was already walking to the door.

They left Chernov alone in the room, with the proof of his crimes spread out around him.

None of them spoke until they were in the elevator.

"Are they here?" Ripley asked Andrew.

"Just pulling in now," he replied.

The mood in the elevator crackled with tension. Andrew stared at the numbers by the door. Ripley seemed to turn inward, his face impassive; hands still at his sides.

They reached the ground floor and stepped out of the elevator just as the arched, glass door opened on the other side of the lobby. Sunlight poured through the stained-glass windows, sending shards of color slicing across the pale floor as three men strode in. All wore dark suits. All were thickly built and moving with aggressive speed.

They spotted the British team the second they walked in.

The man in front had threads of silver in his dark hair and an air of authority that marked him as the leader. He kept his eyes on Ripley as the two groups approached each other.

Emma found herself memorizing the men's features. The wedding ring worn by the second man. The pale blue tie worn by the one in charge. The scar on the face of the third.

Each group gave the other wide berth, moving elaborately out of the way to make space. The temperature in the bright, fragrant room seemed to fall by degrees as the two groups neared.

Ripley inclined his head in a crisp, fleeting nod. The dark-haired man did the same.

Nobody who hadn't been watching them both would have seen it. Even if they had, they couldn't begin to imagine what that slight gesture meant.

The British team walked out through the elegant glass doors at the precise moment the Russian group got into the elevator.

And, just like that, the deal was done.

38

"I JUST WANTED TO see how you are," Emma said into the phone.

"Well, I am fine." There was pleasure but also a hint of suspicion in her mother's voice on the other end of the line. "Are you sure nothing is wrong?"

Emma bit back a sigh. They'd only been talking for a few minutes, but her mother had somehow deduced that she'd had a hard day. Calling had been a mistake when she was feeling this strange and emotional, but she'd needed to hear her voice.

After the encounter with Chernov, they'd returned to London on the next train. It seemed like a good idea not to be in the same town with quite so many Russian Intelligence agents.

When they arrived in London, none of them had wanted to go home. It had been Andrew's idea that they go for a drink.

"Pub, I think," he'd said mildly as soon as they were in a taxi, and nobody had objected. Not even Ripley, who *never* went to the pub.

But once they'd settled into the bar she'd felt an overwhelming urge to hear her mother's voice, so she'd slipped outside to make the call. And now she was standing on the pavement outside the Red Lion pub in the shadow of Big Ben, trying to find a way to politely hang up on her.

"Look, I have to go back in. The others are waiting. My boss is there."

"On a Saturday night?" Her mother sounded skeptical. "What is happening that you go drink with your boss on a Saturday? You know, ever since your accident you are very strange, Alexandra. I think you don't tell me the truth about everything."

"Mama . . ." Emma sighed. She'd had to find a way to explain her injury after she was shot, so she'd invented a car accident. Maybe this had triggered her mother's usually relaxed parental instinct because suddenly she was questioning everything. "I'm really fine. My boss really is inside. We all really had to work this weekend. And I really, really just wanted to call and tell you I love you. Is that so wrong?"

"I suppose it is not." Her mother's tone softened. "You go talk to your boss. But be safe. Or I will be angry."

"I promise."

Emma hung up and let out a breath. She didn't know why she'd needed to call her so urgently. Maybe it had something to do with standing so near to Chernov, and knowing how close she'd come to death at his hands. And that now he, himself, could face death because of what she and the others had done.

She ran her fingers through her hair. It was her own toffee-brown hair: she'd taken the wig off in the cab.

It was a chilly night, but the cold air felt good against her skin, and she leaned back to breathe in the mixture of river air, exhaust, and cigarette smoke that, for her, was the true London perfume. A red double-decker bus grumbled by and for some reason it looked beautiful to her. She found herself noticing other things tonight, too. The ornate Victorian streetlights glowing amber. The sturdy stone government buildings all around her. To her left, Parliament's soaring spires glowed golden against the dark night. Across from it, Westminster Abbey hulked pale and eternal. Crowds strolled by, talking and laughing, taking selfies in front of statues, and it all felt pleasantly, wonderfully normal.

"It's good to be back," she told the sky. Then she straightened and walked into the pub.

The Red Lion is a Victorian inn, packed with civil servants from the surrounding government buildings during the week, and tourists at the weekend, but somehow Andrew had found them a table at the very back. She threaded her way through the mostly young and really quite drunk crowd that filled the room with a constant roar of conversation to where the others were tucked away in a quiet corner.

"There she is." Jon motioned her over to the chair next to his. "I ordered you a pint. Had to guess what you wanted so I got lager. Girls like lager, or so I'm told."

It was impossible not to like him. He had a mischievous smile she found herself returning before she realized she was doing it.

"Lager is fine, but whiskey is quicker," she quipped, sitting down and taking a long drink.

"I could get you one of those, too," he said amiably. "My people are not opposed to a bit of a tipple, as you know."

"My people as well. We like a drink." Adam's glass was already half empty. He drank the way he walked: steadily and with purpose.

"I think it's fair to say the entire UK population is not entirely averse to a bit of a splash now and then." Andrew's glass of Guinness had been only lightly sampled while she'd been outside.

Ripley alone had forgone beer and was drinking a scotch and soda on the rocks. He sat at the end of the table, watching the rest of them with interest. Catching his eye, Emma lifted her glass to him. "My mum says to tell you hi."

He gave a short laugh. "How is your mother?"

"Fine. Although she sometimes wonders why working at the Foreign Office is so time-consuming."

Knowing laughter rippled around the table.

"My parents think I work for Border Control," Jon confessed.

"My girlfriend thinks I work for the Department for Transport," Adam growled. "Sometimes I wish I did."

The mood was jolly, but there was an indefinable element beneath it all. Like a cold undercurrent in a warm ocean. The laughter died quickly.

Emma was the one to broach the subject they'd all been avoiding. "What do you think they'll do to him?"

Andrew and Ripley exchanged a glance.

"Chernov was listed on the flight manifest of an Aeroflot flight that left Paris for Moscow an hour ago," Andrew revealed.

Adam gave a low whistle.

"So they're taking him back home." Jon didn't sound surprised.

"They'll charge him with corruption," Ripley said definitively. "The other crimes will be covered up because it would embarrass the government. They don't want their heroic spy service associated with philandering. They'll focus on the money, and that's enough." He considered the amber liquid in his glass. "If they feel forgiving, he'll spend five years in prison. If they *don't* feel forgiving, he'll spend much less time there. And that will be the end of Grigory Chernov."

"Either way, it won't be pleasant," Andrew said, and took a long draw on his pint.

"I don't like the idea of that bastard surviving," Adam said. "He always finds a way to get out of trouble."

"This time it might be a little tricky to walk away," Jon said. "It's hard to walk with both your kneecaps broken."

"Death would be better for us," Ripley said. "Grigory doesn't have the word 'forget' in his vocabulary. I'm counting on the Russian government to do what it does best."

A few weeks ago, Emma might have been shocked by this ruthless assessment, but now she thought about Elena and Michael, and her own rage at Chernov, which had only been sated when she'd seen him humbled and terrified in that hotel room. And she was not shocked.

But she didn't believe Ripley wasn't emotional about what was happening, despite his world-weary tone. After all, old enemies are like old friends—we miss them when they're gone.

"What about you, Ripley?" she asked. "Can you forget?"

"I think some crimes can never be forgiven," he said. "It would be a disservice to those who were lost. But we take our revenge in unexpected places and that has to be enough." He turned to Emma, his eyes knowing. "Isn't that right, Makepeace?"

"A wise man once told me that every day can be revenge, if you do it right," she said.

"Sounds like good advice," Jon said.

"I'll drink to that," Adam agreed.

At the end of the table, Andrew raised his glass. "To revenge done right."

They all lifted their glasses without hesitation.

"To revenge."

ACKNOWLEDGMENTS

I have no idea how many real spies I've met, and neither do you. That's the thing about spies—they walk through your life without leaving the tiniest proof that they were ever there. They get what they came for, and then they move on to the next job. I suppose this is the thing that fascinated me most, during the brief period when my world collided with theirs: how few traces they left behind. I always wondered what it would be like to live a constant lie. And that was the beginning of Emma Makepeace.

Emma might never have come to life, were it not for the brilliant teams at Penguin Random House. I owe huge thanks to the wonderful Selina Walker and Venetia Butterfield at Penguin UK. I also owe enormous gratitude to the fantastic Anne Speyer at Ballantine Bantam Dell. Their wise edits and brilliant suggestions truly helped to bring the story together.

I also owe many thanks to the film and TV crew at Ink Factory, who shared my love for Emma before a single publisher had even seen the pages. My gratitude goes to Katherine Butler, Maggie Boden, and Steven Williams. I can't wait to see what you create!

As always, all thanks and love to Madeleine Milburn, Liv Maidment, and Hannah Ladds at the Madeleine Milburn Agency. You are the dream team! It's a joy to work with you.

And finally, to my husband, Jack Jewers, who makes me believe that anything is possible: all my love forever.

Ava Glass has worked as a writer and editor throughout her career. For a period of time she worked at the
Home Office as a communications consultant, focusing
on counterterrorism. This was when she first became
fascinated by the art of spying. *Alias Emma* is the result of
that fascination. Ava lives outside London, in a town
much favored by spies as it's so perfectly ordinary, nobody would ever think to look for them there.

avaglass.uk
Twitter: @AvaGlassBooks

ALIAS EMMA

A READER'S GUIDE

AVA GLASS

Random
House
Book Club

Because
Stories Are
Better Shared

Hello!

I just wanted to write a quick note to thank you for taking the time to read *Alias Emma*. This book has been a long time coming. Over a decade ago, I worked for the British government in the office that oversees some facets of intelligence work. I was not a spy myself, but I met spies. Or at least I think I did. It's hard to tell with spies; they are incredibly deceptive. My time in that world was brief, but it has stayed with me. There was one spy in particular whom I have never forgotten. She was young and extremely smart. She exuded confidence. I couldn't imagine being that fearless. That indomitable. As the years passed, I often wondered what became of her. Did she stay in intelligence? Was she put in great danger? Is she still there—the eyes and ears of the British government, disguised as an ordinary person? In *Alias Emma* I got to imagine what it was like to be her: To do a job that requires you to lie fluently. To risk your life constantly. To step in and out of other people's lives without most of them knowing they'd ever met a spy. I have to say, it was a lot of fun to write—and I am writing more! Keep an eye out for *The Traitor*, coming soon.

All my best,
Ava

QUESTIONS AND TOPICS FOR DISCUSSION

1. The plot of *Alias Emma* is intrinsically tied to its setting in London, as Emma Makepeace tries to evade the ubiquitous CCTV cameras throughout the city. Did the writing successfully evoke this environment for you? What was your favorite and least favorite part of the setting?

2. What were your initial impressions of the characters and how did your perception of them change as the story developed?

3. How does the representation of The Agency align or differ from your preconceived notions about the world of spies?

4. How does the novel play with and subvert female stereotypes and archetypes?

5. Both Emma and Michael live their lives in conversation with how they view their parents' lives: Emma as a spy like her father and Michael resisting his mother's business as an informant. How did this influence their decisions during *Alias Emma*? Did that hinder or help them in their mission?

6. Talk about the novel's structure, which is set over the course of a day. How does this influence the pacing of the story?

7. Was there a scene in the book that stuck with you the most? If so, which one, and why?

8. If you were making this book into a movie or TV show, who would you cast in the lead roles?

9. Were you satisfied by the ending? Why or why not?

EMMA MAKEPEACE'S SURVIVAL GUIDE

One thing I loved about writing *Alias Emma* was figuring out how Emma could not be dead by the end of it. I'd write a scene and then spend ages finding a way for her to survive. It was like a perpetual puzzle. Along the way, I learned a few things. So, here are a few tips from her to you, for living through an intense Russian spy operation:

- Expect the worst to happen. If you expect the worst, you'll have a plan in place when it all comes down. Everyone needs a plan.
- Your plan should include a go bag, filled with the most useful supplies. These should include cash, a change of clothes, a flashlight, a disguise, lock picks (just in case), and a weapon (for emergencies).
- Hide your go bag somewhere you know it will not be found. This place should not be in any way connected to you or anyone you know. A small, badly serviced underground parking lot is a good place to hide it.
- Teach yourself how to pick locks! There are videos on YouTube, and you can buy tools on eBay. You never know when this will come in handy.
- Remember that chocolate bars are reasonable meal replacements.

- A moving target is hard to find—stay on the go and you'll make your enemy's job much more difficult.
- Remember the Rule of Three: You can survive three minutes without air. You can survive three hours without shelter. You can survive three days without water. And three weeks without food. But I don't recommend trying any of this.

IF YOU LOVED *ALIAS EMMA*,

read on for a thrilling excerpt of
Ava Glass's second thriller featuring Emma Makepeace,

THE TRAITOR

COMING SOON FROM BANTAM BOOKS

1

EMMA WAS PART of a small intelligence unit so secret it didn't have a name. The Agency didn't appear on any government lists. It wasn't in any phone book. Only a handful of very senior officials even knew it existed. The reason for the secrecy was obvious, once you understood that the Agency's work focused on identifying and stopping Russian spies working inside Britain.

Lately, that work had been constant. Tensions between London and Moscow were the worst anyone could remember. Everything felt dangerous—as if the world had become flammable and each nation clutched a lit match.

In that febrile atmosphere, the Agency's work was silent. Invisible. And absolutely necessary.

At twenty-eight, Emma was the youngest intelligence officer on the team. She'd only been with the organization three years, but after an undercover operation last autumn in which she'd single-handedly fought off a Russian assassination unit, her star was in the ascendant. She was being trusted with bigger operations. And as she parked in front of a glass-and-steel apartment building so close to the River

Thames the blue-gray water reflected in its windows, she had a feeling this was going to be one of them.

There were no police cars on the street. No ambulances. Just one lone guard stood by the door and she recognized the unmarked black van used by MI5's forensics team parked near the corner.

Other than that, there was no evidence of any activity.

Whatever had happened here, the Agency didn't want anyone to know about it yet.

It was June, but the damp air had a chill to it, and Emma buttoned her jacket as she walked to the front door. England was never ready to accept summer until July arrived. It had to be dragged into the warmth against its will.

The Special Branch officer outside the front door gave her a doubtful look as she approached.

"Emma Makepeace," she told him. "I'm expected."

He scanned her fingerprint on a glossy black device and glanced at the readout before reaching into a bag at his feet and handing her a respirator mask.

"Put this on before you go in," he said. "The lifts are safe to use."

Emma stared at the mask, her nerves tightening as she absorbed its significance.

"Can you tell me what happened here?"

The officer shook his head. "They'll explain when you get up there."

Going inside suddenly seemed like a terrible idea. All the same, Emma pulled the mask over her head, tightened the straps, and walked through the door.

As she stepped cautiously across the empty lobby, her breathing rasped heavy and loud through the protective webbing. The room had high ceilings, stone floors, and modern leather chairs, all of it artfully designed in muted shades. It looked expensive.

By the time she reached the lift, her heart was racing but her hand was steady as she pushed the call button.

On the sixth floor, she found more subtle decor and absolute silence. Her footsteps echoed as she walked to number 652. She hesitated for a moment, bracing herself, before opening the door and stepping inside.

The apartment was small and filled with soft, gray daylight that streamed through tall windows. The walls were white and completely bare of art. The living room was empty, aside from a sofa. There was a faint, unpleasant smell she could just make out through the protective filter. Something sweet and sickly.

"Ah, excellent. You've arrived." Charles Ripley appeared from a hallway on the far side of the living area and removed his mask.

Tall, with graying hair, in his navy-blue suit and forgettable tie, he might have been mistaken for an estate agent. That was intentional. Looking ordinary is the best thing a spy can hope for.

Nobody knew as much about Russian spies as Ripley, and there was no one Emma trusted more. Right now, though, his craggy, angular features gave her few clues as to why she was here.

"We've got a bit of a delicate situation," he said. "As you can probably tell."

As he spoke, three forensic investigators in white moon suits emerged from a room behind him carrying equipment bags. They shuffled toward the living room, their progress blocked by Ripley.

The one in front spoke first.

"Excuse me," the woman said, her Essex accent muffled through her mask.

"Oh, I do beg your pardon." Ripley stepped aside.

"No worries." In the living room, the woman paused to pull off her protective visor and hood. Beneath it, she was perspiring, strands of fair hair clinging to her red cheeks.

Emma knew her as Caroline Wakefield, a scientist who worked under the Home Office. Her specialty was chemical weapons.

"We're finished. It should be safe now but I'd wear your gear in there just in case." Glancing at Emma, she added enigmatically, "Weirdest bloody thing I've seen in a while. I wish you both luck getting to the bottom of it."

With that, the forensic team lumbered to the door with a rattle of equipment cases and a swish of white fabric.

When they'd gone, Emma gave her boss a quizzical look over the top of her mask. "Well, are you going to tell me what's going on?"

"I'll do better than tell you," he said, stepping back. "I'll show you."

Motioning for her to follow, he pulled his mask back on and headed down the hallway to a large bedroom. The decor here was as minimal as the living area—there was nothing but a chair, a dresser, and a double bed where the sheets were thrown back, as if someone had just leaped out of it.

The windows were wide open but the sickly-sweet smell she'd noticed in the living room was more noticeable.

Smudges of fingerprint dust stained the doors and windows. The low, five-drawer dresser had been shifted away from the wall, and it was clear some drawers had been opened. The few things on top of it—a bottle of cologne, a leather tray—had been dusted for prints.

Otherwise, the room looked perfect. Nothing was broken. Nothing was damaged or knocked around. Everything appeared almost unnaturally tidy.

The only odd thing was the suitcase on the floor. It was dark and very large—the sort you'd take on a long trip. Or a journey you weren't planning to come home from.

The top of the case was open, and what Emma saw inside was so unexpected it took a second for her brain to grasp what she was looking at.

It was a man, naked, kneeling and bent forward. His hands lay open helplessly at his sides. His skin was as white as paper.

Ripley gestured at the corpse. "This is Stephen Garrick. He worked for the Neighbors."

Emma drew in a sharp breath. "The Neighbors" was Ripley's term for MI6.

"What the hell happened?" she asked.

"That is the question we need to answer." Ripley's tone was flat.

Emma's mind spun through the possibilities. Chemical weapons were suspected or Caroline wouldn't have been there and the masks wouldn't be necessary.

She walked carefully closer to the suitcase and circled it to get a better look. "Who found him like this?"

Ripley pulled a black antique cigarette case from his pocket but didn't open it. "A cleaner came in early this morning on her regular visit. Garrick wasn't here, as far as she could tell. The suitcase was locked and sitting right where it is now. When she tried to move it out of the way, she couldn't lift it. She phoned Stephen Garrick, but his phone was switched off. This was unusual enough that she contacted Garrick's father. He owns the flat." He paused, looking at the cold, pale shoulders that tilted up out of the suitcase. "When the father arrived, he tried to open the suitcase, but it was locked with a padlock. In the end, he was the one who called the police. Eventually, at his insistence, they cut the lock. And found this."

"Jesus." Emma bent over to get a better look at Garrick.

"Don't get too close," Ripley cautioned, his voice sharp.

Instantly, Emma straightened and stepped back. But in that second she'd had time to see that Garrick's face was contorted and bloated, his tongue protruding grotesquely. His arms and shoulders were as smooth and unmarked as a child's, but his face told a different story. One of pain and fear.

She looked at her boss. "What did they use on him?"

"We believe it was a nerve agent, but we haven't identified it."

Emma shuddered. She didn't want to be in this room, this apartment, or this building. The use of nerve agents by Russian spies was infamous, and she knew if it was novichok that had killed Stephen Garrick, even minute traces could be enough to cause permanent damage to anyone who encountered it.

Sweat beaded her brow as she forced herself to stand still and look again at the sparsely furnished room, focusing on the details. The process steadied her breathing.

"This all feels wrong," she said, slowly. "It's almost theatrical. Why the suitcase? What's the message?"

"My thoughts precisely." Ripley pointed through the open door, down the hallway to the living room. "There's no evidence of a break-in. The front door is the only access to the flat, and it was triple-locked."

Emma walked to the open window and looked down, breathing in the outside air deeply. There was no balcony. The glass-and-steel wall outside was smooth and unscalable.

"I don't think they got in this way," she said, turning back around to survey the smudges of fingerprint dust. "Did forensics find anything?"

"No fingerprints. No DNA," Ripley told her. "Only minute traces left of the chemical they used."

A targeted assassination, then. Well planned and perfectly executed. But why? This sort of murder was usually saved for those the Russians believed had betrayed them. And to betray, you must first be part of something.

You have to be on the same side.

"What did Garrick do at Six?" she asked.

"He was a numbers analyst."

Emma's eyebrows rose. Numbers analysts were low-profile civil servants—basically accountants.

"Why would the Russians want to kill a numbers analyst?" she asked, bewildered.

"I think it's obvious. Either he was taking Russian money and not giving them what he promised, or he stumbled on to something he wasn't supposed to find." Ripley cast a dark glance at the suitcase on the floor and the pale body folded forward, as if in prayer. "There's one thing I can say for certain. If the Russians are willing to murder a British intelligence officer in his home, then none of us is safe. Who knows what secrets he might have revealed before he died?" He met her gaze. "We have to catch the people who did this. And we have to make them pay."

2

EMMA MAKEPEACE WAS born to be a spy. It was in her blood.

In the chaotic years after the fall of the Soviet Union, her father had been a spy for Britain, sharing information he believed might prevent a nuclear war. But he'd been found out, and Russia had no patience for traitors.

Emma had still been in the womb when her mother fled Russia, forced to leave her husband behind in order to save herself and her unborn child.

Emma had been only months old when two British intelligence officers came to their house in the south of England to tell her mother that her father had been summarily executed before he could get out of Russia.

Russia never forgives or forgets. And neither did Emma.

Her mother, in mourning and desperate for her young daughter to know her father as she had known him, taught her.

In soft, velvety Russian, she told Emma of her father's bravery. And how much he had longed to meet her. "He will watch you always, whatever you do," she promised.

As a child, Emma hadn't believed it was possible for her father to see her fail at algebra or do well in history, but she did believe in revenge. And she devoted her life to making the Russian government pay for breaking her mother's heart.

She rushed through university before enlisting in the army, where she joined a military intelligence unit. There, her fluency in Russian, Polish, and German marked her as someone with promise.

That was when Ripley had identified her as a potential agent. On the day she left the army, he offered her a job.

Over the years, her concept of revenge changed. She no longer believed the best revenge was to find the person who pulled the trigger, or even the one who had turned her father in. Instead, she took vengeance one case at a time. By making it much, much harder for Russian spies to operate in her adopted homeland.

When she left Stephen Garrick's flat that morning, Emma drove across London to a small, secure car park a short walk from the Houses of Parliament. A shorter walk in the opposite direction took her to a long, crescent-shaped road lined with redbrick Victorian buildings. This was deep in the political heart of the city, and most of the houses were occupied by think tanks, lobbyists, and businesses connected with government. Simple door signs in brass or wood held enigmatic names that betrayed little about what might actually go on inside. One of the signs read THE VERNON INSTITUTE. Emma opened the unassuming door beneath it and went inside.

The small entrance hall held nothing except a second set of doors. These were modern, and made of thick, bulletproof black glass. Emma stepped forward and stared directly into the small, electronic device mounted on the wall. After a second, a light blinked green, and the doors unlocked with a clunk.

A low hum of activity greeted her as she walked into the main office.

The room was long and narrow, leading into a corridor holding a number of smaller offices. On her left, a straight staircase with an oak banister led up to more offices.

Emma paused to drop the car keys into a box by the door where a handwritten sign pleaded: PLEASE CLEAN VEHICLES BEFORE RE-TURNING.

Spotting her, Esther, who handled the Agency's communications, pulled off her headphones. "Ripley says to go straight up," she said. Her voice was the steady monotone from the phone that morning.

"Thanks," Emma said. But instead of heading up the steep stairs, she bypassed them, and turned into a small, windowless room where the walls were lined with metal shelves holding rows of electronic equipment. The air smelled strongly of fresh espresso.

"Hi, Zach," she said, holding out the pen camera from the bank job that morning. "Got something for you."

A skinny twenty-something with an unruly mop of dark curls glanced up from the four computer monitors arranged in front of him like a shield wall. He wore a Metallica T-shirt under his suit coat, and bright blue Converse trainers.

"Awesome. How'd it go?" he asked, taking the pen. The word "PEACE" was tattooed across the back of his fingers.

The surveillance operation from the bank already seemed a long time ago, but Emma said only, "It worked like a dream."

"It's a tidy little piece of kit." Zach unscrewed the end of the pen, extracting a microchip scarcely larger than a piece of glitter, which he dropped into a device on his desk. "A bit old-school, but it gets the job done. Can't ask for more than that."

He turned the screen so she could watch as a dozen images of the young Russian materialized, stuffing cash into the leather holdall.

"Nice," Zach said, scrolling through the pictures. "Very clear. Who should I send these to?"

"Send them to Adam. I'm off that operation now."

"Oh, so they moved you to the MI6 agent?" Zach gave her an interested look. "Caro from Forensics dropped off some images earlier of that suitcase set-up. That was messed up."

Remembering the pale shoulders jutting out of the suitcase, Emma suppressed a shudder.

"Here's the thing I don't understand," Zach continued. "How the hell did the killers find out he worked at Six? Those spooks are dead serious about hiding their identities."

"Give me a little time." Emma turned to the door. "And I'll tell you exactly what happened."

Ripley's oak-paneled office held only a large desk and two leather chairs. The room held the faintly sweet haze of smoke from his Dunhill cigarettes. There was nothing on his empty desk to indicate whose office it was, or what took place there and yet, somehow, his personality was indelibly etched in every inch of it.

When Emma walked in, her boss was on the phone, and he waved her to a chair.

"Yes," he was saying as she sat down. "Send him straight up as soon as he gets here."

An arched window behind the imposing oak desk offered a view of tilted red Westminster rooftops and the gray-blue English sky.

As he listened to the other person on the phone, Ripley slid a file across his desk to her. The word CONFIDENTIAL was stamped across the top.

The first page held a picture of a slim, fair-haired man with wide blue eyes who bore only a faint resemblance to the pale, tormented body she'd seen that morning. In this image, his skin was flushed with health. Straight hair the color of straw tumbled across his smooth forehead, and a slight smile curved the corners of his lips.

Ripley put the phone down, pulled a cigarette from the slim, black case he always carried, and lit it.

He'd once told Emma where the case came from. He'd worked for MI6 in Russia in the dying days of the Cold War. Back then, many bitter ex-KGB agents had used him for revenge against their own government, giving him valuable secrets they'd protected for years.

One man in particular had surprised him by coming forward. For years, the man had been assigned to follow Ripley and find evidence that he was a spy, rather than, as his cover would have had it, a junior diplomat. Ripley had enjoyed losing him in Moscow's notorious traffic, or dodging into dark alleyways and then emerging in the light. But on multiple occasions, he admitted, the man had outsmarted him. On one memorable day he turned up at the address where Ripley was headed to, arriving before Ripley got there, and giving him a jaunty wave when he walked up.

Ripley believed him to be a brilliant spy on the wrong side of history. It turned out the man, whom he'd never identified, agreed. One day he slipped Ripley a stack of documents which could have cost him his life. They explained precisely how his department worked. Who ran which office, where they lived, what he thought of them. It was a goldmine.

When Ripley asked him why he'd done it, the man handed him his cigarette case.

"You've taken my country and my beliefs, you might as well have everything," he'd said with a bitter laugh.

When Ripley later opened the black case, he'd found, in addition to five Russian cigarettes, a razor blade. He still kept it there, behind his Dunhill blues.

"Always have a weapon you can easily reach," he'd said, when he first showed Emma the hidden blade. "Someplace they're unlikely to search."

And as she sat in the high-backed chair, flipping through Stephen Garrick's file, Emma could feel the short-bladed knife tucked inside her right boot. She'd only ever had to use it once, and on that night it had saved her life.

There were no more than twenty pages in the file—very thin for a background brief on an MI6 officer—but Garrick had only been with the department two years, and his role was minor. Emma flipped through the pages quickly.

"His salary was modest," she noted. "But that was quite a posh flat. Can't be cheap."

"His parents own it," Ripley reminded her, reaching for his lighter. "His father is a very wealthy man. And, unfortunately for us, he has vast political connections."

Her brow creasing, Emma flipped back to the front page of the file again. "Garrick . . . Wait. His father is Lord Garrick?"

Ripley's nod was tense. "This case is going to get far more attention than we'd like."

Emma couldn't argue. John Edward Garrick was a famous investor and property owner. He didn't just invest in corporations, though, he also invested in politicians. He paid a lot to all the political parties, and in return his views were listened to.

This case was going to end up in the press, and it was going to catch fire.

Before she could say as much aloud though, someone knocked on the office door.

"Enter," Ripley called in a cloud of smoke.

A portly man with thinning hair and a round, likable face stepped inside.

"Andrew." Ripley motioned him in. "I'm just briefing Emma on the Garrick case."

"Oh, excellent." Setting the bag down, Andrew took the chair next to Emma and ran a hand across his thinning hair with a sigh. "I've got to say I'm glad to have you on this operation, Emma. It's an ugly one. We need our best."

In a neat gray suit, with a laptop case slung over one shoulder, Andrew Field could have been any London office worker midway through a particularly busy day, but there was nothing ordinary about him. He was a highly trained Russia specialist at MI6, with an encyclopedic knowledge of that country's secret service.

"Any news from forensics?" Ripley inquired.

"I've asked Caroline to brief us," Field told him. "She should be here shortly."

"Do you have any idea who was behind this?" Emma asked.

"Not yet," Field said. "We're examining CCTV footage around the house now, but I don't think we'll find anything. If it was the GRU, they're too professional to be caught out that way."

Ripley exhaled a stream of smoke. "You haven't found anything useful in Garrick's emails?"

"Stephen was a back-room investigator. As far we can tell, he never knowingly met a Russian agent. His entire team has been taken to secure locations until we get some information." Field paused, his eyes meeting Ripley's. "I've had C on the phone already asking me what the hell happened, and I haven't got an answer."

"C" was the head of MI6.

"Dammit, this is just what I was afraid of." Ripley's face darkened. "They'll all be in here before long. MPs. The Home Secretary. We'll have to bar the door." He blew out a distracted stream of smoke. "Your people have checked the obvious things, I assume? New girlfriend from Russia? New mate who was terribly interested in everything in his past?"

"We've been working through Stephen's contacts all afternoon," Field told him. "He had vanishingly few close friends. No new love interests. His last relationship ended eight months ago, apparently amicably. Since then there seems to have been no one."

"I suppose we have to consider the possibility that he hid political beliefs from us," Ripley suggested. "He was a very bright young man. He would have been capable of deceiving our background check when he was hired."

"We have no doubts about his loyalty." Field's demeanor didn't change but a new edge entered his voice. "He was extremely well vetted. If he was a closet Russia sympathizer we'd have known."

Ripley's brow lowered. "That is not necessarily the case, Andrew."

The air in the room seemed to cool by a few degrees. They all knew how much was at stake. If Andrew was wrong, and Garrick was a double agent, then Andrew's job was on the line.

Emma was almost glad when someone knocked at the door.

"Enter." Ripley's voice was as sharp as a gunshot.

The door swung open and Caroline Wakefield stepped inside. The forensic scientist's expression was studiously blank but Emma thought she saw a warning in the depths of her blue eyes as she closed the door behind her.

"The results are back on the chemical used to kill Stephen Garrick," she said. "It's a bit unusual, so we ran it through twice. We're certain it was VX."

"VX?" Ripley looked stunned.

Emma's mouth went dry.

VX. Full name: Venomous Agent X. She'd studied it during her time in Army Intelligence. It was a twentieth-century chemical weapon, developed at Porton Down during the Cold War. Absorbed through the skin or inhaled in even the tiniest quantities, it disrupted the nervous system, paralyzing the muscles so the victim couldn't so much as draw a breath. Death by asphyxiation was the inevitable, excruciating result.

It was banned by the United Nations, but that never made much difference to things as far as Emma could tell.

Ripley turned to Andrew. "Did we know they had stockpiles of VX?"

"I think," Field said, "at this point, we should assume they have stockpiles of everything."

"There would be something elegant about using a weapon we invented, I suppose," Ripley observed.

"The personal touch," Field agreed.

Emma barely noticed their dark humor. She kept thinking of Stephen Garrick's face, contorted with pain until it was unrecognizable. There had been nothing elegant about it.

Field turned his attention back to Wakefield. "Was there anything else in the flat? Any other substances?"

"We're still running final tests but so far we've found nothing," Wakefield told him. "It looks like a clean kill."

"If you find anything at all, let me know immediately," Ripley ordered. "And make sure the apartment building is safe before the residents return. What have they been told, by the way?"

"Gas leak," Wakefield said. "The usual story. So far it's staying out of the press."

Ripley nodded. "Good work, Caroline."

When the forensic scientist had gone, Ripley and Field exchanged a glance. "It's not the GRU, then," Field said. "VX is too old-fashioned for them."

The GRU was the Russian military intelligence branch—the one responsible for most assassinations carried out abroad in the name of that country's government.

Ripley didn't look convinced. "They could have used it for deniability."

"Why the suitcase, then?" Beneath his thinning hair, Field's high forehead furrowed. "That was designed to draw attention."

Emma picked up Garrick's file again. "Maybe we can figure out who if we understand why. The answer has to be in his work."

"Yes, that's my thinking as well." Field turned his small, piercing eyes to her. "The problem we have is that Stephen's skills were quite . . . unique. It's hard to explain, but I'm not sure anyone in my office truly understands his reports."

"His file contains the word 'genius' several times," Emma said.

"It's not an exaggeration, I assure you." Field pulled his laptop out of its case and opened it, typing quickly. "This is from a report he wrote two months ago on an operative who was funneling Russian government money from Dubai into London." He turned the device so Emma and Ripley could see. The page was covered in long, intricate formulas that took up every inch of space. "The Home Office was absolutely baffled when they saw it. Stephen had to sit down with them to explain it, but once they got it, they banned the target from the UK for life and handed the file to Interpol."

Ripley gestured at the screen with his cigarette. "Who was it? Could he have found out about Garrick and taken revenge?"

"Only if one of my people told them, and that's impossible." The crisp tension returned to Field's voice. Emma had never seen him this unsettled. He was rarely rattled.

Ripley must have noticed, too, because he quickly moved on. "What other cases was Garrick working on?"

"What about this one?" Emma held a page from Garrick's file. "He was investigating the daughter of a Russian government official who was supposed to be in London working for an international charity, but Garrick traced money from her charity directly to Russian Intelligence. She was banned, too."

Ripley made a dismissive sound. "We do five cases just like it every year. What else?"

"There's only one other," Emma said, turning to the last page of Garrick's file. "An investigation into two Russian oligarchs. Nothing seems to have come from it. It looks like the whole thing was canceled before it finished."

Field grimaced. "It was a bit of a bastard, that one. The investigation ran for months and found nothing concrete. Then we had budget cutbacks, and it wasn't considered a good use of funds to keep going." He glanced at Ripley. "You know how these things go."

"All too well," Ripley agreed, morosely.

Emma flipped back to the start of the file. "Nothing Garrick worked on seems likely to cause the Russians to take this kind of action. They're obviously making a statement. But why?"

"That's the question we want you to answer," Ripley said. "Find out what we're missing. Retrace Stephen Garrick's last days. Did he meet someone we don't know about? Make promises he couldn't keep?" He gestured at Field. "We'll work with you on this. But we don't have much time. The heat is going to come down from above, and it's going to come down hard. Before that happens, we need to know who killed him and why. Most of all, we need to make bloody sure nobody else ends up dead."

3

EMMA SPENT THE rest of the day immersed in Stephen Garrick's life. Andrew Field sent her a link with secure files on every case the dead man had ever worked on. In all that paperwork, she could find no evidence of where Garrick had gone wrong. He'd been meticulous. Even obsessive. She didn't see a traitor or a fool in those pages: she saw a man in love with the truth.

By the time she finished going through the files, daylight had faded to black outside the window.

Picking up the phone on the desk she'd commandeered, she dialed three numbers.

"Hey, it's Emma," she said. "I need a favor. I want to look at the CCTV footage on the Garrick case. Can you find it for me?"

"Sure, come down," Zach replied. "I'll hook you up."

Ten minutes later, she was in his small office, watching as he typed with dizzying speed, only glancing up at the screen occasionally.

"I want to look outside his house first," Emma instructed, rolling a chair closer to his. "Start with the day before he died."

He glanced at her. "You're tracing all his movements?"

She nodded. "I've got to understand what he was up to. Nothing in his file gives me any indication what was really going on."

Zach frowned at something on the black screen in front of him, muttering under his breath as he typed a machine-gun volley of clicks.

While she waited, Emma looked around the room. She'd rarely spent much time in here. Zach hadn't been with the Agency long, and the previous tech specialist hadn't been particularly friendly. The walls were covered in metal shelves, holding stacks of unidentifiable equipment. A short, black safe squatting in one corner was where Zach kept the technology nobody knew they had.

Emma liked him. He was only a year older than her, having been recruited by MI6 while still hacking his professor's computers from his halls at Cambridge. He'd confided to Emma once that he hadn't been sure he wanted to work for the government at all because he didn't like the political party in power. But then his recruiter had described in blunt terms three recent deadly terrorism attacks prevented in London by intelligence work, and he'd changed his mind.

Zach was a caffeine addict, and even at this hour the room held the rich scent of coffee. Emma, who had been up since six that morning, felt her mouth water.

"It smells so good in here I could drink the air," she said.

"You want coffee?" Zach gestured at a sleek black-and-silver pod coffee machine on the shelf to her left. "Help yourself. Be careful, though. The purple pods will blow the top of your head off."

By the time Emma had filled a cup and sat down again, Zach's thirty-inch monitor showed a clear image of the street in front of Stephen Garrick's building, and he was scrolling quickly back through time. On the screen, people walked jerkily backward, cars drove in reverse, and birds flew by tail first.

Emma lowered herself back into her chair and wheeled it closer to get a better view.

"This is yesterday morning," Zach told her.

Emma took a sip of coffee, watching people going in and out of the apartment building—a woman and a man, a man alone, three men, a man in a suit, a woman in jeans, all moving quickly as the footage scrolled forward in time.

"Actually, I'm going to make myself a coffee. Take over." He slid the mouse to her. As he got up he added, "I think I'm in the mood for purple. I can sleep when I die."

As the coffee machine whirred back into life, Emma barely noticed. She was watching day become night, and the street in front of the Edwardian building in Hammersmith going still. There were lights on in some of the windows, and she counted up to Garrick's sixth-floor flat. The lights went off at two in the morning. And then, thirty minutes later, switched on again.

"Interesting." Zach sat down next to her, his eyes on the screen. "That's his flat, isn't it?"

Emma nodded, staring at that glowing window. Behind the curtains, someone was torturing Stephen Garrick. Spraying a nerve agent in his face and watching him die in agony. Then stuffing his body into a suitcase, and deep cleaning the room. But why?

They scrolled back and forth in time. Just after four in the morning the lights in the flat were switched off again. Job done.

Nobody went in or out through the building's front door at any point during those hours.

"Creepy," was Zach's assessment. He glanced at Emma. "You want to keep going?"

"Yes, let's go back a few days. Maybe we'll catch someone running surveillance or breaking in."

He set the film to scroll back. Night became bright afternoon and then pale morning.

Ordinary-looking people walked in and out of the Garrick's building. Cars drove by. Delivery vans made U-turns and sped away. Taxis idled and then drove off. Boats roared by on the blue strip of the Thames on the left side of the screen.

Emma blinked hard to keep her focus, opening her eyes just as a blue Prius rolled by. The sight of it triggered something in her memory.

"Stop!" she ordered.

Zach paused the recording with just a corner of the car still on the screen.

"That car." Emma tapped the screen. "I need to see the registration number."

He scrolled back until the full number plate was visible. "You got something?" he asked.

"I'm not sure . . . " Emma flipped Garrick's file open and rifled through it until she found the description of his car. The plates matched.

"That's Garrick's car," she told him. "When did this happen?"

Zach checked the timestamp. "This is two days ago. About eighteen hundred hours." He leaned forward, studying the car. "He's just pulling in? Where's he going to park?"

"There's a small car park behind the building," Emma said, looking up from the file. "He'll probably go in through the back door. Is there a camera there?"

"Let me check." Moving his coffee aside, Zach opened a second window on the monitor and quickly typed something Emma couldn't see. A series of numbers came up on the screen, and he grimaced as he read them. "No camera behind the building."

"That must be how his killers got in." Emma thought for a moment, and then pointed at the car. "He's coming back from somewhere. I want to know where he's been."

"Not a problem," Zach said. "I can track the car. It'll take a little while, though."

"If you're sure you've got the time?" Emma said, already knowing what his answer would be.

"Hey, it's either this or sitting at home playing Grand Theft Auto," he told her. "Personally, I'd rather find a killer."

For Emma, watching him work the footage, expertly tracking Garrick across London, brought back memories of the night nine months earlier when the Russians had hacked that same CCTV system and used the cameras to hunt her down. On that occasion, the city's famed

Ring of Steel surveillance system had been her enemy. Tonight, it was her friend again.

The work was going to take time, so Emma ordered pizzas (vegan for Zach), and went out to buy two cans of Pressure Drop beer from the shop down the road. When the food arrived, Zach ate quickly, holding a slice of pizza delicately in his left hand and typing with his right.

"The ANPR system is good," he told her between bites, "but it needs a bit of massaging. You've got to tell it exactly where to look or a search can take days. I don't want it searching Scotland."

ANPR was Automatic Number Plate Recognition—it could search any CCTV in the country for a particular license plate and link up a journey from start to finish through hundreds of cameras.

"I'm limiting the search to London." Zach typed a code into the system, and then hit enter with a decisive thump. "Now let's see what we've won."

The dark screen churned. Slowly, images began to appear, each showing a tiny square of street at a different time of day.

"Here we go." Zach dropped the pizza box into the bin, wiped his fingers on a napkin, and leaned forward, typing hard. Immediately, the images rearranged themselves on the screen—some bright with daylight, others gray with rain, and a few dark and glittering with headlights.

Tapping the top image he said, "This is about five hours before you spotted his car."

"Let's see it." Emma moved her chair closer to his and rested her elbows on the desk as he hit play.

The screen lit up, showing a street in Kensington. It was bright daylight, just before noon. Cars, taxis, and buses jousted for space in eerie silence, and then stopped as a traffic light turned red.

"There." On the screen, Zach tapped his finger against Stephen Garrick's blue Prius, which moved slowly in heavy traffic.

"I'm going to speed this up," Zach said, and typed a brief staccato command. The car jerked forward, speeding across the metropolis until, abruptly, it stopped, and the Prius was parked on a street, surrounded on both sides by modern buildings that towered over it, casting it in shadow.

"Where is this?" Emma asked.

Zach pointed at the data to the right of the screen. "St. Edward's Street, in Pimlico."

Emma pointed at the CCTV image. "Can you zoom this? Is he still in the car?"

Zach typed quickly, and the computer zoomed in on the blue car. Even with the shadow and reflections off the windscreen they could both see Garrick in the driver's seat, his blond hair glinting. As they watched, he raised a black object to his eyes and directed it up so that, startlingly, he appeared to be looking directly at them.

"What's that in his hand?" Emma asked.

Zach's brow creased. "Binoculars, I think."

"What the hell?" Emma breathed. "Is he running surveillance on someone?"

"That's what it looks like." Zach watched the dead man with interest as he raised the binoculars again. "I think he's watching someone in that building." He pointed at a brick structure on the right side of the screen.

Picking up her phone, Emma typed a secure message to Ripley. *Who was Garrick surveilling in Pimlico? He was following someone there the day before he died.*

She turned her attention back to the screen. "Can we speed this up? Let's see how long he stayed there."

Zach sped the footage forward until the Prius angled out of the parking place and shot away.

"Look at that." Zach pointed at the timestamp on the camera. "He was there more than four hours."

Emma stared at the blue car. "What the hell was he doing? Numbers analysts don't run surveillance. They're office guys."

Her phone buzzed and she picked it up to see Ripley's reply: *Garrick wasn't following anyone. He was on extended leave for two weeks before he died.*

"Check this out." Zach tapped her arm. He'd already opened another of the CCTV files and was following Garrick's car down a different London street. He'd sped up the footage, which was rushing forward on a rainy day.

"When was this filmed?" Emma watched the blue Prius dart around a stopped bus.

"Two days before the clip we just watched." Zach pointed at the screen. "He's at Trafalgar Square. Who drives to Trafalgar Square?"

"Spies." Emma kept her eyes on the car, which was turning at high speed into an underground car park. But the footage ended there. "Shit. We'll lose him."

"Oh, ye of little faith." Zach opened a second window and typed something quickly. A moment later, another window opened. "Here we go. This is the same camera. We should see him when he comes out."

"There!" Emma pointed at Garrick's distinctive blond hair as he emerged from the pedestrian exit of the garage, walking quickly, his face tilted down.

As they watched, he headed down the Strand, near the private bank where Emma had been only that morning, threading through the crowd, just as she'd done, visible and yet invisible, unnoticed until he reached the distinctive recessed entrance to the Savoy Hotel. A few doors away, he stopped in front of a shop, leaning back against a wall, pretending to look at his phone. He stayed there, trying to blend into the scenery, as the minutes ticked by.

Emma, who had done the same thing many times, albeit with much more skill, was baffled.

"He's definitely conducting surveillance. But that wasn't his job. Something else was going on." She stood up. "I need to talk to Ripley."

4

Emma waited impatiently by Ripley's desk as he and Andrew Field watched the footage Zach had sent up to them. Ripley's expression remained impassive, but Field watched for only a few seconds before turning away and typing something on his laptop, a cigar clenched between his teeth, his expression dark.

"Does anyone know what he was doing?" Emma asked. "Who could he have been following?"

"What did you say the street is called?" Ripley asked.

"St. Edward's Street," Emma replied. "In Pimlico."

"I can have someone check on it." Ripley reached for the phone but Field's voice stopped him.

"I think I know what he was doing there." Field turned his laptop around so they could see the image on-screen of a dark-haired man. He was tall and heavily built, wearing a designer suit, his striped shirt unbuttoned at the throat, revealing a thicket of chest hair. He had pale skin and a prominent mole on his right cheek. His eyes were hidden behind sunglasses.

"Andrei Volkov owns Riverside House on St. Edward's Street, in

Pimlico. He uses the penthouse flat as a bolthole when he's in London." A new tension lay under Field's steady voice. "Until last month, Garrick led a team investigating him."

Emma leaned over to study the image more closely. "I remember that case from Garrick's files. Wasn't Volkov suspected of selling chemical weapons?"

"We were trying to prove that Volkov and Oleg Federov were acting as black-market arms dealers for the Russian government and using the UK as a base." Field's voice was measured. "We believed they were selling chemical weapons to a number of unsavory governments. Afghanistan, Iran, Syria—a real rogues' gallery. An interested party warned us that they were encouraging those governments to use the weapons against us." He glanced at Ripley. "Revenge, apparently, against NATO."

"This is the investigation that was shut down before it finished?" Ripley was watching Field closely.

"Yes. Budget cuts meant we couldn't keep spending money with nothing to show for it," Field said. "We simply ran out of time."

"But these images were captured a few days ago," Emma pointed out. "The operation was over by then, wasn't it?"

"The operation has been over for weeks," Field's voice rose. "Stephen should have had nothing more to do with Volkov after that. Where else did he conduct surveillance? Did you say the Savoy Hotel?"

"Yes." Emma said. "On the ninth. At one in the afternoon."

Field glanced at Ripley, something unreadable in his expression. "Volkov often has meetings at the Savoy."

"Right." Ripley picked up his phone and dialed. Despite the hour, it was answered almost immediately. "Sam! I hope I haven't woken you. This is Ripley. I need a favor. Can you find out if a man named Andrei Volkov was at the Savoy on the ninth of this month?" He listened briefly, and then said, "Yes, the ninth. It's a bit tricky—he may have just been at the bar or restaurant." He paused. "Of course. I can wait."

Emma's phone buzzed and she glanced down at the screen. It was a message from Zach.

I've gone back through the last two weeks. Garrick was on that street in Pimlico nearly every day.

When she showed it to Field, his expression tightened visibly. But before he could respond, Ripley ended his call and looked across his desk at them.

"Andrei Volkov and Oleg Federov had lunch together at the Savoy the day Garrick stood outside." There was a pause and then he added, "I suppose that's it then."

"You think they killed him?" Emma shifted her gaze from him to Field. "Volkov and Federov?"

Neither man responded right away. Field stared at his cigar, which appeared to have gone out. Ripley looked past her at the wall over her shoulder. Both seemed lost in thought.

"I don't understand. Why would he follow them?" Emma pressed. "The investigation was closed."

Field spoke first. "Andrei Volkov and Oleg Federov have a massive organization together. Their finances are incredibly complex; dozens of shell corporations funneling money all over the world to hide what they're really doing. Only Stephen could begin to understand it. It was the biggest thing he'd ever worked on. He didn't sleep. He didn't eat. He became obsessed. He believed there were actually three people in this organization. Andrei Volkov, Oleg Federov, and someone else—someone he couldn't identify. Someone British, with connections. Possibly inside this government. But he could never find proof. And then the operation was shut down. He took it very badly." He paused. "A week later, he announced he was taking a temporary leave from work."

"When was that?" Ripley asked. "Remind me?"

"Two weeks ago," Field said. "His supervisor thought Stephen was suffering from stress. He was glad he was taking time off. But it appears he couldn't let go."

Emma could see it all in her mind. She'd read the files. Andrei Volkov and Oleg Federov were both tightly connected to the Russian government. Federov, in particular, was notorious. He was ex-FSB, and known to be a thug. Either man might easily have noticed Garrick the first time he staked out the Pimlico building. He was so obvious.

The whole time he was following them, they must have been watching him. When they figured out he worked for MI6, they must have assumed the entire British spy agency was responsible. Killing him with a nerve agent in the middle of London, leaving the body hidden in plain sight . . . Suddenly, it all made more sense.

"The suitcase was a distraction," she said, piecing it together. "They wanted us to think it was the Russian government doing the killing, so they made it look like a GRU assassination."

"That poor fool." Field threw his cigar savagely into the ashtray. "That stupid, stupid fool. Why wouldn't he just let it go?"

Ripley alone seemed unaffected by the situation. "I must say, I'm astonished Volkov and Federov would take the risk of killing someone who worked for Six," he said thoughtfully.

Field met his gaze. "What are you thinking?"

"I'm thinking if those men took that sort of a risk, then Garrick must have been right about them."

There was a pause. The air in the room seemed to shift, charging with sudden electricity.

"If those men really are dealing chemical weapons from the middle of London . . ." Field began.

"This case should never have been shut down. It needed time to run." Ripley picked up his cigarette case and turned it slowly in his hands. "We have to do what Stephen Garrick couldn't. He went after the money. We should go after the men. His death gives us that opportunity."

"We must assume they interrogated Garrick before they killed him," Field reminded him. "He will have told them at least some of the truth. They'll expect us to come for them."

Ripley didn't blink. "So, we'll have to be careful."

Something unspoken passed between them. The two men had worked together for thirty years—their relationship was closer than some marriages Emma had known.

Field broke the silence first. "In order to arrest them, we have to prove Volkov and Federov are personally involved in selling weapons. Stephen couldn't prove it and he was a genius."

"Stephen Garrick wasn't us." Ripley's voice held a note of finality. "We have other ways of getting what we need."

His words hung in the air, swirling like smoke.

Finally, Field pulled a box of matches from his pocket and struck one, sending a faint scent of sulphur into the air. Holding it steady, he relit his cigar, drawing hard until it smoldered.

Turning to Emma, he said, "I guess you'd better get ready. Looks like we're about to attempt the impossible."

5

OVER THE NEXT twenty-four hours, they considered multiple ways to get close to the two Russian men. Andrei Volkov was part owner of a five-star hotel near Waterloo Bridge called Mine, which charged eight hundred pounds a night for the cheapest room overlooking the traffic-clogged streets. But Ripley dismissed the idea of placing anyone from the Agency there with a terse "It won't get us to him."

They toyed with the idea of placing someone inside one of the Russians' houses as a cleaner or personal assistant. But each man owned multiple properties and stayed on the move, traveling from one country to the next by private jet or yacht, protected by guards who served as a private army. They were never in any house for long. Their money made them as untouchable as gods.

In the end, it was Emma who came up with the idea. It was the day after Stephen Garrick's body had been discovered, and she'd been rereading Andrei Volkov's file, searching for a crack in his life she could step into. Finally, she'd thrown the document down, and said, "It seems to me he lives on his yacht more than in any of his houses."

There was a long pause as her words sank through the smoke that filled Ripley's oak-paneled office.

Ripley glanced at Field. "Could be an option."

Field, who'd been slumped in a chair, red-eyed with exhaustion, straightened. "Not could be. Is. I know someone who could make it happen. But we'd need the right person. Young. Good-looking."

In tandem, he and Ripley turned to Emma and studied her speculatively. They were like a pair of old druids. They didn't even have to speak aloud.

"We'd have to train her up," Field said, thinking aloud. "And it would have to be quick because they'll know we're coming for them. They're going to run. But she can handle it, can't she?"

Emma opened her mouth to agree but before she could speak, Ripley held up a cautioning hand. "Hang on. This is one hell of a risky operation. She'd be completely cut off. Isolated."

"But think of the access." Field said it almost reverently. "The crew on those yachts live alongside the owners. There's nowhere for them to hide. It's perfect."

"There'll be nowhere for Emma to hide, either." Ripley's voice rose. "If we're right, these men have already used a chemical weapon on one British agent and there's nothing to stop them from doing it again."

"But—" Field tried to interrupt but Ripley spoke over him, suddenly furious.

"I don't give a damn about access. Emma would be too exposed out there."

Field's forehead furrowed.

Ripley turned to Emma and said abruptly, "You should get some rest. Go home. I'll call you when we know more."

Emma wanted to refuse but she knew there was nothing to gain from arguing. Ripley knew what she was capable of. And he must be able to see how much she wanted this.

And yet, when she stood up, her feet dragged. With her hand on the door, she turned back. "For what it's worth, I want to do it. I know it's got risks, but I can handle it." Ripley's face closed, but she kept going. "We can't let them get away with this. If I'm the right person for this operation, send me."

Emma used the Agency's car service to take her home. In the back-seat, she tried to understand Ripley's sudden resistance.

She knew how dangerous it would be to go undercover on a boat that might well hold the man who killed Stephen Garrick. In the wrong hands, it was a suicide mission. She was one of the youngest people at the Agency, but in the last year she'd proven herself more than once.

As the car crossed Westminster Bridge, she looked down at the water glittering blue and gold in the late afternoon sun, and remembered a frantic speedboat chase on the river nine months ago. That was the last time she'd had an assignment that put her life on the line. Since then, she'd been given soft jobs—light surveillance, easy targets. Ripley hadn't said anything about it, but she got the impression he had been giving her time to heal, physically and mentally. That was what she hoped, anyway. The worry, of course, was that he'd lost faith in her for some reason, after the job that nearly killed her.

Reaching up, she touched the smooth skin of the scar on her left shoulder, where the Russian bullet had hit her. And for the first time in a while, she thought about Michael Primalov's hands, gentle but firm on her skin as he dressed the bullet wound in her shoulder. He'd been bewildered by the ruthlessness of her world, as she'd fought to keep him safe from the spies intent upon killing him.

The two of them had formed a bond that night. A bond only sur-vivors can understand. And yet, although she'd thought about him many times since then, she'd never once tried to find him. He and his parents had been given new identities, new lives. Tracking him down could put his life in danger again.

But now and then, when she was very tired, Emma allowed herself to wonder what might have been, if absolutely everything had been different.

Nothing, she told herself firmly, as the car pulled up in front of a white Victorian building in the Crystal Palace neighborhood of south London. Nothing would have happened.

Their lives were too different. Even if everything had been fine and he hadn't needed to go into hiding, it wouldn't have mattered. They couldn't be together. She could never have told him the truth about her work. And he would have hated being deceived.

As she climbed the steps to her flat, she put Michael out of her mind. She'd worked thirty-six hours straight, and every part of her longed for sleep.

The small apartment, with its polished wood floors, simple furniture, and pale walls, had an anonymous feel. The furniture was from a mainstream chain; the framed print above the sofa of Piccadilly Circus on a rain-soaked night was a mass-produced image.

When she'd moved in two years ago, she'd loved the built-in bookshelves on either side of the fireplace, but she'd never had time to fill them. They were as bare and glaring as an accusation.

Emma had never much minded the fact that she had no time for reading. No time for hobbies. But looking at her home now, she didn't like how much it resembled Stephen Garrick's starkly empty flat.

The apartment was rented in the name "Emily James." Emily worked as a civil servant for the Foreign Office, or so the landlord believed. But he didn't really care, since the rent came through right on time every month. That had little to do with Emma, of course.

When she'd first begun working for the Agency, she'd had a meeting with someone from MI6 who helped her set up a bank account in a false name, through which all her bills had been paid ever since. A portion of her income went to that account each month, ensuring that nothing was ever overdue.

Debt was a door temptation could walk right through, and intelligence officers weren't allowed to have any of it. Even their credit card statements were monitored.

In a strange way, Emma thought money was beginning to lose its meaning to her. When she needed it on a case, Ripley gave it to her, stuffed in envelopes. In her own life, she had no desire for more of it, and no time to spend what little she had left after her bills were paid.

She was too tired to keep thinking. Wearily she turned off the lights and crossed the room, stripping off her clothes as she walked, falling into the cool sheets with a sigh of relief.

Her last thought was that Ripley had to let her do this job. If he didn't, there was no point in staying with the Agency. She hadn't become a spy to watch Russian children carry money around London.

Seven hours later, when the phone woke her up, she couldn't remember dreaming at all.

"Makepeace," she said, thickly, raising herself on one elbow.

"I need you to come into the office." It was Ripley's voice, tireless and crisp. "You're going to France. You may be there several weeks. Best if you throw away the milk."